FLAMES OF MIRA

Paperback edition published in 2023 by Solaris
an imprint of Rebellion Publishing Ltd,
Riverside House, Osney Mead,
Oxford, OX2 0ES, UK

First published in 2022 by Solaris

www.solarisbooks.com

ISBN: 978-1-78618-961-5

Copyright © 2022 Clay Harmon
Map design by Gemma Sheldrake

10 9 8 7 6 5 4 3 2 1

A CIP catalogue record for this book is available from the
British Library.

Designed & typeset by Rebellion Publishing

Printed in the United Kingdom

FLAMES OF MIRA

CLAY HARMON

SOLARIS

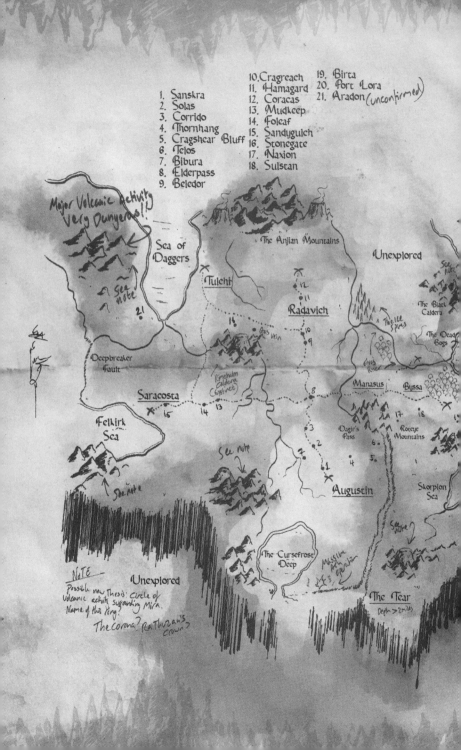

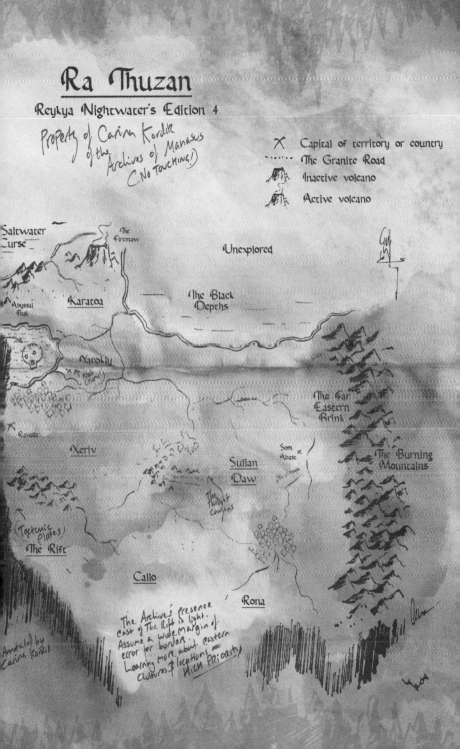

Part 1: Ig

Chapter 1

TONIGHT I WOULD put an innocent man to death.

Magnate Sorrelo and his guards bulled through the crowd as I struggled to keep up. Commoners congesting the trade district did their best to clear a path for him—the heat in the magnate's eyes made it clear he wanted blood.

We reached the epoxy shop's front entrance, where light glowed in its dirty windows, broken up by the shadows inside. The guards pushed through the door, and Magnate Sorrelo paused, waiting for me to catch up. *It's him or it's both of you*, his glare said. So it had gone with the others. The air inside the shop smelled of citrus and warm earth, and two craftsmen behind a counter spoke with a group of customers, all of whom froze at our arrival.

The magnate's cousin hunched over a vat of steaming resin near the back wall, bat-hide gloves covering his arms up to the elbows and sweat glistening on his shoulders. He turned at the sudden silence and realization dawned on him.

"Bolivar," Magnate Sorrelo said.

Bolivar white-knuckled the stirring rod, and I readied myself to defend the magnate. Part of me hoped Bolivar attacked. If you had to die, best do it with your feet under you. "Please, Sorrelo," he said, releasing the rod, letting it sink into the resin. "Don't do this."

Magnate Sorrelo swished a hand, and I forced myself to follow one of the guards behind the counter to grab Bolivar's arm. "You are being formally charged with aiding and abetting in a plot to stage a coup to overthrow me," Sorrelo said. He twisted a ring on his forefinger, as if dismayed by the difficult choice. All I saw was excitement.

"That's ridiculous. You're family." Bolivar tried to pull away, but it was half-hearted, like he still refused to believe what was happening.

Sorrelo nodded, but not to him. With the guard's help, I guided Bolivar to the exit while Sorrelo and his second guard followed.

A growing crowd waited outside. The epoxy shop sat in the heart of Augustin's trade district, on the sinkhole's first level, where Bolivar's arrest would attract the most attention. The district's torchlight danced on the faces of worried and angry Augustins, many of whom cared deeply for the magnate's cousin. Bolivar always volunteered around the city, despite being an Adriann; his job in the epoxy shop wasn't even paid.

"What now?" Bolivar asked. "Is it the Lid? Is that it?" The shaking words undermined the outrage he tried to project. Every political prisoner arrested over the recent months had stayed in the prison cells pocketing the top of the sinkhole—a week near the darkness of the surface and most lost a foot or two to hypothermia.

"No," the magnate said. "Death by ash, or by ice?"

Bolivar's arm flexed under my grip. "I-I'm sorry?" he asked.

"You heard me. Pick now. Ash or ice?"

The crowd's whispers faded, replaced by the faint roar of the chasm's waterfalls. Sorrelo had never skipped a trial before, and I could feel the heated and horrified glares from hundreds of onlookers start to envelope us. Their attention dug into me, moving around the rocks of acid in my stomach. Fhelfire, but I always hated standing in front of an audience, and the feeling was multiplied a hundredfold knowing what they were about to witness. Nothing could be done about it, though. If I didn't play my part in this arrest, the magnate would torture me to death before killing Bolivar anyway.

"I'm *not* trying to overthrow you," Bolivar said. "And I'm no reformer. I want my trial."

"Pick, or I'll pick for you."

"This is insane. You can't just accuse someone of a crime and decide they're guilty. It doesn't work that way anymore."

The lines in the magnate's face deepened. "Ash it is, then."

Bolivar yanked violently as the guard and I dragged him across the street toward the stairs leading from the first level ridge to the chasm floor, and he nearly slipped out of my sweaty palms. "Help!" he screamed, feet skidding over colorful mosaics—mosaics I'd watched him build for the city—but nobody intervened.

We reached the uneven volcanic rock of the chasm floor, and I nearly lost my grip a second time. I repeated to myself that this was no different from the others I'd killed for Sorrelo. *Just another notch on the belt.* Over and over I whispered it, working it in between labored breaths, the straining of my arms hiding how badly they trembled. Augustins crowded the railings rimming the sinkhole's vertical walls, scrambling to catch a glimpse of the spectacle, and wooden platforms carrying goods between levels slowed as tradesmen paused in their work.

A river of lava waited for us on the field of black stone. Bubbles of gas ruptured on its surface, and as we came closer to the execution platform built against its shore, Bolivar craned his neck toward the crowds. "Please," he yelled. "Stop him. Anyone. It'll be the end of Augustin—"

The man restraining Bolivar's other arm punched him in the nose. Bolivar stumbled and hit the ground, dribbling red spit on the platform before struggling back to his feet. I tried to help him up, my hand still a vice on his wrist.

"Please," he croaked again.

The guard's next strike landed under Bolivar's armpit, hard enough to crack ribs, and I let go before I was thrown to the ground too. Bolivar whimpered, smearing blood onto the glassy obsidian, and the guard brought his steel-toed boot back.

I grabbed the guard's arm while my foot pushed down on top of his boot, catching him off balance and rooting him in place. He twitched like he wanted to hit me, but had the smarts to avoid interrupting the magnate's performance in front of half the city. All I could think about in that moment was how I would come for this man in some damp side alley, or in the washroom of some backwater bar on the fifth level while he drank himself stupid, and the magnate would never find out.

But killing this guard wouldn't help that awful feeling creeping into my body that worsened with each wheeze Bolivar squeezed out.

"Ig," the magnate said. Sweat beaded on his brow, reflecting the lava's light as he watched the two of us.

"Yes?" I asked, struggling to keep the resentment out of my voice.

"Don't mess this up."

He faced the people of Augustin. Waterfalls leaking from ice on the upper walls fed into the lava, the steam obscuring parts of the crowd. Sorrelo would draw this out as long as possible—at least until someone from the audencia showed up to stop him. Or at least try to. "Times are different," the magnate boomed. "Don't think I haven't noticed the toll these past months have taken on you. But consider this a moment of respite from my authority. Sometimes the decision of who lives and who dies shouldn't rest on the shoulders of those in power, whether that be myself or the audencia."

Bolivar's quivering calmed as he watched his cousin. I could almost feel the hope coursing through his veins.

"My personal attendant has been called before the eyes of the city to make the final decision," Sorrelo said. "Should he decide that Bolivar deserves life, all he has to do is say the word and my judgment will be annulled. Ig is a commoner living outside the politics of the court. A true voice of objectivity. If Bolivar's life should be spared, no harm shall befall him or my manservant. The audencia will make sure I will be judged accordingly, should anything happen to either party. Accident or otherwise."

Bolivar's eyes shined, tears cutting into the dirt on his face. "Not like this," he said to me. "My cousin is sick in the head."

His hopeful gaze intensified, but he didn't continue. To him, every moment I spent deciding the right thing meant more of a chance at survival. I experienced a near-overwhelming urge to knock the guard into the lava, throw Bolivar over my shoulder, and run for the main gates. I didn't want to kill an innocent man. All I wanted was to keep him away from Sorrelo.

It didn't matter what I wanted though. Sorrelo needed Augustin to think he wasn't alone in believing Bolivar deserved death—a reformer in his eyes. The reformers had been hounding the capital for months, torching businesses, beating loyalists to the Adriann family half to death, planting the idea that it was time to put the monarchy to the sword. Now Sorrelo was in a kill-or-be-killed frenzy. Why he thought Bolivar was helping the reformers, I had no idea, but I couldn't expect him to be kind enough to tell me.

And knowing his reasons changed nothing. Before the arrest, the magnate had bound me with a Word to follow through with the execution. In truth, I could either kill Bolivar, or the flesh magic tying me to Sorrelo Adriann would kill me.

I gestured for the other guard to step away. This was mine alone to carry. Then, with all my strength, I pulled an innocent man to his feet and shoved him to his death.

A scream echoed up the walls of the chasm—the sound of someone encountering an unstoppable force. The viscous material ate into him, his skin rupturing and hissing from explosive evaporation, accompanied by pops of bubbling fat. His body convulsed until there wasn't enough left of him to move around. The river swallowed him in twelve heartbeats. Hardly more than a few seconds. A whiff of meat passed over us, cleansed away by wind from the nearest waterfall.

Chapter 2

SORRELO PATTED MY forearm as he passed, and the guard offered me the sweetest of smiles before he followed. I bristled. *Ezequiel, rank of Co Priero of the royal guard. Works second shift.*

Thousands of spectators had packed themselves along the ridges of the cylindrical chasm, but the bottom of the sinkhole remained perpetually barren, and Sorrelo picked up the pace to leave the open ground. Lingering on the field was dangerous; sheaths of ice grew along the sides of the sinkhole, like massive sword sculptures hundreds of feet long, and occasionally the river's heat would weaken the ends until ice broke off and debris as large as houses would shatter against the chasm floor.

The booing started when we were halfway across the field.

It sounded uncertain—only about a third of the crowd participated, though I couldn't tell if it was because the others supported Sorrelo or because they didn't have the spine to join in. Augustins cried out as city guardsmen struck them with saber guards and gauntleted fists, and the soldiers accompanying us moved in front of the magnate protectively. Augustins watched me with hateful looks, shouting obscenities, but I suppressed a gleeful laugh despite everything.

Maybe the magnate wouldn't get away with this after all.

We climbed the steps where the din started to fade. Sorrelo looked around, pleasantly surprised, until we reached the top and saw the real reason people had gone quiet. Mateo the master smith, his shaggy hair framing his face and blending into his red-brown robes, stepped out of the crowd, expression as brittle as granite. Everyone nearby bowed their heads toward the master smith—everyone except me, the magnate, and his personal guards.

"May I have a few words with you, Magnate Sorrelo?" Mateo asked with cold politeness.

"Of course," Sorrelo answered, eyes sweeping the crowd of eavesdroppers, the threat in his voice clear.

Mateo came closer and brought his voice down. "Dealing with Bolivar was the audencia's job, not yours. Why? What was the point?"

The only man with enough political power in Augustin to rival Sorrelo's stood three feet in front of us, but instead of respecting this fact, Sorrelo stepped forward in challenge. "Isn't the Foundry's support of me unconditional? Or is that untrue?"

Mateo's pause was barely noticeable. "You're right... as always. The Foundry's loyalty to the magnate is never in question." He eyed me, his attention molten, and I fidgeted as he looked ready to say something. Bolivar had been his friend. Instead, he turned toward those around us who hung on his words. "Fheldspra would despair to gaze upon so many idle bodies."

Every commoner within earshot looked down, some even turning to leave. To worship Fheldspra meant to follow the tenet of mastering one's chosen craft—I wouldn't be surprised if some of the commoners were more afraid of failing the master smith than angering Magnate Sorrelo. The magnate frowned at the people leaving, but before he could say more, the master smith spun on his heel and disappeared in the press of bodies.

More guards appeared and started pushing open a path for the magnate toward the second level's stairwell, and further along the ridge it was like the master smith had never reared his head. Commoners shoved at each other for a chance at a face-to-face with the passing guard, some held up torn bandanas of Augustin red, and others shouted "asha'iso" at me. A word from the old tongue, and one of the few I happened to already be familiar with. Murderer.

An object struck the back of my head and I stumbled. I'd been tailing the entourage, and I turned to find a teenager standing in the path as it started to close, the tendons in her forearms standing out and her posture daring me to fight. A spot behind my eyes started to ache.

The guards didn't notice the girl, too focused on helping Sorrelo push through the crowd. She advanced and raised her fists. "Saior Bolivar was good," she said, her commoner's accent heavy. "Better than magnate. Didn't deserve what you gave him."

I never tricked myself into thinking people might not hate me for throwing Bolivar in the river. I'd lived most of my life unwanted, so I was better trained than anyone to guard against hatred. Still, the grief in her eyes dug deep and sharp, and the need to shout the truth into the chasm dug even deeper. I was flesh bound to the magnate, and refusing his Words meant death. Not only was it impossible for me to admit this though, but flesh magic didn't exist in this part of the world. They'd call me as deranged as Sorrelo.

It was impossible for me to take what I wanted, but maybe I wouldn't have to. If the crowd was any indication, she'd get her justice soon.

"I'll stop this. I promise," I said. I wasn't too sure what the promise meant, but in that moment the words felt right. I hurried after the entourage.

"That one, I think," Sorrelo said, pointing to a woman chanting "butcher." Her expression wilted. "That man too," the magnate continued. "Oh, and that one."

Guards collected commoners from the crowd and shackled their wrists, the protests jilting. The prisoners were led to the bottom of the second-level ramp, where a neat-looking man with spectacles waited. The acid in my stomach churned. It was Olevic Pike, Augustin's Listener. "I trust you'll glean what's needed from these dissenters and find who's leading the reformers?" Sorrelo asked him.

Olevic eyed the line of crying Augustins over his spectacles and shook his head, his mouth a thin line. "Truth sits upon the lips of the dying. If they know something, I'll find it." A girl of perhaps nine or ten poked her head out from behind his legs to look at the prisoners, and Olevic caressed the top of her head. Olevic's daughter, who went everywhere with him, even to his listening chambers. Olevic left her side and approached a trembling old man with scraped up shins and a bloody nose. He put a hand on the commoner's shoulder. "The innocent have nothing to fear. This I swear. And if you're guilty... well, that's irrelevant, is it not?"

The old man's trembling stilled and he nodded, sniffling. "Yes, saior."

As I watched the guards form up in preparation to escort the two dozen prisoners up the ramp, it all clicked into place. Sorrelo had Bolivar killed to provoke those who most hated him out from hiding. It was his way of digging for a new lead on who was leading the reformers. But yelling slurs at the magnate was a far cry from plotting his death.

"Ig, come," Sorrelo said. He stepped away from the entourage and said in my ear, "Make sure the prisoners get to the interrogation rooms safely. Return to me once Olevic's work is underway."

The man didn't even trust his own guards. His paranoia was getting worse.

Shouting turned to murmurs, turned to whispers, and most of the crowd broke up, headed back inside the torch-lit alleys of the trade district and back to their lives. The magnate followed us to the second level, then broke off with his royal guard while I followed the Listener to the next set of stairs. The listening chambers waited in the East Vine Vale District on the third level, where creeper vines crawled across alley ceilings and glowing quartz crystals were embedded in the walls for light. The alley opened to a plaza, the listening chambers standing next to one of the guards' barracks. Inside the listening chambers, the guards shepherded everyone into a pen, but Olevic grabbed the shirt sleeve of the old man with the bloody nose before the prisoner could move through the bars. "You first."

"Don't know anything," the prisoner said in a shaky voice as Olevic pulled him into the adjacent room. The room didn't have much, save a table of straps in the center, a counter of tools that shined from the glowing white quartz that hung from a chain on the ceiling, and a chair in the corner. A sparse room for easy cleaning. The room didn't even have a door. "Sit," Olevic commanded, and his daughter took a seat in the corner.

I leaned against the entryway while the guards helped the old man on the table. "I h-this necessary?" the old man asked. "Answer your questions, no need for any'a this."

"It's a matter of following procedure," Olevic said. "That's all." I could already see pieces of his mask slipping away, the feigned sternness and bullshit concern melting, replaced by an eagerness that made his hands work just a little too fast as they tightened restraints and pulled hard on the straps. My uneasiness worsened. Call Sorrelo what you wanted, but he wasn't an Olevic Pike.

"Wait!" someone said as they rushed into the listening chambers. A young man—hardly older than a boy, really—with a shaved head and a thick, manicured beard, stopped beside me. Sorrelo's son, Emil, the princep of Augustin. "Why are you doing this?" he asked Olevic.

"You'd think you would recognize your own father's bidding by now," Olevic said.

Emil turned to me. "It's true? You killed Bolivar?"

"He was helping the reformers," I said. It was easy to say something you didn't believe when you practiced it enough. "You know how much Bolivar disliked your father."

His dark eyes hardened, but he didn't argue. Only he and Sorrelo's other two children knew about the flesh magic binding me to their father. He had to know me well enough to realize I wouldn't have killed Bolivar without a Word. Right?

"Please," the prisoner said, lifting his head off the table, the only part of his body not strapped down. "Help."

A small whine left Emil's throat. Even as Augustin's princep, he couldn't supersede his father's commands. Olevic ran a finger along the line of instruments on his table until he picked up a serrated knife. "Do you know what I find interesting?" he asked as he approached the prisoner's legs. "The city can lose its mind when men like Bolivar Adriann are executed without a trial, yet I can pluck any old commoner out of the crowd and play with his flesh and bone without hearing more than a peep."

"This isn't necessary," Emil said. "He doesn't know anything. None of these people do."

Olevic bent over until he was eye-level with one of the man's knees. The prisoner tried to thrash, pleading in the old tongue and crying, but his legs couldn't move more than an inch off the table. Olevic grabbed the man's kneecap, pressed the knife's edge to its base, but paused when I stepped forward. "This is an interrogation, not your entertainment," I said.

Olevic straightened. "My life's work is built on parsing true intentions," he said to me. "The city may be fooled, but I'm not. Strange how you threw Bolivar into the river, yet your true feelings were written into every step you took from that river. It's all over your face even now. You have a lot to gain from Sorrelo's death." He came closer, pointing the knife at me, the tip parting several strands of fabric on the front of my robe.

"Careful," Emil said. "My father's attendant doesn't fall under your authority."

"I know, I know. But how about this, Ig. You can save this man from the table if you let me interrogate you instead."

"Ig isn't a reformer," Emil said in a low, threatening voice. "That I can promise you."

Olevic shrugged. "Don't look at it like that. I'm offering him a chance to save this man. That's all."

The man on the table looked at me, a bubbling cauldron of fear with a dash of hope, his eyes a mirror of Bolivar's. Maybe some time under Olevic's knife would do me some good, help me forget the hollowness that deepened in the base of my chest. The men and women I'd killed for Sorrelo had tricked me into thinking I could kill without remorse. Oh how wrong I was.

But for the second time this passing, there was nothing I could do. Sorrelo had given me a Word to return to him as soon as Olevic's work was underway—even now, I could feel that mounting pressure in the base of my skull, like a phantom hand pushing its fingers where soft flesh met bone, threatening to strike. Waiting to see how long I would disobey. If I waited too long, the magic would kill me.

"I can't," I said. "I have to return to the palace."

Olevic let out an exaggerated sigh. "If you say so." He returned to the table, pushed his spectacles further up his nose, and glanced at his daughter, who was digging at the grime lining her fingernails. "Cate," he said sharply. "Pay attention. Learn now so you may succeed tomorrow."

Her posture straightened, eyes gluing to the old man, and Olevic winked at me. "What do you know of the plot to usurp Sorrelo Adriann?" he asked the man, looming over the table.

"Don't know anything," the man said, his words explosive. "Swear."

Olevic's daughter watched her father grab the man's kneecap once more and squeeze with bloodless fingertips, her mouth slightly ajar, and I grabbed Emil's hand, pulling him out the room just as the screaming started. The other prisoners clung to each other while they listened to the sounds of shrieking and pleading and pounding of flesh on rockwood float through the open doorway.

"I'll kill him," Emil almost snarled when we were on the ridge outside. "Men like Olevic should not be in charge of asking those kinds of questions."

"Sometimes the people who are best at a job are the last ones to seek it out," I said. I knew that better than anyone.

Emil fiddled with the charm dangling from the belt loop on his hip—an iron ring interlaced with silver, too large for his fingers. A trader from Xeriv—a country built on hopelessly corrupt trade, like the six territories before the Sovereign turned them into Mira—had given it to him as a gift. I always found the gift strange, considering that Xerivians and generosity were like water and oil. "It was my father, wasn't it?" he asked. "He made you kill Bolivar."

"He gave me the Word right before we went to the epoxy shop." We started along the ridge. Mist from the chasm's waterfall beaded on the vines and moss above our heads, dripping into my hair. "He knew how the commoners would feel about Bolivar's death. He tried to pass the buck onto me. He also wanted to find more people to feed to Olevic."

"Bolivar was one of the Foundry's most devoted members," Emil said, sullen. "Mateo isn't going to like this." Conflict between Sorrelo and Mateo always made Emil uncomfortable. Emil had apprenticed under the master smith for years, toiling away in the Foundry in the hopes of becoming a smith and joining the order. He'd grown close to Mateo—close enough for the magnate to force Emil to end his apprenticeship.

"Mateo already spoke with your father," I said. "It went as well as you'd expect."

We moved down the stone steps lining the third level ramp, toward the palace. "I'm sorry for how my father and Olevic treat you," he said. He stopped me, moving one step down until I was standing over him. "For how everyone treats you. I can't take it anymore. I'm making you a promise, Ig. Once I'm magnate, I'm doing everything in my power to release you from your flesh binding."

Uneasiness knotted me up, almost worse than the rocks that had piled inside my stomach over the course of the passing—a feeling that always crept in when the topic of my freedom came up. I'd been a servant since the age of twelve, a servant in this country and to Magnate Sorrelo for the last two years. It gave me purpose, and what was life without purpose? Grey and indifferent. Meaningless, if Little Me had a say in the matter. Losing my purpose was almost too much to think about. "Can we talk about something else?" I asked.

"I'm serious. I'm going to be magnate, and I hate to say it, but it might happen sooner rather than later. You deserve to make your own choices for once in your life."

Emil had no idea the things I'd done for his father. Nobody did. Only the Adriann family knew about my flesh binding, but only Sorrelo Adriann knew I was much more than a personal attendant who kept his itinerary up to date and made trips for him to the trade district. Secrets inside secrets.

"I'm always going to be by somebody's side," I said. "It's what I want."

The front of Emil's bald head wrinkled as he frowned with those last words, then he shook his head like he didn't know what to do with me. "You could be by my side. You could take your freedom one step at a time, see how you liked it."

Emil was young, hardly older than nineteen. The only things kids his age understood was idealism and how to make promises they couldn't keep. And life could be worse than serving the wealthiest man in the Augustin territory.

My uneasiness graduated to nausea. *Bolivar's eyes, full of hope, thinking I had the power to stop an innocent man from dying. His shirt rough under my fingers as I threw him in the river.*

Chapter 3

THE PALACE SAT on the second level ridge in the Clover Hollows district, its façade of red marble twinkling with enough white jade and torchlight to be seen by anyone in the chasm with a direct line of sight. We threaded between onyx pillars and entered a hallway lined with torches that reflected off murals carved from silver and gold veins running through the walls. Nobles working the palace—civil intendants, lower chamberlains, and keepers of the Adriann trust—watched us pass, but their attention was cursory at best. Some probably had no idea an execution had occurred. It was sad and a little ironic. To them, ignoring what made them uncomfortable suited them just fine. They were in the best position to make a difference and were the least likely to care.

The commoners knew about the execution, though. Charcoal marked the foreheads of the guards standing attention and patrolling the halls. It was a custom many orthodox believers of the Foundry practiced after the death of a smith, but Bolivar hadn't been a smith, just a follower.

Emil's sister Sara waited at the door to the magnate's atrium, looking composed with her dark braided hair resting on one shoulder. She knew better than anyone how to wear a mask. She wore a grey-and-white coat made from pitch mink fur over a black jerkin of bat leather—the comforts of a lady masking the suit of a mercenary. "Wait in line if you're waiting to speak to Father," she said.

"What do you want with him?" Emil asked.

"Oh, I just wanted to let him know I might be able to prove if Bolivar was guilty."

"Not that it matters anymore," Emil said bitterly.

"Who knows, it might convince someone or another to stop trying to hang Father from the rafters."

I hated the possibility that Sorrelo had been right. Even if Bolivar was a traitor, he'd still deserved a trial. "I have to see the magnate," I said.

"Now's not a good time. He's speaking with the primordia. Nektarios decided to drop in."

"Oh, fhelfire," Emil breathed.

Sorrelo didn't like me hanging around when Nektarios was in town, but that sentiment wasn't a Word, so much good it did for the pressure building at the base of my neck. The magnate was afraid of the primordia finding out about flesh magic, probably because he was worried the Sovereign might try to replicate it on him. Not that it would make much difference. The Sovereign and his sycophantic primordia could already do whatever they wanted to the territories' rulers and to everyone else.

I put my hand on the door, but Sara grabbed my wrist. "If you prefer your skin attached to your body, I wouldn't."

I pushed my way inside. Polished, mosaicked marble spanned the length of the room and centuries-old frescos stared down at us from the ceiling. Streams of lava bubbled along the walls in stone aqueducts, sloughing the length of the throne room and disappearing behind the granite throne. Sorrelo stood on the dais leading up to his throne, speaking with the primordia, his arms folded behind him where Nektarios couldn't see him clenching his own wrists. Both men looked in our direction as Emil and Sara followed me inside. Sorrelo grimaced, but he had to have known this might happen.

Nektarios wore the features of a man in his prime, with a body chiseled from stone and a face I knew at least three people had written songs about. He was lithe like a dolomite panther and wore faded black leathers. The deadness in his shorn hair was one of the only things that gave away his age. There was even less life in his lupine yellow eyes. "Emil. Sara," he said. He frowned at me. "Who is this?"

"My personal attendant," Sorrelo said. "What I know, he knows. He is permitted here."

"Oh? And that is up to you, when it is my message that is at risk of compromise?" The primordia left the dais, the marble somehow creaking as he strode toward us. Primordia were like mountains incarnate—they could break a boulder in two just by standing on it. I instinctively moved up until Emil and Sara were a step behind me.

Nektarios stopped close enough so that when he took his time to look me up and down, the smell of lilac crossed the space between us and filled my nostrils, making me feel light. He didn't wear vambraces or a long sleeve under his chest guard, and his bared muscles ground together like rock when he crossed his arms. Where my ponytail was unkempt and wisps of hair sometimes tickled my face, there wasn't a strand on his head that was out of place. Looking him in the eyes for too long made a phantom ladle stir something warm in the back of my chest, but I imagined he was used to that kind of reaction by now. "You killed Bolivar Adriann, did you not?" he asked.

"I did."

"You know it is the audencia's responsibility to put to trial and execute suspected criminals, yes?" He set his hand on my shoulder.

Under his grip I sensed the faint trembling of someone trying to keep the slightest change in grip from breaking bone. Before I could answer, Magnate Sorrelo said, "A magnate can take extreme authority during extraordinary moments in history." His brown sandals tapped across the marble as he joined us. "We already uncovered two plots to take my life in the last six months. We will need to nip this in the bud if I want to hold my rule."

"Magnates have long memories, it seems," Nektarios said without looking away from me. "Their little brains stuck two hundred years in the past. A time when they could do as they pleased without consequence." He flashed his teeth at me. "It felt good, did it not? I bet the smell did nicely to cut through the stench of sulfur."

Bolivar's eyes, shiny with tears, glistening with the river's fire. "Not like this."

"You're not here because of the execution," I said. "You're fast, but you're not that fast. It takes someone like you, what, a few passings to get here from Saracosta? The death of someone outside a magnate and his children makes no difference to you or the Sovereign."

The primordia's hand twitched. Light enough for him to barely notice and hard enough for my shoulder to purple by next passing. I struggled not to flinch. "I am here to pass a message along. That is all." He patted the side of my face, his palm slapping painfully against my ear and cheek. "I am done, so now I may take my leave."

He walked through us instead of past—I bounced off his side while Emil and Sara stepped away so he wouldn't knock them to the ground. The royal guard was already opening the door for him by the time he reached it, and his exit was finalized with the echo of rockwood settling back into its frame.

"Rotten all the way down," Emil muttered.

"What?" his father asked.

"Nothing."

Sara stared at the door like she was waiting for Nektarios to come waltzing back in. Lava bubbled in the aqueducts while we waited. Finally, she asked, "What was that about?"

"Politics," Sorrelo said. "Favors. A small one this time, for the Sovereign's son, Bilal. I'm requested to send fifty of my best soldiers to Saracosta to be trained as Bilal's personal guard."

Sara snorted. "A three-hundred-mile journey for *that*? I swear, the only thing the Sovereign seems to have on his mind lately is that boy."

"Let's hope it stays that way. Visits from Nektarios have become infrequent."

I frowned at Sorrelo as he made his way back to his throne, his red ermine robe swishing over marble. The start of a thought wormed its way in my head—that if the Sovereign put him in his place, these reformers wouldn't exist in the first place—but I squashed it fast. Sometimes Sorrelo liked to ask what I was thinking with a Word, and that's when I learned the price of insubordination. Best to push the bad thoughts down and deep.

The magnate moved up the steps to his granite throne and collapsed on the cushion, leaning on his knees and rubbing his face. Sara marched after him until she was on the dais, head tilted up. "I know you forced Ig to kill Bolivar with a Word."

Sorrelo looked up from his hands. "And?"

Emil followed his big sister, stepping more carefully. "Father, don't you think killing Bolivar was a little hasty?"

"Yes, Father," Sara continued. "Stop talking like a bureaucrat and start acting like you just grilled your own cousin in front of the whole city without blinking."

"Shut it," Sorrelo hissed. "Now." If anyone else had said those words, they would've been tossed in the Lid. I was just amazed to see Emil and Sara agree on something, even if Emil was having a much harder time at it.

"Didn't you say outside you could prove Bolivar's innocence?" I asked.

Sara rounded on me. "Don't think you're in the clear. You more than anyone would have reason to throw my father in the river, and you just got to practice on Bolivar. You didn't get a taste of something you liked, did you?"

"Sara," Emil said. "Stop."

Sara glared at her brother, but Emil didn't back down.

The magnate gave a wave of his hand. "Ig will never want to betray me. It's not in his nature. Now tell me what you learned about Bolivar, Sara."

"Trusting someone with nothing to lose," she muttered. She made a point to turn her back to us, then pulled a slip of paper out of her pocket and rose halfway up the steps. "Bolivar spent time with a drinking buddy named Tuli Dempra who went missing while you were... investigating Bolivar. A convenient time to disappear, I'd say. Tuli owns a place on the fourth level, but we found nothing worthwhile when my men ransacked it." She ascended the rest of the stairs and handed the paper over. "Here is an address for a suspected rat hole of his on the eighth floor. I bribed a whore for that, so you be the judge on how reliable the information is."

The magnate took the paper and started nodding as he read it. "Good, Sara. Very good."

She landed on the bottom of the steps and set her hands on her hips. "Well, that's all the information I have," she said to me. "If you want to tip off any reformers before my father sends out one of his goons, best hurry. In the meantime, I'll be drowning my sorrows in the nearest bar. A family member recently passed, in case you were wondering."

She left. Sorrelo turned to his son, who lingered. "Is there anything else you would like to add?"

Emil swallowed. Sorrelo seemed to be the only person in the world he was afraid of, primordia included. "No, sir," he finally said.

"Then leave."

The doors to the atrium shut behind Emil, and the sound of crackling flames and lava filled the silence. Hundreds of men and women in the ceiling's fresco hung over us, judgment in their eyes.

"Let me look into Tuli Dempra," I said.

"I would have expected you to want a break after earlier."

"I'm fine." My heart thumped as I looked at the paper crumpled in Sorrelo's hand. It was too late for Bolivar, but not for the people Olevic was interrogating. He'd ply them slowly—I'd seen him work before, and the stretch of time between sessions was just important as the sessions themselves. I could exonerate them before he crippled and maimed the whole group.

"You don't sound fine," Sorrelo said. "You sound the opposite, actually. Disappointing, considering how you serve me."

Bolivar kneeling on cut knees, torso shaking as he sobbed, head bowed. The magnate knew this was nothing like the reformers I'd hunted down for him. They'd made their guilt clear before finding me looming in their shadows. "You saw how the crowd reacted," I said. "The execution only made the people you want to scare angrier. You don't want to give them more reasons to start a coup."

"You think they have reasons?"

I didn't bother lying, since he could just force the truth with a Word. "Yes."

I braced myself for his anger, but Sorrelo only rubbed at the bridge of his nose. "Why can't everyone be as honest as you? Sometimes I think you're the only one I can trust. People need to believe I can take criticism. A good ruler must be able to take any news that is hard to hear."

Serving Sorrelo was my purpose, but maybe there was room for more. Maybe I could advise him. Nudge him in the right direction when times like these came. "You could step down. Make the announcement now and it could placate the commoners while you prepare Emil for the throne. Augustin loves your son. They'll be happy with him as their leader."

His expression darkened. "Ig, kill Emil."

The weight of the command pressed against me. The pressure built toward a crescendo every moment I refused to obey, and my vision turned glassy with tears in anticipation of my doom, the phantom grip squeezing tighter, tighter, tighter on the back of my neck, threatening to blossom.

I gasped as I fell to the ground, overwhelming pain blinding me. My mind raged, lightning lancing behind my eyelids, and I focused all my energy on counting upward. Somewhere between seventy and eighty I would succumb to a coma, and then death, according to my old masters.

I spent every waking moment doing whatever it took to avoid this agony, but I couldn't kill Emil. Not him.

"I change my mind," Sorrelo finally said as the number sixteen bounced inside my skull. His voice sounded far away, at the other end of a cave.

Waves of relief washed in, but I stayed on the floor, catching my breath. "Punishing you by flesh magic can be very inconvenient at times," Sorrelo said. "This roundabout way of forcing you to disobey gets tiring." He stroked the patchy whiskers of his beard. "But it makes me wonder sometimes. If I punished you enough times, would your desperation to end it get the best of you? Would you ride the pain over and over or would you give up and try to kill my son?"

I struggled to my feet with wet, ragged breaths. Dizziness made me waver and my chest seize, and I vomited onto the stone. The magnate didn't care. His marble floors had seen plenty of my vomit already. "Find Tuli Dempra," he said. "You'll extract as much information from him as you can, and then you'll kill him. Remain unseen and tell no one of this task. And Ig, you'll perform this in a way that would be of most benefit to me."

His Words settled on my shoulders like a blanket. They nestled deep inside my bones, and they would stay there until I killed Tuli Dempra, or Tuli got himself killed some other way. Sorrelo's last command was important, and he included it with every set of Words—it guaranteed I wouldn't find a way to double-cross him.

As I turned to leave, he spoke again. "I mean it when I say

you won't be seen. Sara tells me she saw you near Bolivar's home when I had you investigate him a few passings back. It's no surprise she's gotten so suspicious of you. It wouldn't do for my children to know you were more than my personal attendant. Especially Sara. The fact everyone underestimates you is what makes you my most precious tool."

I paused, unsure if the compliment was intentional or if he was playing with my head again.

"Go," Sorrelo said. "Find the people who want to kill me. And thank you."

With a nod, I left the chamber.

Chapter 4

As CRUEL AS Sorrelo could be, living in Mira was a luxury compared to my life growing up in Sulian Daw. The magnate let me roam the city whenever work for him dried up; a step up from my life under the cultists he stole me from, who locked me in their compound every minute I didn't break my back for them. For that I would be forever grateful.

I turned down a dark stone alley near the palace, where homes lined a path that swayed like a centipede. The air was calm and smelled of sweet pinesap flowers. Pyremoss grew in the crevices where the walls met the ceiling, and the red, shimmering moss guided my way. I stopped at one of the supply sheds used for maintaining the piping running between levels, and after locking myself inside for several minutes, emerged as Jakar or Hossa.

I'd traded my servant's robes for a maroon-colored cowl and coat, which hid pieces of black beetle carapace that rubbed against my shoulders and chest in a satisfying way. If I closed my eyes and focused on the way these strange clothes fit me, the name Jakar almost felt like *more*. Like I was a different person. "Jakar" was known by no one, really just a moniker over anything else, not that Sorrelo would've cared enough to know. One of my few precious secrets that left a smile on my face every time I had the chance to act him out.

As Jakar the Mercenary, I allowed myself the dumb fantasy of taking the identity, even working up the courage to picture myself living outside the capital, and that's how I passed my time on my trek to the eighth level, working pretend jobs with my score of invisible friends. The humid heat from the river and perpetual glow of the bottom levels dispersed as I moved up the stairs toward to the sinkhole's mouth, red and green nebula smearing the blanket of stars in the sky and Ceti twinkling down on the capital, the brightest star of them all. Ice crusted the metal railings I leaned on for support, numbing my palms, and it bearded building fronts along the ridge, an occasional gust from Ra'Thuzan's surface hitting me like a slap to the face.

My breath came out thick as smoke and foot traffic had reduced to a trickle by the time I reached the eighth level. Further along the ridge, Tuli's hideout waited through a veil of mist leaking from the tip of a nearby ice sheath. Frost condensed on my clothes and the whiskers on my face as I approached the hideout, and I clenched my teeth from the cold.

I noticed a man bundled in several layers of clothing on the doorstep to a general store a few doors down. He stood, clutching his coat to his body, and when he passed me, the hairs on my neck stood.

I followed the alley running along the side of the rat hole's façade, then pressed my back to the wall and counted to thirty. When I peeked out, the man was leaning against the walkway's railing fifty feet away, coughing over the edge.

He was casing the place. Maybe one of Sara's men? A reformer? But why would a reformer be watching their own rat hole?

I erred on the side of caution. There was always another way in.

Inside the alley, nothing indicated the place along the rock wall where the rat hole ended and the next house began, so I stopped at the neighboring door and knocked. No one answered. I cupped my hands and peered through the grimy windows. Only darkness waited inside. A place without pyremoss or even fire usually meant abandonment.

I cupped the steel lock in my hand and waited until it vibrated and opened with a click.

A smith somewhere on the ground level had put so much care and work into this lock. What would Mateo say if he knew a nonbeliever of the Foundry—a foreigner, no less—wielded the same elemental power as him and his smiths?

The hinges squeaked as the door swung inward. Dust had made its home everywhere, and the wall connecting the house to the rat hole sported a soot-stained fireplace. I knelt into the fixture, crawling through ash and pressing the palm of my hand to the back. I closed my eyes.

The composition felt like... sandstone, with injections of limestone. It'd be hard to move, but not impossible. I took a deep breath, then pushed with my palm until my hand started to sink into the stone.

The rock swallowed my arm like thick mud. I slid my other hand in through the rock until my elbows disappeared. My palms faced away from each other, like I was swimming and preparing to propel myself forward. The rock was cold as ice at first, but it started to warm from friction as it ground against itself to move out of the path of my hands. With a groan, I pulled the rock open.

The more space I wanted to create in the rock, the more compression I needed. That meant more heat. Elementals like myself could funnel away heat generated by composites they could control, making them temporarily immune, but if a rock contained ninety-percent of what I had power over, the remaining ten-percent of vitrified rock could still cause extensive burns. Sparks generated from compression friction bit at my arms, but I gritted my teeth and soldiered on. The sediment was warm as coffee by the time I'd created enough space to crawl into. Newly-formed white stone covered the interior, covered in stress fractures—sandstone turned into metamorphic rock. Marble. I began the process again. A few of these nooks would get me out of one building and into another.

Cold, delicious air caressed my face when I reached the other side. Poking my head through the hole, I found the one-room rat hole empty. I widened the hole until I could crawl through and climb to my feet, and I stretched my aching muscles and dusted off my clothes. The place was small, poorly insulated, with moisture collecting in the corners where lightcaps grew, casting a teal-white glow on the room. A cot lay in the corner with several layers of blankets stacked on top. The perfect place for squatting to escape heat from the guards. A lockbox and a gas lamp sat on a desk of mycelium wood beside the cot, and I sat in the seat.

Writing utensils and a small pile of bits and standards sat in the lockbox, grime collecting in the grooves of the coins. I ran my fingers over the desk and felt the curves of handwriting engraved on the surface. Mycelium wood was fragile. Judging by the criss-crosses and flourishes of scratches, someone had done quite a bit of work here.

If the dust and the undisturbed mold collecting at the base of the door were any indication, this hideout hadn't been visited in several passings. Maybe Tuli skipped town before Bolivar was even arrested.

I gripped the edges of the desk. It rattled, revealing a dark space in the wall that the desk concealed. Fungus in the wood that a craftsman had failed to kill sometimes survived in poorly-crafted mycelium desks, which resulted in mold eating into rocky surfaces in direct contact with the wood. And someone had hollowed out one of these erosions. A thin stack of papers lay hidden inside the dark space, and I pulled them out.

They were journal entries detailing meetings between Tuli

and Bolivar Adriann. They played card games in a hostel frequented by visitors from Mira's other territories, and Tuli had been trying to learn details that would get him some one-on-one time with the magnate, like guard counts and patrol schedules. The handwriting looked painfully familiar, but I couldn't recall from where.

One entry said, *Met with the magnate's cousin on the eighth of First Northern Sway, at approx. 14 a.p.* So about three weeks ago. Fourteen after passing, a usual late hour for drinking. There was no mention of collaborators or if Tuli had help, but the journal repeatedly mentioned prayers for good fortune, and that the work they did was to spite their "brothers and sisters."

Referring to a nonrelative as a sibling was common back in Sulian Daw, but in Mira, people saw it as strangely intimate. Only the smiths of the Foundry called each other brethren.

Was a smith trying to overthrow the magnate?

I frowned at an excerpt from the last entry: *No matter how drunk Bolivar gets, he is unwilling to share key details that could get me alone with Sorrelo Adriann. He may be a dead end. Other possible avenues? The magnate's manservant?*

My heart skipped. There was no rational reason to be afraid, but I couldn't stop thinking about what the magnate would do if he thought I was a reformer, of the pain of my flesh binding hurting me over and over again. I stood there, trembling, and nearly ripped the entry into pieces.

No. The magnate would never believe I was helping them. He knew I couldn't lie.

The reformers had considered approaching me for help. How close had they come to finding me in some dark corridor inside one of the districts? Now that half of Augustin had watched me throw Bolivar in the river, the chances of it happening were nonexistent.

The paper crinkled in my hand and I slapped the sheaf once against the wood, overcome. Nothing here would help me unlock the pen of prisoners in the listening chambers.

I crawled through the tunnel and left the abandoned house. What would Tuli think if he found a tunnel of marble carved into the middle of his hideout? Only primordia could bend and break rock like that, and a magnate's punishment was an unpleasant dream compared to the horror the primordia were capable of unleashing. Maybe Tuli would assume one had blown through here and discovered his journal entries. That was a funny thought.

I passed the man patrolling the ridge. He was too concerned with watching his step and grumbling from the cold to look at my face.

SORRELO SAT AT his dining table, digging into seared salamander, roasted slug, and sweet potatoes. A massive chandelier hung above our heads, glittering with red and white light, made to resemble the moon, Saffar. It cast a bloody hue onto the food the magnate stuffed into his mouth. "This stays between you and the family," he said between mouthfuls as he studied the journal entries.

I'd expected as much. If evidence implying Bolivar's innocence somehow got out, one of the few remaining threads that kept the peace would break. *At least Sorrelo would have more protestors to give the Listener*, I thought, struggling to keep the bitterness off my face.

"This last part is interesting," he continued. "The rebels were thinking of recruiting you."

"Apparently."

He leaned back in his chair and chewed on his sweet potatoes. "If I had cause for concern, you probably would have forgotten to give me this page. Or burned it."

"You're right."

"Do I have cause for concern? Tell the truth, Ig."

"No."

"Good," the magnate said. "Now go eat. Come back prepared for your next job."

"Yes, magnate."

In the kitchen, I smiled politely at the other servants as I sat down, many of whom wore streaks of charcoal on their foreheads. They offered a few insincere nods before returning to their food. I brought my attention back to my food, trying to keep their looks from bothering me.

I had to consider the possibility I wouldn't be able to save the people Olevic was interrogating. But what could I do? Wait around until another lead presented itself?

I stared at the table knife, imagining it sliding into the soft skin under Olevic's jaw. That was always an option.

There was no Word stopping me from killing Augustin's Listener, but it was about as close to disobeying Sorrelo as I could get, and it was treason, and all the magnate needed to do was ask the right question and I'd have to tell him everything. The pain that would ensue wouldn't hold a candle to Olevic's table.

The knife shook in my hand, and I set it down.

The atrium was echoing with voices when I returned. The magnate sat on his granite chair, scrutinizing Sara and Emil as they stood side by side below him. "A smith?" Emil asked. "Really?"

I stopped within the shadow of a pillar, leaning against an engraving of Fheldspra creating a prison of fire for The Great Ones within the Black Depths, watching. Sorrelo noticed me but didn't comment. He motioned to one of the guards and the man brought the journal entries to Emil.

"And what could those possibly be?" Sara asked her brother, exasperated.

"It… looks like entries of Tuli Dempra meeting with Bolivar."

Sara's attention switched to her father. "Where'd you find that?"

"One of my 'goons' found it in Tuli Dempra's rat hole."

She scoffed. "*Batra*. I had men staking out the place. They would have seen someone entering, and if they did and didn't report it, someone is taking a swim."

For once, Sorrelo let out a genuine laugh. It sounded lofty. The kind of laugh belonging to a street performer reciting a libretto, or to someone who wasn't a sociopath. It was one of his endearing qualities that made him charismatic when it suited him. "You'll never change," he said. "But I don't want you to. It makes you predictable. Of course I knew you'd stake out the place. I have ways around it."

She tensed in retort but stopped herself. She usually kept her attitude to a minimum while guards were present. "Why are we here, then?" she asked. "Let the Listener or one of his interrogators look into this lead."

"No. This involves a member of the Foundry. Emil is close with the master smith, which means he can learn more through his friendship than anyone else could with knives or hammers."

"Look at you, Father. Being humane for once. But I disagree. You need to squeeze right now. Don't let them fly away."

Emil lowered the papers and frowned. "I don't believe it. A smith really wrote this."

"So go find this mysterious smith," Sara said. "I have better things to do."

"This is about more than saving Father, Sara. We're in danger, remember? The reformers are going to drag our bodies through the streets if they get the chance."

"You're going with your brother," the magnate said. His attention moved to Emil. "If you can't find Tuli Dempra in the Foundry, you're going to set an example to the smiths by arresting Mateo."

I bit back a groan. Emil and Sara stared wordlessly at their father, and even the guards started at the proclamation. An arrest of the master smith was the worst thing that could happen to Sorrelo. He wouldn't have to wonder if there'd be a coup, as there'd be riots in the streets before Emil and Sara could even return to the palace.

"Father," Emil said. "The Foundry's been loyal to the

territories' magnates for eight-hundred years. Even the Sovereign respects the smiths enough to leave them alone. Besides, we don't have the authority to arrest a master smith of the Foundry. Only Fheldspra can judge someone like Mateo."

Sorrelo rose from his seat and slowly descended to the dais as he wrung his hands. He only wrung his hands when he wanted to hurt something. "He's housing a traitor. If he needs motivation finding Tuli Dempra, some time in the Lid will give it to him."

Emil and Sara stood within striking range, but the magnate didn't expel the energy simmering under his skin. Sorrelo Adriann never hit his children. In fact, his rage always washed past them. He seemed to believe it made him a better father. Maybe it did.

His gaze settled on me, and his children finally noticed me. "Take Ig with you," Sorrelo said. "He makes the smiths nervous. He'll keep Mateo off balance."

Sara turned her back to Sorrelo and regarded me coolly. Emil opened and closed his mouth several times like he wanted to argue, but the words didn't come.

"There'll be consequences if you don't find the people trying to kill me," Sorrelo said. Emil and Sara were too consumed by their own thoughts to notice him staring at me.

Chapter 5

"FATHER'S AN IDIOT," Sara said as we entered the misty warmth outside the palace.

Emil walked like he was headed for a death sentence. "This isn't happening."

Sara veered away from the ramp to the trade district, approaching a man leaning against the palace's corner pillar. The stranger was eying a pack of guards patrolling the second level and wore a red-and-grey doublet that was a common style among the Augustin nobiletza. His clothes were moth-eaten and stained upon closer inspection. "Where's Vyn?" Sara asked.

The man pointed at someone smoking a cigarette at the ridge's railing near a set of stairs. Vyn watched one of the waterfalls leave dark spots on the river's lava, then coughed into his sleeve, and I recognized him as the man surveilling Tuli Dempra's rat hole.

Sara's friend fell in step beside her as the princepa led us toward Vyn. "What are we doing?" Emil asked, but Sara ignored him. I tried to mask the hesitance in my stride. *Remain unseen*, Sorrelo's lingering Word whispered in my ear.

Vyn nodded to the princepa, smoke streaming out of his nostrils, but his face fell when he saw her expression. "Saiora?"

"You fucked up, friend."

"What you mean?"

Sara studied him as she deliberated, then nodded in my direction. "Do you know him?"

I resisted the urge to look down. "Nãu," Vyn said. "Why?"

It made no sense that a small part of me was sad he didn't recognize me. When I dressed as Jakar ot Hossa, I was always surprised by how easy it was to don the confidence of a free man. But when I wore these robes, acting like someone else turned into this insurmountable thing. Even the way I walked changed, I'd noticed.

I was Ig through and through, I realized, swallowing back the phlegm in my throat. Best not to dwell on such facts.

"What's this about, Sara?" Emil asked.

"Nothing. Just something I need resolved. Vyn, go wait for my orders by the tetaro downstairs."

Vyn flicked his cigarette and disappeared down a nearby stairwell. Once Emil wasn't thinking so much about Mateo, he might realize Sara suspected I was the one who recovered Tuli's journal entries and was angry at Vyn for letting me slip through his fingers, but at least Vyn had put those suspicions to rest. For now.

Sara turned to her friend in the nobiletza disguise. "Do you remember that kebob place on the fifth level, over in the Corridor of Keys? *Kebob Da'Pin*. There's a storage shed next to it with a hole in the back where people draw water from one of the rivers. Take care of Vyn and dump him there when you're done."

"You're kidding me, right?" Emil asked.

"Go," Sara said to her friend. The man wilted under Emil's gaze, but headed for the stairs anyway. Before Emil could protest, Sara set a hand on his chest. "There's a story here. I caught him selling cigarettes laced with Ash to some kid last week, so he was going to die one way or another. I just wanted to extract some use out of him first."

Emil joined me at the railing and leaned over, searching the trade district on the first level. Vyn paced in front of one of Augustin's play stages—a theatre stage for children's plays—and Sara's friend joined him. The railing creaked from Emil's grip. He and Sara had a fifteen-year-old sister named Efadora who lived in Manasus, and if Emil had caught anyone offering her drugs, he would've broken their spine with his bare hands.

Sara had been smart to make Vyn wait in front of the tetaro. It really drove the point home.

Emil let go of the railing. "There's too much frontier justice going on lately. He should have a trial."

"Too late now. It'll be a 'he said/she said' at this point, and I'm not risking Vyn going free. I'm taking care of him whether you want me to or not."

Vyn followed Sara's friend until they disappeared in the crowd, and Emil turned away, gaze sharp enough to cut. "Just do me a favor and arrest any drug dealers you come across in the future. Don't add them to your fucking payroll." He headed for the staircase. "Let's find Mateo."

If Emil knew what I knew, he'd find the company Sara kept less surprising. I was one of few who knew Sara moonlighted as Mira's Hand, the rising star in Augustin's smuggling rings.

Up until recently, organizations like the Torsell Gang or the Ortavella Runners had controlled the smuggling game, until Mira's Hand had carved a mark in the industry by carving up Torsells and Ortavellas. But while Sara profited off moving the drugs the gangs sold, she broke the backs of those who hired her if she found out they sold to children. She also stole from the nobility, leaving coin and other gifts for the poor living in the Barrows on the seventh and eighth levels, stamped with the Mira's Hand symbol. The commoners loved Mira's Hand almost as much as they loved Emil.

Sorrelo was the only member of the nobility who knew about his daughter's alter-ego—a fact I'd learned by chance while running an "errand" for the magnate. When it came to lawbreaking and his children, he pretended the two didn't mix. But it was why Sorrelo didn't want Sara, and by extension Emil and Efadora, knowing I could move steel, break rock, and more. They knew of my flesh binding to their father but not how to control me with a Word; the power would pass to them once he died. And according to the magnate, once his daughter 'matured and let her streak of rebellion run its course', he'd consider letting his three children in on the fact I was an elemental.

On Augustin's first floor, the tunnel out of the city gaped at us like the mouth of a whale shark. Countless caravans and travelers followed the deep ruts out of the sinkhole and descended into the crust's extensive cave system. We entered the start of the tunnel, and a hundred feet down the gentle slope there was a line of stone columns and flagstone steps built into the left wall. The Foundry. It was a dry heat down here, the glow of a hundred fires and forges blasting heat onto the road like a furnace.

We moved up the flagstone steps and passed through the columns. In the main chamber, forges lined the side walls where smiths worked in brown robes, their frames bulky from the fire-resistant clothing underneath. Dozens of traders from across the territories, and even a smattering from Callo and Xeriv and other countries beyond The Rift, browsed freshly made tools and weapons that littered long, granite countertops along the back wall. A procession of commoners were being led through a side hallway—only the wealthy could afford Foundry steel, but a temple waited farther inside the sanctuary where every believer of Fheldspra was welcome.

We crossed a floor checkered with dark volcanic rock, each black tile embedded with a rune of carved ruby as long as my arm. Near the back, Emil caught the arm of a passing smith cradling a box of chisels. "I need to speak with Mateo," he said.

"Sorry, saior, he's—" The man took in our group. "Dedra!" he yelled over the din.

A smith perked up at the call and weaved through a trio of patrons. "Yeah?"

"Princep and princepa're here to see the master smith."

Dedra paused when he took me in, but nodded. "Sword, please."

The Foundry forbade any weapons beyond the trade area. Emil hesitated before unstrapping the blade from his belt and handed it to the smith. Judging by Sara's expression, she and I shared the same thought—how compliant would Mateo be if we had to arrest him? He knew as well as anyone what a prison sentence from Sorrelo Adriann meant.

We walked through halls of black and brown rock. Most were natural, but some had been carved out with explosive pyroglycerin, courtesy of the cartographers from the city's Archives. Channels for magma had been cut to flow off the river, spreading throughout the Foundry like arteries. Ancient pyremoss on the ceiling cast red, orange, and white light onto the hallways.

Dedra stopped. "Mateo's tending to two smiths taking the rhidium trial. Not a place for manservants."

"A valid point," Sara said. "One we'll promptly ignore. Keep going."

The smith offered an embarrassed bow and continued onward. "Ignore the screams."

It didn't take long for the cries to reach us. We entered a candlelit chamber with four stone slabs and bodies writhing on two of them. Mateo stood at the foot of the slabs, accompanied by a physician, who was only there to record the time of death if a smith passed. No known salve could suppress the agony each smith endured to become a metal worker. Something I had personal experience with.

Mateo nodded toward the Adrianns and offered a subdued smile. "How are you two doing?"

"We're fine," Emil said. "Can we talk alone?"

The master smith's strained look made it clear he didn't want to leave the apprentice smiths' sides. Sheets of sweat covered the young man and woman, both of them wearing urine-stained pants. The man moaned and gurgled, and the sounds tapered as his eyes rolled around in his head.

"He's dying," I said.

"We're all dying, Ig," Mateo said. "Hopefully we do something with our lives before that time comes, like Isak here did."

Emil watched the dying smith, and his eyes lost focus. It wasn't difficult to know why—he'd confided in me late one night over Saracostan cigars about the guilt he could never get over. Almost every member of the Foundry harbored survivor's guilt of some kind, but Emil's ran deeper than that.

Shortly before I came to Mira two years ago, the princep had undergone his own rhidium trial after starting initiation into smithhood. But then Sorrelo pulled Emil out before the final induction ceremony. Sorrelo witnessing the master smith slowly replace him as a father figure played a big part, but Emil believed his father had strung him along so the magnate could have a fighter outside the Foundry who could manipulate steel. And Sorrelo had gotten what he wanted— there was a reason people now called Emil "Rock Snake." All it cost was his relationship with his son.

"Come," Mateo said. "Isak will stay with us a few more hours."

We followed the master smith down the hall to a small chapel farther inside the sanctuary—a place exclusive to the smiths. Ratty blankets covered the dirt floor in the middle of the room, where smiths would press their foreheads to the ground during prayer, believing it connected them to Fheldspra deep within the core. A pulpit and dais sat at the head of the room, and a ten-foot stream of magma fell from roof to floor behind it.

Mateo's voice echoed in my direction as I circled the room.

"Sorrelo should've taken a smith with him when he passed through The Rift to treat with Sulian Daw. It's always hard to get good information on your country. Are Som Abast's skies really red?"

The smith never showed interest in Sulian Daw and its capital city, Som Abast, far as I knew—the Foundry valued strengthening one's household over proliferation in the bigger world, which I suspected was rooted to all the quake activity in The Rift that kept Mira so isolated from the rest of the world. "Som Abast translates to Bloodreach if that answers your question," I said. "The sky is red enough to plot out Saffar, but in that part of the world they call the moon Ulugh."

"I hear the people of Sulian Daw are violent."

Ah. He was trying to figure out the man who killed Bolivar. "People make their own assumptions about my people when they hear what Som Abast means in Miran. Sulian Daw is misunderstood. It's easy to judge if you look at their culture based on Miran standards."

I continued toward the magma fall at the end of the chamber. It spat and splashed onto the rock near my feet, and I noticed a plaque built beside it. *Stone makes a man; it breaks a man. Fire claims the soul. Fuse the two, a promised few; bear burden Fheldspra's toll.*

"Please step away from there," Mateo said. "It's dangerous."

Mateo had maneuvered to within several strides' distance, poised to grab me. The smiths saw magma as sacred, so maybe there was something significant about this particular fall. Or maybe this was his chance for a taste of revenge after what I'd done to his friend Bolivar.

No, he had disliked me since my arrival to Augustin. I didn't move.

Emil fiddled with the iron ring hanging from his belt loop. His gaze kept returning to the sacred falls behind me, his discomfort clear.

"Enough distractions," Mateo said once I stepped away. "Why am I here?"

Emil moved to the pulpit. "Do you know someone named Tuli Dempra? He's a smith. Presumably someone who serves here."

"No."

"How chummy are you with those who serve beneath you?" Sara asked. "Any strangers you might not know about?"

"Everyone here is a brother or sister. It's hard not to see them that way when you sit through their rhidium trial."

Emil ran a palm across the worn, dirty pages of the Sky Scrolls still open on the pulpit, expression wry. "You need to double check. Even if Tuli Dempra doesn't exist, or it's an alias with no official record, you need to find him somewhere. Anywhere."

"You want me to lie? Why?"

"Our father thinks someone in your order wants to overthrow him," Sara said. "There's evidence suggesting he might actually be right. We're under orders to arrest you if 'Tuli' isn't found. To set an example."

Mateo looked from Emil to Sara with a small smile, like he couldn't tell if they were joking. Then the smile fell. "Your father is going to get everyone killed. Tuli Dempra doesn't exist, and even if he did, anyone who sacrifices as much as we have to be a part of the Foundry would never distract themselves with politics." The statement echoed through the chamber, swallowed by the rush of falling magma.

"And here you are, in need of someone who would."

Emil stepped off the dais. "I'm sure Tuli is a false name. You can't be positive at least one smith isn't corrupted."

"I guess it's possible." Mateo tucked his shaggy locks behind his ear. "Give me a few weeks so I can investigate."

"It has to be now. I'm sorry, Mateo."

"Then I'm sorry too." He and Emil stared at each other for a few moments, until Mateo faltered. "There's no getting around this, is there?"

Sara pulled a bundle of twine from her back pocket and stepped forward, but Mateo put his hand up. "No restraints. Let me go with you two to the palace as friends. If anyone gets a whiff of this, it'll be the beginning of the end."

Mateo made the necessary preparations for his absence but told no one where he was going. We reached the main chamber where the smell of coal smoke and burnt honey hung heavy in the air as a smith worked the bellows to a nearby furnace. Nobody paid much heed to the princep and princepa escorting the master smith across the floor. I expected resignation at the thought of killing Mateo, but the idea of throwing him in the river only filled me with dread.

I couldn't execute another innocent person, I realized. It would break me.

A line of men passed through the pillars at the entrance, shouldering their way toward us. Swords scraped against scabbards, and the shop floor emptied as the Foundry's patrons rushed out of the way. Suddenly we faced a semi-circle of warriors, the space between the pillars behind them too crammed with bodies to offer escape. The men wore no colors, bore no insignias. Mercenaries.

"Do you know anything about this?" Emil asked Mateo over the din of panicked whispers. Mateo only shook his head. Other than the magnate's royal guard, no one could have known we were going to arrest the master smith.

The lead mercenary planted the tip of his sword against the floor and rested both hands on the hilt. "Speaking on 'half of Augustin, the son and eldest daughter of Sorrelo Adriann are hereby sentenced to imprisonment, and should they resist, death."

Emil's hand moved to his waist, but his weapon wasn't there. "This is treason," he said, scanning the crowd for more threats.

It was the coup, I realized. It had begun.

Chapter 6

WE WERE LESS than halfway across the floor of the Foundry's main chamber, the countertops of freshly forged blades waiting just a short sprint behind us, but if one of us made a break for it, the mercenaries would be hard on our heels.

Emil took a step toward the men. "Tell me who your leader is." He faced the apparent leader—a man clad in secular steel, standing apart from three others dressed in leathers. Four razor-sharp edges hovered a few strides away from Emil, polished until they almost glittered, but he barely seemed to notice.

"Don't worry 'bout that, princep. Simply surrender yourselves for judgment."

"No."

"One more time, 'n I'll ask politely—"

"I choose to die."

The leader clenched his jaw like he was trying to decide what to do. The ring of commoners struggled their way to the exit, but too many had paused to watch, boxing the others in. The leader raised his blade and chopped downward.

Emil swept his hand in front of his face, deflecting the sword with an open palm. The tip of the blade *tinged* off the floor, and the weight behind the swing left the side of the man's head exposed. Emil's fist connected with his opponent's neck and sent the man sprawling.

Before Emil could snatch at the dropped blade, the other three pounced.

Emil moved like water, pushing and deflecting the steel with his elemental power. His sword arm swiped at each weapon gracefully, but his other hand was less practiced—one of the blades found its way through, drawing a line down his forearm and flinging blood across the floor. Emil barely flinched. He lunged forward and shouldered his opponent, which sent the man stumbling backward. The rebel crashed into the line of bystanders, then roared in frustration and swung, his blade slicing through the backs of two merchants and dropping them to the floor.

The one wearing secular steel moved to his feet and backed away, a hand pressed to his neck, while two of his friends moved to opposite sides of Emil. The princep tried to keep them both in his line of sight, but was forced to focus on one while the other came from behind. I jumped forward. The man tried to bring his steel to bear, but I smashed into him and we hit the ground, his blade clattering against rock. I grabbed a fistful of his hair and smashed his head against the ground, and he tried to wrench my hand away, but I was stronger. He twisted his body around, locking his legs around my neck and putting me in a chokehold, and then I was the one trying to pry him off, the meat of his leg pressed against my throat.

I was terrible at hand-to-hand, and Sorrelo's earlier Word prevented me from using my power in front of others, so I could either let the man choke me to death or break loose and let the Word's punishment kill me. The choice was obvious. I let my grip go slack.

The rebel let out a sharp sound, halfway between a shout and a gurgle, and his hold loosened. Emil stood over us, the knife he was holding buried in the rebel's side. He helped me to my feet, but immediately pushed me out of the way as a rebel came at us swinging. Then hands were grabbing me from behind, dragging me back, and I found Mateo pulling me toward Sara, leaving Emil's side unprotected. Was Mateo a reformer?

A smith who had been working one of the forges pushed her way through the frightened merchants and commoners, a hammer hanging from her grip. The mercenaries hadn't noticed her, too focused on surrounding the princep, and the newcomer gripped her hammer with both hands as she moved in behind the mercenaries. She yelled as she swung, and the hammer connected, caving in the leader's skull and spraying brain and blood across the rune-carved floor. People screamed as the rebels turned to face their new enemy.

Other smiths entered the arena, having left their forges wielding hammers, chisels, and other makeshift weapons.

"You'll stay away from Master Adriann," one of the smiths said. "Surrender yourselves so that you may be brought to trial."

The mood shifted. Suddenly, the three remaining men looked vastly outnumbered, but they remained lax. One grinned. "Do smiths bleed same as the rest of us?"

Other rebels pushed past the pillars, knocking people down as they joined the first three. The number swelled to over a dozen, all ready to kill. Emil stepped away, and more smiths moved to join their brothers and sisters.

Blood dripped from the smith's hammer as she stood over the fighter with the crushed skull. "What do we do, master smith?"

All eyes moved to Mateo, and there was no hesitation in his voice. "Protect the Adrianns."

The rebels surged across the Foundry's floor, and we melted behind the newly formed line of smiths. "Follow me!" Mateo commanded as the rebels smashed into the smiths, swords clashing against tools.

We moved through the Foundry's depths, and the halls blended together as we rushed through crimson light interspersed with the white-hot glow of exposed magma flows. We reached a wrought-iron door covered in a strange pattern of interconnected parts. Mateo touched the barrier with both hands, and the parts started to click and move like a performance of metal. The door was one giant lock. One last click vibrated the iron, and the barrier disengaged from the frame. He pushed inward. A room on the other side couldn't fit more than several people, and crates of vials lined the back wall, glittering from the magenta-hued torches flickering on the walls.

"This is where you keep the rhidium," Emil said.

Mateo pushed the door shut behind us, and the metal chimed as the locks moved back into place. "Yes. Keep it to yourselves." He flipped over a rug to reveal a hatch as intimidating as the door. He placed his hands on the barrier, like before. "Help me, please," he said to Emil.

Even with both men straining and grunting, they barely managed to lift the trapdoor. Below, a tunnel glowed with faint light. "This will take us to the palace," the master smith said.

Emil climbed into the hole, followed by Sara and me. After I jumped in, Mateo followed and lingered on the last step, struggling to nudge the door enough for it to fall downward. He ducked before it could crush his head. We descended several steps and arrived in a tunnel wide enough for two men to walk abreast, the ceiling only a foot above Mateo's head, the tallest in the group. Whereas rock supported the walls of Augustin and the Foundry, packed dirt made up this passageway, and clumps of earth hung from the ceiling by threads of plant roots. Untrimmed patches of young pyremoss cast a dull light that strained the eyes.

Mateo led the way. "I can't believe I didn't know this existed," Emil said. "Does it lead anywhere other than the palace?"

"It connects several of the city's landmarks. From here you can reach the palace, the Archives, the Guild of the Glass, the physicians' halls, The Tempurium and some of the trade schools. The magnates from before the Sovereign established Mira put it here so their agents could move uninhibited. Or so I'm told."

"Father should have told us about this," Emil muttered.

I made no mention of how intimately familiar I was with these tunnels. The passageway started to slant upward, and we reached a room where several routes branched off. Mateo stopped. "The reformers made their move, which means your father's in danger." He pointed to one of the hallways. "That way leads to the throne room. Is that where Magnate Sorrelo is right now?"

"Most likely," I said.

"Is there one that leads to other parts of the palace?" Emil asked.

"Yes," Sara said. "That one leads to the library. Why do you want to know?"

Mateo and Emil started at the statement, but I was hardly surprised Sara knew about these tunnels. I was just happy I had never run into her down here. It would've been an awkward conversation. "You saw what those reformers did back there," Emil said. "They killed bystanders, Sara. What do you think they're going to do to the nobiletza in the palace?"

"You're going to help the nobles over father?"

"Father's been obsessed with protecting himself since this all started. He's surrounded by his royal guard and the chamber commander at all times. Other parts of the palace don't have that same kind of protection."

If the coup had begun, it would mean a fight in front of the magnate and whoever was with him. It would mean using my elemental power out in the open. "The throne room's designed to be barricaded," I said. "All of you can secure a place for the nobiletza and then find me and your father."

The group looked at me in unison. "You want to go alone?" Mateo asked.

"The magnate will be fine, and Emil needs all the help he can get."

Emil shook his head. "This is the magnate we're talking about. I'll take the risk by helping the others first, but that's crossing the line. I don't need Mateo. He's better off with you."

I didn't press further. Nobody questioned my request, but Sara's gaze lingered on me. The two groups parted, and I followed Mateo through the passage leading toward the throne room. As we ran, I prayed my lie about the barricade would somehow become reality, and that I wouldn't need to reveal my closest guarded secret in front of the master smith of the Foundry.

Chapter 7

"EMIL SHOULD'VE COME with us," Mateo huffed as he navigated the tunnels. "He's well meaning, but if the magnate is killed, that will mean even less protection for the nobiletza if the reformers take over the city. What if Emil is too late?"

I prayed that was the case. "You don't seem like someone who would give up easily."

"I don't like the magnate, but the Foundry made an oath to serve Augustin's ruler. If I give my life, Fheldspra will be waiting for me in the next life. I don't know what will await you."

The smith didn't know that the people who raised me since I was twelve, the Ebonrock cultists, included Fheldspra in their pantheon, but now didn't seem the time to mention it. Both organizations dedicated their lives to the mastery of a craft, too—the Foundry mastered the forge and the Ebonrock the flesh. "You saved me back there," I said between breaths. At first I thought he'd grabbed me to keep Emil separated and vulnerable, but as far as he knew, I was a helpless manservant. Those mercenaries would have cut me apart.

"It's what Bolivar would've done."

That did its job to shut me up.

We reached the end of the tunnel, where a lever protruded from the rock. Mateo pulled it, but nothing happened. He pressed his hand against the keyhole, but shook his head in frustration. "I can't get us through."

"The magnate doesn't want anyone who knows about these tunnels having access to his throne room." I pulled out a key made of a silver-tin alloy. It wasn't as durable as a typical key, but Sorrelo had been adamant that none of the palace keys be made of steel.

"You have a lot of power for Sorrelo's personal attendant," he said uneasily.

"I've never agreed and disagreed more with a statement."

The stone wall ground to the side, revealing a storage room lit by an aqueduct of magma circling the circumference of the room. It was one of the antechambers leading into the throne room. We rushed through and arrived in the main chamber to find shouting.

But only one person shouted. Sorrelo sat on his chair, pointing aggressively at the royal guard and the chamber commander braced against the pounding from a poorly barricaded door. "Where are the men who were supposed to relieve you?" he asked.

The chamber commander had heavy bags beneath his eyes. They must have been past the end of their shifts. "I mean no disrespect, saior, but there's a rebellion going on right now. Now is not a good time to look into it."

"You're saying you had no idea you had potential deserters among your ranks? That reflects poorly on you, Chamber Commander."

The chamber commander—Rikardo was his name—ignored the banging on the door and faced the magnate. "Saior, it seems we're the last two men standing between you and death, so I suggest you stop yelling."

Rikardo didn't seem to know about the escape tunnel, and I wondered how long the magnate would have waited before fleeing. He'd been cutting it close. Sorrelo's mouth hovered open for a retort, until he noticed us standing at the entrance to the antechamber. His body relaxed. "Where are Emil and Sara?"

"Emil needed his weapons. Sara is helping him," Mateo said.

"And how long will that take?"

A bang on the door loud enough to startle the guards cut him off. The wood cracked, and the tip of a battering ram appeared in a growing hole. Rikardo and his companion stabbed their spears through the breach, eliciting a scream from the other side. Mateo climbed the steps toward the magnate, and I remained off to the side, near the magma funneling around the edge of the throne room, watching the guards continuously shove their weapons into the hole.

"Accept Fheldspra," Mateo said quickly. Another crash. "I know how you feel about theology, but please, if you accept Him, He'll forgive you when you arrive home."

"You think I might die?" Even now, the magnate knew this wasn't the end. Didn't the master smith find it odd Sorrelo didn't try to flee?

"Whether you die now or much later, the burden can be lifted now. Please."

Sorrelo studied the man. "This means a lot to you, doesn't it?"

The master smith nodded. "Yes, magnate. I know we've had our differences, but everyone deserves a second chance."

The magnate feigned consideration until he snorted, the sound ugly. "I'm not a good man, Mateo. But I've accepted my nature. It can't be changed. I'll leave my place at Fheldspra's side to those more deserving, like my children." He motioned for Mateo to leave, and the master smith nodded again, frowning as he moved down the steps to take his place beside me.

When the guards attempted to pull their spears out of the breach, they grunted as the rebels held onto the other end of the shafts. The rebels won the tug of war, yanking the weapons away. The guards drew their short swords and waited for the barricade to fall.

"We can still flee through the tunnel," Mateo said to the magnate.

"No need," Sorrelo said simply.

I thought maybe Mateo would finally break and berate the magnate, but the master smith only watched the splinters fly off the door. "During the Schism the smiths swore to serve the throne second only to Fheldspra. I'll protect you, but I am not afraid to die either."

Sorrelo's brow rose. "I appreciate that."

A deep crack from the doors vibrated the floor, and the entrance swung open, followed by six men bearing short swords who hid behind their shields. They faltered when they found the magnate accompanied by two guards and two servants.

Rikardo and his comrade shouted and charged. Rikardo managed two strokes before taking a blade in the armpit and another to the base of his neck. His subordinate only managed one before crumpling to the floor, blood pouring from the hole in his face left by a spiked shield.

The line of men didn't advance. Instead, they broke to allow a newcomer to join the confrontation. Olevic Pike grimaced, taking in the carnage with sad eyes.

Sorrelo released a sharp breath. "Olevic?"

"You're alone," the Listener said, glancing at the master smith, then at me.

The muscles in the magnate's neck tightened. "I gave you everything," he said through clenched teeth.

"Favors buy you a following. Strength of character buys you loyalty."

"Drop the act," I said. "You don't have to put on a face for the master smith. He said he would die for the magnate."

Olevic's eyes narrowed, then the concern melted, his demeanor shedding like a skin. He smiled. "Mateo was a little too close with the princep anyway, so perhaps it's for the best he goes into a ditch with the rest of you."

"Have you even considered what the Sovereign might do

if you kill the Adriann family?" Mateo rumbled. I'd never heard him raise his voice before, or look so angry. "His primordia will tear the territories down and build them up again if he thinks anything threatens the peace."

"The Sovereign won't do shit. So long as the territories get along and Augustin doesn't break out in civil war, he will let this slide. And who would go to war for Sorrelo Adriann?" He laughed. "Last I heard, the Sovereign's too busy spoiling his son to step foot outside Saracosta. Isn't it you who told me that, Sorrelo?"

The magnate descended the throne, sliding his blade from the ornate scabbard at his side. The soldiers' shields rose a degree, but the magnate kept his movements slow and deliberate. His knuckles whitened on the sword's grip, and for a moment he looked ready to charge. Olevic didn't move as he stood in front of his rebels, amused. "Ig," Sorrelo said.

My time had come.

The magnate threw me his sword. I could feel the wavelengths of iron pulsing as it arced through the air. He had tossed it too short, and I caught the spinning blade, my steps awkward. "Kill my attackers," he said. "You have permission to do so in front of witnesses."

It was my first time using the Adriann family blade. The hilt was made of pale bone, wrapped in dark leather, with a gemstone in its pommel that was black as the void. The blade gleamed faint blue in the light—rhidium lined its edge, the alloy caustic enough to dissolve flesh. "This is rich," Olevic said.

"You tortured them," I said. "Even though they were innocent. They could have been fighting for your cause and it wouldn't have mattered."

"I'm sorry. Who?"

I shivered, the rage building. The people he'd maimed would remember him for the rest of their lives, but to him they were a footnote. Realization finally glimmered in his eyes. "Ah," he continued. "Well, if you think I would have risked raising suspicion before the big event, you're stupider than I thought."

A man trying to fly under Sorrelo's searching eye wouldn't have looked the way he had while strapping that man to the table. I looked past the group, where a massacre waited in the hallway outside. Nobiletza covered in bloody clothing, twisted up like marionettes dropped on the floor. I recognized some of the victims—wards to Augustin's secretariats. Children no older than thirteen.

"Ig," Sorrelo repeated as a warning. I wasn't in a direct path between the soldiers and the magnate, but the rebels didn't take advantage. We had nowhere to run as far as they knew, and they were enjoying the moment.

"That servant killed Bolivar," one of the rebels said. "He dies for Sorrelo, won't be unwillingly."

A man wearing a sergeant's patch left the line of soldiers and moved past Olevic, approaching me. "Don't want to harm you," he said, his commoner's accent thick. "Give me the weapon. Let us cut this cancer from the throne, then you go free."

I met Olevic's eyes, but he just shrugged. He would never let me leave alive, but the sergeant believed he could get away with mercy. The sergeant waited, as though seeing if I would surrender, then brandished his sword. "Won't forget how you took your vows so seriously. May Fheldspra judge you accordingly."

I inhaled deeply, settling into a fighting stance, feeling the smooth marble through the soles of my shoes. The stone pressed against the edges of my elemental senses, its resoluteness flowing through me. The soldier paused at the sudden change in my demeanor.

He charged, attempting to barrel me down with his shield. Maybe he still wished to disarm me instead of going for a killing blow.

His sympathy would mean his death.

I ran forward and propelled myself into the air, and my

body twisted to dodge his shield as I swept my weapon toward his exposed head. The magnate's blade made a clean cut as I sailed past him.

My feet touched the ground soundlessly, and I moved into a defensive posture. The men froze, and their sergeant's head bounced off the stone and bumped into the back of my foot. A second later, the sound of plate hitting rock echoed through the chamber as the sergeant's body crashed to the floor, and the smell of chemical burns wafted in my nostrils.

Olevic turned tail, pushing through his line of subordinates and running into the hall. He tripped over a body, but recovered and disappeared while the rebels were still adjusting to the sight of their friend's decapitated body. I thought of the way the sergeant had sized me up; a soldier trying to save a slave from his master.

Maybe I could have prevented all this if I'd thrown myself in the river long ago.

Whispers of pain nudged me onward. My work was still unfinished.

Before the rebels could think to attack, I stepped toward the aqueduct of lava. They stilled as they watched me dip my hand into the molten rock—down I went, the sleeve of my servant's robe catching fire, burning until it smoldered at the shoulder. The air rippled with heat, warming half my face. When the lava reached my elbow, I stopped.

My forearm glowed when I withdrew to face the magnate's enemies. Globules of deep, deep red dripped onto the marble as I once more stood before them, the magnate's sword in my right hand and half of my other arm coated in fire and rock.

"You're no servant," one of the soldiers said. "You're primordia."

"No," I said sadly. "I'm something else."

The closest one raised his shield and moved carefully. The five others flanked him. I flicked my hand toward him, the magma weighing my arm down, and released a chunk. It stuck to his shield and the wood burst into flame. He dropped his weapon and struggled to pull the shield off as his friend passed him. When the second man came within striking distance, he swung. I danced to the side, parrying a blow and striking him in the face with my molten fist. He fell to the ground screaming, wisps of smoke trailing from his hands as he clasped his skull.

While the first continued to wrest the burning shield from his arm, another unhurt rebel ran toward me. I made a pushing motion with my open palm, and the man flew backward, plate crashing against the stone wall.

I could increase my power exponentially by drawing heat from the elements within the lava I was bound to, but if I wasn't careful, too much energy would rip through me, killing me. Or I could feed too much heat into my elemental power and accidentally draw from my own body, killing me that way too. It was a precarious balance. There was also the problem of my skin blistering from the elements inside the molten rock I wasn't bound to. If I didn't end this fight soon, the lava would start eating into my flesh and bone. The four surviving rebels didn't move, though, surveying the man who had been thrown into the wall. The back of his head had broken, leaking blood mixed with white onto the floor, and the survivors expressed a range of emotions, from horror to fury. I couldn't wait. I leaped forward, swiping at the one who had discarded his shield, but he blocked it. I kicked at the burning shield, flipping it up—it didn't hurt him, but the surprise sent him off balance, and I stuck my blade into the opening he left on his stomach.

The wails of two dying men filled the chamber as I faced the remaining three. Their training finally kicked in—they advanced in a semi-circle, accepting that they fought an elemental wielding powers only rivaled by the Sovereign and his primordia. If I let one move behind me, I was dead. Already the cocoon on my arm felt like dagger points digging into my skin.

They attacked together. I parried a blow with my sword and another with my coated arm. The blade scraped along the magma's surface, pressing it against my skin, and I growled at the horrible pain. Before the third man could strike, I lashed out with my coated arm, as if swatting at a cragwasp, and released more magma from my hand. It flew forward, smacking the man in the face and engulfing it. The molten rock clinging to his skull muffled his screams.

The remaining two pressed the attack, and I backpedaled as I struggled to defend myself. They swung in rhythm, advancing simultaneously, and the man to my right who attacked my sword arm stabbed viciously. Emil knew proper swordplay, not me, and I could already feel my parries lagging.

I took deep breaths, trying to center myself and overcome the exhaustion from flinging the rebel into the wall. With a roar, I pushed once more.

Both men's weapons sailed toward the opposite walls and struck the stone with a sharp *clang*. Before either rebel could back away, I swung high, and the tip of my blade sliced through their necks, spraying blood onto the floor.

I released my hold on the lava, and it sloughed off my arm and into a smoking pile on the marble. Pale blisters and cracked flesh covered me from fingers to elbow. I took a step back and collapsed onto the marble floor, breathing hard as blood sizzled from the two pools of blood meeting vitrified rock.

Sorrelo stepped down from his throne. "I'll never get tired of seeing you work."

The color had drained from Mateo's face. His attention wasn't on the magnate—it switched from my burns to the lava to the dismembered and burning bodies, his eyes having trouble focusing on any one detail.

According to smith scripture, when The Great Ones rose from the great underground ocean, the Black Depths, a select few were chosen to wield rock and magma as a defacement to Fheldspra, and to work as their agents. To him, only the soulless could do what I just did.

I kept my arm in front of me, whimpering as I crossed the room toward one of the antechambers, the master smith shying away as I passed. In the supply room, a jar of pyremoss gel sat on a top shelf, which was kept here in case any nobiletza became a little too interested in the aqueducts and hurt themselves. I uncapped the jar and slathered it on my skin, then returned to the throne room, where Mateo stood stock still, staring at the carnage.

The magnate ripped a strip of cloth off one of the dead rebels and retrieved his rhidium sword where I'd left it propped against a pillar. He wiped the gore off the blade as he joined Mateo. "So, master smith, what did you just see?"

Mateo stared back. "I don't understand. Only the primordia can control rock, and they're evil."

"The world is a big place, master smith. But the correct answer is 'nothing.'"

"I... I don't know how that's possible."

"I'm sure you'll find a way." He discarded the bloodstained cloth and sheathed the sword. "The smiths made an oath to the territories' magnates, remember? You're supposed to advise and support us above all else. Excluding serving Fheldspra, of course. So, when I tell you to never utter to anyone what you saw Ig do, and I mean *anyone*, you'll obey me, yes?"

Mateo's expression firmed up. "Yes."

The sounds of fighting in other parts of the palace started to fade. It sounded like Olevic had ordered a retreat. If he had, it wouldn't last long.

Emil and Sara rushed into the room. Scrapes and bruises riddled Emil's skin, his expression detached and drained. Sara, on the other hand, moved with restless frustration until she took in the sight of the splintered barricade and the dismembered bodies. Emil paralleled her puzzlement. "Father? You're all right?" he asked.

"Rikardo and his man fought like madmen," Sorrelo said. "Mateo said they worked hard with their blade work, enough to earn their spot in the next life. Or did I misquote you, master smith?"

Mateo nodded without comment.

"You burned yourself, Ig."

Emil moved to my side, carefully grasping my hand and bicep. The sheen of pyremoss gel covering my damaged skin was glossy. "Had to protect myself with one of the torches," I said weakly. "Didn't work out so well."

Sara knelt before the decapitated sergeant's body, and her nose wrinkled, the chemical aroma still lingering. "You killed this man, Father?"

"Despite what you may believe, I'm not useless," Sorrelo answered. "What is going on in the rest of the palace?"

Emil dropped my arm. "Reformers are murdering the nobiletza. It doesn't matter if they're supporting you or not." He turned to the carnage in the hallway and didn't speak for a few moments. "Most of the royal guard are still loyal. They're rounding up the nobiletza by my orders."

"I wonder if I could teach Olevic a thing or two about his chosen craft," Sara said.

Olevic never struck me as someone who wanted Sorrelo's seat, just a man with simple tastes that involved a table and a bit of steel. But I supposed I didn't know the man very well, and becoming magnate meant getting away with things that could never fly under Sorrelo's rule.

"Let me find him, Father," Emil said. "I'll hunt him down. He can't get away with this."

"Are the rebels winning out there?" his father asked.

Emil nodded.

"Then our priority is finding safety. We can't run headlong into a situation that Olevic has had time to plan for. We're leaving before the reformers regroup."

"If Sara knows about those tunnels, others might too. It's too risky to go down there."

Sara studied the pile of cooled magma in the middle of the room and the vitrified rock stuck to one of the rebels' heads.

She knelt before the body, poking at the face with her dagger. Before she could ask questions, Sorrelo said, "There's always another way out."

The magnate moved to where the aqueducts fed into a pool against a wall and reached behind the bench built against the basin to grab something. Stone ground against stone and the lava receded. A stairway of glowing red stone appeared that seemed to lead into a dark cavern, the air inside it shimmering. I hadn't even known about this passage. "That looks dangerous," Emil said.

Sorrelo jumped onto the stone. "It's also on a timer. You have forty-five seconds." The soles of his boots sizzled as he climbed down and ducked under superheated stone, and a sound echoed from the door in one-second increments, like rock tapping against rock.

I hiked up my robes and leapt after him. The rock started eating through my shoes, and it reeked of trapped gasses like a rancid inferno, the heat so oppressive I couldn't breathe. Fresh, damp air greeted me on the other side, where fireflies roosted in the tunnel's crevices near clumps of lichen and sparkling granite. The air changed from cool to frigid as wind blasted us from deeper inside the cave. Mateo entered the cave last, and the wall of red stone swung upward, slid into the ceiling, and concealed us in a strange calm.

"We're safe in here?" Emil asked.

Sorrelo rummaged inside an alcove and pulled out an unlit torch and a container of paste. "Safety is the absence of violence," he said. "Impossible to really prove." He dipped the end into the jar, and as soon as he stuck the torch into the air, hundreds of fireflies dropped from the ceiling and swarmed the sugary food. The light revealed an archway carved into the wall with words chiseled along its edge that wasn't the old tongue or ancient Sihraan. It looked like some sort of proto language made from a blend of pictographs and letters. Beyond the arch was a shallow chamber, where the light illuminated cobwebs covering busts of exotic animals that didn't exist in any book I'd seen. But this was typical, I'd heard. Ancient ruins filled the territories—so many, in fact, that cartographers tended to only record those that provided defensible shelter.

The light also revealed several chests of supplies. Sorrelo lodged the torch in a crevice and sat down to pull off his scorched boots. "There's clothing for everyone here. I'm now a trader fleeing the coup with my servant and a friend from the Foundry. Emil and Sara, you're my hired swords. Decide on a persona that best fits this story."

"You put a lot of thought into this escape plan," Emil said.

The princep changed into mercenary garb, with interlocking pieces of beryl scorpion chitin. Sara didn't change out of her climbing leathers but traded her mink coat for common pigmy bear. I fastened on a set of heavy boots and changed into a tunic and pants. Mateo stayed in his smith's clothes.

"You're trying to get yourself killed, aren't you?" Sara asked her father. Sorrelo wore a shoulder pelt of sable over a maroon colored dress shirt that was tied together with a leather girdle laced with silver thread. The clothes of a wealthy merchant.

"This scabbard is the only thing that will allow me to carry the family blade safely, and I need an outfit to match it or it will look suspicious. Now quiet. This isn't the time for your attitude."

"You could always leave the sword behind."

"No!" Sorrelo, Emil, and Mateo said at the same time. "It's one of six blades of its kind," the magnate said. "It could fund a small army if we needed it to."

Mateo's expression strained at Sorrelo's words—the Meteor Blades, owned by the magnate of each territory, held religious significance to the Foundry. He'd be horror struck if the magnate sold it, but he didn't argue.

"Stupid is as stupid does," Sara muttered.

"This path will take us to within a few miles of Sanskra," Sorrelo said. "We'll hide there until we know we can return."

"And if we can't?" I asked. The Listener had been surgical in his attack, striking the palace with relatively few men, and at the perfect moment. Members of the audencia, Augustin's other branch of government, had to have helped him. The thought made me sick, of Olevic Pike having friends in the right places. Or maybe the only thing his associates saw when they looked at him was a man of the lower levels. Sometimes it wasn't about who you were, but about who you knew. And Olevic was capable to the right people, the type of man who could do what others didn't have the stomach for.

"We'll return," Sorrelo said, then went quiet before adding, "I have a backup plan, but first let's find out what's happening to my city."

The narrow, sloped tunnel steepened, and we picked our way down the treacherous path while a deep rumbling permeated the rock. "That sound is just runoff from the ice sheaths," Sorrelo said. "No need to worry."

The comforting words were alien coming out of his mouth—nonchalance and Sorrelo Adriann didn't mix. Maybe he realized he traveled with the last four people he could trust.

The group was quiet, breathing lightly, too wrapped up in their own thoughts. As I thought of blood-slicked bodies crumpled in heaps outside the throne room, a thought soured my stomach. Where would I be if the reformers had arrested or killed Emil and Sara at the Foundry? I would've had a chance to escape. Sorrelo would be dead by now and his children never would've had the chance to learn how to use my bindings.

I'd have nowhere to go, nothing to do, with no purpose. And I'd had purpose every passing since I was twelve years old. I shivered. My elemental power would disappear too.

It was the final rule to my flesh binding, to show that not even my power belonged to me, just like everything else in my life. If I ran, my power would fade after three passings, only coming back once my flesh came into contact with my master's again. A simple handshake would do. It was the one rule about my flesh binding I hadn't known about—and I'd learned it the hard way two weeks after Sorrelo brought me to Mira after kidnapping me from the Ebonrock, when I got lost in the capital, still unable to speak Miran. The Fiador Fianza's bounty hunters found me on the fourth passing, shivering in a leaky basement.

The magnate didn't punish me that time. He was more understanding back then, more forgiving, when we were still getting to know each other and his patience wasn't so thin. So it went with relationships.

The tunnel opened up, and we approached a ridge overlooking a massive cavern littered with several farms. Mushrooms dozens of feet tall stood like monoliths, illuminated from below by magma pools and clusters of glowing amber quartzite among groves of coral trees. A mushroom waited several feet below us, a narrow gap between it and the ridge.

We jumped from mushroom to mushroom, descending to the shortest stalk where a coil of rope waited. Darkness clung to the tops of the mushroom heads, which made it difficult to watch my footing. Sulian vision was weaker compared to Mirans'—my eyes were predisposed to the bright, bloody light of the Burning Mountains that shrouded my old home.

We touched the cavern floor, where silky-skinned mole-rats scavenged crevices for tubers to eat. Their backs came to my waist, and I ran my hand along their spines as we walked by. Mole-rat and titan armadillo farms resided in the cave networks above the Granite Road and was where most of Augustin's meat came from. Not a likely place for reformers to search, but our group didn't exactly blend in around here, and a farmer might connect the dots and sell the information for a small mountain of money. Some of them watched us even now. I prayed Sorrelo didn't notice and put me to work silencing them.

"Those soldiers had to have been something else," Sara said. She'd snuck up to join me.

"I'm sorry?"

"The guards who killed Olevic's strike team. I wish I could've seen how that battle played out. Can you describe it to me?"

Sara never acted this conversational, but I didn't complain. Sara didn't like to talk to people; rather, she challenged them. I'd always admired the way she wasn't afraid to say what was on her mind, sometimes watching from the corner of the throne room while she argued with other magnates' representatives, or hardlining delegations from beyond The Rift through her interpreter. "I was distracted while I was looking for pyremoss gel for my burns. Sorry."

"Ah. Well, it's too bad you hurt yourself like that. You were the opposite of clumsy when I saw you outside Bolivar's home last week."

She was fishing for information, I realized. "I was trying to avoid getting killed back there. I did pretty well for myself, considering the others."

She glanced behind us, toward Mateo who walked beside Emil. "All those unattached limbs and heads back in the throne room couldn't have been agreeable with the stomach, master smith. If you ever need to talk, I'm good at listening. Better than Olevic, I bet."

"My smiths are in danger," Mateo said in a small voice. "This whole ordeal has been difficult, so forgive me if I'm not in the mood to talk."

Sorrelo didn't show any concern while he listened from the rear of the group, but he had to have known Mateo and I wouldn't talk.

"This whole thing stinks like batshit," Sara said under her breath.

Chapter 8

WE ENTERED A cavern that was wide and low like an inverted bowl, with a lake in the center that filled up most of the cavern. A path led across the lake where the town of Sanskra sat on a rocky plateau, radiating like a flaming beacon, minerals twinkling on the cavern ceiling like stars in an open sky. Our group weaved through staggered wooden barriers on the island's edge, where guards nodded to us in acknowledgment, and all three Adrianns angled their faces downward, masking the gesture as respectful bows of the head. The guards didn't give them a second glance.

It wasn't hard for the Adrianns to blend in. They were a family of Augustin averages, shorter than the typical person from the northern territories like Tulchi or Radavich, with black hair and round cheeks. Emil was the only problem—not many men shaved their heads around here, and combined with his heavyset brows and thick beard, he had a habit of standing out. He kept the hood of his cloak draped over his head.

Several stone foxes with harnesses were tied to a nearby hitching post, their fur ash-grey and irises milky-white. They lapped at a trough of water or gnawed on cured salamander meat, and one yawned. The people, on the other hand, walked the streets with a nervous energy. It seemed news of the coup had finally traveled far enough on the Granite Road to catch up with us.

We reached an inn built from cave wisteria lumber, its roof a carpet of vines and purple leaves. "Can you get inside the capital without notarized travel papers?" Emil asked.

"The coup's chaos should hopefully solve that problem," Mateo said. His plan was to head back to the city, traveling mostly through one of the fishing tunnels running parallel to the Granite Road, then enter the city in disguise. Even if he was recognized, he wouldn't have to worry about being arrested unless Olevic wanted his coup to end as soon as it had started.

"Don't be followed on your way back," the magnate said. The master smith nodded and headed for the nearest stable.

I booked us a room in the back of the inn—a place for meetings favored by sellswords needing a place to drink and scheme in solitude. The others filed in and settled themselves at the table while I lit a fire in the hearth.

"Let's talk contingencies," Sorrelo said.

Sara leaned against the hearth's mantel while I stoked the flames. She already smelled of wood smoke and, oddly, of oil. "There are towns in the territory that will give us asylum, but that isn't much of a long-term solution if it turns out Olevic has Augustin in his greasy little fingers."

"You're right. If that's the case, Magnate Jancarlo of Radavich will help. My brother Lucas is close with him. Convincing him to aid our family won't be difficult."

Nobody pointed out the obvious flaws in the kind of aid Sorrelo had in mind. Assaulting Augustin with another territory's army would be next to impossible—the city was mostly corridors and long passageways, where six or seven men standing abreast could easily ward off an attack. Augustin had only one entrance, and it could stop an attacking army almost as well as solid rock. The gates of every capital had a similar design, which meant war was rare between territories—the northern territories, Radavich and Tulchi, fought the last major conflict almost seventy-five years ago, and it was a war of attrition until the Sovereign put an end to it single-handedly.

I could carve my way into the capital, but enough rock stood between Augustin and the surrounding cave network for it to be a several-weeks-long job.

"There's always Tulchi," Sara offered. "I hate to say it, but they like us more than Radavich does. Uncle Lucas might serve Magnate Jancarlo as his secretariat, but 'sympathetic' isn't the word I'd think of when Jancarlo comes to mind. Especially with other territories."

"Radavich is our solution. They have the largest army and the most economic pull, which means they'll be handy in negotiations. Magnate Jancarlo can always threaten an embargo if assaulting Augustin won't work."

"What about Efadora?" Emil asked. "We can't assume she'll be safe in Manasus."

"Yes, we can assume that," Sara said. "She's a big girl, and Manasus has good relations with our family anyway. Magnate Bardera will take care of her."

"Sorry if I'm a little hesitant to trust Bardera after what happened with Olevic. Efadora has a claim to the throne too, so it would make sense for the Listener to go after her."

Sorrelo stirred. "Traveling to Manasus would severely delay our plans. Your sister will be safe."

Emil didn't argue, but I watched his jaw work while he stared at the fire. Spurning help and ignoring advice was his little sister's favorite pastime, but from what little I'd seen of Efadora before she moved to Manasus, she was as resourceful as her sister. She could take care of herself.

Emil played with the Xerivian good-luck charm, turning it over in his hands. "If we want to get to Radavich without being identified or getting killed by bandits," he said, "we'll need to go through Dagir's Pass."

"Dagir's Pass?" I asked.

"It's a path that takes us near the surface. It's treacherous and the path is too rocky for most caravans, so bandit ambushes are rare."

"We'll need a guide, which means we'll need money," Sorrelo said. "Sara, you know where the family cache is. Find us someone afterward. One we can trust at least to some degree. We'll want them ready to go in case Mateo brings back bad news."

Sara made a flourish with her arm and left. Sorrelo rose from his chair, unsheathing his knife, and stabbed it onto the table. He pointed a finger at his son. "You're cutting that off."

Emil's hand went to his beard and he grimaced, but Sorrelo was right. Facial hair could be hard to hide, and young men like Emil spent enough time grooming their faces that people tended to notice.

A trading post next door carried shaving gel, and once back inside the meeting room, I proceeded to scrape the oiled bristles off Emil's jaw. The procedure sharpened his cheekbones and revealed an angular jaw that had been squared by his beard. Within minutes I was looking at a boy I always knew existed—a young man trying to save a father who didn't realize he needed to be saved. Sorrelo sat in the chair next, and after I was done with him, I tossed the clippings into the flames.

The two men looked eerily similar side-by-side, so much so that I felt a stab of fear when Emil met my eyes. He smiled and some of the fear dissipated. "Does everyone's face always feel this cold?" he asked.

Did I look like my father? I hadn't seen the man since I was twelve—his face only a fuzzy, degraded picture. It was the same with my mother. I hadn't thought about them in a long time, but seeing how Emil was such a bundle of similarities and contrasts to his father, it was hard not to.

Life before the Ebonrock sometimes felt like a vision I'd made up to cope with what the masters had done to me. How could I prove it really happened? I'd been a slave longer than

I'd been alive, to the point Mother and Father might as well have been moving statues. If they existed at all.

"Did you learn anything about Tuli Dempra?" Sorrelo asked. He leaned in his chair and propped his boots onto the table, which looked odd, because the magnate was not a man who relaxed. He had been acting differently since we left Augustin.

"No," Emil said. "There were no smiths in Augustin by that name. We were arresting Mateo when Olevic's men confronted us."

The light danced in Sorrelo's eyes as he stared into the fire. "That journal belonged to someone."

"Maybe he wasn't a smith," I chimed in. "Just because he was religious doesn't mean he was from the Foundry."

"What do you mean?" Emil asked.

I glanced at Sorrelo, who gave me a nod. "Fheldspra exists in different forms all over Ra'Thuzan. People in Sulian Daw worship Him too, but He's called Fedsprig there. Isn't He worshipped in multiple religions across Mira?"

"No, not religions. Cults. You think Tuli Dempra might be a cultist?"

"Could be. They hide in the upper levels of the capital, right? A journal written by a cultist might've read like a smith's." Cults were common enough in the deep tunnels and dank caves of the crust to make this a possibility, but I didn't point this out due to the sour look forming on Emil's face. He didn't seem to like thinking about the similarities between the Foundry and Mira's cults.

"The writing on the note looked familiar, but I can't put it together for the life of me," he said. "If it isn't a smith, I'm betting it's someone in the audencia, considering they write up the city legislature."

"I recognized it too," I said.

Sorrelo tapped his fingers against the table. "That wasn't important enough to mention when you brought the journal to me?"

"I wasn't sure," I answered. The longer he stared at me, the tighter the nerves in my stomach twisted.

"Wait," Emil said. "Ig's the one who followed Sara's lead? Why? You could have sent the provosts, or the guard, or even asked Olevic, which I suppose is a good thing you didn't. Ig is just your manservant."

For once, Sorrelo faltered. "The man can't disobey or betray me. He's obviously suited for sensitive jobs."

"Does he usually do 'sensitive' jobs for you? Sara said she saw him investigating Bolivar's home, but I told her she was probably wrong."

"I don't owe you an explanation."

"I'm going to succeed you eventually, Father. What's so wrong with keeping me in the loop? The more you tell me, the more helpful I can be."

"You wouldn't help if I told you everything. You'd only hate me."

"At least I'd be better equipped to protect our family from people like Olevic Pike."

Sorrelo moved to his feet and planted his fists on the table, the light dancing on half his body. "Do not question me. I know what I'm doing. As soon as the people stop noticing how I keep you at arm's length, they'll think you're complicit, and then you'll lose them. That can't happen. I won't let it."

"And the cost of our relationship is just an afterthought then, right?"

Hearing how small Emil's voice became, and seeing all that exposed youth on his face, was like looking at a different Emil. The real Emil. Sorrelo's fists squeezed, his blood playing colors under the skin. "Shut your mouth. You don't know what you're talking about."

I stirred. "He's being honest. Take it easy."

I was better practiced than anyone at recognizing when the magnate started to feel truly angry. Most of my time in Sorrelo's presence was spent hyper-focused on avoiding whatever might trigger him, and so I saw at once how his body tensed in a dozen subtle ways. I imagined him giving me the one Word I couldn't follow—to kill Emil—and forcing its punishment on me. A spike of fear shot through me from gut to brain. I'd overstepped. I'd been doing that more lately.

The magnate's gaze shifted from me to Emil, Emil to me. He took a seat and stared at the fire.

The door opened and Sara entered, accompanied by three strangers. "Meet my new friends," she said as she sat against the coffee table.

The group was oblivious to the awkward tension in the room, or they pretended it didn't exist. The first stranger, a tall, gangly man with eyes the color of emerald, bowed deeply. He had the looks and mannerisms of a Bys. "I'm Crane, the short one is Fern, and that's Dellix."

The brittle look on Emil's face dissolved and he crossed the room to offer his hand. "I'm Sharif. Pleased to meet you, saior," he said, donning a commoner's accent.

"You need help getting through Dagir's Pass?"

"We'll know in the next couple hours. Would like to leave as soon as possible if we do. That acceptable?"

"It's short notice, but we're used to it. We've finished our work in Sanskra anyway. Are you trying for Manasus or Radavich?"

Emil glanced at his father, as though hoping the magnate would reconsider retrieving Efadora first. "Radavich," the magnate answered, speaking in a low and gruff voice, not taking his eyes off the fire.

Crane adjusted to the new authority in the room and bowed once more. "Very well, sir. And may I ask your name?"

"I am Sario."

Crane waited for the magnate to meet his eyes, but when Sorrelo didn't, he continued. "A pleasure, Sario-hos. There's a fee of twelve standards per hour for keeping us on retainer, and the trip from here to the backend of Dagir's Pass on the Radavich side will cost four hundred."

Sorrelo waved a dismissive hand. "Fine."

I tensed. The magnate should have let Sara or Emil negotiate the terms for the trip, since his kids would've known the guides would start high and expect to be bartered down. Our group could afford the four hundred and fifty some-odd standards, but Sorrelo had just flaunted his wealth.

"Our supplies are still in the room where we're staying, but we'll wait here for your word. See us in the main hall if you need anything," Crane said. He bowed once more and led the other two out.

"They're courteous," Sorrelo said in the ensuing silence. "I don't see why we need three though."

Sara grabbed an apple out of a bowl on the dining table and returned to her spot. "They've been together a long time, apparently. Package deal."

"Fine," the magnate said. "The two of you will go find us any supplies we might need for the trip."

"That sounds like a job for Ig, father."

"He'll be running his own errands."

I could feel Emil's attention on me, and I made a point to ignore it, but that only brought me face-to-face with Sara's eyes boring into me instead. She tossed the half-eaten apple into the fire. "Let's get this over with, Emil. And try not to work too hard, Ig."

Emil followed his sister from the room without a word.

"Those guides," the magnate said. "I want you to find the room at whatever inn they're staying in and see if they're hiding any secrets. I don't want to travel with anyone who might try to rob us."

"Yes, Magnate."

I turned to leave, but the magnate continued, "There will come a time when I'm gone and you'll be passed down to my children. Ig, tell them how much I—" He stopped. "Make sure they know I cared."

I was at a loss on how to respond, but Sorrelo made it easy by dismissing me with a sharp motion of the hand. I left.

In the hall leading to the bar outside, I spied the group of guides through some wooden pillars drinking rice beer and laughing with one another. I usually needed time to prep my persona, but not now. Maybe it was the excitement about traveling through the crust for the first time and the exhilaration from standing up to Sorrelo. I didn't even need to change into mercenary garb. I cracked my neck and took a deep breath, then pulled up a chair and joined the group.

They paused in their drinking. "You're that servant who works for the nobleman trader, right?" Dellix, the fatter one with thinning hair, asked. "Barely noticed you in the corner earlier."

"Yep, that's me," I said. "Name's Jakar. But I'm no servant. Just a steward who handles Sario's business affairs. Schedule meetings and whatnot, make sure he shows up in a timely manner."

"Steward, servant, what's the difference?"

The men laughed and I cringed. Even with a thousand backstories at my disposal, for some reason I'd picked steward. "I'm kidding," Dellix said, and clapped me on the back. "We all have masters we answer to."

"Yeah. I guess so," I said slowly.

"Ignore Dellix," Crane, the tall, lanky one with the emerald eyes, said. He was the leader. "You can't take anything he says personally. Would you like a beer?"

"No, but thank you, saior," I said. If I accepted a drink from a Bys, I'd be expected to stay awhile. "I'd be happy to buy you three a round though," I added. If I remembered correctly, it was considered rude if I didn't offer a drink in return for declining. My knowledge of the territories' customs was all secondhand from watching interactions around the capital, but it was exciting to be out in the world using that knowledge. It was almost as if I really was Jakar.

"No, no, don't worry about it," Crane said. "Fern only drinks Ferician orujo, and we'd rather not break your coin purse. No offense to whatever Sario-hos pays you, but Fern can barely rub two standards together because of that palate of his."

Fern shrugged. "Life's about enjoying the little things. I'll get myself killed long before I have to worry about a retirement fund."

Dellix leaned forward, his chair groaning beneath his weight. "So how do you like employment under Sario-hos?" He laughed after emphasizing the title.

Crane knocked him on the shoulder. "Enough of that. I'm starting to think you might've had one too many. We need to stay nice and crisp for this job."

The men stayed at ease, and Crane threw a handful of nuts into his mouth. They had some sort of opinion of 'Sario-hos,' but was it enough to warrant suspicion? We needed guides to get through Dagir's Pass, and if we ditched these men out of paranoia that they knew Sorrelo's identity, who knew if we'd find someone else.

"If you're not drinking, why are you sitting with us?" Fern asked, not unkindly.

"Just getting some fresh air. Being around the same people all the time can get repetitive."

"Daniela doesn't seem the boring type," Dellix said. "Quite the opposite, actually." He nudged Fern in the ribs, and Fern grinned to himself before taking a sip from the small cup before him.

They were talking about Sara. The slimy edge to Dellix's words irked me until I realized I had no reason to feel irritated by Dellix trying to cozy up with Sara, or to feel defensive at all. The princepa could take care of herself. "Where's all of your equipment?" I asked.

"I don't feel like lugging our shit around while we wait," Crane said. "We'll check out before we leave. We'd be hanging out at The Caterpillar right now if Dellix here didn't get us kicked out for playing grabby hands with the server."

Dellix displayed a checkerboard of yellowed teeth when he smiled. "How was I supposed to know she was just giving me the eye for a tip?"

"You're a real bat sometimes, my friend."

I stood and bowed. "It was nice talking to you three. Looking forward to these next few passings together."

They raised their drinks in acknowledgment, and I moved for the front door.

I dodged a group heading into the inn and stepped onto the single rutted road that weaved through town. The number of Sanskra patrollers had tripled since I'd last been outside. Short-faced salamanders—stout creatures covered in cords of muscle—pulled carts alongside me as I walked down the street, and the merchants riding them spoke in hushed voices. While nobody panicked, people hurried instead of walked, glancing toward the side of town closest to Augustin's capital. I wondered how much longer Sanskra would remain safe.

All these people were free, embodying possibilities of the kinds of lives I could live if my bonds were broken. But none of them looked interesting. What purpose in life did they have? Simply being free wasn't enough, would never be enough.

I rubbed my eyes. Why was I even thinking about my flesh bindings? Down that path only lay madness. It must've been precipitated by my conversation with Emil and Sorrelo. Under normal circumstances, my desire for freedom rarely came naturally and needed to be summoned. Maintained. Hatred toward servitude was too exhausting otherwise. Those who hated me for wanting to serve Sorrelo didn't understand that I'd needed to so I could stay sane.

I'd killed a dozen men and women for Sorrelo over the past several months, and on those passings when I'd hunted them down, I jumped at a chance to help the magnate. I strangled and slit throats without more than the thought to keep the blood off my clothes. What if my victims were as innocent as Bolivar?

Oh, fhelfire. I couldn't think about that. I was flesh bound, which meant I was not the one who really killed those people.

Bolivar's screams as he fell. Mangled bodies outside the throne room, limbs twisted under torsos.

The Caterpillar was built at the edge of the plateau against the lake. A line of wrought-iron placements held crackling flames at the front of the building, and several people sat on the inn's patio, drinking from horns, their tables smelling of sizzling, spiced meat. I slid into a dark alley beside the inn that funneled the wind traveling across the lake, peeking through each window as I made my way to the rear. An empty room waited on the backside of the building with three packs stuffed in the corner and a stack of four-ounce cups sitting on the desk next to a near-empty bottle of orujo.

Lightcaps crusted the inn's overhang, their glow reflecting off the glass of the three vials I removed from the belt under my tunic. I uncapped the first vial and began pouring the catalyzed rubidium hydroxide in a horizontal line across the wood. The wall sizzled, acid emitting violet sparks that danced onto the gravel.

When working a job for the magnate, nine times out of ten the only barriers I had to concern myself with were the rockwood structures comprising a typical Augustin household, or the rock the house was built into. Whether I could mold the stone depended on its elemental composition, but my power almost never worked on organic compounds. Thus, I had to rely on alternatives if a wooden wall stood in my way instead of an iron lock or solid rock.

With a single kick the weakened section broke away, and I waited several moments, listening to the black water lap against the plateau's edge behind me. I moved onto my stomach and crawled inside.

Low voices permeated the door as I worked my way through each pack, searching for anything incriminating. There was lots of climbing gear. Snake jerky and other packaged bits of stale rations. A couple of timepieces built by the Tempurium, both needing calibration. A large vial of fish liver oil, essential for long treks where lack of access to proper nutrition could cause bonebreaker disease.

I sat on one of the beds after several minutes. Sometimes Sorrelo's paranoia created a lot of unnecessary work.

Outside, I reached through and struggled to shimmy the desk in front of the hole, then fit the missing piece of wall back in place. Someone would notice eventually, but hopefully not until we left Sanskra in our memories.

Gravel crunched behind me, and I turned to find a knife at my throat. A man in black pushed me against the wall and my head bounced against the window, rattling the glass.

It was Mateo.

Chapter 9

"WHAT ARE YOU?" Mateo asked.

The flat of his blade pressed against my throat, its edge daring to bite if I tried to resist. There was no rage in his question. I pushed against the weapon with my elemental power and found him pushing back, as if he'd been waiting for me to do so.

He stepped away, his face a pale glow from the lightcaps. "So you can control metal like the smiths. How?"

There was something satisfying about his reaction. "You know how. Emil isn't the only metal worker in Augustin who isn't a smith."

"You're no metal worker. That title is reserved for men and women who have dedicated their lives to Fheldspra. Tell me how you can command molten rock or I'll spread your secret."

"Didn't you swear to Sorrelo that you wouldn't?"

His expression surprised me. Anguish. "Please, Ig. Foundry doctrine says you're an agent of the Great Ones, and that crime goes beyond any obligation I have to the magnate. Convince me you're not corrupted."

Mateo was letting me argue my innocence, even after what

happened to Bolivar. "All right," I said after a long moment. I waited for him to lower the knife, but he didn't relax. "I don't bleed answers, so you can put that away."

He didn't make a move. Out of good faith, I dropped my guard and moved to the railing separating us from the lake's edge. "First off, the magnate's the only one in Augustin who knows I'm an elemental. He kept it a secret from his children."

"He's that paranoid?"

"He doesn't want his children knowing what I can do before they…" I couldn't tell Mateo about my flesh binding.

He finally lowered the knife. "Before what?"

Moss on the rock gave way to water lilies, algae, and eel grass growing along the water's edge, but from what I knew, the shoreline dropped beneath it almost vertically, the lake hundreds of feet deep. The rock was slick as ice too. Once someone fell in, there wasn't much hope for getting out without help. Something to consider. "Before his children inherit me."

"Tell me about your power over rock and magma, and where it came from."

"I'm bound to it the same way you're bound to metal, or the cartographers are bound to quartz, or the chronographers are bound to salt, or how any of the bindings in the other trade schools exist. Is that so hard to believe?"

"It is, because to have power over rock and magma makes you the same as the Sovereign and his primordia. The Foundry would openly condemn them if we knew we could survive their retribution, but we're not afraid of you. Tell me where your power came from."

"Nothing about it is evil." I leaned against the railing and took a deep breath. Sometimes it was easy to forget how morally complicated bindings could be in this part of the world. I would have to be careful with my wording. "Take the Seedheart Lodge in Saracosta. They bind with feldspar and then they can perfect the soil they use to grow medicinal plants for the physicians' halls. It isn't feldspar they're really binding to, though. They bind to something called potassium. When some of their horticulturists die during the ritual, it's because the rhidium they ingested alongside their feldspar sample ended up pairing with the wrong element inside the feldspar, an element that doesn't exist naturally in the human body."

Mateo frowned, the gears turning in his head. "You can apply that same logic to the Foundry's rhidium trials."

I'd picked the Seedheart Lodge because the Sovereign founded it, hoping it would make the truth easier to accept, but he'd connected the dots quicker than I expected. I nodded. "The element smiths are bound to is iron, not steel or any other metal."

His frown didn't go away. "That is not new information."

"Iron is one of the few elements you can mine in its pure form, but for organizations like the Archives for instance, their cartographers don't know they aren't bound to quartz but to silicon. Silicon doesn't manifest in its pure form naturally, so people don't know it exists. But that's how I can control magma and certain types of rock. I'm bound to many of its elements. Like I said, not evil."

"What elements are those?"

The minerals twinkled in the cave roof, and it was almost like we stood in Augustin, the sky bursting with stars at the top of the chasm. Talking about this felt nice. Liberating. "I'm bound to iron, silicon, calcium, sodium, potassium, and magnesium."

"Does that mean you underwent six binding rituals?"

"Yes."

"Impossible. Cartographers and horticulturists and chronographers throughout history have attempted the binding rituals of other organizations. There wasn't a single survivor in all those centuries."

"No offense, but Mirans have a lot to learn about elemental power."

Mateo sheathed his knife and joined me at the railing. The lightcaps highlighted his profile and shadows collected in his crow's feet. The wrinkles of a teacher. "Are you saying there is something I could do to ensure my apprentices can survive their trials?" Guilt haunted the edge of his voice.

"Yes, but binding rituals are traumatic by nature, so there's always a risk of death. If you want your smiths to bind with iron, then use pure iron. Don't use steel. Steel only risks the rhidium mixing with the wrong element, and that will kill them."

He snorted, staring at me like I'd glossed over some fundamental fact. "Steel is the most important part of the rhidium trial. The apprentice uses Fheldspra's fire to forge a tool or weapon of their choosing, then they ingest shavings of it with the rhidium, which binds them to He Who Warms as much as it does the metal."

I mused on all the elementals in history killed by ritual. "Believe me or don't. All I know is that I'm bound to certain elements that by themselves would kill most people. Ritual had nothing to do with it. It was the medical skill of my old masters." The trials had been the most horrifying moments of my life, even with the blackouts and the blanks in my memory. The more common an element in the human body, the deadlier the binding ritual—I was told the calcium trial killed me twice through my induced coma. Fortunately, my old masters were very good at reviving overworked hearts.

"Sulian Daw is more than I expected," Mateo said.

"My masters belonged to an organization called the Ebonrock. They weren't from Sulian Daw. They set up shop in a city, kidnap or buy up some of the children, then turn them into elementals and ship them away before moving on. And before you ask, no, they've never been west of The Rift."

"So anyone could bind with six elements and control Fheldspra's fire? Ridiculous."

The last word was spoken softly. He sounded distant. Sad. I rose a hand to show my blistered forearm. "Almost. There's still one more element I'd need to bind with to have near total control over magma. Oxygen. And nobody would survive that."

"Did the Sovereign's sycophants gain their power from your old masters? They do what you do."

"I know very little about the primordia or how they became elementals." Nektarios reeked of power that was a total mystery to me. "There's something wrong with their bodies too. They have strength and speed unrelated to elemental power."

Mateo stared across the black lake. A breeze swept through the cavern and he pulled his robe closer to his body. I suffered in silence, like usual. "Why are your old masters doing this?" he asked.

"Doing what?"

"Creating elementals. Is your purpose for existing to earn money from the highest bidder? To serve men like Sorrelo Adriann?"

"No. Sorrelo stole me." I gnawed at my bottom lip. How could I tell this man who worshipped Fheldspra that I and the other Sulian children I'd grown up with were created to find his god's enemies?

Fheldspra, Brexa, Terias, and other gods found in and outside Mira existed in a hundred different forms across Ra'Thuzan, but one pantheon that never really changed was the Great Ones. The Unmade. The *mora gula*. Myths from a dozen different cultures hinted at ancient, colossal horrors residing within the vast underground ocean of the Black Depths, far east of The Rift, beyond the edges of the most remote civilizations. Men and women throughout history rumored to encounter a Great One only found insanity, supposedly—simply hearing their names in their native tongue caused all manner of illnesses, sometimes death.

The Ebonrock had no problem throwing body after body at proving the Great Ones' existence. The stupidest of stupid quests, but it would've killed me regardless if I hadn't escaped.

"Why were you created?" Mateo asked.

"We were created to explore the Black Depths and to find the Great Ones."

He stiffened. "Really?"

"Really. But my former masters have been at it for a long time. Centuries, I think. They worship Fheldspra like you, but they don't believe the Great Ones were some opposing force that came to be during the creation of Mira to balance the light in the core. They think Fheldspra created the Great Ones."

He backed away and rested a hand on his knife. Maybe I'd misjudged how he'd react. "Mateo, please," I said. "Just because I was raised by fanatics doesn't mean I am one."

His robes billowed as he walked toward the alley leading back to the street, and I sprang after him. I should've known this would happen. "I don't care what you think of me, just as long as you know I'm trying to help Emil and Sara."

He didn't answer, and when we entered the light of the street, I saw his scowl. I stepped in front of him. "Please tell me you'll keep your word and keep this a secret," I said.

"You won't have to worry about that." He didn't sound angry.

Mateo pushed the inn door open and bee-lined for the back room. Our guides still drank at their table, and they nodded at me as I followed the master smith. The magnate was in the middle of speaking with Emil and Sara, the three of them standing over a collection of packs.

"Good timing," Emil said.

Sara finished clipping her pack's clasps. "Any chance the Listener slipped on a patch of ice and broke his neck while we were gone?"

Mateo pulled out a chair in front of the fire and sat, posture melting into the seat. "I spoke with some of the smiths. The rebels who attacked the Foundry are dead, and so are six of my smiths. The city's in chaos and the Granite Road is packed with refugees. It was the only reason I managed to get in and out unnoticed."

"Large numbers fleeing the city? Maybe the commoners actually do care who rules."

"They're fleeing because there have been casualties on the upper levels. My smiths tell me most of the guard are taking orders from a sergeant-at-arms, Susa Rozelia. She's done a good job keeping the people safe, and there's been intermittent fighting between her and the reformers. Word has it Olevic is trying to schedule an emergency session tomorrow for the audencia where he'll make a formal announcement. The lower districts are on lockdown and most of the nobility have barricaded themselves in their homes. The first level is a mess." He grabbed a nearby horn of water and took a long drink.

"That doesn't sound like the kind of environment conducive for our return," Sara said. "Unless Fheldspra is interested in divine intervention."

Mateo wiped the dribble from his chin. "Olevic's made a mess, but one thing is obvious. A significant portion of Olevic's force was made of sellswords. I have no idea where he found them, but they and the military the audencia controls are a problem. And Olevic has friends in the audencia. We don't know how many. It could be the majority for all I know."

Sorrelo pushed the head of his ring into the table, carving out a line. "Damnit."

"A cragwasp can kill a human if it stings in the right place," Sara said. "We can sneak in and kill Olevic, and anyone in the audencia who supports him. Assuming we can still get through the front entrance."

Commoners huddled in the listening chamber's cell, trembling in terror, listening to an old man screech and struggle in the next room over. Olevic Pike's eyes, a little too wide as his hands worked at the table straps. All those people could very well be dead by now. The thought sent a thread of anger needling through me, standing up the hairs on my neck as I thought of how I could pull Olevic apart in ways not even he would expect. I would be the magnate's cragwasp if need be. I would kill the plotters and schemers in the audencia too if it meant putting an end to the fighting.

"There's a back entrance into Augustin that leads into the Foundry," the master smith said. "But if there's a mutineer among the smiths, Olevic will know about it."

We all started at the information. "Why didn't I know about this entrance?" Sorrelo asked.

Mateo looked down. "I'm sorry, Magnate. The tunnel is prone to cave-ins during quakes, and the entrance lies at the top of the twists."

"The twists? Might as well not bother then," Sara said.

The twists were a series of corkscrew shafts running along the outside of Augustin's north side, starting at an entrance off the Granite Road. The place was commonly mined for tin, but was impossible to travel through if one didn't know the right turns to take.

"If we can find a cartographer who's loyal, the twists won't be a problem," Emil said.

Sara clapped her hands together. "Perfect. One problem down, twenty to go."

For several moments, metal clicked against wood as Sorrelo tapped his ringed fingers against the table. "We can't risk going into Augustin right now. It'll be too easy for Olevic to trap us."

"That risk is a guarantee if you want what's yours again," Sara said. "Getting trapped in a tunnel is an occupational hazard."

"If we're going to retake the throne, we'll have to place our trust in someone," Emil added. "We can't do this on our own. There are people in the city who still believe in our family."

I thought of the crowd that had looked down on us during Bolivar's execution. How many of those faces would have fought for the Adrianns if they returned? The answer didn't bode well for the father, but Emil was a different story. He was cut more from Bolivar's cloth than anyone else's.

The magnate studied his children. "I'm well aware that we can't single-handedly take back our city, but we can't put our lives in other peoples' hands either. My brother Lucas is the only person outside this room I know I can trust. Radavich is where we need to go."

By the time we traveled to Radavich, convinced Magnate Jancarlo to aid us, and returned to Augustin, Olevic would have had control of the city for several weeks. But what else could we do?

"If we leave, the people will get comfortable under Olevic," Emil said. "Maybe we should strike now while passions are high."

"Nobody will forget their favorite Adriann," his sister said. "Augustin'll take you in with open arms and bend over for Father like usual."

Emil ignored her. "Ultimately, it's up to you," he said to Sorrelo. "Do we stay or go?"

Sorrelo rose. "Augustin needs to cool down." His attention shifted to Emil. "This is an important lesson when it comes to rulers. People idealize the past. How they see me will only improve over the coming weeks."

"Assuming Olevic shits the bed," Sara said.

"No. It doesn't matter how well you rule. They'll always find a reason to hate you."

The room went still until Mateo broke it. "Do I have your leave to make a few more preparations before we depart?"

Sorrelo nodded. Mateo rose from his chair and left. After the door shut, the magnate turned to his children. "The two of you, do the same."

Sara's gaze moved from him to me. "There's nothing left to do. You're shooing us away so you can talk to Ig."

"You're right. Now go."

"Father," Emil said. "If we're going to have any chance of getting out of this in one piece, you need to keep us informed."

I realized Emil viewed me as a confidante and not a colluder.

Judging by Sara's expression, her suspicions fell closer to the mark. She headed for the door. "C'mon, Emil. I have theories I want to share with you."

Emil lugged himself to his feet and mouthed *good luck* to me.

The two left, once more leaving me alone with the magnate. Sorrelo cracked his neck and rubbed his own shoulder, relaxing in a way he hadn't before. "So, what did you find out about our guides?"

"Nothing important. They like their inside jokes, but they don't work for Olevic or the reformers. I don't think they suspect who we are either."

"You're sure?"

I nodded. The men didn't seem to think highly of him, but neither did Mateo I suspected, and the master smith always did his job.

Next would come Sorrelo's Word for me to share every little detail, but instead, he put his face in his hands and rubbed his eyes with his palms. "You were right."

"I'm sorry?"

He exhaled slowly. "When you suggested I step down. I could have avoided all of this and Emil would've had the audencia's blessing." He wrung his hands, staring at his callouses. "When did I become this man?"

A small sound escaped my throat. Was this the same Sorrelo I had served for the past two years? He'd been acting so differently since we left the city.

He looked up, and the expression on my face must have been the wrong one, for his own darkened. "It doesn't matter. You wouldn't understand. Leave me."

I bowed my head quickly and headed for the door.

Outside, Sara leaned against a support beam. "So how'd you really burn yourself?"

Emil was nowhere to be seen. "I told you."

She stepped up to me, but I didn't flinch. "What's going to happen when my father dies and you're still bound to my family? Emil, Efadora, and I will just give you orders, and the flesh binding does its magic?"

"Ask your father."

"What if we give you conflicting Words?"

"It would kill me, probably, unless all of you agreed to get along." It was the only outcome that made sense, and it was one that made me squirm just thinking about it. My life these last two years had been constructed around avoiding the flesh binding's punishment at almost all costs—the rare occasions I disobeyed a Word was when Sorrelo ordered me to kill his son to force its punishment on me. Every other Word from the magnate I'd followed, begrudgingly or otherwise.

Sara, Emil, and Efadora didn't see eye-to-eye on most things, so I couldn't imagine what it would be like to have the three of them trying to share me. I probably wouldn't last a month. There was only one person I was meant to serve, and where I came from, flesh bound slaves never outlived their masters.

"Your secrets will be my secrets eventually," she said. "Promise." She walked off to join the guides at the table. They laughed after she said something too low for me to hear.

Chapter 10

WE FOLLOWED A trail of caravans along a stone path that cut through the north side of Sanskra's lake. Beyond the water, a gravel road descended into a wide-mouthed tunnel leading to Thornhang, the next town over. A set of steps branched off from that road, up and up toward a network of old lava tubes headed for the surface, to Dagir's Pass. Our group broke away from the stream of travelers and began climbing the rocky steps.

Inside the old lava tubes, fireflies swarming our torches danced lights on black ponds of melted ice, dripping from the stalactites above our heads, and igneous boxwoods and winterberries pushed against our legs as we passed. Occasionally water would splash into my hair like an injection of ice that sent shivers down my spine.

"You don't look Miran," one of the guides said to me. It was the shorter one named Fern.

"I'm not."

"Figured as much. Not such a strange thing to a man who travels for a living. Whereabouts are you from?"

"Som Abast. It's the major city of Sulian Daw."

He scratched his head. "You speak Miran better than

anyone I've met from across The Rift. Sulian Daw's part of the far eastern brink, yes? I heard about the Sovereign sending one of the magnates there to establish trade a couple years back."

"That's the one."

"Never met a Sulian before," Crane, the tall one, said. "I'll be honest—I expected men like you to be different."

"How so?"

"They say Sulians throw every foreigner onto the surface to prove they're worthy enough to enter the city. Anyone who survives is then worthy enough to be thrown into the lakes instead. They also say you make the best damn coffee in Ra'Thuzan, so I suppose you take the bad with the good."

It was the first time hearing a compliment about my homeland. I remembered once trying to explain that the surface winds by Sulian Daw didn't kill like they did here—that someone could survive for up to a half-hour outside before succumbing to the cold—but explaining this only reinforced the idea among some of the more skeptical Mirans that I was an idiot. "Even if that was true, how would that say anything about my personality?"

"Crane is just surprised you're so well-mannered," Fern said. "To be honest, so am I. And now I'd like to apologize on behalf of our little group for making untrue assumptions about you."

I failed to subdue a smile. In a world without my flesh binding, what would traveling with these three be like? It exhilarated me to think of having someone beyond Emil as a friend.

"How far was the journey?" Crane asked. "Did you pass through Callo or just Xeriv? You had to have traveled through the Twilight Canyons, right?"

"I wasn't navigating, and I wasn't permitted the information."

He made a face like he didn't believe me. "You a serf or something?"

"Er, yes. Sort of."

"Oh." Crane's eyes shifted toward Sorrelo, who walked a dozen feet ahead beside Mateo. Though the Sovereign had outlawed slavery at the start of his reign, the wealthy worked around this by offering serf contracts—travelers would agree to serve the merchants and nobles to garner passage through the endlessly confusing tunnels throughout Ra'Thuzan. Serf contracts and even slavery was rampant east of The Rift, but most people in Mira had low opinions of serf contract owners.

"Well, don't you worry," Fern said. "We'll take good care of you."

An odd thing for him to say. "Do you think there'll be trouble?"

"There's always trouble this far out from the capital. The outskirts might as well be their own territories. Always expect the worst, 'specially after Bibura."

"Bibura?"

"You know, the massacre."

It took a moment to remember the disjointed reports the magnate had received about Bibura over a year ago. Bibura had been an Augustin town to the west until raiders overran the place and murdered every man, woman, and child. It was suspected their motive involved Augustin's Mercantile Guild and the guild's supposed love for stockpiling wealth inside a secret vault under the town. The rumor wasn't unfounded—before the Sovereign established Mira, trade guilds were their own empires, hoarding treasure like abyssal fire salamanders from Sulian kids' stories. The Mercantile Guild had been around for centuries, surviving Mira's founding and the Merchant Wars that followed, which meant they could have caches all over the territories. Whether the raiders found one was an answer only the Mercantile Guild knew.

Judging by the way these men kept observing the magnate, I realized there might have been a reason Fern had mentioned Bibura. "Did you know anyone from that town?"

"Dellix's parents lived there. Lived in Augustin barely a season before they were killed."

These men thought Sorrelo belonged to the Mercantile Guild. "Sario isn't part of the guild," I said, keeping my voice low, "It doesn't look like it, but he does business out of Augustin's third level. He's a moneylender for the lower class."

"Men who dress like that always have ties to the Mercantile Guild. Call us backwoods illiterates, but we were all city kids at some point. He smells of corruption worse than Dellix's pits."

"You're wrong."

"Well, I suppose it depends on Dellix." He turned to the third member of their group. "Do you feel reassured, my friend?"

A smile crept onto Dellix's face. "Call me adequately relieved."

Did these men agree to guide us through Dagir's Pass so they could settle an old score? "If you're planning on doing anything other than guide us through the pass, I'm telling you as someone who'd benefit the most. Don't try it."

They frowned at my sudden aggression, and Fern made a sound of disgust. "Never thought I'd hear words like that from a slave."

His words stole my momentum. Crane shook his head. "You're turning into a disappointment. Remember who you're dealing with? In Byssa, we break the knuckles of anyone who proves themselves false in a deal. That principle's followed me into this profession as well. For you to insinuate otherwise is extremely rude."

Their disdain made it clear they wanted me to leave, so I did.

Was I reading them wrong? That possibility didn't agree with the instincts currently telling me not to turn my back on the blades strapped to their waists. I could either voice my suspicions to the magnate, which would result in a death sentence for these three men, or stay quiet and keep an eye on them. I glanced back at the princep and princepa, and found Sara watching me. Had she keyed in on the same thing I had, or was she just interested in my secrets like usual?

I moved up to walk between Mateo and Sorrelo, who headed the group, and found them focused on their strides and breathing. The master smith grimaced but said nothing. Sorrelo wiped at the sweat on his brow and sniffled. "You're not even winded," he said to me.

"Years of labor in Sulian Daw will do that," I said, replaying the conversation with the guides in my head. What did our group look like to them? At a glance the primary threat was Emil. The magnate was armed but clearly just a talker. There was also the master smith and me. The smiths didn't train in armed combat and I looked like a simple attendant. They had warmed up to Sara, but it wasn't hard to imagine what they wanted from her if they thought they could kill the rest of us.

"You're strong," Sorrelo said.

For a second I didn't understand him. The magnate had never complimented me unless it immediately followed the death of one of his dissenters. Warmth crept up the sides of my neck and I struggled to look his way. "Uh, thanks."

"You should be Emil's," he said between breaths. "After we retake Augustin, he'll take the throne and I will be his advisor, which means you'll be passed on to him. I won't need you anymore." He punctuated the last sentence by looking me full in the eyes, but it wasn't hard to read between the lines. He was willing to give up the flesh binding.

When I'd first arrived in Augustin, I'd fantasized about hearing those words too many times to count. They were supposed to break me down until I was crying at Sorrelo's feet or fill me with happiness to the point of delirium, but the words only sat dead in my ears. It was shock, a distant voice in my head said. He was giving me the one thing I'd wanted in the last two years.

"Things are different now," the magnate continued. "This trip has given me perspective. It's showed me just how heavy the eyes of the world felt on my shoulders. There's a certain charm to obscurity, and it took a coup for me to see it. If you live too long without breaking the routine, you forget how easy doing so is."

The tunnel straightened and the slope nearly leveled out. Dellix broke away and sat on a rock, reaching for his foot. "I need a moment."

The words sobered me up. It was obvious Crane and company were going to try something, and every moment I didn't act was more time for them to put their plan into place. The pressure of a Word didn't push me to confront them though. Sorrelo had commanded me to protect him in the past, but Words weren't forever—they did something to the brain when the command was given, but brains could adapt over time. Could heal. A Word could fade after months, and at some point along the way Sorrelo had forgotten to reinforce the command. Had forgotten that I'd once wanted to disobey. I didn't blame him.

My heart hammered in my chest, tripling in cadence over the span of a few moments. There was a choice in front of me I'd never thought was possible. Crane and Fern stood next to Dellix, who fished at the inside of his boot with a finger, and Emil and Sara milled next to me. All I had to do was say a handful of words and Sorrelo would be safe—I'd be helping a man who was willing to give me up, step down in the best interest of Augustin, and let his son rule.

"While we're stopped," Crane said. "I might as well take this opportunity to impart a gift to our new friend."

The group didn't realize who Crane was referring to until they noticed the guides focused on me. The three men unsheathed their swords, and Emil barely had time to grip the hilt of his weapon before Fern hacked at the princep. The strike would have killed if my dagger hadn't been there to parry it.

No one's weapon was handy to deflect Dellix's and Crane's swords as both plunged into Sorrelo's chest.

The magnate gasped and crumpled to his knees. Sara screamed. Dellix and Crane spun to join Fern, who spat in my face. "Unappreciative prick."

The man hadn't seen me pull the vial of liquid from my belt. I flicked the container and the glass exploded against his neck, spilling its contents everywhere. The vial wouldn't have broken against his soft flesh—I'd used elemental power to apply pressure on the silicon in the glass. He screamed from the rubidium hydroxide covering his neck, jaw and ear, and he brought his free hand to the burning flesh, swinging wildly at Emil.

My action spurred Emil out of his trance. The princep's blade sang, faster than I'd ever seen a blade travel, Emil roaring as he side-swiped at Fern's weapon. Sparks flew and the force of Emil's blow sent Fern's sword flying. Crane and Dellix flinched as Emil hacked into Fern's shoulder.

"Shit," Crane said, stepping back to put distance between himself and the Rock Snake. Dellix didn't notice the Adriann daughter move in from the side. She looked at me furiously as she stuck her dagger into Dellix's spine and twisted. Dellix let out a half screech, half moan as he fell.

Crane moved his back to the wall as Emil advanced on him. "How did you knock Fern's sword away like that?" His gaze fell on Sorrelo as the magnate leaked blood into the dirt, and on Mateo, who desperately tried to staunch the magnate's wounds. Blood had already started to pool on the rock beneath Sorrelo, and his eyes fluttered. Crane's eyes finally settled on the Meteor Blade, and his mouth fell open. "Ah, fuck me to the depths."

"You have no idea what you just did," Emil said, and he stepped forward and swung with all his might. Crane tried to block, but encountered an invisible resistance that prevented him from raising his blade all the way. He could do nothing against the force of the blow that nearly bisected him.

Sara pushed me and I stumbled backward. Her knuckles whitened on the dagger's handle. "How could you let them get away with that?"

"Sara, leave Ig alone," Emil said.

She faltered when she noticed her brother kneeling over their father, and she hurried to their side. I stayed away and checked on the dead men. The aroma of chemical burns hit my nostrils—what little part of Fern's neck and face not covered in blood continued to sizzle from the catalyzed rubidium hydroxide. The other two wore masks frozen in pain.

These men had answered old prayers.

Sorrelo's eyes went in and out of focus. Mateo ripped open the magnate's shirt to reveal gouges below Sorrelo's rib cage that pulsed with blood, and the smith and princep stacked their hands atop the wounds to apply pressure. "I thought you screened those fucking guides," Emil said to his sister.

Sara's fury vanished. "I did," she answered coolly. "They were a group of nobodies. They had no reason to attack."

"Well, clearly someone gave them a good reason."

"Why didn't you protect Father?" she asked me.

"You need to stop eyeing Ig like it's his fault," Emil said. "He saved my life."

Sara didn't move, apparently still waiting for an answer, but all I did was stare at Sorrelo as the blood drained from his body. Did I feel guilty? I… didn't know what to feel.

"Ig," the magnate whispered. "Help."

I rushed to rip strips of cloth from my tunic and fashion a bandage. The occasional buffet of wind touched my exposed arms, prickling my skin like needles while I wrapped the cloth around Sorrelo's torso. Emil and Mateo continued to maintain pressure on the wounds, and blood appeared on the magnate's lips, streaming down his jaw and dripping off his earlobe.

"His lung's pierced," I said.

"What does that mean?" Emil asked.

I only shook my head.

Emil and Sara sat at their father's side for the next minute, holding his hand and talking to him in small voices. Sorrelo had trouble forming words, and his eyes roamed his surroundings. He was afraid. Still, he tried to talk to his children, and they answered with distressed nods and shakes of their heads, or with words too low for me to hear. Sorrelo's chest rose and fell, rose and fell, and then it stilled. It wasn't until my heart started racing did I notice I'd stopped breathing a while ago.

Emil cupped his father's cheek. I watched his throat contract and bulge as he whispered something, and I realized it was the Augustin death chant. *Seri do-neuro, filepa mor fiera-di Fheldspra*. Words from Augustin's old tongue.

Emil rose and continued onward, disappearing behind the bend. His sister repeated the ritual and touched her father's face. When she finished, she stood to face me. "Why didn't you stop them? You knew they were planning something."

Mateo had been busy wiping the blood off his hands. She turned on him. "What is he, Master Smith? He's not just a servant. He knows how to fight, doesn't he?"

He stayed silent.

"Kill yourself," she said to me.

I didn't move. "It doesn't work that way," I said. "Even if you knew how to give a Word, you can't make me take my own life."

She almost replied, until she noticed Mateo waiting for her to speak. The man was clearly confused, but I wasn't interested in offering an explanation. Neither was Sara.

Emil came back, crestfallen but with a better hold on himself. "He deserves a burial," he said.

A burial was next to impossible—the old lava tubes we traveled through were made from solidified magma, making it too hard to dig into. I could have created a hole with my powers, but not while they were around.

The tunnel started to reek of gore and intestinal acid. The

guides' mutilated bodies lay a short distance away, leaking bloody fluids that slid down the slope and soaked into the fronds crusting a nearby pool. Mateo investigated the alcoves branching off the tunnel, but they were only several feet deep. "This trail obviously leads to Dagir's Pass. If the wrong people find him, it will be an arrow pointed our direction. We can't bury him, but we need to get rid of the body."

"Remove the head and make the face unrecognizable," Sara said to me.

Mateo and Emil gaped at her. Emil gave a sound of disgust and walked off once more.

"You don't find that overkill?" Mateo asked.

"No, I don't. And why does it matter? We have someone to do it for us."

The master smith blanched but didn't argue. "Stay with him so he doesn't run off," she said, then left.

"I don't know why she thinks you would run off now, of all moments," Mateo said once we were alone.

I stared at Sorrelo. "Who knows."

"I'll be watching from over there, I guess."

Mateo held a firefly torch while he sat on a boulder fifty feet away, turning his body so he wouldn't have to watch. I didn't need the torch for my work—enough lightcaps grew here to provide an uninhibited view of the scene. Sorrelo looked so small in the way he had curled into himself, like a bag of leathery flesh wrapped in fine clothing and stale rage. I retrieved a sword from Crane's hacked body and stood over the magnate. Then I swung.

Crane's blade was dull, and it took two swings to sever the spine in Sorrelo's neck. As I watched the head roll a foot from the body, I felt nothing. Wasn't this supposed to be satisfying? Seeing his face separated from the rest of him looked so wrong. The magnate had been many bad things, but he had always been full of life.

"What's wrong with you?" I whispered as I recovered a knife and knelt over the severed head. "You're supposed to be ecstatic. He's dead. He is dead. *Dead*." I went to work carving up his face, cringing as I did so.

My gloom dogged me as I finished my work and picked up Sorrelo's head by the hair. Farther up the path near Mateo, a series of cracks lined the left side of the tunnel—deep holes that tapered to nothing or expanded into hidden cavities. Popular places for wolf spiders to make their homes.

Mateo watched as I threw the magnate's head into one of them.

Ice melt trickled through centimeter-wide spaces on the ceiling, and I used them to clean the blood off my forearms. The water hurt my skin, but I gritted my teeth and did my best to remove the gore.

"Are you all right?" Mateo asked when I joined him.

"Sorrelo and my old masters made me do worse." These tunnels acted like a funnel for wind, and it wouldn't be long until the stench warned away anyone farther down the path, or convinced the wrong people to follow.

"Why did Sara think you would suddenly run off?"

We started walking. "Couldn't tell you."

"Is there any way I could convince you to disobey her?"

"You want me to leave?"

He stopped. "Yes. Power corrupts, and if you want Emil to have the best chance to rule Augustin with a good heart, you can't serve him and he can't know what you are. What would happen to my home if Emil turned into his father?"

His home, he'd said. Not ours. "Emil's nothing like Sorrelo."

"For now."

It took a moment to puzzle out what he was thinking. "You really think I'm an agent of the Great Ones, don't you? I told you, I'm not a disease."

"Maybe, maybe not, but we can't take the risk."

The curve of the tunnel where we had come from waited invitingly. It would have been so simple. All I had to do was walk away.

But if I did, what would I do? Where would I go? To live life independent of the Adrianns, or of my old masters... how would I even start? My elemental power was tied to the Adrianns and would fade in three passings, turning me into just another man. A Sulian stuck in a foreign country. Everything I knew about Mira outside Augustin's capital was through books.

I would barely last a week.

An old man thrashing on a table, the glow of amber quartz glinting off the Listener's knife as Olevic leaned over. The memory made me dig my fingers into the palms of my hand until they ached. That was all the purpose I needed: to kill Olevic Pike and help Emil, my best friend, retake the throne.

Helping the princep meant doing something the masters of Sulian Daw would have never permitted me to do. To affect something I actually cared about.

Once again I glanced down the tunnel leading back to Sanskra, where a black pit of endless choices waited. Some people were meant to lead, so it went, but there were others who were always meant to follow. Freedom was useless to someone like me.

"I'm sorry," I said. "Emil needs me."

The master smith's nostrils flared. "We'll see."

Chapter 11

By the third passing, being on the constant move had battered us down and shortened our tempers, and the winds funneling through the tunnels and caves had evolved from nipping to cutting. Fortunately, guides weren't needed to find World's Grotto Inn—the last vestige of society before the pass—but getting to the other side would be impossible unless we found someone else to hire.

The twinkling lights of the inn appeared around a corner, and Sara let out a sigh of relief. "Oh, black winds. Finally. No more sleeping on rocks."

The tunnel widened into a cavern, with World's Grotto resting against the left wall. Only lightcaps grew at this elevation, which shined a ghostly pallor on strips of ice that grew between rips across the ceiling that looked as though some colossus had raked its claws across it. Distorted stars peeked through the ice.

My teeth chattered violently by the time we reached the inn. Long-haired yaks clustered in groups within the straw of the stables adjacent to the inn, and two guards sat on chairs beside the front entrance. They wore furs draped over fighting leathers, each wielding fauchards—spears with wide, wickedly curved blades instead of pointed ends.

"We could steal those yaks," I muttered as we approached the guards.

"Agreed," Sara said.

Yaks were common pack animals for high elevation travel, and could in some cases navigate the terrain better than a cartographer. No doubt these ones knew the far side of Dagir's Pass like the backs of their hooves. But they moved slowly. We'd be forced to kill anyone who chased after us.

The guards nodded toward us as we reached the door—without Sorrelo's ridiculous ensemble, we blended in for the first time. Inside, mercenaries smoked white sage from pipes and drank from stone mugs by a hearth, and traders sat separately among the tables littering the floor. Only one group had the distinctive, stout features of Augustins, but were probably headed the opposite direction, back into the territory. It was unlikely anyone had beat us here if they'd been fleeing the city.

"Hello, saior," Emil said to the man behind the counter. "Two rooms." The owner took us in, but I couldn't tell if his suspicion was of the general or the specific type. "Fifty standards per room, per night," he said in a lilted voice.

As Emil pulled the money out of a pocket in his cloak, Sara stopped him and turned to the owner. "Are you trying to skin our asses? Rooms like these should cost thirty-five, maximum."

"Don't like it, go somewhere else."

Sara leaned forward, and for a moment, her body tensed like she wanted to hit him. But the anger dissipated and she put on a sweet smile. "Look, our group's been sleeping in the dirt and the cold, so piling into one room to save ourselves some money isn't a problem. I don't see a sign for an occupancy limit either. Would you rather make fifty standards from one room, or seventy from two?"

He leaned forward. "Forty-five per room."

"Forty."

"Forty-four."

"Forty."

"Fine," he growled. He left the counter for the back room.

Sara backhanded her brother in the shoulder. "You have no concept of the value of money, do you? Don't think that because you're not dressed like the damn Sovereign, people aren't going to try stiffing you. Father's ignorance in Sanskra painted a target on his back, so try not to do the same."

Emil took a breath as though to argue, but nodded instead. "I'm sorry."

The owner returned with our keys, and Emil set the pile of greenish-gold coins on the counter. Outside our rooms on the second floor, Emil handed the keys for one room to Mateo and me, keeping the other keys for himself and Sara.

"Emil, trade your key with Ig," Sara said. "I'm staying with him."

We paused. "What?" Emil and I asked at the same time.

"You heard me. I want our servant staying with me."

"Why?" Emil asked.

"To serve. Obviously."

"What does that mean?"

"Want me to spell it out for you? I figured you would have already learned this lesson from a girlfriend or two. Or at least allowed them to sit you down and explain how it worked."

Emil eyed me. "I have nothing to do with this," I said.

"If you say so." He switched the keys.

"Don't be a prude," Sara said as she opened the door. She gestured for me to follow, and I walked inside. The door creaked shut and she locked it.

She set her hands on her hips. "So. Here we are. Alone."

"We are." I swallowed hard, my attention moving from her feet upward, tracing the curves of her legs and her hips, up and up until I reached her face, where I found her smirking. We'd been hitting the roads hard since Sanskra, Sorrelo's death was still fresh, and Sara hadn't shown me an ounce of interest before. Why now? My body didn't much care for the answer though as it realized the situation it was in. My skin prickled. Heat ran up my ears and down my thighs. I hadn't been intimate with someone in years, not since Quin.

Did I want this?

My attraction toward Sara had grown over time, evolving from respect to admiration to something more, but I'd hardly acknowledged it due to the despair of serving Sorrelo. But now Sorrelo was dead.

Yes, I did want Sara. Badly. The thought of being close to someone, of being wanted, nearly overcame me, and the room suddenly felt five degrees warmer. Sara moved by, brushing past me and grazing my hand, the skin on the back of hers feeling cool, my own skin hypersensitive, her hair smelling of wood smoke, and she sat on the bed, letting out a moan of pleasure and straightening her legs until her joints cracked. Her eyelids fluttered until her gaze settled on me, inviting. "Father would've flayed us alive if he found out I tried to seduce you. You're very responsive, you know that?"

My hands covered the front of my pants.

"We have things to discuss," she said.

"Like what?"

"So, so much," She rolled up her sleeve where a bloody bandage was waiting underneath, and she untied it, pulling it off to reveal a maze of red lines carved into her flesh, half-scabbed over. It was a series of whorls and intricate patterns, and in the center was the word *Ig*.

My heart skipped. "How'd you find out?"

"You know that first passing after Father died, when we made camp? I snuck off during my watch and went back to Father's body. I knew he had a scar, but didn't give it much thought until I got a better look at it right after the coup, when we were switching disguises."

"A flesh sacrifice isn't enough to issue a Word."

"I mean, obviously. I did this to myself almost three passings ago and none of the commands since seemed to do the trick. But I think I have it figured out." She spoke before I could argue. "*Ig*," she enunciated, "sit on the floor."

A pressure appeared like a cold hand on the back of my head, and it intensified with every moment I didn't obey. I sat on the floorboards, shaking my head to myself.

She withdrew a sharp breath. "Amazing."

A hundred regrets churned through me like a mudslide, so obvious to me now that I faced being enslaved to an Adriann again. But the thought of helping Emil had been so liberating—for the first time in my life, I'd had a purpose I cared about.

Why hadn't Emil shown an interest in my flesh binding? He, Sara, and Efadora now had the power to issue a Word, so long as they made a flesh sacrifice to the name of Ig. However, Emil never bothered to learn more about my flesh binding. Of course Sara figured it out first. The princepa continued, "It's so obvious now that I think about it. I mean, how often do people refer to someone they're talking to by name?" The mattress whined as she leaned back. "I'm guessing 'Ig' isn't your real name. What is it?"

I ground my teeth before answering. "Jakar."

"Hmm. I'll just call you Ig. I'll have to anyway if we want to keep this to ourselves."

"You don't want to tell your brother?" The ensuing sensation was like falling. I should have told Emil everything, even if it meant Sara finding out.

She scoffed. "You don't know my brother as well as you think. It's for the best."

"How could that possibly be for the best?"

"You didn't know my father before you fell into his hands. You brought out the worst in him. You can help us retake Augustin, but Emil doesn't need you to rule. We don't need you bringing out his demons."

She sounded like Mateo, and the thought almost made me laugh. "Telling him about the flesh binding depends on you," she said. "If it turns out you're just a personal attendant? Emil can have you then. I already have enough people around my fingers."

"I'm sure you do, Mira's Hand."

For the first time since we'd met, shock crossed her face. "You know about that?"

"No," I said, my tone deadpanned.

We traded fierce gazes for several moments. "This'll be interesting," she said. "Ig, I want you to tell me everything you did for my father."

The pressure appeared once more. "Fine," I said.

My FIST RAPPED on Emil and Mateo's doorway a couple hours later. Emil answered, and his lips drew into a tight line. "Hi."

I was too tired to care about the awkwardness. "Can we get a drink downstairs?"

"Sure. I couldn't sleep anyway."

The stairs creaked as we descended into the smoke and voices of the bar. Fewer people occupied it now—exhaustion likely shadowed most arriving at World's Grotto, just as it had us. I ordered two rice beers and brought them to the table near the fire where Emil waited.

"You don't usually drink," Emil said as I took a sip from my mug.

"You're right. This is a special occasion."

The princep took a drink as well, and I realized how that must have sounded.

I would have done anything to tell Emil the truth, but Sara had covered her bases. After I'd shared with her Sorrelo's secrets, she'd moved on to my own. Little had been safe. Once satisfied, she'd spent the rest of the time experimenting with her commands until she was comfortable enough letting me leave, knowing I wouldn't share anything she didn't want me to. Emil would have to continue thinking I'd slept with his sister.

Looking back, I was angry with myself for wanting Sara. She'd done little more than offer mild insults over the past two years, despite ample opportunity to abuse me like her father had, and it'd tricked me into thinking it could've meant more.

"We haven't had a chance to talk since all this started," I said. "Alone."

Purple rimmed the princep's bloodshot eyes. "We've been busy, but busy keeps the mind off home." He took another drink and ran his thumb along the mug's rim. At first I worried he wouldn't want to talk, until he finally spoke. "I'm a bad son."

"Why?"

He checked his surroundings before answering. "I've been having dreams about killing Olevic Pike every passing since Father died. I've been trying to figure out why, and I realized part of me thinks I'll have an easier time reclaiming the capital without Father in the way. Is something wrong with me?"

"Those dreams don't say anything about who you are. They say something about Sorrelo. He wasn't... a pleasant person to be around. You're nothing like your father if that's what you're worried about."

He took another drink. "I'm more like him than I let on. I just hate that part of me enough not to act on it."

"You can't control what pops into your head. Nobody can. People should be held accountable for their actions, not their thoughts."

He offered a humorless smile. "If it's worth anything, I haven't once thought about your flesh binding. Father never told us how to issue a Word and I'm glad. I want it to die with him. It's not the same as undoing your flesh binding, but once I'm magnate, we'll figure out how to truly free you. I promise."

Instead of answering, I took another long drink. Emil could always tell when Sorrelo had forced me to withhold information. *Ig, give no hint to anyone that you're bound to my Words,* Sara had said.

Commands like these always muddled my brain. While nobody could command me to want something, if the command required enough effort from me to complete, sometimes I found my desires changing anyway. Part of me *hoped* Emil wouldn't find out.

The idea tied knots inside me. No matter how bad things had gotten as a slave, at least I'd had my mind to count on most of the time. But times like this, when fulfilling a command required so much of my mental capacity, I wondered if my wants evolved simply to lessen the chance of experiencing terrible pain.

Dark corridors of Augustin and darker homes, creaking through doors as I slipped into sleeping homes. Separating the flesh of throats. The drip of poison from vial to food. Believing I was doing the right thing. Jumping at the chance to help Sorrelo, knowing those people were guilty.

What if I'd tricked myself into thinking I wasn't a monster?

No, no, no, I thought. Mateo was wrong about me. I was Sara's puppet and I didn't want to serve her. Emil would find out what she'd done eventually, and once he did, I would be his and we could focus on excising Olevic Pike from the Augustin throne.

"Are you all right?" Emil asked.

I realized I'd had my eyes closed. "My arm hurts."

"Ah." He eyed the sleeve covering the burn. "How's it healing?"

I lifted the sleeve partway to show the pale scarring and lingering blisters. Pyremoss gel accelerated the healing, but now we traveled at an elevation too high for pyremoss to grow.

"Sara said some things to me," Emil said. "She thinks you're not who you say you are. That you might've had more of a hand in helping my father during the coup than you're willing to admit."

"She's right," I answered after a few moments.

"How so?"

"Your father had someone train me with a sword, but he

didn't want anyone knowing. He would have probably died back in Augustin if I didn't ambush those rebels in the throne room. Having everyone see me as just a servant was one of the tricks he liked to hide up his sleeve."

Emil reached across the table and gave my hand a squeeze. A rare gesture in Mira, one that made me miss the casualness of physical affection in Sulian Daw. It had been so long since someone had touched me in kindness. Maybe Emil knew this. "Well, *I've* always seen you as much more than a servant. It was obvious since the first passing you came into our family. You were half-insane when we took you from Sulian Daw, and to see how much you've changed, how much stronger you've become despite Father's punishments... I'm in awe of you, Ig." He scoffed. "Sometimes when I'm scared or nervous, I picture you in the same situation working through the problem with ease, then suddenly I know I can do it too."

A buzzing grew in the base of my chest, and I focused on Emil's palm as it sat rough and warm over the top of my hand. I inspired him? He was Augustin's future magnate and I was some kid from the Nochi slums of Som Abast. I used to wonder how I looked to those around me, and the answer had always been a skulking, trembling attendant hiding in Sorrelo's shadow. Was I wrong?

He peered into my cup. "I was going to get you another drink, but you're barely halfway through your first one."

"I'm not much of a drinker. It's hard to get down."

He smiled. "It's only rice beer. You could get drunk off bush apples if they were left out for too long."

I tipped my cup toward him and drained it.

The front door groaned as it opened and closed, sending a gust of wind swirling through the bar.

There were three of them. They paused to survey the room, and the light danced on their faces, cutting into the shadows cast by their wide-brimmed cordovan hats. The choice of wardrobe was as out of place as it was distinctive. Augustin bounty hunters.

I almost turned back to face Emil, but resisted the urge. It would have been odd not to act curious about the arrival of men from Augustin's Fiador Fianza—a professional organization operating out of the Sandstone Wing in Augustin's third level. Their footsteps fell heavy beneath the weight of chainmail hidden inside brown overcoats that reached their knees, and naked falcatas hung from their belts. No sane guard would have let such heavily armed men into their establishment, but most made exceptions for Augustin bounty hunters. Sorrelo Adriann had always openly supported the Fiador Fianza.

Two pairs of eyes passed over us in their search, but one pair didn't. The man they belonged to broke away from the group and headed our way. I turned back to Emil before he could reach for the dagger he'd brought downstairs in lieu of the Meteor Blade—he'd left the rhidium sword upstairs where the scabbard wouldn't draw attention. "Don't attack," I whispered quickly. "They don't recognize you. They would've drawn their swords."

Each bounty hunter joined different groups throughout the inn. Chainmail clinked faintly as the man sidled up behind me. "Mind if I join you two? Wanted to ask a few questions."

"Feel free," Emil said.

The man turned a chair around and straddled it. He had long brown hair that curled over his ears, and an unkempt beard with a streak of blond through it. "Name's Micah. Pleasure to meet you both. I promise I won't take up much of your time neither. To whom am I speaking?"

"Elzo," Emil said. "That's Agnal."

Micah nodded to me in respect. "How long you two been staying here?"

Emil answered again. "Half a passing or so. We've been due to leave, but it's hard to summon the courage, the way the wind's blowing."

"Ah, solé." *Understood.* "Where you headed?"

"To Thornhang, then to Cragshear Bluff."

"Not the capital?"

The princep shook his head. "Cities don't interest us, nor anything else on the Granite Road."

"What does interest you?"

"Pardon me, Micah, but our business is our own."

Micah nodded, and I relaxed a bit. Emil was playing it smart by not spilling his guts. That would have been suspicious. "Fair to say you have a writ for one of them yaks out there? Would like to see it."

I took a turn to answer. "We're not using a yak."

"So then neither of you are traders if you don't have wares to carry. How'd you manage to find your way through Dagir's Pass?"

"I'm a cartographer," I answered. "If you have to know, that's our reason for traveling. We're headed to the Tear to catalogue some Sihraan ruins rumored to be along one of its cliffs. It's something we'd rather not advertise." It wasn't the best lie—I could imitate a cartographer's powers, considering my bond to silicon, but Sara had forbidden me from performing such a feat. I prayed they didn't ask for a demonstration.

Micah let out a *hmph*. "Strange thing to keep secret. The Archives has the territories' blessings to move freely through the crust."

"No offense, but the city's idea of cartography isn't grounded in reality. People don't appreciate someone rolling into their hometown and recording every detail on a map. Especially ruin folk. Men are more dangerous to me and my friends than any wildlife or cave-in."

"Gotcha. I appreciate the candor, saior."

I didn't know much about the Archives, and I was dredging up the information as quickly as I was giving it—when cartographers weren't hired to guide caravans, they hunted down Sihraan ruins or worked on a thesis for their chosen field of study. They like all elementals didn't need Tempurium timepieces to track time, and they could navigate tunnel networks that chewed up and spat out the hardiest explorers, making them invaluable… as well as a giant target for the folk who populated Sihraan Empire ruins. Ruin folk killed cartographers on sight. I couldn't remember much else, but as long as I knew more than the bounty hunter, that's what mattered.

"Well," the bounty hunter said. "Just letting you know there's been a recent change in leadership at the Augustin capital. A man named Olevic Pike is now standing magnate for the territory."

"What's that supposed to mean?" Emil asked.

"Means the Adrianns no longer hold the throne."

"What happened?"

"Olevic Pike overthrew the Adriann family and placed them under house arrest until a trial can be started."

It seemed the Fiador Fianza didn't want word to spread that they were on our trail. "Unfortunate for the Adrianns," Emil said. "Not that it matters to us little folk. What do you think, Agnal?"

"Someone better needed to take the magnate's place," I said simply.

A shadow of stubble covered Emil's jaw, making him look much younger than before, and only someone who'd dealt with him personally could have recognized him. But what about me? My long hair, which I normally wore in a ponytail, was hidden in a cowl wrapped around my head, and I'd allowed a patchy beard to grow. However, I couldn't do anything about my ash-grey skin. I'd been told I bore a resemblance to the people of Callo, but if these men had been specifically told by Olevic to look out for someone like me, my appearance should have given us up the moment they stepped into World's Grotto. Olevic would have been an idiot not to emphasize how dangerous I was, and my description should have been at the top of their list.

"Since we've been honest with you, would you be free to do the same?" I risked asking. "Who are you hunting?"

"Why so interested?"

"Try traveling so near the surface for a week with the same company. You start thirsting for a change in conversation. No offense, Elzo."

"None taken," Emil said.

"Sorry, friends," Micah said. "Join the Fiador Fianza if you want a piece of the pie. Can't risk loners nabbing our bounties." He rose to his feet and turned the chair around, pushing it in. "Careful heading toward Thornhang. There was a murder that way. Killers're still at large."

His attention moved to the stairwell, toward the sound of footsteps. I turned to see Mateo descending, but the smith paused when he noticed the intensity of Micah's gaze on his smith's robes. The bounty hunter looked from Mateo to Emil, then back again.

His hand moved to his waist, but Emil lurched, flipping the table and sending the man stumbling. Emil had his dagger out before Micah could recover. Mateo pounded up the stairs.

The other bounty hunters drew their weapons and backed up their friend. "Set it down," Micah said to Emil. He had his free hand in front of him, as if calming a spooked stone fox. "You're wanted alive."

Emil glanced at me as my feet moved into a fighting stance, then at the long, glossy steel in the bounty hunters' hands. Panic filled his eyes, which transformed into rage. "Back off," he said to me.

"Emil—"

"Out of the way, slave, or I'll cut you out of the way."

I shuffled to the side of the room, but none of the bounty hunters reoriented themselves, only having eyes for Emil. When I was out of harm's way, Emil's shoulders relaxed a degree. To the Fiador Fianza, it seemed I was just a harmless manservant.

Olevic could not have sent these men.

Emil threw the nearest chair at the group and darted up the stairs. The other patrons scrambled as the bounty hunters sprang into action, who knocked over chairs and tables and left cracks in the staircase as they bounded up it. Micah lingered behind, falcata in hand, watching me press myself against the wall.

It was hard to resist the urge to fight back when Micah grabbed me by the shirt and pulled me toward the exit. Sara's Word left me impotent to use my elemental power in any obvious way, so there was a good chance the bounty hunter could kill me if I fought back. "My employer figured you for dead in the riots back in Augustin," he said. "Sorrelo Adriann never struck me as the sentimental type."

Micah kicked the door and brought me into the cutting air outside. My breath blew out like smoke, whipped away by winds that seemed to freeze the hairs on my skin. The guards had retreated to the stables to stand warily in front of the yaks.

"The magnate trusted me. Besides, it was either follow him or be killed," I said.

He guided me toward a hitching post nailed to the ground where the inn's wall blended into the stables, where stone foxes waited with the bounty hunters' gear. "Interesting you would use the past tense when referring to the magnate. He dead, *ami*? Would explain the bodies we found."

I tensed at the slip up. "Please. I was forced into all this."

"Says the man I found drinking beers with the magnate's son. Don't play me for an idiot. You killed Bolivar Adriann."

"And you just sent two men after the Rock Snake. How do you expect that to turn out?"

"Perfectly." He shoved me toward the inn guards standing in front of the stable's awning. "Hold onto him," he commanded, and the guards obeyed, each setting a free hand on my shoulders. Micah rummaged through a pack hanging off his stone fox's saddle and pulled out wrought-iron shackles. He locked them onto my wrists. Returning to his mount, he untied something hanging off the fox's far side, then came back with a crossbow.

Glass shattered as a pack flew out to land on the purple wisteria leaves covering the stable roof. Mateo's profile could be seen as he used what looked like a dresser leg to clear the shards rimming the window frame.

He didn't notice Micah as he gingerly climbed out the opening and hung from the frame, feet still several feet from the stable roof. The master smith let go, dropping onto the sloped surface and almost rolling off the side. As he pulled himself up and untangled the robes from his legs, he peered over the awning to see me between the two guards. His eyes found Micah, who had backpedaled for a better angle of the roof. The bounty hunter raised his crossbow.

"No!" I screamed, twisting out of the guards' slackened grip. One reacted faster than the other, gripping his fauchard and sweeping it toward me as I turned to face him. I leaned back and caught the blade with the chain linking my wrists together. The weapon bit into the chain but didn't break through, and I gasped from the agony as the cuff bit into my burnt wrist, but grabbed the spear's haft and yanked it out of the guard's hands. I jabbed viciously, and the butt connected with the guard's face, breaking teeth and cartilage. Jumping to the side, I turned the spear around and faced the bounty hunter, who had the crossbow trained on my chest. The disarmed guard whimpered on the ground as he held his face, and the other one sneered as he aimed his spear at me.

Another body bounded out the window, landing lightly onto the stable roof. Sara. Micah moved his weapon from me to the princepa, uncertain. If he shot me, he'd have nothing to threaten the others with.

"Kill him," Micah commanded.

The other guard needed no convincing. I jumped to the side as he thrusted, and I attempted to hack him at the shoulder. The chain between my wrists prevented me from widening my grip enough to sturdy the hold on my weapon. As our fight meandered onto the field, patrons from the bar filed out of the inn—traders guarded by their hired mercenaries who held an array of weapons. They watched us with wary eyes, sandwiched between the chaos within the inn and the chaos without.

If I didn't free my hands soon, the guard would kill me. The chain jingled as I sprinted away to put a dozen feet between us, and I focused on the metal of his blade with my elemental senses. He charged. When he raised his fauchard to swing once more, I brought the haft up to block and flicked my wrists so that the chain wrapped around the wood.

The chain caught between the haft and the guard's blade, and it broke along with my weapon's haft. I discarded the broken butt and grasped the shortened spear, wrists now free. "Thanks," I said, grinning. I smiled through the painful vibrations that shot up my arms.

The guard let out an angry breath and charged again. The shortened handle allowed me to bring the weapon up faster, and I sidestepped as he jabbed, bringing the blade down on his head until it cut through skull.

I faced the bounty hunter when I managed to pry the edge from the guard's head. The other guard still lay on the ground dazed, blood leaking between fingers that covered his nose and mouth. Micah swung his crossbow wildly from Sara and Mateo, who still watched from the stable roof, to me. Emil was still inside the inn.

I felt for the steel located in the bolt strung in his crossbow—it existed on the edges of my awareness, too far to manipulate. Then I started running. The distance gave him time to aim, and he pulled the trigger, the crossbow jerking back.

I swung the fauchard, and it let out an ear-piercing shriek as the bolt hit the flat of the blade and deflected to the side. Micah brought his crossbow up when I closed the distance, but the swing from my blade broke his weapon in half.

The bounty hunter desperately brought his arms up, unable to find time to draw his sword, but I leveled the fauchard at his face, noticing a long dent in the fauchard's blade.

The princepa landed on the ground with a grunt. "Grab his sword," she said as she joined us.

I grabbed the hilt of the blade at Micah's side while Sara hovered her dagger near his neck. My chest heaved from the fight, but the winds cut right through the haze of heat, causing me to shiver. Micah glowered at the onlookers lingering near the front of the inn. "Kill these flame-forsaken shits!"

"You should have killed him in the inn," Sara said to Micah. "Greedy bounty hunters usually make for dead bounty hunters."

"Who sent you?" I asked him.

He spat on the ground. "Take our contracts at the Fiador Fianza seriously, we do."

A commotion erupted at the inn's entrance, and Emil appeared, clothes steaming with blood as he stormed toward us. A deep gash ran along his shoulder and part of his left ear was missing. The edge of the Meteor Blade glowed blue in the dim light.

When he reached us, his foot connected with Micah's chest and it sent the man sprawling. "Who the fuck sent you?" he asked as he stood over the bounty hunter. The rhidium edge hovered dangerously close to Micah's skin, close enough for the man's nostrils to flare as he smelled its caustic scent.

Sara stepped away from her brother, and I followed suit. I'd never seen Emil this angry before.

Micah put his hands up. "Name was Tuli."

Sara laughed. "I think there's a smith haunting us."

"You don't work for Olevic?" Emil asked.

The bounty hunter shook his head. "Listener approached us about finding you, but we'd already signed another contract."

"It seems hard to believe you'd refuse to help the Listener after he just staged a coup. We're the most valuable bounties in Augustin right now." He didn't say it suspiciously.

Micah propped himself up by the elbows. "Don't mean to

point out the obvious regarding your father, but if the Fiador Fianza was known for breaking a contract, Sorrelo Adriann would've torn us down to the bricks."

"He knows your father is dead, by the way," I said to Sara.

Sara checked the crowds, some of whom were scrambling to ready their yaks to leave. Mateo managed to climb off the stable roof and started preparing our packs. The inn's guests and the master smith kept a healthy distance from each other, and the remaining inn guard was nowhere to be seen.

Sara pushed the tip of her sword into the flesh beneath Micah's chin. He gurgled and his eyes rolled back, blood pouring over her steel.

"Damnit, Sara," Emil said.

The mercenaries guarding their employers faced us as the traders worked beneath the stable awning, but none seemed interested in attacking. Sara came up behind me as Emil and I rummaged through the packs slung over the bounty hunters' stone foxes. "I might need you to steal a yak from one of those traders before they leave," she whispered.

A dozen men guarded at least as many traders, all of them clustered inside the stables in a flurry of limbs and low, furious voices. The traders continually glanced our way. They feared me, though they had no reason to. As soon as I attacked one trader for his yak, the other men-for-hire wouldn't hesitate to fight, and unless I had access to a lava pool, they would easily kill me.

"Here," I said after finding a piece of thin, folded leather.

She took it and examined the writing. "A map."

"They're bounty hunters from the Fiador Fianza. You don't think they came all this way without buying maps from the Archives?"

Emil found a black flower salve in his pack for the wound on his shoulder, along with some bandages. Mateo lugged our supplies onto the bounty hunters' stone foxes as the princep shoved the black mush into the gash, and I started tying the wrap around the wound.

"The sooner we leave, the better," Mateo said, eyeing the others. "I don't know if they recognize us, but they know we have bounties on our heads. They might consider picking up where the bounty hunters left off."

"Hey!" someone yelled from the inn's entrance. The owner clutched his clothes close to his body and crossed the icy rock. When he reached us, I realized he wasn't clutching his coat, but a hurt arm. The wound didn't soften the anger on his face. "You killed Kahey and them bounty hunters. My inn's been wrecked to shit too. One'a you better pay up or the next group of bounty hunters riding through here're gonna know I'm doubling whatever price is on your heads."

"Ig..." Sara started.

I stepped forward before she had a chance to finish. My fist collided with the bottom of the owner's jaw, sending him sprawling onto the ground, unconscious. She looked at me, considering, then shrugged and moved to help Mateo. My heart beat faster in that moment than when I'd been fighting. Sara was going to make me kill the innkeeper and I'd made my own choice instead. It was strange and exhilarating.

Emil shook his head. "Not good enough," he said, pulling out a coin purse and hiding the money inside the owner's coat. He turned to the people still inside the stables. "Someone should help this man before he freezes."

Mateo, Sara, and Emil mounted the bounty hunters' stone foxes, and I stole the coat Micah had been wearing over his chainmail before climbing on behind Emil. Emil held the reins with his good hand while I carried the torch.

The princep shouted the 'go' command—"*Shé*"—and the animal took off, headed for the tunnel at the other end of the cavern. Behind me, I could hear the other foxes panting.

We headed toward Dagir's peak, toward uncertainty.

Chapter 12

ICE COVERED THE walls, swirling with the light from our fire. I nestled closer to the flames, almost to the point of burning myself, but I still couldn't remove the chill, my body to the point of jackhammering. All I wore was the stolen coat over my tunic and pants, but it felt like I was sitting naked in the snow.

Rock and ice created a domelike cavern with a translucent ceiling that glinted with stars and nebula on the other side. It was a landmark, according to Mateo, called the Cathedral, where ancient smiths called oredancers once mined rhidium, the mine depleted millennia ago. Emil had also said it was a sinkhole like Augustin. Along the walls at the sinkhole's base, soot-streaked wounds scored the rock where people had set off pyroglycerin over the centuries, and side tunnels littered the cavern, completely iced over. All except two. A fork in the road waited at the far end of the sinkhole—one way headed into the Radavich territory, the other into Manasus.

Last passing we rode through the peak of Dagir's Pass, traveling through old lava tubes threading the surface. But the roofs were caved in, covering the ground with debris and exposing us to the elements. I still hadn't recovered from that terrible cold, but years working beneath my old masters had taught me to think clearly through all forms of pain. Part of me had appreciated the black, jagged peaks of Dagir rimming the sky. They had to be the only reason we survived traveling through the pass, acting as a windbreak against the gusts on Mira's surface—winds that normally killed within minutes.

Emil pulled a bedroll off one of the foxes, shoulders trembling, and laid it out next to me. "Get inside," he said.

I did as he said. He warmed himself next to me, head bowed in exhaustion, and scooted closer to help. "Are you going to survive?" he asked, only half-kidding.

"I'm in a better spot than I was last passing."

The master smith returned to the fire to throw more lichen onto the flames and left again—he and Sara, both wearing yak furs they'd pillaged from Fern and Crane, gathered whatever lichen grew in the few spots not covered by ice. I would have helped, but I could barely stand after having clung to Emil on the back of the stone fox for hours with only my pants to protect my legs.

"What was in the sky last passing?" Emil asked in a tired voice.

It took a moment to figure out what he meant. "You mean the storm clouds?"

"If that's what they're called. They made the sky so dark."

"You only see those near mountains. It's too cold for them to form in most of the territory." It had been years since I'd seen clouds obscuring the always-present blanket of stars. Storms were normal in Sulian Daw, but only because the city sat so close to the Burning Mountains. It wasn't until I'd arrived in Augustin that I realized how unique they were.

My shivering calmed. Emil moved closer until he was almost sitting on me, and soon his body calmed too. "You've been quiet lately," I said.

Emil wrung the haft of a hammer he'd discovered near the pyroglycerin blasts. The oredancer tool was ancient, its alloy pre-dating techniques established at the Foundry's inception eight-hundred years ago by several factors. "I lost control of myself back at World's Grotto," he said.

"Everyone has a temper. You're allowed to lose it every once in a while."

"All I wanted was to kill that man after I almost died," he said quietly, almost too hard to hear over the crackling fire. "We needed information from him, but for a moment I didn't care, and all I wanted was to hurt him." He watched the stone foxes for a long moment as they licked at patches of ice nearby, their reins lodged beneath a boulder. "Have you ever been that angry before?"

I nodded. Anger and hate had overwhelmed me a few times in my life, mostly when I was with the Ebonrock, but hatred ran too hot to sustain. Accepting what my life had become was easier after realizing that.

Mateo and Sara joined us with their armfuls of lichen, and each sat on the remaining two bedrolls. There were only three, but I had no problem sleeping with the foxes tonight. They were dirty but likely warmer.

Emil broke the silence. "I'm going to Manasus."

It didn't surprise me—Emil had wanted to find Efadora since the start. "You may have to," Mateo said as he stirred the fire. "If this Tuli Dempra fellow sent bounty hunters after us, he might've sent some after Efadora too."

Earlier, Sara had found a copy of the contract in one of the packs, and it turned out "Tuli" had paid a substantial sum to have the former magnate and his children captured.

"I'll go with you," I said.

Sara started, but Mateo cut in, "Emil is going to need my guidance on his trip too."

"As much as I would love the peace and quiet, I can't go to Radavich by myself," Sara said. "Soon as the first group of bandits sees a lone woman traveling the countryside, they won't hesitate to make friends."

"You're right," Emil said. "And it turns out Ig can handle

himself. He'll go with you and Mateo and I will go to Manasus."

I stewed on the decision but didn't argue. Sara would have found a way to take me with her anyway. "Do you think Radavich will help with your father dead?" I asked.

Nobody answered. From my understanding, Lucas Adriann had been close with Sorrelo, but cared very little for the rest of the family. Lucas would also be essential in convincing Radavich's magnate that helping was worth the risks that came with inter-territory conflict.

The frowns on Emil and Sara betrayed similar thoughts.

"Let's get some rest first," Emil said. "Then we'll part ways."

Later, as I sandwiched myself between the backs of two dozing foxes, I stared at the spires of ice running up the sides of the cavern, conjoined into a monolith dozens of feet thick. Distorted wisps of clouds floated by, lit by the passing of the moon, Saffar. I fell asleep thinking of Sara. It wasn't too late to show her she didn't have to treat me the way her father had. We could start this off the right way.

A few hours later, I woke to Emil shaking me. "It's time to go," he said, fogged breath blowing into my face.

My legs creaked like old leather when I stood. He was working at the knot of twine on his belt loop, and when it came loose, he handed me his good luck charm. "Take it."

The dark iron ring sat on my palm, its silver trim as shiny as liquid mercury. "I can't. You've been carrying this around for half your life."

"I have. And these past ten years have been very kind to me. Much kinder than they've been to you." He closed my fingers over the charm with both hands. "I want you with me, but I can't always get what I want. At least part of me can go with you instead."

He wore a look that dared me to argue, a look I'd seen Sorrelo wear, and I couldn't help but smile. I tied the twine around my neck and tucked the ring into my shirt. The metal burned like ice, but a warmth overshadowed it. So this was what receiving a gift felt like. "Thank you."

Preparing for the trip didn't take long, and Sara worked with an excited energy while she harnessed her mount. Mateo and Emil were taking two of the foxes, and I would be riding behind Sara on the third.

We stood at the road's fork, each of our foxes surefooted on the ice. Emil had the map, but Mateo had copied it onto a spare piece of parchment for us. "Be safe," Emil said. He looked at me when he spoke.

"You too," I said, anxiety filling in the gap my words left behind. I wanted to say more, but how to say it in front of the others? I didn't want to travel to Radavich without him, and being stuck alone with Sara for the next several weeks was the last thing I wanted. Emil and I were supposed to stay together.

Emil's fox took off, followed by Mateo's, and they bounded down the tunnel out of sight.

"Finally," Sara said. She heeled the fox and it jumped forward. The darkness swallowed us, eating into the light of the torch I carried.

Part 2

Chapter 13 – Efadora

WHILE SETTING OUT the pottery display under the awnings outside the shop, I caught Niall staring at my legs for the third time in an hour, the creep.

"Aleena," he said. I stopped pushing the display shelf I'd been rolling toward the front door and answered my fake name with an expectant look. "You set that one closest to foot traffic," he continued. "Angle it so they get a real good look at them bowls. Got it?" His gaze did another one-two from the top of my body to the bottom.

"Yes, Het Tulp," I said, the words colored with barely suppressed disgust, but the old bat was oblivious as usual. I pushed the shelves of bowls, teapots, and ornaments through the entryway.

Niall owned a porcelain repair shop on the ridge of the city's fourth floor. His business was tucked against the Stone Tendrils—a cluster of hexagonal basalt columns cutting through the Manasus capital from the ground floor to the seventh like packaged sticks propped against the sinkhole's wall. For the past week, I'd spent an hour each passing helping him open and close up shop. I was younger than the average girl he liked to employ and assault in his back office, but lucky me, he'd offered the job anyway.

A line of vases rattled as I pushed the last display shelf against the front window. "All done," I called through the open entryway. "Can I get my pay now?"

"Course," Niall said, only a shadow in the dimly lit shop. He still hadn't lit the brazier in the middle of the floor. "Don't got no money on me though. Gotta get it out back. C'mere."

The inside of the front room smelled like ceramic and lacquer, and the office in the back glowed like honey from bulbous fungi on the ceiling. I waited in the doorway, watching Niall make a show of pretending to search through papers on his desk. His hair was grey and limp from age, but he had enough old-man strength in his limbs to overpower me if he got the jump.

He turned, hand moving halfway toward the hilt and sheath strapped to his side. "Yes, come. Come inside."

I didn't move. "Where's the money?"

He hesitated, but pulled out a set of keys from his jacket pocket and knelt before the safe under his workspace. The safe popped open with a click, and several seconds later, he rose with a handful of standards. "Here. Now."

I approached, noting the way he leaned forward, his hand cocked. He grasped the hilt of his knife when I came within arm's reach, body halfway turned to hide it, but I was ready.

I slipped my fingers into the brass knuckles in my pocket and brought my fist out, connecting with the wrist of his knife hand as he brought the blade in front of him. He yelped and the knife clattered to the floor. The brass knuckles on my other hand crashed into the digits clutching the money, sending coins bouncing and rolling across the floor. His yelp turned into a gasp and then a wail. One more punch to the ribs and mouth for good measure, and my work left him drooling blood and spittle on the floor with a low, constant whine on his lips. I stepped over him and grabbed at the safe's contents. Even if robbing Niall blind hadn't been on the table, knocking him senseless made it all worth it.

I pulled a small, hand-carved box from the safe and opened it. Nestled in the blue velvet were several nuggets of platinum ore, which Niall used to create platinum-laced lacquer to repair pottery for his customers among the nobility. I let out a laugh of triumph. The rest of the Titanite gang would shit themselves when they saw my haul.

"Ragworm," I said, giving him a kick. "Touch any more girls and I'll kill you. Got it?"

He answered by coughing out bloody spit. I picked his keys off the floor, and the man seemed to finally come to his senses once I locked the door behind me. Muffled yells and vibrations from his fists penetrated the rockwood. I headed for the entrance, nearly skipping from excitement.

A figure appeared in the entryway. "Shit," I said. Even through the dim embers of the brazier, I knew right away it was Meike.

"Efadora?" my personal guard asked. Niall's muffled screams answered her, and that's when she noticed the box in my hands.

I tried to slip past her, feinting to the left then going right, but I moved too slow with the box in my hand. She grabbed my shoulder and yanked the box away, causing the keys to fall to the floorboards. "Pick 'em up," she said.

"You pick them up."

"I do that and you make a run for it. Pick 'em up and let him out." She noticed the brass knuckles still on my hands, and added, "Give me those."

She confiscated my weapons, and I grabbed the keys and unlocked the office. Niall burst through, face red with flushed skin and blood smeared on his chin. He staggered toward me, but stopped when he noticed the box in Meike's hand.

I eyed the platinum longingly as Meike handed it over. "Sorry if she disturbed you, Het Shopekep," my guard said. "Be taking her now."

Niall pulled at his shirt to show the blood staining it. "See what she did? Nearly killed me. Punish the bitch."

Niall must've thought Meike was a city guardswoman come to stop a robbery in progress. Meike pulled me away by the wrist, and I looked back to see Niall smiling with teeth painted red.

I knocked over every piece of porcelain within reach outside the shop. Niall stormed out, crunching over thousands of pottery fragments on the mosaicked ground, and shouted a chain of curses as we walked away.

"You'll pay him back for that," Meike said.

"You made me, just now. That platinum was mine. I hope you know you really screwed me over."

"Sure I did. Fifteen-year-olds have all sorts of uses for shiny stuff like that, I'm sure."

"You'd be surprised." I let out a small whine as I imagined showing up to Titanite emptyhanded. They would've loved me for the rare metal, bought a bottle of ahkavit and fish cakes with just a fraction of what it was worth and celebrated late into passing's fall, talking about how the Augustin princepa had more grit than anyone else in the gang.

"It frustrates you knowing I won't listen, doesn't it?" I asked. "It must make you angry. Angry enough to hit me, I bet."

"Nice try. Magnate Bardera would brand me if I laid a hand on you."

I could have told Meike that Niall was a pervert, but it would have been my word against his, and Meike hadn't liked me from the get-go. It wasn't hard to guess who she would've sided with.

Bardera had attached Meike to my hip two weeks ago, following news of Augustin's coup, and Meike had done everything in her power to ruin the life I'd built in Manasus.

But she was playing a losing game. The Titanite gang needed me, and I still had plenty more creeps throughout the city to con.

"Magnate Bardera wants to speak with you," she said, leading me toward a set of metal stairs spiraling down the levels.

"Bardera has news about my family?"

Her grip on my wrist tightened. "*Magnate* Bardera. She earned that title. Best use it."

I shoved my foot through the middle of Meike's stride. Her armored shin collided with my leg, waves of agony making me gasp, but she tripped and let me go to catch herself. I took off before she had the chance to recover.

Commoners and nobility alike struggled to move out of my way as I sprinted across the city and down each level, Meike hot on my tail. Her ragged breaths faded into the chaos of foot traffic circulating the chasm, and soon it was just me and the press of bodies, the air reeking of hot stone and the grassy scent of pack animals, bear and dolomite panther bones clacking from the wind as they hung from chains along the ceiling. The Manasus capital was smaller than Augustin's, which meant more people packed in a tighter space, and I struggled to squeeze between food carts that smelled of spices for mole-rat kebobs, cave lobster tail, and meat pies. Down another metal stairwell I went—tricky to hurry down compared to the wide stone ramps in Augustin, but trickier for someone bogged down in steel. I checked my flanks, but Meike was nowhere to be seen.

A blanket of wet heat filled the bottom floor, making everyone move just a little bit slower. The soldiers guarding the palace entrance frowned at me, but didn't say a word when I ran past. I found Magnate Bardera in her atrium, sitting on a bench at one of the long wooden tables in the middle of the throne room's floor, drinking from a stone goblet and bent over her meal, broad shoulders draped in wildcat furs. The woman was built like a boulder. The kind of person who could kill someone five different ways as soon as she knocked them off their feet.

The magnate smiled when she saw me. "Ah, Efadora." The expression faded. "Where is the sergeant?"

I shrugged. "Haven't seen her for almost a passing. Why?"

"Do you mean Meike hasn't been watching you?"

"Was she supposed to?"

The echo of metal and heavy footfalls reached us, and Meike wheezed into the chamber, her auburn hair damp with sweat. For a moment I thought Magnate Bardera would yell at her, but Bardera turned to me instead. "Keep her close. Don't run off like that."

"Is there news of my family?"

She eyed me, but gestured to the opposite side of the table. "Sit, please."

I wriggled my way onto the bench facing her, and she steepled her hands, fingers studded with obsidian rings laced with ruby, made to resemble lava, hefdolla tattoos like perfectly symmetrical stains on the back of each hand. "It's about your uncle, Lucas."

"What about him?"

"We received a message from Radavich. Magnate Jancarlo declared support for Olevic Pike to rule Augustin. We have reason to believe Lucas was the one who convinced him."

Magnate Bardera watched me, as though waiting to see how I would react to this betrayal. "Why does that matter?" I asked.

"He's your uncle, Efadora. What he's done is terrible and you needed to know."

My uncle had been close to my father before moving to Radavich, but I'd never really cared for the man. "I just want to know if this affects my father's claim when he tries to retake Augustin."

Bardera's expression fell. "Let's find your family first before we worry about how he'll get his seat back." For the first several passings, she'd treated me like a kid in denial, but eventually accepted the fact I didn't believe my family was dead. All sorts of rumors were circulating, but for some reason, Bardera decided to believe the one about Olevic Pike executing them in the throne room.

She popped a radish into her mouth. "There's something else, too," she said after she swallowed. "My men believe there's a plot to... remove your claim from the Augustin throne."

"You mean assassinate me?"

Again she studied me, as though the information would physically weigh me down. "Yes. My men interrogated a group of Augustins who tried to sneak into the city without notarized travel papers. They said there was a bounty that wants you dead."

"How does it work if Olevic puts a bounty on someone under the protection of a magnate?"

"That's something I'll have to work out with him. He knows Manasus is small, that we're not in an economic position to push Augustin, let alone punish any bounties he puts on your head. But this danger is why I have no choice but to forbid you from leaving the palace until Olevic and I can reach an understanding."

My skin prickled and a nerve stirred in the pit of my stomach. "You don't want me to leave here? At all?" Augustin was two weeks' travel on the Granite Road if a normal courier rode on foxback, and I didn't want to think how long negotiations would take between the two capitals. I looked back to see the magnate's royal guard take small steps to bar the room's entrance, and even Meike loomed behind me. They knew me too well.

"I'm sorry, Effie," Magnate Bardera said. "It is the only way to keep you safe. You're in danger."

The red glow of the hallway leading to the exit called to me. What would Sara say if I let myself become some princepa locked away in a castle? Running with the Titanite gang was my life, and having a place with them would be impossible if I went missing for a month. They'd be miserable without me.

They needed me. Everything I'd built in Manasus would be ruined.

The magnate reached across the table and touched the top of my balled fist. "It's for the best. I don't know what I would do if I lost you."

I became a ward in Manasus because of the stories I'd heard about Magnate Bardera. She was headstrong and ruthless, someone who recognized the benefits of an equilibrium between the syndicates and the cities. Faults above, she'd even earned hefdolla tattoos before she inherited the throne—prestigious markings reserved for the underbosses of the criminal underworld, a symbol hearkening back to the old merchant currencies from before Mira's founding. There was no doubt she'd done enough to earn herself a prison cell ten times over if anyone found the right dirt on her.

That Bardera wasn't the one I'd come to know, though. This one was as stimulating as every other member of the nobility. I was fifteen, but she treated me like I was half that age.

"Would you like some food?" she offered.

I shook my head and climbed off the bench. My sleeping quarters were the only place that interested me right now. Meike still stood in the way, and I realized how much time I'd be spending with her if the magnate had her way. "It hurts me to say this," the magnate continued, "but if I hear that you've disobeyed my wishes to stay in the palace, you'll receive two lashings as punishment."

I'd gladly take the whip if it meant getting out of my cage, but Meike was the type to make those lashings count. Maybe doing as I was told and staying in the palace would be for the best.

No. Sara had lived a harder life, had done harder things when she was my age, and chose that path despite the option to be Daddy's Girl. She'd handled a few dances with death— was handling it now, wherever she was—and so could I. She expected better from me.

"What am I supposed to do while I'm locked up?" I asked.

"Your tutor keeps asking me why you've been skipping your lessons, so start there. We have a library, and the palace has direct access to the Foundry, which I'm permitting you to enter. The smiths would protect you just as well as any of my guards."

Magnate Bardera expected me to meet with Tutor Yalkin? I preferred Meike's company over the sound of his voice. The library and the Foundry were even worse. I would die of boredom long before any assassins found me.

Five soldiers appeared in the room, sporting crisp uniforms and freshly cut hair. Bardera had taken an intense interest in her military lately, inviting a squadron to dine and drink with her every passing. The signal our conversation was over.

"Why are you dressed as a commoner?" she asked me as she waved the men and women over. "Go clean yourself off. Your outfit is unbecoming for prinzessa."

I pulled at the iron ring to my room, the rockwood door swinging open and revealing a tall, gawky figure on the other side in a ratty light blue shirt and rough-fabric beige pants. Carmen. I started forward, almost pouncing on her to give her a hug out of relief, but stopped myself. I'd promised myself to never indulge in those kinds of gestures once I joined a gang.

"What's wrong?" I asked.

Carmen checked over my shoulder and must have noticed Meike behind me, for she kept her mouth shut. I moved to close the door, but metal smacked against wood as Meike set her gauntleted hand against it. "Behave yourself," she said to Carmen.

"You think she's going to try to cash in on my bounty here?" I asked. "You're my guard, not my nanny. Mind your business."

Meike opened her mouth to respond, but I slammed the door on her face. "C'mon," I said, and motioned to the bedroom.

Carmen sat on my bed while I threw off my shoes and padded to the copper bathtub in the corner. A hot bath sounded too good after my encounter with Niall—the man had barely touched me, but I still felt dirty. The water scalded my fingertips as soon as I turned the spigot, and I leaned against the tub's edge while I waited for it to fill. "So what's the problem?"

"You need to stay away from Titanite."

"Why?" I asked. Carmen knew better than anyone how I planned to lead Titanite before the turn of the year. Filching Niall's platinum had been just another step in that direction—it would've brought in more money than anything the gang had stolen in months.

Again I thought of Sara, of how she'd been smuggling schorl dust out of Augustin by the time she was my age. If I was going to impress her, I'd have to move beyond platinum fast. Another reason why I couldn't stay in this flame-forsaken palace.

"Söres got word from his *bredah* in the Regheta gang that there's a bounty on the prinzessa," Carmen said. "Nobody in Titanite's given you up, but I don't..." She trailed off, fishing for the right word. "*Vertrua nes*. No trust. There is an opportunity for Söres and the Regheta gang, hera. He smells blood in the water."

It took a second to pick up on what she was saying. "You think Söres might use me as an in to the Regheta gang?"

"Regheta is big time, yes."

I peeled off my tunic and trousers and slipped into the bath, groaning when the water swallowed me to the neck. The only thing more satisfying than heart-stopping cold was the scorching heat. It couldn't be lazy, lethargic heat either—it needed the intensity that sent tingles through my nerves and made my jaw muscles clench to the point of aching. The heat had an added benefit of helping me forget the slime in Niall Tulp's eyes. Black winds, I hoped I would never have to deal with his type again, but I knew that was too much to ask for.

"I can't stay away from Titanite," I said once I'd adjusted enough to breathe. "I'll just have to move up my plans to take the gang from Söres. It might be hard to convince some of the members, but if you're there to vouch for me, we've got a real shot as long as you're not afraid to break a couple of Söres's bones. If I disappear now, I might as well never come back."

"Better'n getting bagged up or a knife to the throat, hera."

"I can handle it."

Söres had made me his number two because I climbed and moved faster than anyone else in Manasus—a decision he would soon regret—and the tunnels and chutes threading the city's interior were like a second home to me. Sara always said to play to our strengths to get what we wanted. How could I use mine to get out of here?

The mattress creaked as Carmen left the bed. "You should stay here where it is safe."

The dirt from my body swirled in the sulfur-scented water. "I can convince Titanite to follow me, but I can't do that if they think I won't take risks."

"Eladora," she pleaded. "Please don't leave palace."

I finally looked at her, but she avoided my gaze. "What aren't you telling me?" I asked.

"What? No." She stared at her shoes.

"Tell me."

She shook her head.

"Tell me," I repeated in a harder voice, trying to sound like Father.

A tear ran down her cheek. And another. Soon her crying showed no signs of stopping. I slid out of the tub and grabbed the robe hanging on a nearby hook, then wrapped it around me as I sat on the bed. Carmen continued to stand there, crying. This was the first time I'd seen her shed tears since I'd met her.

"What's going on?" I asked.

She let out a shuddering breath and met my eyes. "*Mi vat.*"

"What about your father?"

"He's involved."

"Involved?"

She still seemed unwilling to talk. What would it have taken to make her open up? Emil would've known, but for the life of me I couldn't put myself in his shoes. So I waited.

She wiped at her cheek and finally relaxed. "Dad doesn't know we're friends. Even if I told, he would not believe. I heard him talk earlier to visitors at *as hus*. Outsiders. They were talking about ways to capture, to kill you."

"That's it? It's not like he's the only one. He must be desperate if he thinks Regheta won't kill him if he tries to grab me under their noses." I'd do what I had to to Carmen's father if he came for me, but she didn't need to hear that.

A new wave of tears came. "That is the thing, though. Söres heard from his *bredah* that the bounty is still a secret in Manasus. That Regheta is working with an Augustin who works undercover for new magnate. If *mi vat* knows about the secret bounty, he must be part of something bigger. You need to stay inside palace, hera."

Keeping an eye out for the Regheta gang was manageable, but whoever Carmen's father worked for could be a different story. How recognizable was I? In Manasus, hair was browner than black, the local cheekbones more pronounced and the faces angular. I was short for my age, and Augustins were already stocky as it was. My hairstyle would give me away most of all. The girls in Manasus let their hair grow past their shoulders, but I hated long hair. It only got in the way. The only long hair on my head were my bangs. Anyone with a basic description would probably recognize me.

I quickly dressed and started digging through my chest of clothes, looking for one of the floppy-brimmed hats women like to wear on the chasm floor to protect them from the mist. "I'll be extra careful once you help me out of here."

"What?"

"The magnate put me under house arrest. She'll whip me if she knows I snuck out."

Carmen took a step back. "Why do you try to leave? Nobody disobeys the magnate."

I leveled a gaze at her through the mirror on my dresser. "I'm the Augustin princepa. I'll be fine. Bardera's too protective and so are you. Just trust me."

She backpedaled toward the door. "No. I'm not helping. Listen to what everyone is saying for once. Stay."

I walked after her as she headed for the exit. She rushed into the hallway, and a gauntleted hand caught me by the scruff of my shirt when I tried to follow. I tried to rip free, but Meike yanked me until I was off-balance, and I tried to put my feet under me while my shirt half-obscured my face. My fist lashed out and caught her in the steel on her thigh, and I hissed in pain.

"Don't touch her," Carmen yelled. I regained my balance in time to watch Carmen try to shove Meike, who barely budged. She managed to hop up and punch the woman in the chin.

Meike released me to turn her fury onto Carmen, who stumbled backward. "No!" I shouted, grabbing onto Meike's arm with both hands. She pulled, lifting me off my feet as I clung to her vambrace. Fhelfire, she was strong.

"Sorry, hera," Carmen said, voice wavering. Two guards appeared at the end of the hall to see what the commotion was about, and Carmen looked at them like a caged rabbit, backing against one of the sculpted pedestals lining the marble walls.

"You made a big mistake just now," Meike said.

"I didn't see anything," I said, still holding her arm. "Say otherwise and I'll call you a liar."

The woman gave me a murderous look, then scraped me off and held me in place by the back of my neck. "What was your fight about?"

"You know, girls fight," I said, considering the ramifications of reaching up and ripping Meike's nose ring out of her face. "Can you let go?"

The guard zeroed in on Carmen. "You let the prinzessa's friends know that any of you who come to the palace again gets a prison cell. Got it, *madchya*?"

Carmen nodded. Once she disappeared, Meike let go and I walked back into my quarters. "You made a big mistake yourself," I said before shutting the door.

I returned to my room, picked the hat off my dresser, and tossed it in the chest. Carmen was just trying to look out for me, but it had meant disobeying me. She should've listened. Sara always said growing close with your subordinates was a recipe for heartbreak. Maybe she was right.

The rational part of me knew I'd made a mistake making a friend, given the ruthlessness required of me if I wanted to make anything of myself, but an emptiness gnawed at my stomach when I thought of life in Manasus without Carmen. I'd kept everyone else at arm's length, the way Sara always said, and it had helped me shoot through the ranks of Titanite like a meteor. But could I let go of Carmen too?

If I wanted to be harder than even Sara, then I supposed I had to.

AN HOUR LATER, I opened the door to find Meike standing there. The woman still stood at attention, attentive as ever, and I couldn't help but see why Magnate Bardera had stuck her on me. "I want to go to the Foundry," I said.

Her footsteps echoed an octave lower than mine as she followed me down the hall. Nobles who worked in the palace gave us wide berths, but they seemed otherwise uninterested.

Slumming it in Manasus had made me privy to all sorts of stories about the nobility I never would've heard in Augustin. A bookbinder operating out of the basement of his seventh-floor bar once told me about the secret genocides the Sovereign performed on the upper caste during Mira's founding. The Week of Stillness, it was called. According to him, thousands of nobles disappeared all at once, replaced a week later by people who didn't speak the territories' original language, Ashait, and who spurned the idea of slavery under an unregulated empire of merchants. The Sovereign built monarchies out of the ruling merchant families of old, who proceeded to teach a new language and way of life to the commoners, a life diluted of customs and tradition. Each territory clung onto some of their old ways, but most of it was lost. The old bookbinder bragged about preserving some of the lost traditions in his books.

"No one knows how the Sovereign did it—impossible, yes—but theories abound about why, hera," he said. "Wash away *divitat*—diversity, yes—and one territory won't lord themselves over another. Sanitize the differences and get everlasting peace, yes."

That was the passing I made Carmen my friend. Good to stay as far away from the nobility as possible.

A single hallway connected the palace to a private entrance into the Foundry. It was guarded by two men with sashes of Manasus green tied to their upper arms, and the glow of white, orange, and red pyremoss guided me as the walls changed from the carefully cut stone of the palace to the more natural curves of the Foundry, its walls glittering with minerals. Meike always stayed a few steps behind me.

"Why go to the Foundry?" she asked, sounding more bored than suspicious.

"The palace is too quiet. Makes it too easy to remember how miserable it is in there." The organized chaos of smiths pounding red-hot metal and pouring molten slag into weapon molds reminded me of the noise in the Pit—Manasus's trade district on the chasm floor. Carmen had laughed at me when I said I was jealous that she lived in the Pit, surrounded by bartering and mischief and revelry beneath the starry sky. Living in the palace was like choking on claustrophobia.

We entered the heat in one of the back halls of the Foundry. Back in the palace, shadows liked to linger in the corners of its halls and corridors and tried to push against the light, but a red glow seemed omnipresent here, as if the Foundry resided within the bowels of a volcano.

I led Meike to one of the cooler areas. The Foundry sported two public shrines—one for the commoners, and another, more isolated one for the royal families that could only be accessed through the palace. We arrived at the shrine, and Meike undid the strap of her sword and propped it against the hallway outside.

The walls were largely made from rippling stone, with a lava fall in the back and a statue of Fheldspra at the front of the room in lieu of a podium. A rudimentary booth of stained wood sat in one of the corners, where people would enter and sit before a mesh-screened window, opposite a smith. They would recite passages from the Sky Scrolls—the Foundry's religious text—and participate in a 'word sparring' to defend their beliefs. A smith in turn would try to twist their opponent's reasoning and poke holes in their argument. Magnate Bardera was the only noble I'd known to give the booth a regular visit.

"What're you doing?" Meike asked when I made my way to the booth.

"Guess."

"You even know anything from the Scrolls?"

"Sure I do. The way I see it, I'd rather get closer with Fheldspra now before I get a knife in the back later."

I entered the confined space and shut the door. Candles lined the walls, flickering from the disturbed air. A bell hung from a hook, which people rang to summon a smith who would sit on the other side of the semi-transparent screen. My fingers explored the edges of the screen instead.

After a few minutes of pushing and prying, the screen popped out of its frame. There was always a way out in a city full of tunnels and corridors, so said Sara. You just had to keep your eyes open.

Peering through one of the narrow holes in the box, I spotted Meike kneeling with her forehead pressed to the ground. Before her was Fheldspra—a statue of a naked, stone person about ten feet tall and made of cooled volcanic rock and glowing ruby, its face featureless. Two concentric rings circled the statue, the smaller ring made up of five stone cubes and the larger made from six. The inner circle represented the five base components that the Foundry claimed all of Ra'Thuzan was created from—fire, stone, flesh, nature, and energy—and the six smaller cubes represented the territories. Meike had removed her breastplate, her torso expanding and contracting with deep breaths.

I climbed through the window frame and poked my head through the narrow entryway leading into an adjacent hall. Old, bright pyremoss crusted the ceiling and shadows underscored imperfections on the walls, but I didn't see or hear any smiths coming or going.

After some navigating and backtracking through the maze inside the Foundry, I came to a door that opened onto the front room, where a crowd of people perused shelves and tables littered with goods, and where a line of smiths worked the forges on the side walls. I entered the crowd, thinking about Meike waiting outside the recitation booth, holding back snide remarks so as not to offend the smith she assumed accompanied me. Wondering when it would be appropriate to ask what was taking so long.

In Manasus, the entrance to the Foundry sat next to the palace, both on the first floor. I weaved through the throng of people along the ridge and stopped before the railing separating me from the Pit, which sprawled across the entirety of Manasus's chasm floor. Hundreds of campfires and bonfires of yellow, magenta, and even white-hued flames littered the trade district, providing enough light to reach the first four levels. The buildings in the Pit were made from rockwood, which was mined from rockweald— an underground root fire-resistant enough that only magma could eat through it. This place would be my future kingdom, and it would put Sara's smuggling empire to shame.

On the chasm floor, I raced through the crowds and entered the perpetual mist covering the south side of the Pit. I entered an alley glistening with condensation, behind a bacara where Titanite scavenged leavenings of bread, and stopped at a stack of barrels beside a closed hatch. It led to a basement beneath an adjacent pawn shop.

The pale glow of lightcaps lit the basement, along with a blue fire flickering from torch holders along the walls. The color was a cheap party trick, but Söres loved the faux-frigid atmosphere it created with the lightcaps. Eight teenagers lounged on pieces of furniture strewn throughout the room, lazing around instead of roaming about the capital scoring loot for Titanite. Another symptom of Söres's leadership. These kids could be better, could be pushed to do great things. I could be the one to push them.

Söres, who sat sideways on a rocking chair, moved to his feet. "*Hala,* Efadora." He looked to the others and babbled something in the old tongue. I had a passing understanding of the old tongue, but it changed from territory to territory, having branched apart from Ashait after Miran became the official language. If Titanite spoke in the old tongue I could pick up on the conversation most of the time, but not when they spoke too fast on purpose.

The others rose to their feet, some stretching their arms and others shuffling out of the way. "Gesmon?" I asked. "Diete?"

Both boys didn't answer, refusing to look me in the eye.

I felt my cheeks flush. "I know about the bounty, Söres. You're not getting the jump on me."

The Titanite leader, who was several inches taller than me, smiled. "Strange that you came back anyway." He took a step toward me.

Where was Carmen? She was supposed to be here. Asserting myself would be hard, and I needed her here to back me up. Her dagger and my bravado should have been plenty to give this group the kick in the right direction.

"Veerla," I said to the girl in the corner, the oldest and strongest member of the gang. "Remember that pigeon drop we pulled off together last month? We ate like the Sovereign for a week after that scam. We do great work together."

Veerla's eyes were hard as diamond. "*I* ate like Sovereign. You go home to your soft life every passing's fall while I sleep in trash by Hera Reslach's Cabaret. You're worth more to me in a bag."

I eyed the line of kids advancing on me, the emptiness in my chest deepening, a knot welling up in the back of my throat. It didn't make sense. I'd put more time into this gang, worked harder than anyone else to make sure our rivals knew our name, and yet over the span of a passing these kids had gone from allies to den sharks caught onto my scent. What did I do wrong?

"How's this going to work?" I asked, my voice thick. "You're going to give me to Regheta and they give you a cut or a place in their gang, just like that?"

"Not your concern." Söres took another step forward and his knuckles paled as his hands balled into fists.

"I trusted all of you with my secret," I said, my voice coming out hoarse. "Don't any of you care what happens to me?"

Söres grabbed for me. I slapped the hand away and ran for the door, but he managed to find a grip on my upper arm as I reached the stairs. My other hand gripped the wall placement holding the torch of swirling blue flame, and my foot lashed out, connecting with his groin. He gasped, and I pulled the torch out of the placement and swung my body around. The iron guard at the end of the torch connected with the side of his head.

He screamed as the powder used to turn the fire blue showered his face, and blue flames licked his ear and hair as he fell to the ground. The others in the gang rushed to kneel at Söres's side while he clutched his head with a hand.

The flames had already dissipated, but pointed edges

rimmed the iron guard, and blood leaked from several small cuts in his hair. The gang members watched me, forming a protective line.

"You really hurt him," Sujan said.

"You're kidding me, right?" I asked.

Veerla grabbed a rock off the ground, Erak a piece of scrap metal. The steps leading out of the basement waited behind me, but I didn't move. "Wait," I said. I couldn't stop my voice from cracking. "Let me take over for Söres. I can double whatever bounty's on my head, easy. You'll have a much better time in Titanite with me at the head."

"Doubt it," Veerla said. "You're easy money right now. Besides, someone boring as you telling us what to do? Would rather throw myself in the depths."

Heat flooded my cheeks. I met Söres's eyes as he sat on the ground with a hand pressed to the side of his head, his gaze full of pain and rage, and for a second I imagined drawing a line of blood across his throat with a knife and watching the life leave his eyes. No one in Titanite had taken a life before, but in that moment I knew I could do it.

The torch clattered to the floor and I ran up the stairs. My heart twisted, a raw nerve as I ran down the alleyway and entered the buzz of people in the nearest street. I'd misjudged my place in Titanite. Horribly. Why didn't they like me?

Sara always said that only those of stone could rise to greatness, and I realized now I'd made a mistake going halfway with my approach. Those who served me needed to be terrified of the consequences of going behind my back. I would make Titanite fear me.

I sniffled, wiping at my eyes as I made my way toward Carmen's father's shop. She was the only person I needed.

Nobody chased me onto the street, where the sidewalks burst with vendors for this passing's farmers' market. I passed tables laden with vegetables, where mist collected in beads of water, and butchers hung pale and bloody cuts of meat from hooks in front of their stalls. Carmen's father owned a tanner's shop on the southwest side, where the food district transitioned into trade goods.

I made a left at the street corner near the tanner's shop and stopped to hide behind the building's edge. The Manasus city watch stuck out in their bulky, dark grey steel and green bandanas tied around their foreheads. Three of them stood outside the shop.

Meike emerged, towing a kicking and thrashing Carmen. I couldn't hear what she said to Meike, but at least she knew not to scream or yell. The only reason for her arrest would have been me, and advertising the disappearance of the Augustin princepa would have earned her a beating.

Carmen's father appeared. His stance was rigid, like he wanted to kill Meike, but he kept silent.

I leaned a shoulder against the wall and rested my head against the cold rock wood as I watched Meike drag Carmen toward the nearest ramp. How ironic for them to arrest my friend but not the traitor she lived with.

Carmen was right. I should have stayed in the palace. And now my bully was dragging my only friend down the middle of the street.

"Well, if it ain't you."

A man with slicked hair, wearing a high-quality tunic and pants, stood behind me—someone who would have made a home on the third level, if I were to guess. He grabbed me before I could scramble away. "No, no. Not so fast."

"Fuck you," I said before biting his wrist.

He yelled, and I hoped it was loud enough for the guards to hear. The man grabbed a handful of my hair with his other hand and slammed my head into the wall.

Chapter 14 – Jakar

SARA PULLED US to a stop next to a crystalline spring full of mossy logs and lily pads where lantern bugs roosted and floated lazily through the air. She awkwardly slid off Cassius, took a few sluggish steps to the rocky shore, and said, "I'm not feeling too great." Then she fell on her butt.

I jumped off the fox. "What's wrong?" I asked, rushing to her side.

"My body hurts," she said, rubbing at her eyes, a glazed look to them.

I brought a hand to her mouth, but she didn't protest. I pulled her bottom lip down until I could see her gums. "You'll be all right," I said. "Promise." I hunted through the bags hanging off Cassius's flank until I found the jar of juice hiding at the bottom. I returned to Sara and offered it. "Drink."

She did as she was told, almost coughing it up as she forced it down. "It's sweet," she said, wiping her mouth.

"Plum juice."

She nodded without comment. Someone like her, a princepa who used to dine on the finest foods of the territories and been offered the ripest, handpicked fruits, brought to her on Foundry steel, likely only learned about the threat of Barlow's blight during childhood schooling and proceeded to never give it a second thought. So it went with nobility. Vitamins from fruit were easy to find to avoid the condition, but it took knowing the right fruits from the poisonous ones while in the crust. I knew as much about living off the beaten path as Sara probably did, but luckily I'd bought some plum juice from an outpost we'd stopped by a few passings back.

Sara nursed her juice while I set up camp against an archway built against the cavern wall. The archway had two statues on each side, thirty-foot tall and standing watch over the cavern, but the tunnel past the arch had collapsed, likely eons ago. The entrance to an ancient Sihraan city if I had to guess. I fed Cassius some jerky and, after gathering up some dead moss and tinder, grabbed some flint out of our supplies. "How are you feeling?" I asked Sara as she sat against the ankle of one of the statues, watching me.

"Better."

"We caught your symptoms early, so you should feel like your old self soon."

She nodded and continued to watch. Soon her gaze felt like a hot wire running directly into my back, and I tried to ignore it while I scraped a rock over the flint, sending sparks into the dead moss.

"Thanks for helping," she said. *Without a Word,* was what she didn't say.

"My pleasure," I answered. In the two weeks we'd been traveling to Radavich, she'd only taken advantage of my flesh binding that first passing at World's Grotto inn. The riding had been hard—wrong turns made down dangerous tunnels that involved a few close calls and some backtracking—but despite all that, she never uttered a Word.

"You know," I said, stirring the blackened Saffar tomatoes that sizzled on the pan. "Mira's Hand has a reputation for mercy and protecting the commoners. It's why she's famous. You could use that fame to your advantage."

"It's all an act," she said. "I'm an ethical drug smuggler *because* it makes me famous. Commoners eat it up like butter."

Sara always struck me as someone who wasn't afraid to speak the truth. For the first time, I doubted that presumption. "Why keep it a secret then?"

She drew lines in the dirt with her finger. "Father would have killed me otherwise."

"It's just my opinion, but I think you should let it be known. It could help your cause when we return to Augustin. And if you and Emil ever went in on a popularity contest? I bet you could give him a run for his money, easy."

She gave me a strange look, staring at me until I had to divert my eyes, a warm nervousness sitting in the back of my throat.

Later, as I was lying by the fire, my mind drifting in and out of sleep, I was nudged back to consciousness by Sara. She stood over me, the light casting half her face into shadow. "Move over," she whispered, even though there was no one to hear her.

She pulled my bedroll open when I didn't move, sliding inside until our bodies were pressed together. My breathing hitched. She touched her lips to the stubble on my neck, sending shivers up my spine. A heavy silence followed, one brimming with expectation.

She kissed me.

Her lips tasted warm and wet, like cured meat and smoke. I answered woodenly, my body still as stone, and she pulled away. "Do you want this?"

I nodded slowly.

She kissed me again. At first my mouth had trouble remembering how to kiss, until I fell into the rhythm of it— the ebb and flow generating heat throughout my body and sending me swaying against her. I was kissing Sara. I was kissing the princepa.

A new energy surged through me, and I wrapped my arm around the small of her back and rotated my body on top of her. She inhaled sharply and kissed me harder.

The kids I'd grown up with around the Ebonrock had experimented through the years, so as my hands explored Sara's body, it was as much an act of remembering as it was of learning. I felt her fingers touch the scars on my upper back, which branched downward from my neck like lightning. On my spine, her fingertips paused where the lightning spelled out *Ig*, surrounded by the same whorls carved into her arm. I felt the muscles rippling beneath her skin, ones that could've only been developed through a hard life, and it sent me into more of a frenzy. She pulled off my clothes, a desperation to her. I did the same.

Musky heat surrounded us as small sounds from Sara's throat echoed across the cavern. Cassius, who slept in a curled bundle nearby, was curious at first, but the stone fox laid his head back down when he seemed to realize we were only doing what came most naturally.

The moment seemed to draw into eternity. I wasn't sure how long our bodies pushed against each other, but only one thought lingered through the haze before the starburst of intensity faded and exhaustion took its place. In those moments, Sara had been vulnerable, and she had needed something from me I didn't have to give her. In those moments, we were equals.

Afterward, I sat on Sara's bedroll, fiddling with the palm-sized figurine I'd found in the dirt. It was of Fheldspra, carved from animal tusk and depicting a sexual union between Him and a god I didn't recognize. How many versions of Fheldspra were lost to history or hiding in Mira's darkest caverns?

I set the relic aside and stirred the embers of our fire, unable to resist a long look at Sara. She looked so innocent, a hint of drool shining on the corner of her mouth while she slept. These past two weeks with her had been nothing like what I'd expected. Sara had been hard on me at first, but that had faded over time until she acted more like her brother than anyone else in her family. There could even come a time when the last of her Words faded and I'd be able to slip away, even if I didn't want to. It was how I'd imagined traveling with Emil would've been like.

I eyed the curves of her body half-hidden by my bedroll. Well, maybe not quite.

Laying with Sara had been unlike those first times I'd coupled with other kids growing up. The princepa knew what she was doing, confidence powering every twist of her hip and every graze of her hand. Pretense didn't exist within her. When she wanted something, she didn't hide it.

We were close to Radavich now. The map placed us not far from the Granite Road, and once there, a few hours' ride separated us from the city. But Sara wanted to make a stop first, her sights set on a hidden place. A place unique to the cartographer's map we'd stolen from the bounty hunters.

And I would gladly help. I would continue to show her she didn't need my flesh binding to earn my loyalty. That I would follow her freely.

I SET MY palm against the wall, the surface damp with moisture. Moss covered the ground, and behind me, brightly colored mushrooms grew beside the small lake that covered half the cavern floor. Fifty feet to my left, tucked along the water's edge, a door brimming with quartz crystals hid inside an alcove—a door that Sara had talked her way into an hour earlier. The highwaymen living in the hideout thought she was a lost traveler on her way to Radavich. Once inside, Sara had found the time to set a chunk of volcanic rock on the other side of this wall, showing me the safest place to burrow through without being spotted.

With my eyes closed, I could sense the quartzite interspersed in the wall, twinkling like stars in the void. In Sulian Daw I'd read somewhere that people from Rona—a city far to the south—called the elemental sight the Eye. In this case, the Silicon Eye. A dozen feet within the barrier, on the edge of my elemental awareness, I caught sight of the volcanic rock, then set to work.

The wall compressed beneath my touch like hard putty, shooting sparks and radiating heat that sent pleasant chills up my arms. The sound of rock grinding against rock would alarm anyone standing on the other side, so I worked slowly. Sara never explained why she wanted to sneak into a cartographer's den, but I trusted her.

A cartographer had blasted this den into existence for a base of operations using pyroglycerin. Normally if they ventured far enough away from civilization without dying from the subterranean creatures infesting places like this, the cartographer would create a new fortified hideout elsewhere and move on. This old den was prime real estate for bandits and marauders since it lay within easy striking distance of the Granite Road.

I stopped to take a drink from the lake. The mist from the falls cooled my brow, and I double-checked on Cassius. The stone fox still lay in the moss behind a rock, staring intently into a cluster of bushes with milky eyes. Something moved inside, and the fox reached out with a paw to swat at the leaves. It was intriguing to see how uninhibiting blindness could be for subterranean animals.

I returned to the dig site. Once the faint glow of heat dissipated, I continued working. An opening appeared—at first only as wide as my finger, and it cracked and sparked as I stuck my hands through and pushed the rock aside. I tried to peer inside, but wooden crates labeled *Glycerol* obscured my vision.

Once I made enough room to crawl through, I pushed at the pile of crates in front of me, and they struggled to slide to the left. A similar stack of cases waited on the opposite side of the room, labeled *Fluorine*. Cartographers used fluorine for chemical mining, usually to dissolve larger chunks of rubble during the construction of a new cartographer den. Another stack of crates had *Nitric Acid* printed in black lettering.

I held my breath. Cartographers used glycerol and nitric acid to manufacture pyroglycerin. These substances should have been long gone if the cartographer had abandoned this den. And if I had worked too quickly and inadvertently vitrified the rock, it could have ignited the crates. Had bandits come across a working cartographer and killed them to take their den?

The light from pyremoss sprouting out of empty, rotted crates mixed with the amber glow of crystals growing out of the room's corners, guiding my way through the hall. Voices echoed from an adjacent room and a burst of laughter followed. Sara's laughter. I hid behind the corner of the hallway and watched for any wandering residents. Nobody living here could have expected someone infiltrating from the inside.

At the other end of the hallway, I hid behind a collection of spades leaning against a desk that concealed most of my body from the room. Sara lounged on a bench covered in furs in front of a fire pit, near a chair with a woman sitting on the lap of a man. The woman wore fur over a short-sleeved tunic, and the man wore millipede chitin. Firelight danced on a tattoo on the woman's forearm—a quill pen dipped into an ink bottle of quartz. A cartographer's tattoo. I knew that two more people lingered somewhere in this hideout, another man and woman, but I couldn't go any further without exposing myself. Sara, who was the only one facing my direction, noted my arrival with a twitch of her brow. I set my hand on the hilt of the dirk I'd stolen from a Tulchi man several passings ago, sliding it from its leather sheath.

"A city girl shacking up with a country boy. Now I've seen everything," Sara said.

The cartographer caressed her lover's neck. "When you get paid like we do, the more enterprising individuals of my organization tend to seek out alternate means of income." She picked at her teeth with a shard of bone in her other hand, a lazy smile on her face. Plates of mostly eaten food lay discarded near their feet.

"She's forgetting how I swept her off her feet," the man said. "Wasn't a business decision. Was love, pure and simple."

The cartographer poked him with the bone shard. "Shut up. You're obsessed with stealing, you know that? You'll steal credit whenever you get the chance."

"Know me well, you do."

"I'm surprised you're this comfortable operating so close to Radavich," Sara asked. "We can't be more than a passing's walk from the city."

The man shrugged. "Raiding ain't risky like it used to be. Some friends-a-friends tell me the Granite Road's been easy pickings since the coup in Augustin. Magnate Jancarlo's ordered more patrols, but business in the crust will be booming these coming months."

So much honesty to a stranger was a bad sign, but the princepa and I already knew they had no intention of letting her leave. "It's been this chaotic because of a rebellion in a different territory?" Sara asked.

The cartographer answered for him. "Augustin's coup proved the magnates' impotence and how little the Sovereign really cares for his kingdom. Magnate Jancarlo and the Manasans haven't been playing nice lately either—tensions between them's been stretched like twine since Radavich declared support for Olevic Pike. Manasus still has Sorrelo Adriann's younger daughter, so you can imagine they shat rocks when they heard the news."

"Radavich supports Olevic Pike?"

The outlaw and the cartographer ate up Sara's shock—conversation must have gotten stale when holed up with the same crowd for so long. But we certainly had been out of the loop. Having spent so much time making our way through Radavich's fringes, it had been hard to stay up-to-date. Half the towns we passed didn't even know about the turmoil in Augustin.

I tapped the flat of the dirk against my pants. My dark clothing blended in with the rock and the low light, but Miran eyesight was sharp compared to a Sulian's. Sara needed to give the signal or the guests in the other room would come striding in and spot me.

"Quit gossiping, Killian," the cartographer said, running her fingers through the man's hair and giving it a playful tug. "He's just parroting what the Archives told me. But would Lucas Adriann still be secretariat if he didn't support Magnate Jancarlo's support of the Augustin Listener? Doubt it."

Sara nodded to herself, but I could see the fury bubbling under the surface. Her uncle had betrayed their family while our entire trip to Radavich was hinged on his help. While I had no ties to the man, I felt rage for the princepa. I should have been angry at the possibility of Emil never sitting on the Augustin throne, but all I could think about was retribution for Sara. To do what I could to alleviate it.

Sara slapped her knee and rose. "Well, dear friends of mine, I believe it's time for me to head out. I'm already late enough as it is, and I need to find my family in the Radavich capital. My uncle in particular."

The cartographer slipped off Killian's lap. "Come now, Sara. You're smart enough to know your business is here with us."

"If I didn't plan to leave, I wouldn't have shared my intent to do so."

Killian laughed as he stood. "Poor little girl in denial. Or maybe you was thinking you'd show us some spine and join the crew. I'll consider it. Not a fan of that southern look, but it's not the face I'm interested in."

Sara stepped to the side, angling the two so their backs faced me. "What happened to the star-crossed lovers? The honest, hardworking cartographer and the ruffian who fell in love with her?"

"Killian supplements me with a nice flow of income from idiots off the Granite Road and he gets his mushroom tugged on by anyone stupid enough to get captured," the cartographer said. "It's a business relationship first, a story of love second."

"I can respect that. Jakar, what do you think?"

Killian didn't move fast enough to dodge my knife as it plunged into his upper back and scraped against bone. The cartographer turned in surprise, and Sara grabbed her and pulled. The woman fell onto the fire pit, screaming.

I took off into the red glow of young pyremoss growing in the adjacent hallway. The closest room was a bedroom, where a man stumbled beside a bed as he tried to slip his trousers on. He brought his hands up in a vain attempt to block my slash, but could do nothing to stop my blade from slicing his throat. The other room's occupant, a woman as bare as her partner, screamed and grabbed a sword leaning against the wall. She managed to block two of my blows before I cut her down.

Sara entered the room a heartbeat later. "Caught him with his trousers down. Literally."

In the lounge room, the cartographer sat with her back against the wall, her leg badly burned. She stared at her lover, who watched the crackling flames in a pool of blood. His eyes didn't move.

"What do we do with her?" I asked Sara.

"Help," the woman said with a trembling voice.

Sara took the dirk from my hand and knelt before the woman. "I thought the cartographers were as principled as the smiths. Craft first, everything else second."

The cartographer's eyes squeezed shut. "The... The crust is a dangerous place. Brutality is how you survive. But... you're right. I lost my way." When her eyes opened, they pled.

"It's human nature," Sara said, patting her on the knee, sounding a little sad. "Everyone loses their way eventually. It's just that sometimes they don't realize until it's too late." She reached up and slit the woman's throat.

As the princepa rifled through the stack of maps on the desk, I took in the scene around us. So much death. The air turned musty with the scent of blood. "Do you think what they said about Lucas is true?"

Sara wiped the sweat from her brow and sniffled as she threw map after map onto the ground. Killian's blood bled onto the pages. "I don't know. Maybe. If it is, that means I'll have to kill him."

Two weeks of traveling for nothing. Emil and Mateo were to wait in Manasus for word of our success, but now I pictured telling Emil to his face how I'd failed. Magnate Bardera of Manasus didn't stock a force capable of retaking Augustin.

"We need to sneak into Radavich and figure out what's going on," Sara said. "We've traveled too far to let a rumor stop us."

"And if it's not just a rumor?"

"Then we go to Tulchi. They dislike Radavich strongly enough that they may help simply because Radavich won't. With Tulchi and Manasus combined, it could be enough to retake Augustin."

I tried to keep the worry off my face. She needed support, not a cynic.

"Augustin won't forget the Adrianns," she said. "I'll die before I let that happen." She left the room.

The last unexplored area, and the only one not afflicted by the seeping aroma of death, contained a table made from a mosaic of stones like an exotic puzzle, held together by epoxy resin. The surface was rough, made for gripping, with two rows of vial racks. A ventilation hood hung from the ceiling, though I couldn't see where it funneled the vapors. A setup tailored to the alchemical needs of the cartographer. Every active cartographer owned some version of a table like this so they could manufacture explosives.

"So you broke in here for the pyroglycerin?" I asked.

"No." She turned and leaned her butt against the table, crossing her arms. "What are the most common rocks found in cities like Augustin and Radavich?"

I hesitated, trying to understand the point to the question, and answered when I couldn't puzzle it out. "Capitals are built inside sinkholes, so limestone."

"And what is limestone made out of?"

"Sedimentary rock. Calcium carbonate."

"Exactly." She slipped her hand into the inside of her coat and pulled out a small vial. My stomach dropped.

She set the rhidium onto the table. "Where'd you get that?" I asked.

"In Augustin, while we were fleeing from those rebels in the Foundry."

"What are you going to do with it?" The question was pointless, but sometimes people asked stupid questions out of a desperate hope of being wrong.

She pulled out something else—a chunk of limestone. "You're going to distill the calcium out of that."

"You want to bind with calcium?"

She nodded.

I stepped back. "No, I can't. It'll kill you."

"Then why are you complaining? You'll be free."

When I offered a flat look in response, she said more seriously, "If you survived the trial, so can I."

"I only survived because I had the Ebonrock fellowship at my disposal. They kept me alive. Somehow. You can't do this without them."

"I'll have you."

Old, visceral memories of cold stone on my naked back as I writhed in agony flashed before my eyes. "If you're going to bind with something, bind with anything else. Bind with iron. You've seen what your brother can do with that element."

She shook her head. "I'm not interested in waving my weapon around like I've suddenly grown a penis. Winning a sword fight can only get you so far in the world."

"But your brother's the Rock Snake. Being a metal worker made him famous." I don't know why I continued to argue. Sara didn't know how to second-guess herself.

She pushed away from the table and the vials rattled. "I'm not looking for some new method to gain equal footing with men who think they're better just by default. I plan to be something else. Now start distilling."

Chapter 15 – Jakar

Fourteen years ago

MASTER-ON-BOULDER STOOD ON his favorite rock, hands clasped behind his back, his body backlit by the ruby glow of the horizon beyond the cavern's mouth. "While suicide is understandable, it is *not* encouraged," he emphasized.

The field we stood on sat on the shore of Obsidian Lake, near the back wall of Bloodreach's cavern, where winds funneling from Outside crashed together and covered the black water with foam. Master-On-Boulder paced on his little rock, garbed in brown robes and hair slicked back in an oily sheen. "Is suicide really such an attractive alternative? It's a death numbed of pain, but you saw for yourself yesterday. There is no changing your mind once you jump in."

He sounded frustrated, but of course the fellowship of masters didn't enjoy wasting time on those who ended up throwing themselves in the lake. Normally stories of the Beast—a tentacled monster rumored to live on the lake's bottom—did enough to discourage kids away, but the boy from last week had been too desperate to care about tall tales. Memories of him still haunted me—during one of our walks, he fled from the group and tried to swim away from the masters. He realized his mistake within moments and tried to swim back, the waves eating up the sounds of his crying. He'd been a year younger than me, maybe less, and the masters didn't think twice about leaving him on the shore. The boy's hands had been covered in blood from climbing over the rocks, his blue body curled in on itself.

It was either swim or climb the compound's walls and receive the beating of a lifetime. One kid at the back of the group still couldn't stand straight after trying to climb to freedom three weeks ago. But I couldn't blame him. I spotted Saristra's Tear—the massive stalactite overhanging Tradevein Plaza, where my kidnappers had grabbed me. An hour's walk would bring me under it. Our homes taunted us from the other side of the walls, calling to us.

Father had promised safety for anyone begging in Tradevein Plaza. The city protected its own, he said. But the Ebonrock and its fellowship of masters weren't from Bloodreach. Where they came from, I had no idea. This compound sat at the city's edge, farthest from Bloodreach's mouth, and had been abandoned for as long as I remembered.

Lightning bugs swarmed above our heads, attracted to the nectar inside the glowing leaves of the emberbrushes littering the field, and Akhilian stood at attention ten feet to my left. He was the only one I recognized from before they took us. He lived in the Nochi slum, on my side of Bloodreach. He had recognized me too, and even though we hadn't talked much, I found comfort in his presence. He seemed to take comfort in mine as well, always glancing at me for reassurance. It made this place a little less alien.

"My children," Master-On-Boulder continued. "The Imbibing is nigh. Be proud of yourselves for staying so strong for so long." Wind whipped at his robes, and the gust swept away a swarm of lightning bugs. "Your time these past few weeks has served to cull those rife with the disease that is so common among those of your social standing."

Did that explain the beatings? Bruises riddled my body, but standing in the cold air, knowing the next beating wouldn't come for hours, made the pain more bearable.

But the respite came at a cost. The Imbibing was coming, whatever that meant.

"It also taught you to live comfortably in an uncomfortable life," he said. "Those unfamiliar with pain have a difficult time adjusting when that pain can spike, and forcing you to endure the ever-constant sweetness of it has made you strong. You have slept little, trained long beneath the fists of the masters, and have endured much. But now you must prove yourselves. Refusal will mean execution. Fortunately, the Imbibing is the easiest part of your stay here. Once you reach the other side, your new life begins."

A dozen masters passed through the pillars of a nearby cluster of buildings to stand before us. "Please follow the closest master," Master-On-Boulder said. He descended his rock and disappeared through the dark entrance of the nearest doorway.

The master standing in front of me—a muscular man with the slate-gray skin of a Sulian—guided a cluster of us toward a nearby door. His complexion stood out, as almost every other master had skin with tinges of different color to them. The master adjacent to him forced Akhilian into a different group, and we looked at each other as our groups slowly diverged on our way toward the buildings.

We left the red light of the barren field and entered the pale glow of lightcaps within. The master led us through a snarl of featureless hallways, which hopelessly disorientated me, until we reached a dead end. Entryways leading into a dozen curtained rooms lined each side. "One student per room," he said in a deep voice.

I chose the doorway at the end, on the left side. Inside was an empty room with a slab of stone in the center. I looked back, uncertain, but the other students had already disappeared into their chambers.

Ten minutes later, the master parted the curtain and entered while I sat on the slab. A whip hung from his side, and it swung gently with his movements. "What is your name?" he asked.

"Jakar."

"You lived in Nochi, yes?"

I nodded. The city had built holes into a hill of rock near Bloodreach's west wall and tacked on the name Nochi—I'd lived there with my parents my whole life, in a home no larger than this room. It was a small community, but the people of Nochi protected one another. It was why Akhilian and I had stuck near to each other, even though we never spoke. We were brothers of Nochi.

Thinking of home made me think of my parents. For the first several passings, I'd cried every time I thought of them. But my body had wrung itself of tears once I remembered father's insistence I beg in Tradevein Plaza. His request had seemed so strange at the time—nobody begged at that plaza, for it was a plaza of the poor, with people no richer than us. And the crime rate was high. He had insisted I'd be safe anyway. He'd sworn the payout would be huge.

And he'd been right. Despair and confusion warred within me when I dwelled on the possibility he had sold me. He and mother hadn't been perfect, what with their addiction to mist lily, but they always gave me a bed if I came home each passing with enough money. They never would have betrayed me.

"There's no reason for me to have known you're from Nochi," the master said. "I saw you leaving there a few days before you were taken."

The man sounded embarrassed, and I answered with a blank stare, unsure of what to say.

"I grew up there as well," he said.

"So you're Sulian."

"The last time the Ebonrock came here, you hadn't been born yet."

"What's all this for? Who are you people? What do you want from us?"

Instead of answering, he moved farther into the room and knelt before me. "You'll get your answers after." He took one of my hands into his and turned my forearm to expose the tender bruises. "One question before we begin. Where does pain reside?"

My mouth quivered as I tried to think of the answer he wanted. "I don't understand."

He pressed a finger into one of my bruises, and I flinched. But he wasn't rough. "Where does pain reside?" he repeated.

"I-In my arm."

He released me and stuck his hand into one of the pouches dangling from his belt. Out came a leaf stuck between two of his fingers. "Chew on this."

I hesitated but stuck it in my mouth. It tasted bitter and the pulp was chewy. Immediately, relief flooded into the bruises on my body. A pleasant warmth appeared on the edges of my thoughts, relieving a tension in my head I hadn't noticed before. I shuddered.

"Where does pain reside?" he asked again.

I shook my head. What was I supposed to tell him?

"That warmth you feel right now. The one that smothered the pain. Do you feel it in your arm?"

"No," I said, cheek still stuffed with the leaf's pulp. "It's in my head."

He smiled. "There you go. That's where the pain resides. It's where all pain resides." He poked my bruise again, but this time the pain was dulled. "Your arm tells your head it wants to hurt, but your head tells it no. Remember this. If you want to learn anything in this place, that is the one thing you must remember. Now spit out the leaf and lie down."

I did as he commanded and pressed my back against the hard stone. He stood over me. "Close your eyes," he said.

I hesitated, but didn't argue.

"Open your mouth."

I obeyed. The sound of him pulling something out of his pouch followed. Then the unstoppering of a vial. Cold glass touched my lips and a cold fire coursed down my throat. I swallowed. The icy fire cut through the warm haze in my head, and the pain throughout my body returned in full force. I groaned but didn't move.

Someone started screaming. It sounded more animal than human. Another joined in, their agony terrible. Then a third. Soon, a chorus of pain rang through the hallways. I tried to sit up, but Master pushed me back down. "Where does pain reside?" he asked, voice barely above a whisper.

"In my head," I said. Why were those kids screaming?

"Hold that knowledge close in the coming hours. Embrace it. Do not forget it."

A static discharge appeared in the pit of my stomach, like little sparks crawling along my insides, radiating outward from where that liquid of ice and fire mixed with my stomach acids.

The lightning began.

My body convulsed as branches of pain hit the sides of my body like a striking thundercloud. The pain faded, and I breathed heavily, desperate for an explanation. But the master had disappeared. Hadn't the pain lasted just a moment?

The lightning struck again, and my entire body clenched. It branched into my chest, and I didn't realize I'd been screaming until I ran out of breath.

I was alone in this chamber with only the songs of the other children to listen to. The pain lashed out again, and my mind went blank. *The pain is only in my head,* I tried to tell myself, but another wave of horror shocked the thought out of my system. No person could have tricked themselves into escaping this.

The Imbibing was supposed to be the easiest part. The fellowship had lied.

* * *

I CAME TO in a darkly lit room, covered in aching muscles and a heart beating so fast, it felt like it would burst out of my chest.

Moving made me aware of a vast new collection of bruises. Even on the undamaged areas of my body, the skin felt tender and uncomfortable against the blanket. I tried to sit up, but rasped and collapsed onto my back. Instead, I turned my head and found other students lying on nearby slabs of stone. They all slept.

"The first ones to wake are always the most promising," a low voice said.

The few lightcaps growing on the ceiling illuminated Master-On-Boulder—the man in charge of all the others. He walked down the nearby row and knelt to rest his elbows on the slab I lay on. "How do you feel?"

"I... hurt. Everywhere," I croaked.

"Good. What's your name?"

"Jakar."

"You're from that slum, yes? Nochi?"

Had the other master told him? I was too exhausted to ask. "Yes."

"Take that as a lesson then, Jakar."

I only stared in response, too tired to understand.

The lightcaps lit the left side of his face. "You will always be meant to serve, but weakness? That's another story. Strength is not passed down from your ancestors. You, and you alone, decide how strong you'll become."

Many other children slept undisturbed around me, but even from this position, I could see how small the group was. "Where are the others?" I asked.

He rose. "Any student who is not in this room is dead."

"You... You said this was the easiest part," I said after him.

He turned. "Far from it, child. In the months between Imbibings, when we work you to the bone and hone your abilities as a laborer, it will be a battle of fortitude. Do not let the despair win out. The Imbibings are different. You either survive the trauma or you don't. Strength alone is what wins. Few find themselves in possession of such a strength."

Memories of the pain haunted me. Half-remembered tidbits of endless hours writhing on that slab while my mind faded in and out. The mixture had kept me in some sort of trance, unable to think clearly, but still fully aware of the horror subjected to my body. "Maybe suicide is better," I said.

"Perhaps."

"You said 'Imbibings.' There's going to be others?"

He nodded and continued onward.

As soon as I had the strength to walk, a master helped me off the bed and brought me to an antechamber where wash buckets waited. That was when I realized how badly I smelled. Stale sweat coated my body, and I had pissed myself more than once. He left me alone with my washcloth.

A little while later, someone new entered the room. She looked like death under those pale, sweat-slicked curls stuck to her skull, and she aimed a tired glance at me as I gingerly rubbed the washcloth along my torso.

She set to washing herself, and I worked up the courage to speak. "Do you know Akhilian?"

She shook her head.

"What's your name?" I asked.

"Quin." She touched her washcloth to a shoulder and winced. "What's yours?"

"Jakar."

The brief exchange seemed enough to sate the two of us, and we continued to clean ourselves in silence. Other kids trickled in, but despite the growing number, few tried to make conversation.

Someone limped to my bucket and pulled a bundled washcloth out. It was Akhilian. I smiled and he smiled back. For the first time, I felt hopeful. Hopeful for what, I wasn't sure.

Later that day, I learned that the trial had lasted several hours, and all of us had slept in that room for three passings.

Almost half of the hundred children who had been shivering on that field beside Obsidian Lake had died.

The Sulian master led us outside and across the field, toward another building. Every structure was identical to the one beside it. Stories had swirled about this compound for as long as I could remember—ones of hauntings, curses, and death. Funny how if a place stayed empty long enough, it developed a personality, and never a good one. This place felt smaller than the reputation preceding it.

I fell in stride with the Sulian master. He didn't shoo me away. "Thank you," I said.

"I'm sorry?"

"Thank you for trying to help."

"That's the first time I've heard a student thank a master."

The man had a reservation about him. He didn't have the same kind of detachment as his cohorts. "Did you have a choice to put us through the Imbibing, or did Master-On-Boulder make you?" I asked.

He cocked an eyebrow at me—he no doubt called the man something else—but eventually shook his head. "Neither of us had a choice. We all have masters."

Memories of screams from the other kids chased me. "I know a lot of the others died, but your advice helped me at least. A little... I think."

"I didn't do it for the others. Just you. There was no time for anyone else."

"Why me?"

"You know the answer. The people of Nochi look out for each other."

Again, I thought of my dad, and for once, the idea of his betrayal didn't shock me. It made me angry. Feeling anger toward him felt wrong, but it didn't fade. I pointed at Akhilian in the middle of the line behind us. "He's from Nochi too."

"Ah," the master said.

The man took the lead once more, and I melded back into the line of students. Why did I want to speak to him? His job was to hurt us. Rage and fear had been close companions my first several passings here, when I could only think of killing the men who had taken me, but it had faded with knowing I had no family to return to.

My parents had sold me.

"That's the longest I've seen a master speak," a voice said behind me. It was Quin. "What did he say?"

"Not much. But he's different from the others, I think. Nicer."

"Do you trust him?"

The expression on her face wasn't judgmental. "No," I said. "He says he has masters too. What he wants doesn't matter."

We reached a room with several rows of benches and an elevated platform with a pulpit at the front. The master instructed us to take our seats, and Quin and Akhilian sat on either side of me. White rocks lay on the ground between our feet—one rock for each student. The Sulian master disappeared through the doorway.

A woman sat in the back corner of the room. She met my gaze, her expression patient, as though waiting for the inevitability of me turning away. Someone like her didn't belong in this place full of masters in simple robes. She wore combat leathers like some of the city's soldiers I'd seen, except it lacked studs and metal linings. It seemed like a good outfit for rock climbing. Her hair was long, too, like typical Sulian male fashion, ending just past her shoulders.

However, it wasn't her demeanor or her clothes that made her stand out. Her hands glowed faintly like semi-cooled molten rock, wrists shackled with metal bracelets where normal skin began. She seemed to be going through the trouble of keeping her hands from touching the rest of her body.

Quinn noticed my fixation and mirrored me. She turned back quickly. "I heard some of the masters talking the other night about getting a visit from 'the kadiph.'"

"What are those?"

"I don't know."

"The fellowship's masters," Akhilian said. It was the first time I'd ever heard him speak. He was soft-spoken, but so was every student here.

Master-On-Boulder walked into the room and took his place behind the pulpit. He looked at the kadiph, and I noticed the smallest crack in his composure. The woman made him nervous. "Pick up the rocks at your feet," he said.

My rock felt brittle in my hands, and I touched one of my fingers to my tongue. It tasted like salt. The master continued, "What would happen if you broke those rocks into smaller pieces?"

His pause implied he was waiting for someone to answer. "You'd... have smaller pieces?" Quin said uncertainly.

"Yes. It is not a trick question, children. And what would happen if you broke those pieces into even smaller pieces?"

Quin was the only one in the room willing to address him. She sounded more confident when she answered a second time. "You'd have even smaller pieces."

"Yes. Good. Did you know that if you continued to break those pieces down over and over again, it would eventually become something else? It would no longer be salt." He watched Quin as he said this, but spoke loudly enough for everyone to hear. "Like a stew you would make at home, rocks are made of ingredients. The salt in your hands are made of two such ones, infinitesimally small, bound together by very, very strong glue. The Imbibing has bound your body to one of those ingredients. You are now able to manipulate this element through something called electromagnetic force."

A student raised her hand. "Elements... like fire, air, and water?"

The Master pinched the bridge of his nose. "No, child. Those are not elements."

Another student raised his hand. "What does 'infinitesimally' mean?" He struggled with the word.

Master-On-Boulder set his hands on his hips and reassessed our group. "Well, I suppose I wouldn't be much of a teacher if I didn't provide at least a basic education."

"Is it necessary though?"

The woman at the back had asked the question. She rose to her feet and circled the room. When she stepped onto the dais, the wooden floorboards groaned from an unnatural weight.

"They need to know these things," Master-On-Boulder said. "This has always been part of the process. You know this firsthand."

"But it shouldn't take years, Master Galleir. They don't need to know much of anything when they're down in the mantel."

"You know how flesh bindings work. A healthy mind is needed to survive both it and the Imbibings, and their stay here is meant to strengthen them physically and mentally. If we allow their brains to atrophy, the whole batch will be lost."

The woman took a step closer. "And I was sent here for a reason. Are you sure you'd like me to report to Father that the process can't be improved upon? Streamlined?"

Master Galleir stood his ground, but was clearly shaken. It was the first time I'd seen any of the fellowship lose control over their emotions. Even when they beat us, they remained calm and serene. "Yes," he said.

She struck him in the cheek with an open palm. His head snapped to the side, and when he recovered, a layer of soot covered half his face, the flesh beneath it angry and burned. But he didn't cry out.

"Are you absolutely sure?" the kadiph asked. Rock ground against rock as she clenched her hand into a fist.

He glared. Her strike had provoked the opposite effect to that which she'd intended. "Yes."

She turned on her heel and headed for the door. Master Galleir watched the entrance for several seconds after she disappeared, wiping at his cheek. "We all have masters," he said to us. "Even her. Never forget that."

He proceeded to forego any vocabulary lessons, instead teaching us about something called electromagnetism, and how lightning in the storms outside the city intertwined with the attraction of metals like nickel or cobalt. He didn't go into detail about how it related to the salt rocks though. He claimed we could manipulate the ingredients inside the salt somehow, but when I concentrated on the rock, nothing happened.

"Did you hear what the kadiph said?" Quin whispered as Master Galleir—the man's apparent real name—talked. "She said we'd be stuck here for years."

"Why would we need to be trained for so long?" Akhilian asked.

"I don't know," I said, but motioned toward Master Galleir. The man had rubbed most of the soot off, but his cheek twitched from his burn. "They can be hurt though."

The realization changed something. These past few weeks, it hadn't felt like slave masters had kidnapped us. It was like we'd been swept away by a force. But with the Sulian Master's kindness and Master Galleir's fear and pain, one thing became clear. These masters were just people, and people could be killed.

Chapter 16 – Jakar

SWEAT BEADED ON Sara's brow, her cheeks gaunt. A glossy sheen covered the rest of her bruised and sickly-looking body—several hours ago I'd had to resuscitate her with chest compressions, managing to revive her after I'd been convinced she wouldn't come back. I'd seen enough of these trials to know she wouldn't survive if her heart gave out a second time.

She lay on the cheap mattress in the cartographer den's bedroom, the place still musty with old death. Before starting the trial, the two of us had cleared out the bodies and thrown them into the pool beside the den's entrance, but only so much could be done about the stains and smells they'd left behind. Sara was still now, and hadn't moved for a long time, her body probably spent from the writhing and thrashing it had done the previous two passings.

I sat on the bed beside her, and the cold rag in my hand moved along her hairline. She let out a faint moan. I set the rag down and cupped my hand against her jaw. She pushed her cheek against it.

People undergoing the binding trial could experience physical stimuli, but how it was processed was unique—every touch, smell, and sound evolved into its own episode, its own vision. Sara could feel my hand against her face, but how her mind pictured that sensation was vastly different from reality.

No matter what you saw though, the pain never changed.

"Sara," I said. Her forehead wrinkled in response.

I picked the rag back up and ran it along her collarbone. She'd been contradicting herself for the past several hours now. Quiet and almost peaceful. Soft and vulnerable. A version of herself from our time beside the campfire.

"Could you ever trust me?" I whispered. The fingers of my free hand interlaced with hers and my grip tightened, but I pulled away. The gesture felt more wrong than the others. It was not something Sara would have appreciated.

I set the rag on the mattress and left the room. Cassius waited in the sitting room, lying beside the fire and gnawing on the femur bone from a grotto tapir I'd hunted half a mile from the den. He'd been sleeping here since Sara started the binding ritual, but he was restless. I sat on the chair beside him and scratched the scruff of his neck. "It won't be much longer. I promise."

I'd heard stories in Som Abast of slaves among the city's aristocracy becoming infatuated with their cruel masters. It was a disease I'd never expected to succumb to, yet here I was, thinking of Sara's smooth skin beneath my fingertips. Was my brain tricking myself into wanting Sara to save itself from future pain?

The heat from the fire warmed the backs of my hands while I hid my face in my palms. Desire was a dead end to the slaves of the Ebonrock. The same with leading, it contradicted a life meant to serve another's purpose. People like the Adrianns and the nobility, and even the commoners, were meant to cultivate family trees, while I remained forever in the background, without friends, without... whatever this thing between Sara and I was. Romance for me was terminal.

A cry sounded from the other room. I jumped to my feet and ran down the hall. Sara lay in a fetal position on the bed. "Jakar—" she began, but broke into a fit of coughing.

I sat beside her. "You're awake."

"Water," she croaked.

I gave her water and food for the next half hour, spoon-feeding her a stew I'd been cooking. She vomited up the first three attempts, but finally managed to hold something down. She didn't speak, content with studying me while I did what I could to keep her comfortable.

Once she found her strength, she limped to the back room where a hole in the ground waited for sanitary needs, and I waited with Cassius for her to emerge. Finally, she appeared at the doorway, the fire dancing shadows on the gauntness of her cheeks, and she shuffled over to the nearby chair and slumped into it.

"How are you feeling?" I asked.

"Like I—" Her chest seized and she coughed some more, and when she relaxed, continued. "Like I met and embraced Fheldspra." Her voice was barely above a whisper. "Fucker's made of fire, in case you didn't know. Wasn't pleasant. I feel like my whole body was tossed down a ravine."

"You had a lot of seizures in the beginning. You hurt yourself."

She nodded. "I heard your voice while it was happening. It... helped."

We sat in silence for a long time. I remembered how my head had floated in a haze during the hours following the trial, as if still trying to adjust to the idea of surviving. She would feel better in several hours' time.

"Where is the nearest limestone deposit?" she asked.

"Not until the city, most likely."

She focused on the far wall. "Which we'll need to sneak into." Her hand fell tiredly off the armrest and Cassius started licking it. She didn't pull away, face still sickly but concentrated. "Territory capitals require travel papers to get through their main gates. Where is the nearest town?"

The map we'd taken from the bounty hunters on Dagir's Pass didn't possess a complete list of the towns surrounding

Radavich's capital, so I grabbed a map from the nearby desk, the parchment spotted with Killian's blood. "Once we get back to the Granite Road, Coracas is half a passing's ride going the opposite direction of Radavich. Beyond that, Hamagard."

"Coracas is too far."

"We could steal someone's papers."

She rubbed her scalp. "Would that work? I've always had an attendant deal with the paperwork when entering a city."

"The problem will be finding people to steal from who won't become a problem later on."

"Knock them out and tie them up," she said.

Her suggestion was a significant step up from the one I'd been expecting to hear. "This is the Granite Road, so we have to make sure they won't be found quickly. We can stash them in this den."

She nodded.

"Immigration officials at the gates put most of their attention on merchants and caravans to make sure goods are taxed properly," I said, "so the guards won't pay much attention to a couple like us. Hopefully."

"Good." She pulled herself up with a groan and knelt over the pack waiting in the corner.

"What are you doing?" I asked.

"Changing. We're leaving soon."

"Let me take care of you for a little longer. You need to rest."

She paused, spending several moments gazing into my eyes, deliberating. My heart started to thump. I pictured us living here passing after passing, happy as the cartographer was with her lover, and a lump formed at the bottom of my throat.

"No," she finally said, sounding stronger. "My uncle is going to regret ever climbing out of an Adriann womb."

* * *

CASSIUS WEAVED THROUGH the field of stalagmites as we followed a downward-sloping path illuminated by the firefly torch I held. My hand gripped firmly onto Sara's stomach, the back of her shoulders rubbing against my chest and her hair brushing against my cheek with each step Cassius took—something I'd actively avoided thinking about these past couple of weeks, but something that sat heavier in my mind the closer I pressed myself against her.

"You're sure you won't kill our marks?" I asked.

"I'd prefer not to."

"But you will if you have to."

She didn't answer, and the sound of the fox's paws treading through the dirt filled the void.

"When does revenge stop being worth it?" I asked.

"This isn't about revenge. And for the record, it's not like I'll make anyone suffer. Except my uncle, maybe. But even when it comes to him, we're doing it because we need Jancarlo's military. Removing the opposition is a necessary part of that equation."

"It's a plan with a lot of risks. Risks that didn't exist when we made our plan on Dagir's Pass."

"What are you trying to say?"

"I'm saying that you're risking your life to take back Augustin. All so that your brother can rule."

She laughed. "This isn't some double-cross to take Emil's place. Seeing how the bottom rungs of the city view the palace makes me glad I'm a smuggler."

"I'm not sure what you mean."

"Did you know that almost no one in the circles I run with remembers the name of my great-grandmother, Magnate Aurora? She ruled Augustin for over thirty years. The city cares about who rules, sure, but people have short memories. I came into this life ready to make a name for myself, so I won't get in Emil's way while he chooses his path to obscurity."

This Sara acted so differently from the one back in Augustin. Old Sara always cast the same shadow as her father, but the Sara I now knew was nothing like him. Sorrelo was stubborn, vindictive, and guarded. Sara too, but she had dropped those behaviors over the course of our trip. The ugliness she'd inherited from him was a tool to her instead of a disease.

"All right," I said. "I want to help however I can."

"You already are, and I don't think you'd have a choice anyway," she said jokingly.

"I know the choice I'd make if I did."

"Say that again in a week."

The ceiling to the tunnel angled downward until it hung only a few feet above our heads, riddled with tiny stalactites like droplets of condensation, and the path hugged us closer until we sat in an orb of firelight surrounded by impenetrable darkness. A half mile later, the tunnel opened up into a massive cavern. The largest lava fall I'd ever seen rumbled on the opposite side, bathing the cavern with an orange glow. Millions of firebugs roosted on the ceiling, and a patch of undergrowth separated us from a smooth road wider than any path we'd traveled in the past month. The Granite Road.

There was never a point along the hundreds of miles of the Granite Road that couldn't support at least five caravans moving side-by-side. Legend had it an ancient river had cut these colossal passages, which the Sovereign and his primordia refined into a trade route at the start of his reign two-hundred years ago. The gesture had been one of the first steps toward ending the Merchant Wars.

Two stalagmites as wide as the ice sheaths in Augustin stood guard beside the tunnel we'd emerged from. No one traveling the road could have noticed us until they moved directly past it. "This is as good a spot as any," Sara said as she slipped off the fox. She tightened the straps holding the sheaths to her stiletto knives in place, stepping through the mossy undergrowth to peek past the right stalagmite. "No one's coming yet—" Another bout of coughing cut her off, and she clutched at her chest as she doubled over. A mist of sweat covered her brow when she recovered several seconds later. She offered a look that dared me to complain.

"Maybe we should do some scouting," I said. "See if we can spot potential targets and wait for them."

She nodded. "As good an idea as any."

She jumped on the fox and guided us onto the road. It didn't take long to find travelers. Two short-faced salamanders pulled a cart fifteen feet tall and covered in sacks of grains and spices, with two traders sitting at the reins. Four guards sat on the back of the cart, watching us, bored. Fifty feet past them, a group of a dozen people traveled on foot, with packs strapped to their backs, and they watched us more warily than the cart owners.

"This might be harder than we thought," I said.

"Maybe. I have an idea."

"What?"

She waited until we were out of earshot of the nearest passerby. "You can break up the rock on this road. All you'd need to do is damage the road until a cart's forced to stop, and then we could jump them while they're dead in the water. We just need to find an unprotected cart."

While granite didn't comprise all of the Granite Road, it did for this stretch. Granite was igneous rock, comprised of primarily silicon. "It might take some time," I said.

"How long?"

"A half hour. Maybe less."

"Let's find marks far enough away to give you time to work, and we'll take it from there." She shook the reins. "*Shé*," she commanded, and Cassius broke out into a lope.

After five minutes of passing caravan after caravan, and even being overtaken by a courier on a fox traveling at full speed, she slowed. "Look," she said.

A salamander pulled a lone cart, accompanied by a single trader and two guards. The cart couldn't support the guards, so they walked on either side of the salamander's head, moving at a leisurely pace.

"One of the guards is a woman," Sara said. "We'll steal their papers."

She waited several more seconds as she studied the caravan before turning Cassius around and sending him into a run. Our hiding spot wasn't far by foxback, but the carts on this road moved at a snail's pace compared to us.

At the tunnel entrance, we waited for the next caravan to pass before I went to work. I knelt in the middle of the road and pressed my hands against the dusting of dirt covering the rock beneath. Sparks flew as the fragile granite compressed, and stress fractures appeared on the ground surrounding me. Sara stood over me while I worked.

"I'll be able to do this with limestone when we reach the city?" she asked.

"More or less," I said between grunts as my arms sunk to their elbows into the rock. Beads of sweat dripped into the hole. "It'll depend on how much calcium is in the composite. It's easier the more elements you're bound to."

She continued to watch as I disturbed the surface of the road with holes and newly created rubble. I received plenty of warning to stop whenever a group rounded the bend, and they eyed us as they passed, but didn't comment. A few carts even had to stop and move around the damage.

"Jakar, stop," she said quickly. A group of men on foxback rode toward us, spears pointed in the air like a retinue of banners, and I jumped to my feet and brushed off my pants. We moved to the side of the road to let them pass, but they stopped before us. They were patrolmen from Radavich.

"Papers," the man wearing the stripes of a third sergeant said.

"Sorry?" Sara asked.

"Papers. *Please*."

"Why? We haven't tried to enter the city."

"You're on the Granite Road, and there's no reason for someone to be on the Granite Road without papers."

Killian had mentioned an increased military presence on the

trade routes. However, the men accompanying the sergeant didn't wear the glazed look of those slogging through their duties—they watched us attentively, as if waiting for a fight.

"All right, let me get them," I said, walking toward the opposite side of the road, where Cassius lay in the vegetation beside the stalagmite. "Do we really need to do this?"

"Yes," the sergeant said. "Traders were reporting two people on foxback moving back and forth on the road. Almost everyone on the Granite Road moves in one direction. Either toward the city or away."

I stopped to face them. "The mayordomo in Coracas hired us to repair this part of the road. That's why we were riding back and forth. We're surveying the area to see what needs to be fixed."

The sergeant eyed the half-dozen craters and the rubble I'd created. "That's fantastic. Now go get your papers."

I walked to Cassius and rifled through the pack, thinking of what to say. Finally, I straightened. "We left them in Coracas."

"That's convenient."

"I would say it's turning out to be very *inconvenient*," Sara said. "Like my friend said, it isn't against the law to travel the road without papers. Just to enter Radavich's capital."

A distant explosion of gas escaping the lake of magma broke the silence, and the sergeant's glove creaked as he tightened his one-handed grip on the reins. "That might be true, but what I find funny is that that tunnel there"—he tilted his spear toward the dark entrance behind Cassius— "likes to spit out bandits. And now the road in front of it just developed a sudden need for repair. So you're either stupid or unlucky. Either way, you're coming with us."

The sergeant nodded to the six patrolmen and they slipped off their mounts, breaking into two groups. "We'll get all of this sorted out," the sergeant said. "If you're working for Coracas, you'll have nothing to worry about, even without papers. We have men who can travel there to verify your story."

One soldier planted the butt of his spear into the vegetation and patted me down. He found the sash tied around my waist beneath my shirt and removed it. He noted the vials of white powder inside one of its pouches, but didn't ask what they were for. As for Emil's charm hanging from my neck, he let it be.

As the soldier tied my hands in front of my body with a loop of rope, I waited for Sara's command to throw myself at these men. Hoping she wouldn't.

She shook her head like she had read my mind. Fighting back would have only turned me into target practice. She offered her wrists to the nearest soldier. "We're not looking for trouble."

"Good lass," the sergeant said. "Radavich has had a recent uptick with marauders, so we're cracking down. I hate to say this, but you will, in all likelihood, be executed if your identities can't be verified."

"That doesn't seem like an overreaction?" I asked, attempting to keep my voice calm.

While another man approached Cassius, who took a step back with a whine, the sergeant answered, "If you were a local, you'd know that suspicion of such a serious crime would be grounds for execution, which is why all the locals make sure to *never* forget their travel papers. Ever since the rebellion in Augustin, Magnate Jancarlo's established a zero-tolerance policy for bandits. If he didn't, we'd get overrun."

"Then I suppose it's a good thing we're telling the truth," Sara said.

Chapter 17 – Efadora

WHEN I WOKE and noticed my hands tied behind the chair I was bound to, my first reaction was to jump up. This turned into a mistake when it felt like a vial of pyroglycerin went off in my skull. For the next several minutes I could only think of the horrible pain in my head as it ebbed away.

My forehead felt sticky and most of my muscles were sore. Pulling with my bound wrists sent a tugging motion to my bound ankles—someone had tied a rope from my hands to my feet to take away my leverage. I was in some sort of supply room, where the air was cool and lightcaps grew in clumps on the wall, illuminating a room full of barrels and crates stacked in organized rows. A place belonging to a tradesman, probably. Several of the barrels lay on their sides on racks, with corks lodged into holes on the lids. Beer barrels?

Why was I alive? Olevic Pike's bounty wanted me dead.

Slight movements sent more stabs of pain through my head, but the rope showed no signs of give, and I couldn't touch my feet to the floor. Once again, I cursed my shortness. Iron hinges squeaked and a door to my left swung open. I was too tired to look at the newcomer, but they made the job easier by standing in front of me. "You're finally up again."

"Who are you?"

The man lowered himself to my height. He had a beard and shoulder-length hair, and chocolate-colored eyes. A slight gut rested against his thigh as he knelt. "We talked earlier."

"I've never met you before."

"Hmm. Must have a concussion. No surprise there."

He wasn't the man I bit, or Carmen's father. That put their operation at three or more. "Guess I'll need to see a doctor then." I wanted to memorize more details about the man, but couldn't do more than squint without shards of light burrowing into my eyes.

"You gotta rest if you have a concussion."

"I can think of other ways to fill my time."

He followed my gaze to the blade strapped to his waist. "So unbecoming for a prinzessa. Didn't all of those fancy people in the court teach you manners?" The contempt in his voice and the way he clipped the beginning of his sentences definitely made him a commoner.

I was being held by a man who sold alcohol and owned a supply room on the fourth floor or higher. If I escaped, I could find this place within a passing.

"I came in to check on you, but guess I'll repeat what I said earlier," he said. "Bounty wants you dead, which means we'll have no qualms about slitting your throat if you give us too much trouble. So be a good girl and maybe you can plea to the bounty hunters to keep you alive. You want that, yes?"

Men like these cost a standard a dozen in the Pit. According to Sara, they used false confidence by claiming all the things they'd be willing to do just to make their targets submit while never having the stomach to follow through. "Most people don't like hurting other people," she'd said. "So throw the fakes off their game by calling their bluffs. They won't know what to do with themselves, and that's the first step toward beating them."

"If you had no qualms about slitting my throat, you would have done it already," I said. "My guards know I visited the tanner's daughter. They'll find a way to trace her father to you, and they'll be here soon. Let me go while you still can."

"Been here two passings, you have. If they were gonna find you, they would have by now." He patted me on the shoulder. "But right you are. I had qualms about killing a teenage girl, but you did a good job at quashing that. Be back soon."

The door shut, followed by the metallic slide of a lock. The agony intensified as I struggled to find any give in the knots, but if I didn't find a way out soon, that man would kill me.

Voices penetrated the other side of the door, too low for me to hear. The chair wobbled while I tried to shimmy my way to the nearest barrel, hoping to find a sharp edge to cut into a rope. I couldn't stop the whimpers from leaving my mouth as I attempted to move the chair. It felt like someone was striking my skull with a hammer every time I jerked to the side.

The voices rose in volume. Someone was yelling. Suddenly, the door flew open, and a man charged in. He grabbed my chair and dragged it back to the middle, turning it. I squeezed my eyes shut to cope with all the sudden movement.

"Why'd they take Carmen?" the visitor asked. I opened my eyes to find Carmen's father kneeling before me.

That's when it hit me. I was alive because they had Carmen. Thank the core that Meike had no reservations about throwing her into a prison cell.

"They didn't tell you?" I asked.

"They dragged her off without a word. Now they want me."

I forced a smile. "They think she knows where I am. If I go missing, she will too."

"Why would she know where the Augustin princepa is?"

"Because we're in the same gang together."

"Liar. My daughter isn't in a gang. Neither are you." His friend stood in the doorway behind him.

"We're not?" I asked. "Then how would I know you had a meeting with your friends about trying to cash in on my bounty on the same passing you kidnapped me? Carmen told me."

"Fhelfire," he whispered. He faced his partner. They looked ready to argue further, but Carmen's father walked away. "Not here, Tomi," he said.

They shut the door behind them. I once again began the slow and painful process of moving my chair toward the pile of crates and barrels, searching for anything that could cut through the rope. But I saw nothing.

After twenty minutes, I gave up. My vision had turned fuzzy, and Tomi and Carmen's father hadn't returned to kill me yet. But it was inevitable. Carmen's father might have been willing to trade me for his daughter, but the others he worked with were a different story. It was only a matter of time before they decided that Carmen's father was more of a complication than a benefit.

THE SLIDING LOCK on the door screeched open, and Tomi entered once again. When he came to stand before me, he didn't notice that while my hands and feet were still bound, I'd managed to undo the rope linking them together. My tied-up feet lashed out, kicking him in the shin. He grunted and shoved me, and my chair collapsed on its side with me still bound to it. My head came dangerously close to striking the rock.

"Calm down, girl." Tomi grabbed the chair and set it upright. "Not here to kill you."

"Sure you're not."

He took a step away but didn't unsheathe his knife. "You're a hot commodity right now. We're backing out of our deal with our current employers. Turns out Olevic isn't the only one with a bounty on your head. Got bounty hunters from the Fiador Fianza in Augustin working for someone who wants you alive. Lucky you, they're paying more."

"I have two bounties on my head?"

Tomi pulled out his knife and cut the ropes tying me down, but not the one binding my wrists. He heaved me off the seat and onto my feet. I started to crumple, but he caught me.

"How're your legs?" he asked.

"Like pudding." The light still hurt my eyes, but my brain hurt substantially less than it had when I first woke. It still unsettled me that I couldn't remember pieces of my imprisonment.

We passed through a hallway flickering with the fire of torches, Tomi supporting almost all my weight. We came into a larger room—one with walls covered in shelves, as well as a cleared off counter and a foyer leading out of the room. He sat me in another chair in front of the counter—this chair short enough for my feet to touch the ground. Five other men waited in the room, one with a red-stained bandage wrapped around his arm. He looked at me with more malice than the others. "I think a piece of your skin is still stuck in my teeth," I said to him.

"Shut up, bitch."

"Behave," Tomi said to me. "It's your best shot at seeing your family again."

"I'd rather scratch that itch between your ribs with a knife," I said.

He shook his head. "All that false bravado. I already told everyone here how you cried over your friends and family earlier. You're a growl with no teeth."

"You're lying."

"You really don't remember? You were downright *sobbing*. Then you started calling out a buncha nobodies from some place called Titanite. Heard you repeating your sister and brother's names too. Got knocked on the head pretty good."

My face grew hot. "I'm going to kill you."

The others laughed, but Tomi's smile faded as he met my gaze. "That's the first time I've seen such a sincere look from a noble. Didn't know any of you cared that much about anything."

Instead of answering, I surveyed my surroundings some more. That's when I noticed Carmen's father sitting in the corner. "What happens to Carmen?" I asked.

Tomi answered for him. "We're going to put out the word that the Fiador Fianza is on their way out of Manasus. Shouldn't take long for the news to reach the magnate. Bardera will send her men out to retrieve you and then Carmen will be released."

"You're going to betray the Fiador Fianza?"

"It's a cruel world we live in. It'll also be a win-win for us all. We get our pay and Rial gets his daughter back. You get to return to the palace too, assuming you aren't killed before the magnate's guard catches your bounty hunters. So keep your mouth shut when the time comes."

Did they really expect the plan to work? The Fiador Fianza was an organization of professionals. They knew all the tricks of the trade, as well as the risks of transporting a princepa. They weren't stupid enough to stick to the Granite Road or any of the secondary channels, and if I was found and returned, I could tell the city guard to arrest Rial and help them find Tomi.

But the plan had convinced Rial to comply.

A door opened at the other end of the foyer and a pair of voices headed toward us. Two bounty hunters rounded the corner, wearing wide-brimmed cordovan hats characteristic of their order. Chainmail hung from their torsos with brown coats that reached to their knees. Augustin-red scarves were tied around their necks. The leader met my eyes and I couldn't help but snort.

"Our payment?" Tomi asked.

The leader looked me up and down. "Why is she bleeding? Has she been damaged at all?"

Tomi untied my hands and helped me up to turn me in an awkward circle. I barely managed to stay upright. "She hit her head and can't walk on her own, but that's all."

"I'm fine," I said with as much composure as I could muster once Tomi sat me down.

The leader nodded. "Good."

"So, our payment?" Tomi repeated. "The princepa is hot

as bowel's fire. The sooner you get her outta the city, the better."

The leader reached into the coat. "Very well."

The sword at his side sung from its sheath and he swung, decapitating the man closest to him—the one who had kidnapped me outside Rial's shop. The skin on the kidnapper's neck and severed head sizzled from contact with the blue-tinged edge of the Meteor Blade.

"There's his share," Emil said after the body thudded to the floor and the head came to a rest halfway between the two groups. "Who else?"

My brother and his companion rushed forward, but my captors reacted quickly, unsheathing their swords and forming a line in a room that had suddenly become too small. Emil advanced slowly, trading blows with the nearest enemy with inhuman force while his companion protected his side. My captors also outnumbered them almost three-to-one.

One of the kidnappers fell, crumpling near my feet and shooting blood from his neck that pulsed onto the floor. "Surrender," Emil said, breathing heavily. "You'll all die otherwise."

Tomi glanced at his friends but said nothing. I focused on the knife strapped to the waist of the slain captor at my feet, and before Tomi could answer, I jumped forward. Judging by how slow he turned, Tomi probably hadn't expected how strong my legs really were. I slid the knife out in one fluid movement and the point slipped into the back of his ribcage. I unsheathed it from his body to stab it into the side of the man beside him, then jumped back before their flailing arms could catch hold of me.

Emil seized on the confusion and charged. The remaining two—one of which was Carmen's father—didn't attempt to hold the line as Tomi and the other man I'd stabbed fell. Rial yanked the knife out of my hand before I could turn it on him, and he grabbed me into a hug and pressed the blade across my chest. Its tip hovered a centimeter from my neck.

Rial backed us against the far wall and stood side-by-side with his cohort. "Don't come closer," he said to Emil.

"All right," Emil said. Tomi lay on his back, blood dribbling from the side of his mouth as he slowly died.

"I just want my daughter," Rial said. "The magnate has her. Lemme leave and I'll pretend none of this happened. This girl is no good to you dead."

"The magnate has her? I can help you get her back. Just drop your weapons."

Rial let out a half laugh, half sob. "You're going to help? You're a bounty hunter. You killed my friends." His grip on me tightened. "Stand back or I'm sticking this blade into the princepa. I'll cut her up so bad nobody will believe it's her. She'll be worthless."

Emil's fear changed into something I'd never seen on him before. Pure, unbridled fury. His blade arced in a strike that he put all his weight behind, aimed at the man beside Rial and me. The captor sidestepped it and elbowed Emil in the jaw, causing him to stumble, but Emil's companion stabbed the captor in the chest before the man could recover.

Rial made a motion to plunge the knife into my neck, but he seemed to struggle against an invisible force. The side of the blade bit into my chest, and I gasped. Emil grasped Rial's wrist, and with a twist, he forced Rial to drop the weapon. Rial let me go and tried to pry himself free to run, but Emil's other hand lashed out, grasping him by the throat. With a roar, my brother threw him backward.

The back of Rial's head struck the edge of one of the stone shelves, and he fell to the floor. Blood leaked through a dent in the back of his skull and he convulsed, face down. Emil's companion, one I vaguely recognized, watched Rial with horror. Emil knelt before me and threw his cordovan hat to the ground to reveal hair plastered to his head with sweat. "I'm sorry, Efadora. I'm so sorry."

"Why are you sorry? You got him." *Him.* The convulsing man on the floor. Carmen's father. My heart sank.

"I don't know what came over me. I almost got you killed." The corners of his eyes wrinkled in disgust with himself. Rial finally stilled.

"But you didn't." I touched a finger to the cut on my chest, making a point that it didn't hurt as badly as it looked.

His companion touched a hand to my arm. "Come," he said. "This is no place for a princepa."

I'd seen my share of dead bodies. They didn't bother me. In fact, I was responsible for two of them, which made me realize that killing didn't faze me. I felt nothing, in fact. But I didn't argue, picking my way through the carnage. Emil remained where he stood as he studied the scene. Why was he acting so strangely? Tomi still lay in the same position he had fallen in, staring lifelessly at the ceiling. "Told you so," I said to the body as I passed.

As the fake bounty hunter led me outside, I remembered where I knew him from. He was the master smith of the Augustin Foundry. But why was he with my brother? We entered an alleyway outside, which led onto the ridge fifty feet to my left. "Where's my sister and father?" I asked him.

"That's a conversation you should have with Emil."

"They're dead," I heard myself say.

"No, no. Your sister isn't dead. Please, your brother will want to answer these questions for me."

Mateo had left out my father's name, which meant something bad. It had to.

Father was dead.

Emil exited the building, which I saw was on the sixth level. He'd abandoned his long coat and chainmail and now sported the fighting leathers he'd been wearing underneath. Despite my skull thrumming in pain to the rhythm of my heart, Emil looked worse off than I felt. "What's wrong?" I asked.

Mateo cut in. "They would have died regardless, Emil. You couldn't have changed that."

"Did they have to die for refusing to release my sister, or because that's all I wanted when they threatened her?"

"A life of regret is a life in the past. A life without progress," I said, pulling a passage from the Sky Scrolls. The master smith seemed surprised, but nodded. However, I could only think about how ridiculous it was that I needed to comfort my older brother.

Emil stopped and pulled me into a hug. "I'm so happy to see you, Efadora. I don't think Magnate Bardera's slept since you went missing. Not many held out hope you'd be alive. We're lucky our lie spread throughout the city so fast."

"About a bounty wanting me alive?"

He nodded. "The best lies are based on the truth. The Fiador Fianza is trying to hunt down me and Sara, but nobody in Manasus knows yet. The Fiador Fianza hates it when outsiders try to take advantage of their contracts."

"That's not the only reason I'm alive," I said. "There's that man you killed who wanted to trade me for his daughter. He convinced his friends not to kill me."

"Ah," Emil said, joy fading.

While we made our way down the levels, Emil explained how they had arrived in Manasus after I'd been missing for a full passing, then decided to use the Fiador Fianza gear they'd acquired after bounty hunters almost killed them on Dagir's Pass. Sara had traveled to Radavich with Father's manservant to recruit an army to retake our city, and Emil's plan was to rendezvous with Sara in Sanskra once we received word from her. Then he broke the news about Father's death. I still wasn't sure how I felt about it.

"I feel bad for him," I finally said as we huffed down a set of stone steps covered in moss and mist. Moving was hard, but the fresh air alleviated some of the pain in my head. Commoners whispered and pointed at us, likely due to all the blood covering our clothes.

"You feel bad for Father?" Emil asked.

"Yes. He hated ruling."

"What are you talking about?"

"You never noticed?" It had always seemed obvious to

me, the way he was so angry all the time. It started after Mother's death. Before, Father would collect a hundred little injustices, and at the end of every passing, Mother would be there to help him talk them out.

"Father always worked well under stress," Emil said.

"No, he was awful at it. I'm surprised you don't remember since you're older. He ruled because he thought he was the only one able to make the hard choices required of the throne. He just kept winding up tighter and tighter until he turned to stone. Making decisions didn't bother him anymore, but he didn't seem to care about anyone either."

He regarded me for a long moment. "You're perceptive. Has anyone told you that?"

"Sara did. By the way, are you sure having her go all the way to Radavich with only Ig was a good idea? It's dangerous in the crust, especially if they're staying off the Granite Road."

My brother's expression fell. "Let's talk about it later."

"What's wrong?"

He shook his head. "Another time."

When Emil marched me into the throne room, Magnate Bardera broke away from the rock garden pond built beside the dais to her chair, where she'd been speaking with the palace's cofferer and his retinue of scribes. "Effie, you're alive!" She ran to me and pulled me into a hug significantly rougher than Emil's. "Thank Fheldspra."

"Ow," I said.

She pulled away. "Is that your blood?"

"Yes. But it's the headache that hurts, mostly."

The magnate faced Emil. "I should've known more about your plan. I could have offered you people I trust. These last few passings have wreaked havoc on my indigestion."

Emil took a seat at one of the tables and took a long, deep breath, cracking his neck. "I couldn't risk it. My sister disappeared while your guards were watching her."

"It was more the gross incompetence of one particular guard that resulted in this whole fiasco." Bardera turned on me, oozing disappointment. "You disobeyed my order to stay in the palace and nearly got yourself killed. I'm sure you remember what your punishment would be. Two lashings."

Emil tensed, but I stepped forward, ready to get this over with. I just wanted to lie in my bed and sleep for a few passings.

"However," the magnate continued, "she's gotten her punishment already. If there was ever one thing I learned growing up, it was that you don't kick someone while they're on the ground."

"You're an honorable woman, Magnate Bardera," Emil said.

She waved a hand. "Honor can't provide the same results as courage. We're lucky you arrived in the city when you did. Efadora would be dead by now otherwise."

"Not a chance," I muttered.

"Excuse me?" she asked.

"Nothing. Where's that commoner girl you arrested? Her name's Carmen. I need to see her."

"She's in the cells. Maybe you should rest first—"

"She had nothing to do with my disappearance. I'm not doing anything else until I talk to her."

The magnate looked ready to argue further, but my brother cut in. "Her father was just killed."

Bardera grimaced. "Very well."

THE PRISON CELLS were next to the Garst Nat, the Mideast Gardens on the third floor, at the end of one of the deepest corridors. A subterranean river flowed along the backs of the cells where prisoners had access to water and a place to relieve themselves. A guard once told me that men and women sometimes tried to escape by letting the freezing water sweep them into the caverns it disappeared into. Some thought the river went all the way to the Dead Bogs or Abyssal Peak, beyond the northeast edges of Mira.

A dull roar of water echoed through the breezy corridor, and the reflection of water danced along the ceilings of empty cells I passed. Emil escorted me—I asked my brother to stay in the palace but he'd insisted. Each step made the rock in my stomach a little heavier, but the feeling was forgotten when I walked past the first cell with an occupant. "So that's where you ran off to."

Meike eyed me from beside the river, sitting on a cot cut into the wall. She was about to say something when she noticed my escort. "I reap what I sow," she said.

"You're holding yourself accountable," Emil said. "I appreciate it."

Meike threw my brother an angry look, but kept quiet.

"Efadora?" a voice called out. The rock returned in full force, intensifying when Carmen's face appeared between the bars of the adjacent cell.

Yellow marks littered my friend's face from half-healed bruises, and her body trembled from the constant cold, but the discomfort didn't show on her face. "*Mi val?*" she didn't hesitate to ask.

"I'm sorry," I said, voice cracking. Why was this so hard? I'd already decided she couldn't be my friend anymore, and none of this would've happened if she'd helped spring me out of the palace. People with true grit, like the leaders of the Ortavella Runners and the Regheta gang, or Sara, cut people out of their lives all the time. So could I.

Gravel crunched beneath Emil's boots as he stepped up beside me. "It's my fault your father is dead."

Carmen angled her face so that the iron bar blocked her eyes, and a shudder passed through her shivering. "He's really dead?"

"He was only thinking of you, at the end."

I waited for her to say something. To start crying, to do anything other than stand there.

She reached through the bars and grabbed my hair, yanking it hard. Emil lurched forward and grabbed Carmen's hand,

and I heard something break in Carmen's grip. She cried out, pulling her limp hand back.

"Why not stay in the palace?" she asked, her voice quiet and almost shrill as she held her wrist to her chest. "None of this woulda happened if you listened. I *told* you, stay in room. I thought we were friends. Now he's dead. It's your fault. All your fault."

Her words were angry, but she couldn't even look me in the eye when she said them. The heaviness in my stomach transformed to nausea, the urge to vomit rising in my throat. I could do this. She needed to know her father had almost gotten me killed and it had cost him. It was the price of doing business in the groups we ran with. "I—"

"Leave," she shrieked. "I never want to see you again." She bent over, her arms wrapped around her stomach, and she started to sob.

I walked away, trembling, my head low and my cheeks burning, not bothering to see if Emil was following. As I passed Meike's cell, I noticed her watching me. "What?" I almost hissed.

"A shame," she said, and returned to throwing pebbles in the water.

I picked up the pace. As I rushed for the exit, I thought of the part Meike didn't say. *It's a shame they didn't kill you.*

Chapter 18 – Jakar

THE STONE FOXES moved at just the wrong speed. Sara jogged while the guards towed her with a length of rope tied to one of their harnesses, but I was tall enough that I was forced into a half walk, half-run that sent me stumbling over and over again. We passed several farms on our way to the city, where shepherds tended to communities of white-furred halite oxen. Both man and beast watched us pass.

One of the patrolmen was riding for Coracas to verify my and Sara's story. We'd been arrested at the halfway point between the town and the capital, so the man had to cover triple the distance to catch up, but he also likely moved at close to triple the pace. He'd serve us our death sentences soon. Sara hadn't spoken since our arrest—she looked ready to keel over, her skin now a sickly pallor and her breaths coming out hard as she watch the swish of the fox's tail in front of her. It couldn't have been more than four or five hours since she woke from her Imbibing.

The Granite Road tapered into a tunnel twenty feet tall, but still wide enough to keep things comfortable for the traffic congesting the main gate. Along the sheer walls on either side were peculiar sources of light—glass orbs sat in sconces where torches would have normally gone, encasing orange flames. I was no stranger to the lanterns made by the Guild of the Glass in Augustin, but these fixtures had no apparent reserve for fuel. We passed lines of silver-spotted llamas tied rear-to-end like sausage links, heavily laden with goods and sniffing the dirt for bugs. Locals staked out spots to sell food, and sounds of sizzling oil on pretzel carts and the spicy, tangy aroma of hummus permeated the air. A din of voices rose from merchants, families, and hired swords milling about waiting for their turn to enter the city. They eyed us, resentful as we passed them all.

The patrol squeezed past the right side of the line, which led to a series of offset stone walls. The capital's entrance. If it worked in any way like Augustin's, the path waiting for us zigzagged into the city, designed for both funneling an invading force and to mitigate any damage if that force attempted to blast their way through with explosives.

Guardsmen gave the soldiers leading us a cursory glance. We traveled down the first corridor, which pushed Sara and me together. "Notice the limestone?" I whispered.

She examined our surroundings and her mouth fell open. For the rest of our walk through the main entrance, I could feel Sara's power gently pushing against the limestone deposits riddling the floor and ceiling. Despite our predicament, I couldn't stop smiling as I watched her test the waters, full of wonder.

The corridors brought us onto a ridge overlooking a massive sinkhole more than five times the size of Augustin. A hole crusted with ice lingered a thousand feet above our heads, providing a window to the stars and to Saffar as the moon passed, the hole about half the width of the rest of the chasm. It was like the city resided inside a giant vase, its body wide and its neck narrow.

The vegetation was rampant, rivaling some of the jungles of the crust. Mushrooms with drooping bulbous growths that glowed with white light towered over buildings, and manmade structures sat among dozens of flowery, moss-covered boulders strewn throughout the chasm floor. While Augustins lived within corridors and alleyways cut deep into the sides of the sinkhole, the neighborhoods and districts here covered the open floor with a smattering of structures crawling up the sides of the walls. It looked as different from Augustin as Augustin did from Som Abast, despite all three cities residing where water had eaten and eroded rock over the course of epochs.

The guards led us down a set of switchbacks toward the ground floor. Sara seemed to be taking in the scenery, but for different reasons—the stone around us was almost entirely limestone. The switchbacks were riddled with locals pestering newcomers with services—from city guides to men with rickshaws offering rides to foot traffic. At the bottom, most of the traffic broke to the left, down a street I presumed headed toward the busier parts of Radavich. The guards took us right, toward a cluster of barracks with crimson leaves matting their roofs. This was our last chance to make a break for it before we were imprisoned, but Sara was still too distracted to notice.

The patrol took their foxes to the nearby stables, and Cassius sniffed the air in our direction as the sergeant led us away, toward the nearest barracks. Inside, the sergeant threw us in two of the three jail cells lining the far wall. "Sit tight while we get this sorted out. Shouldn't be much longer now," he said. He still held onto the items they'd confiscated from us— Sara's stiletto knives, my dirk, and the sash the patrolman had removed from my waist. He set them in an evidence chest beside his desk and started sorting through the stacks of papers on his desk.

A single set of bars separated Sara from me, and I leaned against them. "I can get us out," I whispered.

"Take the lead then, captain," she whispered back.

"Keep your head down."

She moved to the back of the cell and sat on the bed, hiding her face between her knees as if trying to nap. My hands gripped the cool, rough metal of the wrought-iron door—an alloy made of what felt like ninety-five percent iron—but a *ting* rang out as Emil's charm stuck to one of the bars. The sergeant looked up and I offered an embarrassed smile. "Sorry." I struggled to detach the magnetized ring, thinking of Emil and how he said he would use the ring as a kid to root out iron deposits outside the city. The next time I saw him wouldn't be soon enough. The sergeant brought his attention back to his paperwork.

Stuffing the charm into my shirt, I brought my focus back to the sash inside the evidence chest. The granular texture of white powder appeared on the edges of my Eye, waiting to be manipulated.

In ten seconds, this man will be dead because of me.

The vials of powder inside the chest trembled. I only had to apply enough pressure to create a spark, and it would ignite the pyroglycerin soaking in the diatomaceous soil. I'd spent my time during Sara's binding creating the compound—combining it with the soil to stabilize the explosive enough for transport. I squeezed my eyes shut, concentrating until I could feel the vein in my forehead pulsing. My fist tightened as I imagined crushing the vial in my grip, and a sweat broke out on my forehead.

"What are you doing?" the sergeant asked.

An explosion of sound enveloped us and a blast wave large enough to rock the entire building rolled me across the cell until I bounced against the cot. My ears rang, my face stung, and my vision spun. The air smelled of dust and metal. I nearly tripped trying to pick myself up.

Remains of the desk covered the sergeant's body, the man's skin slicked with blood and peppered with glass and shards of wood. Sara stood, wavering, and shook her head to regain her bearings. I set my hands on the wrought-iron bars and started to pull, my shoulders popping as pain washed into my arms. Blood touched my lips as it dripped from my nose, but the iron started to give, bending outward.

The bars scraped against my body as I slipped past. The keys to the cells hung from a hook by the door, and Sara's cell squeaked open after I unlocked it. She hurried toward a set of cabinets and the window above them. "We can sneak out through here."

A fox whistle hung from a ring by the front door, and I grabbed it and wrapped it around my wrist. Sara stole the side sword from the sergeant to clear out the shards of glass rimming the windows.

Footsteps pounded up the stairs. One of the patrolmen appeared in the doorway, and he looked down at his superior's mangled body. "Escape!" he bellowed.

The man had changed out of his armor and wore a leather tunic and cloth pants, so he didn't weigh much when I collided into him. We sailed over the top of the steps and landed in the dirt, my body punching the air out of his. I punched him once as he gasped for air, and readied another swing, but Sara appeared at my side, the sergeant's sword she'd stolen sliding into the man's chest. His face twisted, mouth sucking for breath and for life. He couldn't be older than Emil, probably still green among the city guard. I couldn't take my eyes off him as Sara pulled me off and away.

Two more soldiers ran out of the nearest barrack, and Sara took off down the street. I followed.

They appeared a block behind us, on foxback and closing fast. I blew hard into the fox whistle and the mounts ground to a halt. The soldiers, who couldn't hear the whistle, began yelling and digging their heels in, but the animals were too confused to know which command to listen to. I blew into it while we ran until I gasped for air and my breathing turned ragged.

We fled without concern for a destination, guided by fireflies flying around glowing bulbs, dangling off mushroom stalks and bushes with leaves the color of rust. Passers-by watched us as the voices in pursuit faded, but the looks became less concerned as the buildings around us started to sag from disrepair and the vegetation grew unchecked. Eventually we slowed to a walk.

Sara stopped in front of a saw mill, where workers cut rockweald root into lengths of rockwood on a lot covered in sawdust. "That's one way to get into a city."

"Half the guard will be looking for us now," I said.

"Then I guess it's a good thing I'm a smuggler and you burgled for my father for a living."

We found a bar a few blocks away—a dingy hole in the wall with a collection of mycelium tables strewn about as though a giant had used them for a game of liar's dice. A faint haze of tobacco smoke emanated from a group of sour-looking men in the corner, the only other occupants in the bar.

"Gotta order something, otherwise you're loitering," the barkeep called out after we sat down. Sara fished out what little pocket change the patrolmen hadn't confiscated and approached the bar. "Four shots of raka," she said. It cost most of her money, but if there was ever an occasion to drink, I supposed now was the time. I watched the man pour her drinks and dump a handful of bits into Sara's palm as change. Instead of bringing the raka to our table, the princepa approached the group in the corner. "For you," she said, and followed with some sort of expression in Radavich's old tongue. "*Delich kadas.*"

Before the men could speak, she left. They regarded the raka, then the largest man touched his forehead with three fingers and gestured toward Sara in the Radavichian gesture of appreciation. He threw one of the shots down the back of his throat.

"So, we're stuck in Radavich's capital with nothing but the change in our pockets," she said when she sat down, "with a warrant out for our arrests. Could be worse."

"That explosion might throw them off our trail. They'll think we're cartographers."

She nodded until her eyes glazed over, and I felt the gentle push and pull of her power. The legs of her chair tapped against the ground.

"The electromagnetic field," I said when her eyes opened.

"I'm sorry?"

"That's how it works. Your elemental power. You exert a force on the element you're bound to or draw energy from it through this field. It's why all elementals can feel the passing of Saffar overhead, because the moon contains every element a human can bind with and it's big enough to disturb that field."

She looked up, her brow furrowing.

"The field comes from electricity and magnetism," I said.

"Electricity?"

I'd forgotten how few people knew about electricity in Mira. I almost used lightning as an example, but storms didn't exist this far west. "You know how some of the metal statues in the palace bite when you touch them? Sometimes they build up a charge. Or the fish that divers will stay away from. The ones that shock."

"Ah," she said, unimpressed. I had no better way to explain though. The fellowship of masters believed electricity could be used as a deep well of energy, but their theories were self-serving, like always. They made no effort to share their knowledge with those outside the Ebonrock.

I continued, "The smiths call elemental power divine magic, or if you're me, it's corruption from the Great Ones. It all comes from the same place though. I tried to tell Mateo, but he didn't care because he already had his answers. People with answers hate asking why *their* answers are *the* answers."

I expected her to ask more about elemental power, but she watched me instead. "Something's been on my mind the longer we travel together. Of all the things I've heard you complain about over the years, it's never once been about the cult you were raised in. Why? Your mind was halfway to the depths when Emil and I rescued you."

The question was strange. It was her first time expressing interest in my past since her fixation on learning about my elemental power on Dagir's Pass. "How often do people complain about the unremarkable things in their lives? I was with them for over a decade. By the time you found me, there was nothing about the Ebonrock that surprised me enough to mention."

She tilted her head slightly and looked away, thoughtful. "People often measure abuse by looking at the victim, which is a real shame for those who cope by acclimating. I hope you know your acceptance of what they did doesn't diminish their actions. It only speaks to your strength."

I touched my tongue to the roof of my mouth, trying to find the saliva that had suddenly evaporated. I swallowed, blinking hard, and the concern in Sara's eyes became too much. Endurance was a static action, one that most people defaulted to without even trying. I had a little too much trouble believing her words.

But she believed them.

"Interesting thought," I said weakly.

"Just something that's crossed my mind a time or two over the years, being Sorrelo Adriann's daughter and all."

Her hands rested on the table, almost at the middle, just past what looked natural. Almost like she was reaching out. So easy to touch. Sara had been deliberate in everything she did, even in dealing with her father, and I had never thought to look deeper into why nothing the late magnate did could bother her. Seemed to not bother her.

She blew out an awkward breath and drummed her fingers on the wood, smile stiff. Funny how we'd gone about sleeping together more easily than this conversation. "Well," she said, standing, "best we don't lose our momentum. We have a lot of work ahead of us if I'm going to get those five minutes in a locked room with my uncle."

The group at the other end nodded to Sara and mumbled thanks when she approached, but paused after she sat with them. "I'm looking for an old friend," she said. "One of the city's jafos. Someone of high business and low moral integrity. Maybe you know him."

* * *

ONE OF THE bar's patrons brought us to a shop owner on the west side of Radavich—a fence, I suspected—who knew the person Sara was looking for. With the simple mention of the name 'Mira's Hand', the shop owner led us down the street toward an inn at the end of the block—an old one that sagged over the sidewalk as if trying to catch a peek of whoever walked through its door. Judging by how well Sara's moniker had compelled the fence into helping, the princepa's reputation was widely known, even in Callo.

"I knew Mira's Hand was famous, but not this famous," I said as we approached the stained door built into a rockwood wall, moss and vines crawling up its sides.

The comment left her smiling. "Fantastic, isn't it? People love the idea of someone working in the wrong places and doing the right thing. Gives them hope. It took all manner of unspeakable acts to get to where I am now." She winked, then a thought seemed to cross her mind and her smile faded.

"What?" I asked. "Is it the bounty?"

"I've just never joined my name with my smuggler's moniker before."

"People need to know a princepa is Mira's Hand. The commoners need to think there are nobility out there who care about them."

She nodded, a faraway look in her eyes.

"*Should* we be worried about the bounty?" I asked.

"I'm always worried, but sometimes you have no choice but to take risks when the stakes are this high."

The inn's exterior was misleading. The back of the building had the fine furnishings of a semi-professional gambling hall, or of a den belonging to a crew doing exceptionally well for themselves. Men and women drunk on orujo carried temperaments dependent on the cards before them, and either pounded the table in rhythm with their hoots or stared at their cards, jaws set. It was the type of place I had to be careful around when on a job for Sorrelo—a place where everyone around me was in on an inside joke and I seemed to be the punch line. An alcove in the back wall sported leather couches, and a man left his place there to meet us. "Leave," he said to the fence.

The fence didn't hesitate. After the door closed, the man before us stuck his thumbs into his belt. "It's been a long time, Hand. Almost didn't recognize you with your hair down." The chaos in the room calmed by a degree, like a black beehive suddenly keyed in on a looming threat. The man was tall, gangly, with grey skin of a lighter shade than mine—Bys, most likely—and wore a skull cap over his long, greasy black hair. One of the crew leaders of the city.

"It has been, Jafo Rodi," she answered.

The jafo bowed his head. "News out of Augustin hasn't been good. Was worried our cargo wouldn't arrive, but I'm glad to see I was wrong. Surprised to see you overseeing the Ash shipment though."

Ash had a nasty reputation—it elicited euphoric hallucinations, coating the lungs and inducing a high that came and went for weeks. Residue from Ash never left the body either. People called the drug 'eight and wait'—several hits turned most addicts terminal, killing them within months. Only certain fungi growing in the southern Augustin territory, near the Tear, produced the main ingredient. "I'm not here with a shipment, Rodi," she said.

"Then why come? There's a hole in the market we need to fill. We don't want the Ortavellas sticking any flags in Radavich."

A few of Rodi's friends perked up at their leader's words, and I saw in my periphery men move their fingers conveniently close to the hilts of their blades.

Sara snorted. "Do you think I'm here to waste your time? I want to hire you for something else. It's a kidnapping job."

"The mark?"

"The secretariat of Radavich. Lucas Adriann."

"How's kidnapping some bureaucrat not a waste of time?"

"Because I'll provide a substantial reward for your help.

Straight from the Adriann coffers."

He waited for her to elaborate, but she didn't. "You want to kidnap and rob the secretariat?"

"Different Adriann coffer. You'll be paid from mine. Lucas Adriann is my uncle."

This caught the attention of the room. "If Lucas Adriann's your uncle, that makes you... Sara Adriann?" Rodi asked. "The Augustin princepa?" He started laughing.

The man was sick with amusement, but the rest of the room continued to dead-eye us. "We've had a productive relationship, Hand," Rodi said, "but you can't expect me to believe you're Augustin royalty. Why would a princepa want such dirty hands? Nobility are soft things. They only care about hiding and living out their soft little lives."

"There's your answer," Sara said. "People don't remember soft." Then she started floating.

Like most buildings in Radavich, the inn was built on limestone, and it impressed me how easily Sara repelled herself off the ground without losing balance. Everyone in the room started—half of whom pulled out their weapons—and Rodi took a step back.

"Jakar?" Sara asked.

Cards covered the nearest table in what looked like a game of truco, crowned by piles of bits and standards. With a motion of my hand, one of the piles clattered to the ground. A standard shot toward me and I caught it, and I raised my hand before me, palm up like an offering. The coin started floating in an imitation of Sara. For theatrics, I made a wave with my other hand, and the coin blurred as it spun.

Someone moved in from my left. The man flew at me, dagger raised, and my hands raised to block. The standard clattered to the floor. I caught the blade between my palms, and the man faltered. "The f—?" he started as he shifted his weight back, allowing me to drop a hand and strike him in the solar plexus. He crumpled to the ground in painful gasps.

Rodi set a foot on the writhing crew member and pushed

at him. "Down, boy," he said as the man continued to make loud and desperate attempts to breathe. "Meet Sal, our god-fearing member of the bunch. It seems he's reacted rather strongly to a non-Foundry metal worker." He kicked Sal playfully. "Coulda been a smith in disguise, Sal. Think next time."

No one else made a move to attack. Sara's feet touched the ground and Rodi watched the princepa expectantly, his foot still pressed to Sal's chest.

"I'm Sara Adriann, daughter of the late magnate, Sorrelo Adriann," she said to everyone. "I'm here on business as princepa. Not as Mira's Hand. That business requires that I speak with my uncle, Lucas Adriann. Help me and you'll have the Augustin royal family on your side."

Rodi stroked his goatee. "There's only one condition, Hand. I'm not calling you Princess."

LUCAS ADRIANN LIVED on the edge of the city, where the ground gently sloped toward the massive wall arcing over us. In Radavich, the nobility lived in four- and five-story houses in the district opposite the city's entrance, as if they had done all they could to separate themselves from the rest of the world. Rodi and I crouched in a snarl of balsa trees within an outcropping of mossy boulders, the leaves non-luminescent and providing ample cover, and we waited in anticipation for the kidnapping of Lucas Adriann to begin.

A system of stairs and walkways surrounded us, covering the sloped district in a grid, constructed of rockwood and connecting each building to the next. The back door to Lucas Adriann's three-story home waited farther downhill, only thirty feet away. We knew of two guards standing at attention at the front of the secretariat's house, but a scout had reported two more inside, along with a cook and a maid. Lucas lived by modest means compared to some of the other nobles.

Ceti shined down on us from the sinkhole's narrow opening with sterilized white light, not unlike the millions of stars it floated among, except ten times more luminous. Below it, Saffar floated by, the red disk crawling toward the edge of the chasm. Saffar's appearance only lasted an hour here, depending on its cycle, but once it came overhead the Tempurium clocks across the city would chime with the new passing. Our plan would be set into motion as soon as the moon touched the other side of the chasm's rim.

"Mira's Hand wants Radavich to attack Augustin," Rodi said. "Nerves of steel, that. I wonder how well she knows her history though. Didn't end so well between Radavich and Tulchi last time two territories went to war."

"I don't think her family sees this as going to war, so maybe they didn't find it relevant."

He grimaced. "Very relevant, friend. But Mira's Hand probably doesn't know the truth, being nobility and all. Happened, what, almost eighty years ago now? The Sovereign loves his revisionist history, so I wouldn't be surprised if it ain't taught in her circles. Stories are out there though, if you know where to put your ear."

"What kind of stories?"

"Stories of genocide. Of how the Sovereign slaughtered every noble in Radavich and Tulchi once he felt the conflict had gone too far. Thousands, dead."

I eyed the matter-of-factness on his face, and he continued, "Murders weren't the end of it, though. Not too long after, the Sovereign brought in his own group from Saracosta to take the place of the dead. Stay in their homes, eat their food, live their lives. Commoners weren't a fan of these strangers, but fear keeps you quiet. Even the magnates and their families had been replaced. And just like that, the war was over. New nobility was much more agreeable, and they carried on living in the cities as though they'd lived there all along." He flitted his fingers through the air, miming the wind. "Life continued."

I'd seen some improbable things in my life, but the jafo's story stretched into the realm of ridiculousness. "So you're saying the Sovereign killed thousands of people and emigrated thousands more from his home territory, all over the course of a week?"

"Pop, and there the newcomers were. It ain't the first time it happened either. Sovereign really went to work on the territories at the start of Mira, during the Merchant Wars. *Hard* at work he was. Other times in history too, if I had to put coin on it."

Not wanting to risk offending him, I let out a *hmm* as though I was considering the story. "If what you're saying is true and the Sovereign replaced the nobility with people who were more peaceful, why are Tulchi and Radavich having such a hard time getting along right now?"

"Nobility weren't the ones who fought the war, obviously. Soldiers came home, they harbored a bit a hate for the atrocities they committed on each other, and over time the circle of life folded those resentments back into the nobility. And if you can count on one constant in life, it's that one group will find any excuse to hate another. Probably why the Sovereign enjoys washing out all our traditions. Harder to hate when everyone's the same. But he's a cancer. Aristocracy is worse, even if they're victims in their own way. I'm not entirely convinced they're even people. Spend any time around them and you feel it."

I'd never come across such strange opinions on the Sovereign and the nobility, but I'd never traveled outside the Augustin capital either. "Mira doesn't war with itself anymore. Is that so bad?"

He spat in the dirt. "Easy to rationalize ethnocide when it isn't your culture getting wiped clean like a bad stain." His attention turned to the walkway. "There's a mass fucking murder of identity going on and the nobility have no idea they're the perpetrators."

He'd stated not a minute earlier that people would find any

reason to hate another group of people, and I was tempted to point out the irony. I kept quiet though. To argue with others was a difficult thing for me at times.

A minute after the edge of the chasm started eating into Saffar's red disk, Lucas's cook appeared in the doorway. He waited impatiently, shifting his weight back and forth, clearly restless. A stranger wouldn't have given his demeanor second thought, but the man suffered from Ash withdrawal.

The footsteps of Cassandra, Rodi's right-hand woman, clacked along the wooden walkway leading behind Lucas's house. She approached the cook with a bag in hand, and they began talking, voices hushed. The cook didn't notice a group of eight men and women move along the walkway farther uphill and sneak down a set of stairs.

As the cook turned toward the group, a knife flashed and Cassandra buried it into the man's stomach. He let out a cry that she muffled with a cupped hand, and she dragged him toward the bushes around the perimeter of the building. The rest of the group entered single file into the home.

Rodi had never mentioned killing the cook. I almost protested, but it wouldn't have changed anything. It took effort to let my fists relax. I wished Sara was here. She was busy collecting money from lenders throughout Radavich that she'd stashed under different aliases, and had trusted Rodi's crew with grabbing her uncle so long as I tagged along. I wasn't sure what reaction I would have expected from her. Part of me didn't want to think about it.

A tiny flame flared, illuminating Rodi's face as he struck a match for his pipe. "You don't have the stomach for this kind of work, do you?" he asked, and took a puff.

My fists had tightened again without me realizing. I had no right to be angry, though. Not with my track record.

"Depends on how you define 'this kind of work'," I said.

"Being whatever person the task requires."

"You and I have different definitions of necessary."

He looked at me like he would an insect pollinating a

flower. "You're soft. Strange, looking at the company you keep. It surprises me Sara would choose to keep you around. Excepting your obvious capabilities, of course."

"At least you're upfront with how you feel."

"Well, when I'm not, that's when you should worry."

The sounds of a struggle erupted from the back door as Rodi's crew carried out Lucas Adriann. The secretariat's movements were sluggish, likely from the rag of ether. Blood covered one of Rodi's men, and seven exited the home where eight had entered.

Rodi led his crew in a wide arc down the hill, traversing the dimly lit, rocky decline through the mossy undergrowth between walkways. Clouds of aphids plagued us until we reached the streets below. Patrols were light this early in the passing, but Rodi stuck to the alleyways, his crew following fifty feet behind. We reached a foot trail where one of their hideouts waited—the narrow alley brought us to an inner courtyard surrounded by shops with rear entrances meant to receive shipments. Most looked abandoned. Rodi's men carried a now limp Lucas up the moisture-slicked steps of the safe house and disappeared inside.

Rodi and I waited at the bottom of the stairs as the last of the crew filed in, and Rodi started to move. He glanced over his shoulder and paused. "Unfortunate," he muttered.

A man covered in rags sat against the wall at the opposite end of the inner courtyard, huddled against a half-rotted barrel and keeping warm with a dirty blanket. He had been watching us, but when our eyes found him, he quickly looked away. Rodi descended the steps and crossed the courtyard, metal sliding against leather, a blade appearing in his hand.

The smuggler knelt over the man and tried to pull the blanket off him. The beggar clutched onto it and whimpered. A glassy sheen of tears covered his eyes as he seemed to realize what Rodi wanted.

My body collided with Rodi's as I shoved him away. "What are you doing?" I asked.

Rodi stumbled, nearly falling, but steadied himself and faced me. The knife glinted. "Dealing with a witness."

"Are you guys coming?" a voice asked. Sara had appeared at the head of the stairs. It took her a moment to notice the stench of aggression between Rodi and me.

When I turned back, the man was already moving. He plunged his blade into the beggar's chest.

Something snapped. Everything turned red, and the color bled into the rest of my body. I charged. Rodi threw a fist, but it glanced off the back of my head as I ducked. I wrapped my arms around him, avoiding his knife, and threw him to the ground. He tried to bring the weapon up, but I kicked his hand. Then I was on top of him, squeezing his neck.

"Ig, *stop*."

The command paralyzed my grip. I relaxed but didn't move off Rodi. The beggar lay in the fetal position, arms wrapped around himself, his blanket stained with blood, and his eyes watched us, full of fear and confusion, the expression frozen. He was dead.

Rodi knocked me off. Instead of attacking me, he turned to Sara as she crossed the courtyard to join us. "Fact he's with you is the only reason he ain't dead right now. If he so much as looks at me wrong again, I show him his insides. Understand?"

Sara nodded. Rodi threw me one last look of disgust and disappeared inside.

"Come on," Sara said, gripping my shoulder. I didn't resist. As we crossed the cobblestones toward the back entrance, a sickness clawed at my insides, the skin on my neck hot and my mind hyperaware of her hand guiding me, old habits making it impossible not to dwell on what her next command might be, if I'd be forced to do whatever I always had to in order to avoid punishment.

She'd given me a Word… after all this time. I looked back, and it was like I was the only one who saw the beggar's body, his bleeding mass now just another prop for the city.

Rodi's crew lingered in the shadows of the safe house, smelling of fungal dust that burned in wisps from pipes glowing red-hot in the darkness. While their spirits sailed high, my fingers buzzed with the sensation of Rodi's thin, fragile skin beneath my grip. Low voices in adjacent rooms burst with exuberance. Laughter. Celebration for a job well done.

The man in the courtyard leaking blood into the dirt, his warm body attracting flesh flies. Rage.

Sara stopped us in front of a door. "What was that back there?"

"What was what?" Bitterness leaked into my voice.

"In the two years I've known you, I've never seen you lose control before. So what was that?"

Why did you give me a Word? I almost retorted, but the question sounded idiotic as soon as I thought it. Instead, I thought on her question and came up short with an answer. Working under Sorrelo had taught me to never act impulsive, since impulse meant punishment. Sara gripped my upper arm, but it wasn't like the hand that had led me through the courtyard. It was gentle. "You just attacked our best shot at retaking Augustin. It doesn't matter what he did. He can kill every vagrant in the surrounding five blocks and there's nothing I can do to stop him. He doesn't work for me right now; I work for him. We need him more than he needs us."

I had nothing to say. Attacking Rodi had been a shadow from the past resurfacing—someone capable of strangling a man in a fit of rage. Someone from a time before my flesh binding. Someone I'd forgotten about.

"We're all right," she said, squeezing my arm. "Let's just forget about it. Eyes on the prize and whatnot."

The words *Ig, stop*, in Sara's rough and commanding voice played over and over in my head. I nodded weakly.

Lucas Adriann lay on a barren floor in a room empty of furnishings and crusted with patches of lightcaps. He groaned as he sat up, rubbing at his eyes. Clarity seemed to cut through the haze, for he brought his knees to his chest and looked at Sara. The princepa and I stood by the doorway, watching him.

"Sara?" he asked.

"Hello, Uncle."

Chapter 19 – Jakar

Three years ago

QUIN, AKHILIAN, CAUBI, and I paused in our work when the distant thunder of a whip echoed into our pit, followed by the sound of men shouting. We climbed out of the dusty hole we'd been mining rocks from and rose onto the icy hill, and I pulled the bandana from my mouth to breathe in the freezing air. Fifty feet away, a slave knelt on the ice next to a still figure on the ground. One of the masters had descended on the two, and he bowed the slave with the lashing of his whip. I squinted, then realized the body next to the kneeling slave wore the robes of a master.

"Son of a bitch," Caubi said, wiping her brow. "That looks likes Hoi. I think he killed a master."

We took off toward the commotion, and other students left their mining holes or ran from the wall we had been building. I picked my way down the slopes rimming Bloodreach's mouth—to my left was the sprawling city, and to my right, a white wasteland painted a rosy hue from the Burning Mountains. We'd been tasked with building a wall that would act as a windbreak for the Raval District—a recently growing arm of Bloodreach built closer to the Outside than any other part of the city. It was brutal yet rewarding work, as it put me closer to Bloodreach's mouth than any other job in recent years. Outside terrified most people—a fear of wide-open spaces was a common phenomenon, apparently—but I found it exhilarating. A thousand cities could have fit within the desert of ice between here and the Burning Mountains.

The whip had ripped Hoi's shirt to tatters by the time we reached him, revealing strips of flesh that had parted from the blows from another master who had rushed to investigate. The slave whimpered, kneeling with his forehead touching the ice, ignoring the body lying beside him. The dead master looked like Master Ledoti, whose blood had already frozen on the ice. A hammer, used to break apart rocks our powers couldn't mold, was wedged into the side of his head above the ear.

A student had never managed to kill a master before. It looked wrong, like I'd suddenly been told wood could melt.

Masters Kax and Bata didn't relent until Hoi was a bleeding, unconscious mess. When they stopped, they breathed hard with their hands resting on their knees, breath billowing like smoke in front of them, and they finally noticed the fifteen of us.

"Back home," Master Bata commanded in his heavy southern accent. Akhilian believed he was Ronan, but Master Bata would never admit it. Rona was a hundred miles south of here, farther down the Burning Mountains, but whether it was twenty miles or a thousand, it didn't matter. None of us had ever traveled more than several miles beyond Bloodreach.

Master Kax tailed us as our group walked down the ice-slicked steps toward the city. Master Bata stayed behind, probably to find a way to dispose of Hoi and their colleague. It was a shame that Hoi had endured so much only to die on Bloodreach's slopes.

After years of hard labor and five Imbibings, only fifteen of us were left from those hundred-plus children who had been stolen. Was Hoi's death any different from the countless others?

Yes, because in several months' time, it was all supposed to be over. Hoi nearly made it to the end.

"Told you they could die," Quin said. She skipped down the black, rocky steps, dodging patches of ice and snow, maintaining her footing and her lighthearted attitude. The wind picked up a draft of warm air from the hot springs to our left as we skirted the city's edge along the southern wall, giving me goosebumps.

"Do you think there's an endless supply of masters?" I asked. Students in the past had tried to kill them, but they'd always failed.

Quin slipped, but turned the stumble into an elegant twist and recovered. "What do you mean?"

"There are twelve masters right now and fifteen of us. If we killed them and escaped, who would come after us? How many kadiphs are there, and how long would it take them to reach Bloodreach when they learned what happened?"

"Keep your voice down," Akhilian said, nodding toward Master Kax walking behind us. The man picked his way along the treacherous steps while maintaining a healthy distance from our group. Symian, Roth, Fendra, and other students walked in packs closer to us, but they were still too far to hear. I trusted them, but not like I trusted the three around me. What we talked about would earn us beatings to within inches of our deaths.

"I'm just saying," I continued, "even if we kill some of them, they can only do so much to punish us. What are they going to do? Execute slaves they spent years training?"

"It only took hours for us to start using our elemental powers after the Imbibings," Quin said. "All this mining and labor helps, but is it really training?"

"What would you call it then?"

Akhilian cut in, "Think of Rhulkaur."

Rhulkaur was a man who spoke with the fellowship on

occasion, and although it wasn't unheard of for the masters to speak to outsiders while we labored throughout the city, Rhulkaur was special in that he was a member of the alaife, the upper caste, who wore billowing cloaks with pauldrons of the finest grotto-wolf fur and white shirts made from silk imported from the Ghost Peaks—a mountain range on the edge of the Burning Mountains, near Rona, where people were rumored to live Outside indefinitely. It meant he was very, very rich, and had no business associating with the simple lifestyle of the Ebonrock.

"I think he works for the city," Akhilian continued. "Think about it. The masters took up a huge swath of land in the city's manufacturing district to raise us, and as far as we know, the city's turned a blind eye. We built that four-story building in the Bejiya Bel district, rerouted two lava rivers along the northern walls, dug countless trenches and repaired dozens of roads, and now we're building walls so Bloodreach can expand. Bloodreach wanted labor and the Ebonrock wanted children. There's an agreement between them."

The idea seemed ludicrous. Not because I didn't believe it, but because the thought of the city offering its own children up to a group of cultists made me angry. Before my kidnapping, my parents had convinced me that the city was the safest place to live, and to trust our leaders, but it turned out they were the danger. The fact they made money off my head was bad enough, but if the city had been in on it too?

I'd only seen the Nochi slums twice in the past ten years, and only at a distance. I could've asked after my parents, but in truth, I didn't care. They were dead to me. Akhilian never mentioned his parents either, so I figured he shared the sentiment.

Akhilian was far and away the most intelligent in our group of four, and I usually trusted his assessments. "We must have been valuable if the Ebonrock is still trying to pay their debt off," I said.

"Or they're paying off the price of a hundred children instead of fifteen adults."

"A price that'll be paid off soon, apparently," Quin said.

The reminder ended the conversation. The masters had told us our last Imbibing would occur two weeks from now, and in several months, all of us would be leaving Sulian Daw forever. The masters spoke of our departure happily. When asked where we would be going, they promised a lifetime of comfort and luxury. Our reward for so many years of hard labor. The idea sounded as alien as it was intimidating. This time next year, we would be living completely different lives.

Akhilian and Caubi were especially sobered from the reminder. Both had nearly died from the last Imbibing, and Quin and I worried over whether they would survive the final one.

"I hate this place," I finally said. "If you're right, Akhilian, then Bloodreach should be burned to the ground. It betrayed its own people."

"I'd hardly consider us members of 'the people,'" Caubi said. "Even when we were, our families were *trelis*. The lowest class."

"Everyone deserves to be treated with decency, no matter their roots."

The hot spring steppes turned into a river, and we followed the path running along its shore, behind the backs of buildings, where we caught sight through their alleyways of people walking the streets on the other side. We were invisible to them, like usual. The river fed into Obsidian Lake, and the ground opened up to the start of the manufacturing district, where workers transported boxes and carts to and from buildings crusted with ice from the wind. These people ignored us as well, even as we walked close enough to brush shoulders with them, but their fear upon seeing Master Kax made it plain to see why. Everyone who worked around the Ebonrock compound knew not to ask questions.

We arrived at the gates of home, where barren dirt and rock

separated the compound from the rest of the city. Master Kax heaved the lock off the gate and pushed the entrance open to let us inside.

At the moment, only one master guarded fifteen students.

If I escaped with my friends, where would we go? Every path and tunnel leading out of Bloodreach contained burrowing millipedes, bobbit worms, and carnivorous plants. We couldn't hide inside the city either. Fifty thousand people lived in Bloodreach, but with enough time, the masters and the kadiphs would find us. It had been a year since we'd seen the last kadiph—they only visited to check on our progress—but they would resurface if need be to reclaim their investments. They were far more dangerous than the masters.

Inside the compound, Master Orino walked toward our group, whip swinging from his belt, but the man had only used it a handful of times in all the years I'd known him. At first, I'd believed he was kind because both of us were from Nochi, but the Sulian master had shown leeway with every student at least once over the years.

Escaping would be suicide, but what if we had a master helping us?

"To your rooms," Master Kax commanded. We headed inside, and the man spoke to Master Orino out of earshot. Master Orino studied our group while he listened to his colleague, and we locked eyes. He didn't look angry as he listened to Master Kax's story. Only pensive.

The other students broke off toward their respective rooms, and the four of us reached our four-bunk bedroom. Akhilian and Caubi slid onto their beds, both immersed in their own heads. I could tell Hoi's death had rattled them—the kid had clearly done it because he didn't expect to survive the next Imbibing. He wasn't the first to attack a master for that reason.

Akhilian and Caubi's confidence seemed to erode with each passing that brought us to the final Imbibing. A strong mentality was needed, as it usually meant the difference between life and death.

Master Orino appeared at our doorway. "Hello, young ones," he said, smiling kindly. "I'm here to assess you because of what Hoi did. I'm sorry for asking, but I have to. Are any of you experiencing a compulsion to kill the masters?" The question was mocking, and his smile didn't fade.

"No, Master," Quin, Akhilian, and Caubi said in unison. My response came a heartbeat later, and everyone looked at me.

I didn't apologize.

"I can't fault you for thinking about it," Orino said. "It's natural to experience these thoughts after what you've been through. But keep them to yourself around the other masters. Students have been killed for less."

"Some of us would risk escape rather than go through the final Imbibing. Master Galleir says it's the hardest."

He studied us for several tense seconds, and I started to wonder if he would leave to tell the others. "Is he the only one who feels this way?" he asked.

"No," Quin said. Her words surprised me. If anyone would survive the final Imbibing, it was her.

"Agreed," Caubi said. A moment later, Akhilian nodded.

Their consent caught me off-guard. We'd entertained these feelings over the years, but I'd never asked if they wanted to escape.

"Why is this the first time I'm hearing about this?" Master Orino asked.

I rose from my moth-eaten mattress. This idea had been mine, and he needed to know who was responsible. Caubi and Akhilian wanted to escape, but they wouldn't have dared try it without my or Quin's prompting. "Do you need us to answer that? It doesn't matter how well you treat us, because you're still a master and we're still slaves. Mentioning thoughts like these is a huge risk."

"Then promise you won't mention it again and I'll pretend

I didn't hear it," he said. He turned and walked off. I glanced at my friends and went after him.

He was a dark figure framed by the hallway's grey stone as he glided away, but he eventually slowed to allow me to catch up. "Help me," I said. "I need to get Akhilian and Caubi out of here. They don't think they're going to survive the next Imbibing."

"Then do what you can to convince them they'll make it, and hope for the best. You'll make it through. So will Quin. Don't drag her into this."

Admitting to a master I wanted to escape had freed something inside of me, and I no longer felt the fear of not being able to help my friends. "You know I can't do that. We need your help."

Master Orino stopped. "Do you know how you sound right now?" he asked. "You can't hide from the kadiphs, even with my help. They're very good at tracking people down, and they can't be killed. They'll find you, torture you, then kill you."

"I still don't understand why everyone is so afraid of them. They're strong, but they're still human. Are you saying they have no weakness at all?"

His mouth opened, and he paused. His lips pressed into a thin line.

"What is it?" I asked.

"There are rumors, that is all. It's been said they fear the storms."

"Everyone fears the storms, Master. Everyone fears going Outside."

"Yes, but obligations occasionally bring one to the city's edge, as you well know. The kadiphs avoid nearing the cavern's mouth at all costs, especially during a storm. Rumor has it a lightning strike is guaranteed to kill any kadiph."

I eyed him. "Lightning is dangerous, regardless of who it strikes."

"I'm only telling you the rumors."

"All right... so all I need to do is pull lightning from the sky."

"You asked, Jakar." He rubbed his brow, then waved me off. "It doesn't matter anyway. Escape without my help and you give me plausible deniability. I'd be signing my own death warrant otherwise."

"And if we did it alone, the entire Ebonrock would come looking for us. The kadiphs too, like you said. Whatever happened to the people of Nochi looking out for one another?"

He hesitated. The deliberation in his eyes spoke volumes, and in that moment, I knew I had him.

Chapter 20 – Jakar

ETHER STILL GLAZED Lucas's eyes, but he rubbed at his face with the heels of his hands and shook his head. "I should've known you'd come."

"Karma is a circle," Sara said. "One of us was always meant to repay you for what you did."

Lucas examined his surroundings. There was no furniture; only lightcaps, moss, and the smell of mold. Nothing he could use to escape. However, he didn't behave like most did in these situations, where panic set in within moments of waking. The man continued to assess. "Olevic Pike said all of you were locked up in the Lid back in Augustin. How did you escape?"

"Olevic never had us. We left as soon as the rebellion started. Of course he would lie, Uncle. He didn't want anyone knowing about his little Adriann problem sneaking through the crust."

"Perhaps..." The man trailed off.

"Jakar," Sara said.

I stepped up to Lucas, looming over him as he peered up at me with those glazed eyes, and I punched him. He grunted as his head snapped back, and I returned to Sara's side. This wasn't like those times Sorrelo had forced me to squeeze information out of his dissidents. This was satisfying.

"How could you do this to us? To my father?" Sara asked.

A line of blood trickled down the corner of his mouth. "If I didn't convince Jancarlo to support his rule, the Listener was going to kill you all. That was my understanding of the situation. Did you want me to spend weeks traveling to Augustin and risk imprisonment so I could see if he spoke true? We've received dozens of reports about the chaos in Augustin that corroborated Olevic's story, and there's only one way out of the city. Olevic's had the throne for weeks, setting it up so his daughter can succeed him as soon as possible, for god's sake. It came down to a judgment call."

Did Sara currently experience the same flickers of doubt? "Olevic is a liar and a sociopath," she said. "He puts on a good show, but it's clear as crystal if you know what to look for. How could you let him take you in like that?" She didn't mention how the Listener had fooled us as well.

"You're right. But none of that mattered anyway."

"How so?"

"You think I betrayed all of you lightly? You're family." The conviction of his words seemed to cut through his haze.

This time I spoke. "So why did you?"

He squinted at me. "You're... You're my brother's servant. Sorrelo told me how loyal you are to our family. *Very* loyal." He turned to Sara. "The Sovereign's primordia, Aronidus, paid Radavich a visit after the rebellion. He ordered Magnate Jancarlo to support Olevic."

"Fhelfire," Sara whispered to herself. "Does Olevic Pike know the primordia forced your support?"

"No one outside this room does, aside from Magnate Jancarlo. I was forbidden from sharing the information as well, so keep it to yourself."

Sara's mouth hovered open, but no words came. The Sovereign had forced Radavich to support Olevic Pike, and he'd done so secretly? At first glance it made sense—

the Sovereign would do whatever it took to ensure peace. But he always made his intentions clear when influencing a territory's politics, as it ensured the magnates stayed on the same page. There was also his son, Bilal, to consider. The Sovereign's top priority these last few years had been readying his son for succession, to the point he seemed to forget to send his primordia to check up on the territories, assuming the territories would play nice on their own, like they always had. To now immerse himself in a game of political intrigue?

"If the Sovereign wanted to avoid war, it would make sense to force our support," Lucas continued, "and it isn't as though we could have said no. Doing so to a man like Aronidus would get you killed rather quickly."

The situation was improbable… but not impossible. Lucas wasn't using the information as a bargaining chip to gain freedom either. He simply stated everything as fact. He sounded regretful too.

Lucas continued, "I don't expect you to care, but these last few weeks have been difficult. Sorrelo and I are close. You and Emil I never really cared for, but you're my brother's children, and that means something to me."

Sara snorted. "I forgot how charming you could be, Uncle."

"Cut the sarcasm. I'm just being sincere. It's all I can do to help you see the truth in my words."

The princepa laced her fingers in front of her, tapping her thumbs together. "Fine. I believe you. It was difficult to understand why you'd blatantly betray your family, since I knew how you and Father were. Luckily, Father wasn't alive long enough to believe you abandoned him."

Lucas paled. "No. You're lying."

"Believe it. He died on our way here."

The secretariat looked sick from the idea—his eyes roamed the room wildly as though reassessing where he was. Sara, on the other hand, stated her father's murder matter-of-factly, unflappable as always. But I'd come to know her over the recent weeks. Could detect the hint of pain and acid in her words. I watched her throat as she swallowed hard, studying her uncle.

Sara knelt before him. "My father's dead, but you still have a chance to help his children." The subtle resentment in her voice was now more obvious. "Convince Magnate Jancarlo to help Emil and me reclaim the Augustin throne."

Lucas let out a sharp laugh, and even though his face was devoid of tears, he looked like he'd been slapped. "Don't be naïve. I told you that the primordia ordered the magnate to support Olevic Pike. You think Jancarlo is going to disobey?"

Sara straightened. "Then we'll go to Tulchi and ask for their help. I'm sure they'd be happy to show they're not as frightened as Radavich when it comes to a few primordia."

Despite her challenge, Sara sounded frustrated. Even I dreaded the idea of traveling all the way to Tulchi only to risk failing again.

"Radavich has been dealing with a growing bandit problem, hasn't it?" I asked. "I've noticed a lot of mercenaries in the city too."

"The Anjian Mountains are to the north," Lucas said. "The capital is the closest city to the northern frontier. The influx in trade with those settlements has painted targets on a lot of caravans over the recent years. Bandit activity's a fact of life this far north."

"Don't sellswords in Radavich outnumber the city guard?"

"Easily. Why?"

"When Olevic Pike staged his coup, a portion of his force were mercenaries. He set a precedent by showing how easy it was to overthrow the city if your pockets were deep enough. Just look at the uptick in violence on the Granite Road over the last few weeks. People are realizing that Radavich's defenses are as fallible as Augustin's. Maybe they'll decide overthrowing the city isn't as hard as they thought. If that happens, you'll already know how helpful the Sovereign will be when it comes to coups."

Sara frowned like she was confused she hadn't thought of the idea first. That was the problem with those brought up in power. They often forgot that those who lived in their city didn't always hold allegiance to it.

"He's right," Sara said. "Magnate Jancarlo has to make an example out of Olevic Pike or his bandit problem will only get worse."

Lucas mulled it over. We had drugged and kidnapped him, and by such account he should have wanted us dead. But the man wasn't volatile like Sorrelo. As he stared at his niece, realizations behind his gaze flashed like light on water. He was actually considering the proposal. "Nobody is organized enough to attack the city. The bandit problem has only been an issue in the crust," he finally said.

Sara leaned against the wall. "For now."

Lucas's eyes were less dilated than before. "I saw the bodies when your men kidnapped me. You killed my bodyguards."

"I wasn't there. Your cook is dead too, from what I heard."

The secretariat adjusted how he sat, wincing. "Those bodyguards were useless if they allowed your friends to do what they did, and I wanted to fire my cook anyway. I might be willing to forgive the fact I was dragged out of my own bed."

"That would be beneficial for the both of us."

Lucas had glossed over the deaths of his employees to talk business, without so much as a second thought. And so had Sara.

No, I couldn't think that way. Sara was her father's daughter, so I couldn't expect her to live like a saint. My job was to help her see the right choices, to help her change.

Sara knelt behind her uncle and cut his bonds, then helped him to his feet. "Can you get us an audience with the magnate?"

"Most likely," he said as he stared at the marks on his wrist. He showed no hint of anguish, but it looked like he had aged considerably over the course of the conversation.

The strength of his bond with Sorrelo had been well known.

We found Rodi and the rest of his crew lounging on a mismatched assortment of furniture in the front room, where the safe house's main door waited. Rodi scratched words into the thick, dirty pages of a journal, and his hand moved toward the dirk in his belt when he saw Lucas unrestrained. But he didn't draw it. Despite being outnumbered twenty-to-one, the secretariat glared at every crew member as he approached the exit. Hand on the door, he turned around. "I will meet you at the base of the palace by the rear entrance in two hours," he said to Sara. He regarded the rest of the room's occupants. "I remember which of you gentlemen and ladies broke into my house. If I see any of you eight again, I'll peel the skin off your fingers and toes."

"Seven," Sara corrected him. "Which reminds me. You may find a body you don't recognize back home. Try not to treat it too disrespectfully."

"*His* name was Hasoko," a gangly man with sheared, fiery red hair said.

The rest of the crew bristled at Lucas's threat, and their bodies stilled, cocked back and ready for permission to string the secretariat up from the rafters. Rodi answered with the slightest shake of his head.

The door shutting behind Lucas sent vibrations through the walls. "My uncle talks to the mayordomos of the territory for a living," Sara said. "Their code of conduct doesn't typically involve shish-kebabing anyone who gives them sass, so he tends to forget how loose his tongue can get at times. It'll eventually get him killed though, if that makes you feel better."

"By one of us, most likely," Rodi said as he stared at the front door. "Should be now. The man's nobility. We can't trust him."

"You're talking to the Augustin princepa. I hope you can see the irony in that."

"You're also Mira's Hand. One of the people. You're no

scorpionfish that's planning to stab us in the back." He took a seat on a worn-out couch occupied by two of his crew members. "Whatever. As long as we get paid, that's all that matters."

"You will, but my uncle is the key to that chest. So please don't kill the key."

The hideaway wasn't stocked with food—not for two outsiders, at least—so Sara and I left to find breakfast. We borrowed two cloaks to obscure our faces, in case the city guard had been given descriptions of the culprits who blew up the patrol barracks.

"Rodi brought up a good point," I said as we walked down the cobblestone causeway. By now, the passing had begun for most of Radavich—streams of commoners ebbed and flowed, and carts clustered in the middle of the street. A lamplighter passed us moving the opposite direction, wielding a long pole to light orbs of glass fixed to the fronts of buildings. "You don't trust your uncle, right?" I asked.

"No, but I think Lucas was the only person in the world my father loved. He'll help us."

Her anger toward her father lost its subtlety in that moment. "Sorrelo cared for you," I said.

She waited expectantly. "He cared? What a nice sentiment."

I tried to say something, anything, to comfort her, but realized I couldn't. Not without speaking kindly of the late magnate. Even if it was a lie, I couldn't push the words out of my mouth.

"Regardless of how ruffled my uncle is," she said, "Radavich's magnate has a legitimate reason to help us. A reason you provided, by the way. Thank you for being a knife instead of a hammer."

"How do you mean?"

"You're a weapon, Jakar. I spent all my time in Augustin thinking you were a hammer, but you're sharper than that. So… I'm sorry."

Part of me cringed at the way she viewed me as a tool,

even now, but I forced myself to recognize the compliment. It was a strange one, but the longer I thought on it, the more it made me smile. She was being kind, I decided.

"I'm going to bring Rodi with us when we meet with the magnate," she said. "I don't want him or his crew thinking we're going to throw them to the wayside as soon as we gain Jancarlo's support. It'll be a show of faith to keep him in the loop. He's the type to have at your back in a tight spot as well."

We passed some city workers trimming the stalks of mushrooms growing along the street, and I waited until we were out of earshot to answer. "Your back, maybe. He acts like there's no chance Mira's Hand will betray him. He's too smart to trust you that quickly."

"He was posturing in front of his crew back there. Making a statement so they wouldn't give us trouble. Lucas knows about their safe house now, after all. They were nervous." Our path brought us onto one of the city's main arteries, and the foot traffic doubled. "There's no way Rodi trusts us," she continued. "I think he's helping us out of self-interest, beyond what he's been promised. It's an opportunity to elevate his status. He hates the nobility, but he envies them too. Wants to be the one with the power for once."

We walked in silence toward a bakery on the street corner. I forced myself to acknowledge that we did need Rodi and his crew, but even with his and Lucas's help, we still needed an entire force to march on another territory, siege a historically impregnable city, and all against the wishes of the Sovereign.

One step at a time.

THE PALACE SAT on a bluff of limestone in the center of Radavich, beneath the bullseye of the sinkhole's opening. Luminescent mushrooms and lightcaps grew in deep grooves running up the rock at a slant, illuminating the rise like a glowing spiral, and a set of stairs dark with moisture zigzagged upward. The building at the top was made from fireproof rockwood, and a river of black water surrounded the base of the hill. The place looked like a fortress. We walked over the footbridge leading to the bottom of the stairway.

"I swore to myself that if I ever crossed this bridge, death would follow," Rodi said.

"They're going to confiscate our weapons as soon as we're inside, but you're welcome to try," Sara said.

I watched Rodi's greasy black hair swing along his shoulder blades like a pendulum as I tailed him and Sara. The man hadn't objected to the idea of tagging along, calling it 'a chance to see the zoo firsthand.' He also pretended our earlier spat hadn't happened, but not because he'd forgotten. I'd met men like him before—people who thought they were clever by playing with their prey's expectations. He wanted to put me at ease; a flytrap luring its prey closer and closer. I welcomed the time when he would strike, because then I would kill him, and I knew Sara would have to let me.

Lucas waited at the foot of the stairs that twisted their way up the steep rock, hands clasped behind his back. He scowled at Rodi but didn't comment. "You're in luck. The magnate is interested in hearing your story," he said to his niece.

"Will he try to capitalize on Sara's bounty?" I asked as we came to a stop before him.

"Your slave never talked this much the last time I visited Augustin," he said to the princepa. "Can I count on you to keep his mouth shut while we're meeting with the magnate?"

Sara asked me the question with her eyes, and I nodded. Lucas turned on the balls of his feet and climbed the steps.

As promised, the guards confiscated Rodi's side sword and Sara's dirks. I carried nothing. They led us into hallways lined with obsidian panels that reflected a spectrum of colors from orbs that sat in sconces on the walls. The same kind I'd spotted throughout the city. "Gas lighting," Lucas said when he noticed our interest. "There are gas veins under the city, and they can be fed into bulbs like these ones." That's when

I noticed the rubber tubing connected to the bottom of the sconce, which disappeared into a hole in the pillar.

Boulders cut into statues and streaked with glittering minerals guarded our path as we approached the throne room. A sudden heat appeared, emanating from a manmade pool of lava built into the middle of the floor. Magnate Jancarlo waited on the other side of the pool, sitting at the head of a long limestone table, which looked like it had been carved out of the rock floor it was connected to. A dozen guards lingered behind the magnate's chair in a rough semi-circle—so much protection seemed like overkill, but Sorrelo's style of paranoia was never unique.

"Sit," the magnate commanded in the deepest voice I'd ever heard, voice echoing through the chamber over the faint bubbling of lava. We walked along the pool and took our spots on the opposite end of the table, Lucas sitting halfway between both parties. The magnate was a handsome man, bald like Emil and with a goatee similar to Rodi's, but where Rodi's looked rough and untrimmed, Jancarlo's was a form of artistic expression. Pale blue veins shone through his milky skin, and his lips were pressed tight against each other.

"Lucas informed me of what happened this morning," he said to Sara. "He made a few points about how supporting the usurper may have indirectly contributed to our bandit problem."

"It's rude to steal other peoples' ideas, uncle," Sara said before turning to the magnate. "Yes, *we* proposed that listening to the primordia might have been a bad idea. Something we saw firsthand on our way here. It's a problem that'll only worsen if everyone thinks Olevic Pike got away with what he did."

The man leaned forward on his elbows and interlaced fingers heavy with sparkling stones. "Be that as it may, you're asking me to disobey Aronidus, which means disobeying the Sovereign. If we march on Augustin, it will leave Radavich vulnerable to them and their army's wrath, and to the bandits outside the city."

"You have the city guard," Sara said. "We only want the military. How often have you needed them?"

"Rarely, but they're a deterrent. Tulchi has never been a friend to us, and relations have only worsened with the growing competition for trade with the settlements to the north and the copper mines along the Snakehallow Ravines. It's unlikely they would attack, but I'd rather minimize the risk."

"All right…" Sara trailed off. "And say I approached Tulchi for help if you refused us. My family already has strong ties with Manasus, but imagine if Tulchi realized they could form an alliance with Augustin and Manasus. That would mean the three territories surrounding Radavich having a bone to pick, now working together. All of Mira knows you're the top trade power of the territories, but how long would that last if every territory you had to travel through in order to trade with the rest of Mira imposed heavy taxes?"

The magnate's nose wrinkled. "Threats aren't the best method for winning me over."

"I'm just telling you the way things are. Tulchi won't attack you and you know it. A garrison is enough to fight off any invading force, and you have outposts in the crust to flank any force Tulchi threw at you anyway."

Jancarlo spun one of the rings on his fingers, thinking.

Sara continued, "That leaves us with those pesky primordia, who likely haven't been detail-oriented enough to know about the growing chaos in the crust. Knock Olevic Pike off his manufactured pedestal and peace is more likely in the long run. They'll understand."

"And if they don't? Will you be the one to break the bad news?"

The sound of bubbling lava filled a tentative silence that followed the question. Of course Sara wanted to say yes, but there was no way of answering the question in such a way without sounding foolish. If the princepa defied a primordia and they punished her for it, would I be able to stand toe-to-toe with one?

Rodi raised a hand, and the magnate nodded. "You can't hear from up here what some'a the people in Radavich say," Rodi said, "but your city guard are a problem too. They rob honest people and call it 'civil forfeiture', or they kill men they don't prefer and claim self-defense. You wanna placate the people while helping Sara? Need to make a change within the city as well."

"I'm sorry, but I thought we were talking about Augustin," the magnate said. "If you think yourself important enough to tell me how to run my city again, you'll be sitting at the bottom of my pool."

Rodi's nostrils flared, but he didn't argue.

"Either way," Sara said. "There are problems that can't be solved by maintaining the status quo. Killing Olevic Pike is in the best interest of everyone. The primordia are as reasonable as they are powerful, and I'm confident they can be convinced of the legitimacy of helping my family."

The magnate pondered the princepa's words. He hadn't mentioned the risk of sieging another territory's city yet, which I found odd. I surveyed the guards standing behind Jancarlo's chair and noticed how tense they looked. They stood at attention as expected, but they gripped the handles of their wooden clubs tightly as the weapons dangled from straps on their belts. Clubs seemed an odd choice too. A few guards moved restlessly, as though in anticipation.

And they were all watching me.

"Sara," I said. "They know."

She frowned. "Know what?"

I recognized that look in their eyes. Sorrelo had given it from time to time, and I'd seen it in the eyes of my old masters in Sulian Daw as well. "They know what I am."

Everyone rose at the same time. I knocked my chair over as I moved away, noting the three guards who had been sneaking into position behind us. Sara and Rodi backed up to stand beside me. The semi-circle of guards behind Jancarlo advanced, but didn't attack.

"How?" Sara asked.

Lucas, who was closest, now had guards behind each shoulder. "How did I know your slave was elemental? How do you think? My brother told me."

"Why would he tell you? His children didn't even know."

Lucas let out a single, sharp laugh. "Because he trusted me. Whether the same can be said about Emil, I have no idea. But my brother certainly didn't trust you."

Sara ground her teeth—a habit she'd inherited from Sorrelo. Lucas continued, "All you've done for years is fraternize with his kind." He gestured toward Rodi. "Commoner trash whose greatest contribution to society will be to feed the worms. Your father wanted greatness from you but Emil was the only one with courage to step up. He is the prodigal son while you're just dressed-up garbage."

Sara's cheeks went scarlet. "Life is so much bigger than all this degenerate shoulder-rubbing among the nobility. This isn't where you find greatness. The reality you're living in in this palace is not the one that's out there."

Lucas snorted. "Believe whatever helps you sleep. The nobility write the history books—the Sovereign made sure of that. Our reality is the one that matters. You lorded my brother's death over me, but in the end the joke is on you. Sorrelo loved me and you were nothing to him. He even told me so."

She looked ready to break Lucas's skull. "My father... he was an idiot. And his stupidity cost him his life." Her voice quivered and the tips of her ears reddened. The vein in her neck pulsed. "If he wasn't so damn stubborn and just told me what Jakar was, then I wouldn't have been so intent on figuring out his stupid secret."

I almost asked what she meant, but she continued, "Want to know the real reason Father died? When he told me to find guides to help us through Dagir's Pass, I hired them to rob us. I always knew there was something fishy about Jakar, and I wanted to see how he would kill them after they put on their performance. Then those guides decided to go off script and kill Father, all because that conceited, condescending asshole wouldn't trust his own children."

I stared at Sara, but she refused to look at me.

"You killed my brother?" Lucas asked. The man started forward, but a guard held him back. "He could still be alive, if not for you? You horrendously stupid girl."

"Jakar," Sara began, but I touched her arm. We needed to know what they wanted first.

Magnate Jancarlo stepped through the line of guards to stand side-by-side with Lucas. "Surrender and all of your lives will be spared."

"Why are you doing this?" I asked.

Another familiar look appeared in the magnate's eyes. Greed. "We're going to send Sara away. We don't care where she goes, but we're willing to spare her life. It won't matter that she was responsible for the death of Augustin's magnate. I'll deny Lucas's need for revenge."

Sara exhaled through her teeth, and Jancarlo continued, "Your commoner friend is free to return to the hole he crawled out of. Call it a show of good faith, and I will give my word to make an effort to improve the monarchy's relationship with the commoners. As for you... Jakar, was it? You will stay here. You will show us exactly how you earned those elemental powers of yours."

So this was about power. Of course. It always came down to that. I corrupted everyone I encountered.

What if Mateo had been right about me?

"You can't make me," I said.

"Yes, we can. You will understand the true meaning of pain otherwise."

Sounds of my laughter echoed through the chamber. The noise sounded foreign to me. When was the last time I had laughed? Truly laughed? "You can't threaten me with pain. Not if I'm not bound to you. Torture me all you want," I said, smiling, the muscles in my cheeks reminding me of how long it had been since I'd smiled so widely. "You're going to regret this."

"Jakar's right," Sara said. My proclamation fueled her resolve. "You'll all die as traitors."

Magnate Jancarlo nodded and the soldiers advanced. I stepped in front of Sara and Rodi, and the leading soldier brandished his weapon. His rockwood club rendered my elemental power useless. Every soldier wielded weapons I couldn't influence, and they wore no material on their bodies that I could use to push them off balance.

The man swung. I dodged and punched his forearm, forcing him to drop his weapon. As I tried to snatch the club off the ground, stars exploded in my vision as someone struck the side of my head. My world turned upside down and I collided with the floor.

Hands grabbed me. I tried to regain my bearings, but my vision blurred. People were dragging me somewhere. The heat in the room intensified, and I realized I'd been taken to the pool's edge. The sharp edge of a blade tickled the bottom of my throat.

A red and orange glow covered the majority of my field of vision. The disorientation started to fade, and I noticed Sara and Rodi had made their way to the opposite end of the room, forced toward the exit by two guards with clubs. Everyone else surrounded me, including Lucas and the magnate. The blade at my throat was rockwood, but it could still easily pierce my neck.

Magnate Jancarlo stood over me like a judge prepared to carry out an execution. The warm limestone beneath my hands and knees was the only thing I could manipulate reliably, but what would I do with that? The lava bubbled almost within arm's reach—maybe I could harness its heat to propel myself into the air, but if I did that, I risked skewering myself against the blade on my throat.

"You lost," Magnate Jancarlo said to Sara. "You have one chance to leave this place without a struggle, but if you so much as take one step this way, I'll order my men to kill you, princepa or no. Your commoner friend included. Got it?"

Sara's image shimmered in the heat as she took in the retinue of guards and the two acting as barricades between her and us. There was no way the magnate would let her leave the city alive and risk an alliance between Manasus, Augustin, and Tulchi—the latter would use what happened here as an excuse to impose heavy sanctions on their rival. But Sara's chances at surviving in the city were better than they were here.

Sara met my gaze. She was the Augustin princepa, and I her servant. If she could continue her quest and retake her homeland, then my purpose would be served. I'd even take Lucas and Magnate Jancarlo to the grave. Somehow. She hadn't lost yet.

"Fuck you," she said to the magnate. She knelt before the pool, and at the same time, I felt the gentle tug of her power. The closer she moved to the magma, the stronger it became. She drew heat from the lava, intensifying the eddy currents of the electromagnetic field all elementals used. But she was unpracticed. I closed my eyes and poured my own power into hers.

Sara screamed, her flesh vulnerable to the lava's kiss. She didn't relent though, and a deep *crack* echoed through the chamber. The guards were distracted, so they didn't notice my hand sneak forward and touch the magma's surface. Adding my powers to her multiplied it a hundred-fold.

Stone broke away from stone, and I heard the panicked movements of the guards around me. The long table flew into the air, ripped from the ground and flipping toward the lava. Bodies broke and flailing limbs struck me as I pushed myself flat against the floor, and stone and flesh were flung into the pool. I opened my eyes in time to see the table splash into the fire. Then came the screaming. It brought back vivid memories of the sound of children succumbing to the Imbibing.

A globule of magma as large as a chair struck one of the remaining soldiers on the sides of the room, and his screaming joined the chorus of Jancarlo, Lucas, and the others. The last, unhurt guard looked upon the scene with horror. The man he served—magnate and highest power of Radavich—disappeared into the fire. The limbs of others ruptured from sudden, massive evaporation as they sunk into the viscous mixture. The table, already red-hot, disappeared last.

Rodi tackled the guard to the floor. He yanked the club away and cocked his arm back to swing. The guard, who couldn't have been older than Emil, started to beg, yelling, "No, no, no," but the weapon hit true. Rodi struck again, and the blow made a wet crunch. Then he struck again.

I grabbed two of the dropped bludgeons and circled the pool, then handed one to Sara. "Thank you," I said.

Sara cradled her arm to her stomach. Bubbled flesh riddled the skin and had turned bone-white, the burn much worse than the one I'd suffered in Augustin. "Are you all right?" I asked.

"My uncle and the magnate are dead," she said weakly. "Never better."

Rodi joined us, still clutching his blood-slicked club. "Black winds, that felt good," he said, a wild, animalistic look in his eyes.

"It might be for the best we get out of here."

We ran down the hall, passing people in connecting rooms who were coming out to investigate the screaming. Two guards appeared ahead. I jumped, propelling myself off the limestone, and I flew toward them, the heels of my boots colliding with their faces. One held a spear, and I grabbed onto it to stabilize my flight, landing on the ground with a pirouette in rhythm with the crashing bodies. The nobles we'd passed earlier stared, frozen. Sara and Rodi ran past, and I dropped the spear and joined them.

I led Sara and Rodi through the snarl of hallways toward the main entrance. "I don't think we'll trick our way outa this place," Rodi said.

"You're right," I said. We entered a hallway full of glass orbs, the palace's front door around the bend. Lucas had taken us through the rear entrance, so hopefully none of the guards at the main gate would recognize us. Still, chances of talking our way out were slim.

I examined the tubing connected to the bottom of one of the wall sconces, then ripped it out.

"What are you doing?" Sara asked as I moved from orb to orb. The flames inside the orbs died one by one.

"Creating a diversion, I think. Hide your weapons and follow me."

We rounded the corner and a group of guards stood at the ornate rockwood entrance leading to our freedom. They watched us while guarding a group of nobility and commoners waiting in line. "What's going on in there?" the sergeant asked.

Sara looked at me uncertainly, but put on her noble-in-distress face. "There's fighting in the throne room," she said. She didn't have trouble injecting distress into her voice, sweat beading on her forehead. "I think a group of nobles are trying to assassinate the magnate."

The citizens shifted uncomfortably. "Fighting? From who? Anyone hurt?" the sergeant asked.

"I'm not sure. We fled before we could see anything for certain."

"Who're you? None'a us cleared you to enter the palace earlier."

Sara opened her mouth to summon her story, but an explosion in the other hallway sent all of us stumbling. Shards of broken statues flew into view and bounced off the wall, and flames licked their way toward us, dissipating before they reached anyone. People screamed and guards yelled, and the citizens fled down the hill. We joined them. Half the guards took off toward the source of the blast while the other half waited at the entrance, unsure if they should stop us. No one did. Luckily, no one noticed the droplets of blood staining Rodi's shirt.

Panic-stricken commoners pounded over the palace's main bridge at the bottom of the hill. When we reached the cobblestone street at the other end, Sara shuddered and let out a whimper as she slowed to a stop beneath a glowing bulb hanging from a giant mushroom. Her composure dissolved, and her arm trembled as she stared at her burned hand.

"One second," I said. I ripped a piece of cloth from my sleeve and climbed down the slicked rocks to the stream's edge, then returned, carefully wrapping the drenched bandage around her hand.

"Need to leave," Rodi growled, eyeing the passers-by on the street corner who watched us.

"We have to cool her arm or she'll go into shock," I said. My tone made it clear it wasn't up for discussion, and I finished tying the cloth. "Better?" I asked.

"Yes," she said, and forced a smile.

A group of six soldiers appeared at the end of the street, running at us. Rodi moved his feet into a fighting stance, but I touched his elbow. The patrol parted and ran around us, racing across the bridge and up the hill. Rodi pulled his elbow away from me. "Don't touch me."

A low-pitched drone filled the air, echoing across the cavern from the palace hilltop—a wind instrument so loud that it seemed to vibrate the insides of my ears. Everyone on the street stopped what they were doing to cup their ears.

It faded, and Rodi muttered, "*Dora-sa,*" under his breath. "The martial horn," he said more loudly. "It means no one can enter or leave the city. Need to go or we'll get trapped in this part of town."

The palace stood between us and Rodi's hideout, so the crew leader led us in a wide arc through the city. We followed a river lined with mushrooms twice my size, fishing boats, and shacks for lobster divers. The crowds thinned with each street we passed.

Upon reaching Mud's Cairn—the district Rodi's hideout lay in—we encountered a barricaded checkpoint at the end of a street manned with half a dozen spearmen. A line of Radavich citizens were waiting to pass through it.

"Fucking city guard," Rodi said. "They'll shake us down. Give us more trouble than we need right now."

"We'll sneak past them," Sara said, and swallowed hard. She needed a place to rest as soon as possible—her complexion had paled further and her breaths came out quick and shallow.

"We're only two blocks from home. Have an idea." He tilted his head toward the sky and let out a chirping sound. Five heartbeats later, another chirp answered back. He waited thirty seconds and did it again. We received another answer, this time closer. "Time to pay our friends in the city guard a visit," he said.

The front of the line brought us into the middle of the barricade, where spearmen surrounded us on all sides. The sergeant, who had a wispy mustache and a yellow bandana tied around his head, held a logbook and a pen. "There a reason you three are trying to cross into this part of town?"

"Our business is our own," Rodi said.

The sergeant closed his book and stepped up to the jafo. "Not anymore. Keep looking at me like that and you'll be seeing plenty of our business though."

"Please," I said, and set a hand on Sara's shoulder. "The martial horn scared my wife while she was working. She burned herself. Please let us pass so we can get her home."

The sergeant turned away from Rodi, and when he saw the pained look in Sara's eyes, his own softened. "Where does she work?"

"Fera do-Sobat," I said, throwing out the name of the place Sara and I had eaten breakfast at hours earlier.

The sergeant approached the princepa and took her forearm into his hands, peering under the wet bandage. "Looks bad. You'll want a doctor. Pyremoss gel or aloe should do it."

"We have aloe at home," I said.

"You'll still wanna see a doctor. Pyremoss gel does better against infections. By the looks of it, she'll need plenty over the coming week."

I nodded. "Absolutely. Thank you."

"Sergeant?" one of the spearmen said. "Can you take a look here?"

The man handed the sergeant a piece of paper and the sergeant studied it. He glanced at Sara and me, then down again. He handed the paper back to his subordinate, and when his hand moved to his side sword, Sara punched him. Her fist connected beneath his jaw, and he fell backward, dropping the book. The city guard lowered the points of their spears.

The sergeant recovered, but gasped when an arrow pierced his shoulder blade from above. A spearman fell to another arrow a moment later. The citizens in line behind us screamed and ran, and the spearmen's heads swiveled as they searched the rooftops for the threat.

The guards' better vision picked out Rodi's crew before I did. The crew members materialized from the darkness of the nearby alleys, illuminated by azure geodes crusting the passageways. They carried all manner of cruel weaponry, smiling as they took their time closing in on the barricades. They outnumbered the guards three-to-one.

One of the guards dropped his spears. "Mercy," he said, and his two comrades followed suit. Swords were strapped to their sides, but they didn't draw them. They bowed their heads forward in submission, and one of them whispered something incomprehensible. Then I heard the name "Fheldspra."

Rodi snuck up behind one of the guards, snaked his arm around the man's neck, and laughed as one of his crew members shoved a knife into the man's stomach, the weapon angled upward so it dug deep into the chest cavity. Rodi let go, and the guard fell to the ground like a ragdoll.

Rodi's crew taunted and hooted at the guards as they killed

them. I stood motionless, focused on counting upward, trying to prevent the red from leaking into my head again, taking a deep breath. *Ignore the impulses*, I told myself. Impulses meant punishment. When I watched these men and women buzz with joy, these people who would help Sara retake Augustin, all I saw was Olevic Pike over and over again. The princepa watched the spectacle, her expression unreadable until she quivered from the pain in her arm.

The Jakar stirring inside me, the one who no longer existed, was getting harder to ignore. Did I want to ignore him though?

Cassandra rifled through the pockets of one of the guards as the man looked up at her, blood bubbling from his mouth. His eyes rolled into the back of his head before she finished. When I looked away, I found Rodi watching me.

I tried to hide my feelings as well as Sara did by focusing on the discarded paper the sergeant had been holding. On it were a dozen sketches of wanted men and women, with surprisingly accurate pictures of Sara and me at the bottom. Below our pictures, an entry that said, *WANTED FOR MURDER/USE OF ILLEGAL MUNITIONS.*

Rodi's crew moved with an excited energy as we headed down the deserted street. I tailed Rodi and Sara, thinking of how much the mercenaries had enjoyed themselves. I trembled the way the guards had, but not from fear.

I SLATHERED PYREMOSS gel on Sara's arm. "We have to go to Tulchi."

We were in one of Rodi's other safe houses—a smaller place where most of the crew was crammed in the adjacent room, a few of them roaming throughout the house, doing who knew what with the drugs they pedaled. Sara and I were alone in one of two bedrooms, the princepa lying on a rotted mattress while I sat next to her, with no light other than a single cluster of amber quartz in the corner illuminating the room, I scooped out another palmful of gel and caressed it over her burn.

"We can't," she said in a low voice. "Rodi's crew wants to collect for the kidnapping job. They'll kill us if we try to leave."

"They won't," I whispered. "You know I can take them." I prayed to Fheldspra that she would let me. I'd had my eager moments hunting for Sorrelo, but that was when my mind had been in a fragile place and throwing myself into serving his purpose came easily. This was not the same at all.

"You really think Tulchi is the answer?" she asked, then winced, pulling her arm back. After a moment she reoffered it and I continued working. "It's not going to happen. It never was."

"Then maybe we should face the fact that Augustin is lost."

Silence settled between us, and muted laughter and clinking glasses from the other side of the wall rushed in to fill the space. Her eyes lost focus, her face almost too dark to see. "We can't let Olevic Pike get away with this," she finally said. "You should understand that better than anyone. My father was not a good man, but he wasn't a sociopath." She struggled with the last sentence, her words edged with annoyance.

"Your uncle was lying, for the record," I said. "Your father never said those things about you to Lucas. You weren't nothing to him." The prospect of saying anything positive about Sorrelo was almost too much to bear, but this wasn't for him. I swallowed and kept going. "He loved you, Emil, and Ffadora deeply. He was just a deeply flawed man."

She showed her teeth through the pain—her attempt at a smile. "I've never heard you talk about my father like that before. You feeling all right?"

"People should be able to voice their understanding of a person without supporting what they've done."

Sara mused for a while, and I wondered if she might believe me. She started breathing hard through her nose—at first I thought from pain, until anger settled into the shadows of her face. "No more talk about my father," she said. "We need to focus on what's important. That means Olevic Pike. The last time men like him ruled the territories without the Sovereign's regulations, they built trade empires by enslaving people en masse and killing anyone who got in their way. Accountability is everything, and the Sovereign is starting to slip in that department. Olevic will put his daughter on the throne and be left to play his table games to his heart's content, then go on to do who knows what once that no longer satisfies him."

"That's interesting," I said. "The fact you brought up slavery. I'm your slave, right? If it's as bad as you say, then free me and show me you can live by your words. We can live as equals. Build a life together as equals."

The words sounded like someone else's, and I almost couldn't believe they were coming out of my mouth as I said them. I'd never considered asking for my freedom before, but the desire grew with each passing second. Sara didn't answer. We could go to Manasus, find Emil and Efadora, and live life one passing at a time. We could continue to look for ways to reclaim Augustin, but we could also take our time, build a concrete strategy, and stay together as a family. We didn't have to spend every waking moment trying to put an Adriann on the throne. *I* didn't have to spend every waking moment with that as my purpose. My purpose could be whatever I wanted it to be.

Sara didn't answer, staring at the wall, thinking.

Chapter 21 – Jakar

JAFA VELMIRA, LEADER of the largest mercenary company in Radavich, Cirk Mezar—'Cat's Eye Company' in Radavich's old tongue—walked with her second-in-command as I led them through the city's industrial park in the city's northeast quarter. The rhythm of her steps lost their usual cadence, and I looked over my shoulder to see her checking our surroundings. I know she wouldn't hesitate to stick her sword in my spine if she thought I was leading her into a trap.

The most powerful of all the jafos and jafas in the city had been the hardest to convince to attend Sara's meeting—most people, even leaders of mercenary crews and companies, avoided this part of Radavich since the martial horn had sounded two passings ago. The city guard had lost total control over the thugs and criminals who now had free rein of Radavich's outer districts.

"The guardsmen are starting to learn," Velmira said as we approached a deserted barricade. Dozens of laborers moved through the checkpoint toward a line of warehouses along Radavich's lake—most businesses had remained open, despite the martial horn, as the palace had given no indication of when the city would end the lockdown. The city was a seafood colony too, subsisting primarily off what they caught in the lake, and people needed to eat.

"The city guard deserted the outskirts and only patrol the housing districts of the nobility and around the palace," I said.

We passed a group of laborers carrying a thirty-foot length of timber toward a loading area of water aqueducts. "Jakar, was it?" Velmira's second-in-command said. She was a tall woman, broad of shoulder and with enough muscle to cleave me in two with the one-hander at her waist. "You sure you know nothing of this meeting? Rumor has it you're close with Mira's Hand. Seems odd she would share so little with you."

"All I know is that the meeting will be worth your while," I said, parroting Sara's words. In truth, the princepa had kept me in the dark, but it had to involve getting her past Radavich's lockdown and into Tulchi. A hard plan that required a lot of bodies.

Dwelling on the fact she'd excluded me from her plans for the first time in weeks caused the ugly feeling in my stomach to worsen.

We reached the entrance to a warehouse built on the shores of Radavich's lake. It belonged to a margrave out on business protecting the territory's northern border, who worked as a distributor for Rodi's Ash operation. I knocked on the door and Cassandra answered. "You're the last to arrive," she said, nodding to Jafa Velmira.

The din of voices dropped a degree when Velmira stepped onto the warehouse floor. A collection of crew and company leaders stood in the center, and a dozen of Rodi's crew lazed against the barrels and crates lining the walls. Rodi and Sara stood in front of the foreman's corner office that they had locked themselves inside of before I'd left to retrieve the jafa.

"Thank you for coming," Sara said to Velmira, who took her place in the middle of the group. All the others seemed to gravitate around the jafa.

"Don't thank me yet. Best tell me what this is about so I can decide if this was a waste of my time." Velmira turned full circle. "Must be interesting if you decided to meet with so many of us."

I ducked beneath an aqueduct that sat on stilts running across the floor, moving away from the congregation. Dozens of crates were stacked on the upper decks rimming the sides of the warehouse, and I leaned against a treadwheel crane used to hoist up whatever floated down the aqueduct. Sara didn't even bother searching me out.

The princepa had changed these last two passings. We'd barely talked—at first she blamed her burn for making it hard to relax, but she spoke with Rodi just fine. The pain almost seemed like an afterthought now. Just like me. We only spent time alone when she let me redress her bandage. Those conversations had been short.

"I have a job for all of you," Sara said. "I want you to help me infiltrate Augustin's capital city and kill the standing magnate, Olevic Pike."

I started. This meeting was supposed to be about recruiting Tulchi, impossible as it was.

A mercenary laughed. So did another. Nobody else joined in. "You wanna kill the man ruling Augustin?" one of the laughing men asked. "With *us*?"

"We'll have the numbers to take the city if everyone helps. Penetrating a city's defenses would be impossible if they knew we were coming, but I know a way in. Once we're inside, it turns into the simple task of locating the Listener. And we have the means of extracting him. I'll need your help to ensure the transfer of power once the Listener is killed."

She was talking about the pathway through the twists that led into the Foundry. If Sara led them through the twists, it would no doubt cause chaos, unless the smiths could be convinced to follow her. The plan was dangerous, but not impossible.

"You want to turn us into an army?" someone asked.

"That's ridiculous."

Sara was the type of person to mirror the merriment of those around her, if only to distract them from her hidden anger. But she didn't joke this time. She held her burned hand close to her body. "Yes. And it's possible. Has anyone noticed what's been going on in the city right now? The chamber commander blew the martial horn, and now the nobility are bunkered down in one section of the city. Why is that?"

Nobody answered. My suspicions were that the nobility feared a rebellion like Augustin's, and had drawn the hand of the law in to protect its gut. Rumors swirled about why the martial horn had remained in effect for so long, but the nobility were always effective at isolating themselves.

It was probably difficult for the palace to conclude the magnate's fate when lava had incinerated all the evidence.

"Magnate Jancarlo is dead," Sara said. "And I killed him."

"Sulf-spit you did," one of the men exclaimed. "And I'm the Sovereign."

"It's true. I killed him because he betrayed me after I asked for his help to retake Augustin for my family. My name is Sara Adriann, and I'm Augustin's princepa."

This bit seemed to resonate. Whispers of Olevic's bounty had no doubt spread through most of the territories by now, and it was no secret Sara Adriann had been roaming the crust. Was it so hard to believe? A few mercenaries—the ones farthest from the princepa and hidden in the press of bodies—set their hands on the hilts of their weapons. But Rodi's crew tracked the guests' movements like predators as they lounged on the barrels and crates.

If anyone tried to cash in on Sara's head, I would kill them.

One of the mercenaries looked at the princepa incredulously. "So how was you supposing you'll pay us? Augustin's hundreds of miles away."

"My family is royalty. All of you will be paid once Olevic Pike is dead and the Adrianns control the throne again."

Another mercenary chimed in. "Some mercenary crews in

Radavich may be fine with IOUs, but I can say for certain that none of the bigger companies here operate under such terms. Pay us half now, half once the job's finished. As men-and women-for-hire, we accept the risk of dying in the crust, but we don't accept the risk of workin' for someone who can't guarantee payment."

Rodi stepped forward. "That's why we steal from the Granite Road. It'll be the greatest heist the territories have ever seen. We'll be our own magnates by the time we reach Augustin."

Everyone gaped at him, me included, and he reveled in our shock. Now I knew why Sara had excluded me from her plans. I found her peering into my spot in the shadows, trying to parse my reaction. So she did still notice my existence. I forced myself to look at the crowd and found most of them still balking at the idea.

"Towns can defend against bandits," Rodi continued, "but what about an organized force of sellswords? Force each town to give up their valuables and continue onward. Rinse and repeat. There're at least a couple dozen towns between here and Augustin and a hundred small-scale settlements. Easy pickings for us, so long as we find our grit and take it."

Some looked at the others, considering. They were starting to take the bait. "What do you think is gonna happen if we go blazing through the territory?" Rodi asked. "After we finish setting our pretty lady here up on the Augustin throne and life returns to normal, no self-respecting merchant or traveler would dare risk traveling without protection, even on the Granite Road. Business'll skyrocket."

"Let's not talk about that right now," Sara said. "I'm only trying to kill Olevic Pike."

"You'll become a legend, Hand. Someone like you up there? You'll have the power of your family name and the love of the commoners."

"Not now," she ordered.

Rodi looked ready to argue the point, but a mercenary cut

him off—a man with a gut that pushed against his leathers, and soft, flabby arms. "I got family in Hamagard right in the path you want us to take. How're you planning to keep people like them safe?"

"No one will be harmed during our march," Sara said. "Those on the Granite Road know how dangerous it is living in the crust. Robberies are a fact of life, and they'll deal with us in stride. Once my family retakes Augustin, we'll pay reparations to Radavich, and all of you will be richer than you could ever dream."

Judging by the worry lining the faces of several others, that man wasn't the only one with family in the path of this beast of a plan, but the last part of Sara's claim seemed to temper their concerns.

Pillaging the Granite Road would guarantee the full attention of the territories, as well as the Sovereign, the primordia, and their armies, but it seemed like I was the only one in the room who saw the lunacy in the plan. Tying a leash to a mercenary army would be like leashing a bobbit worm. Innocent people would die. When it came to pitching such a terrible plan though, this was the group to do it to. The greed in their eyes was clear.

This idea had been Rodi's. Sara wanted her revenge on Olevic Pike, but didn't want to risk asking Tulchi, and Rodi had convinced her this was the only way. These mercenaries needed to realize that only disorder and violence waited for them if they took to the Granite Road.

The head of the snake had to go. And if I wanted to discourage these people from marching on the Granite Road without it, best make the statement loud and clear in front of their eyes. There was no time to plan. I had to do this now while there was still doubt.

I moved out of the shadows and beneath the stilts of the aqueduct, calmly enough for no one to notice. "I'm in," Jafa Velmira said. "If Magnate Jancarlo is dead, now's the time to organize. I'm tired of being holed up in this city anyway."

Circling the edge of the crowd, I grabbed the handle of a dagger strapped to the side of a mercenary as I stalked past him. Cassandra watched the crowd from beside Rodi, looking almost bored, and my grip on the dagger tightened.

The cook outside Lucas Adriann's home staring at Cassandra with hollow eyes, shifting his weight in desperation. Her blade flashing into his stomach over and over again.

Cassandra inhaled sharply when my blade slid into her back, and she turned to see me standing there. The din of voices distracted Rodi enough for him to not notice me nudge Cassandra to the side. She obeyed dumbly as her hand reached behind her, as if scratching an itch. Then I pounced.

Rodi caught my wrist as the blade flew for his throat. He swept my legs from under me and sent me crashing onto the rocky floor, and before I could overcome my surprise, he was on top of me, knee digging into my back. He hammered at the back of my hand with a fist and forced me to let go of the dagger. I gritted my teeth and took the pain in stride, but didn't say a word.

"You already made your intentions clear," he said into my ear. I tried to turn my body over, but he put more of his weight into his knee. "Remember what I said the consequence would be?"

He picked up the blade slicked with Cassandra's blood, but in my periphery, I saw Sara grab his arm. "Don't. He belongs to me."

The man yanked his arm free, and the dagger's tip pricked the back of my neck, followed by the sensation of warm blood trailing down to my collarbone. "Fucker needs a blade in the ear," he said. "He's only gonna be trouble if we take him with us, elemental or no."

"He won't be trouble. I promise."

An old anger rose in my bones. Rodi had no right to decide whether I lived or died. He was nothing—a pawn in Sara's game, and now a body standing in my way. For a moment, I no longer cared if he tried to plunge that blade into my neck. I was stronger than him. I wasn't a victim to the whims of a stranger. I wasn't the cook who'd worked for Lucas.

I was my own person.

My fingers dug into the rock as they curled inward. The pressure of the blade on my neck increased, and the point pushed deeper into my flesh, but Rodi gasped as his strength folded. The stacks of crates creaked and the ground trembled. My head hurt as I pushed with all my might—I would bring this place down on my head, if only to scare everyone off. They would receive my message one way or another.

Elementals couldn't manipulate elements inside organic matter, but they could still draw in their heat. I drank in the warmth from Rodi's body as he pushed his knee into my back, transforming his energy into power. Deep cracks appeared in the warehouse floor, sending pulleys swinging and a stack of barrels to the floor. Swords and daggers flew out of their sheaths, slicing at legs and arms. Rodi gasped and crumpled to the floor beside me.

"Ig, stop!"

Fear of the Word cut through me like a hot knife. I stopped. Voices rose as mercenaries retrieved their weapons and clutched at superficial wounds, but many watched me in silence. Rodi's crew rushed to their leader's side. The man shivered violently and his eyes rolled around in his head.

"Cassandra's gone," one of Rodi's crew members said. "If Rodi goes too, I'm opening Jakar's throat. Don't give a shit what you say, Hand."

"What is he?" someone asked.

Sara knelt down as I turned on my back. She gripped my wrist with her unbandaged hand, and I couldn't tell if the gesture was meant to connect us or to make her feel like she had control. "Are you trying to ruin everything?" she whispered.

I couldn't bring myself to answer. It made me sick to think of the irritation in her voice as she'd yelled the word 'Ig.'

"We have a shot to remind the territories that the Adrianns still exist," she continued. "You're twisting my arm here."

She took a deep breath and stood. The mercenary's question about what I was still lingered in the air—Cassandra lay face down in a pool of blood, already forgotten by everyone except Rodi's crew. For a moment I thought Sara might hold onto our secret, but I was wrong. Again. "He is elemental," she said. "And so am I. Jakar, stand up."

I shook my head.

"Please stand up."

I only looked at her.

"*Ig*, stand."

I picked myself up but refused to break her gaze. I sensed the cold rage from Rodi's crew as they hunched over their leader. No doubt they would attack me if Rodi didn't wake up. I hoped I was that lucky—I knew Sara would let me kill them, and then it would ruin her plans. The muscles in her jaw clenched and unclenched. A tic of hers when she was conflicted.

But she wasn't conflicted enough.

"Ig, turn around and face everyone."

I shook my head. She was better than this. But I obeyed anyway.

"Ig, tell them that if they choose to follow me, you will use your elemental power to ensure we succeed."

The sway of Sara's commands over me entranced the crowd. With power like mine, pillaging the Granite Road wasn't such a daunting feat anymore, and I watched as confidence slowly replaced their alarm. I hated them, I realized. Hate was a feeling I hadn't acknowledged in years, not since I'd last seen a kadiph, and it was strange. Invigorating.

The pressure mounting in the base of my skull pushed the feeling out, though. "If—if you choose to follow Sara," I said, my voice wavering, "I will use my elemental power to ensure you succeed."

My alien power scared these hardened men and women,

but the princepa's total control over me contaminated that fear. The hate seeped back in. I would find a way to kill anyone in this room who chose to follow Rodi and Sara, one way or another.

"He's bound to me," Sara said. "It's old magic that comes from his homeland, and he's incapable of disobeying under pain of death."

"This makes no sense," a mercenary said. "The man can't disobey you? That's impossible."

"It's as possible as the primordia moving rock. He's the most powerful of all of us, and with him and the rest of you, we'll take Augustin."

The conviction in her voice broke me in two.

"Fuck this place," someone finally said. "Invading a city's insanity, but we can at least rob our weight in riches before then. I'll go."

"Aye," another said. "Let the primordia come. They can't stand against an army and your elemental. Sovereign's probably too wrapped up in his boy to notice anyway. He's as weak as the magnates."

The proclamation startled some. How often did someone speak of the Sovereign as anything other than all powerful? But the more they chewed on the idea, the less it seemed farfetched.

Several minutes later, most of the mercenaries reached a consensus. They would follow Sara. Rodi hadn't woken from his stupor, and someone laid a blanket on top of him. I refused to turn around and face the princepa. Maybe I could help her see the consequences of her plan before we reached Coracas, the first town in their path.

"The primordia will come," I said over my shoulder in a low voice. "They'll kill us all."

"They're welcome to try."

"People in the crust will die."

"They'll know who Mira's Hand is, which means they know I'm a champion of the commoners. They'll submit."

She was under the delusion these mercenaries would listen to her and restrain themselves on the Granite Road, all because she was Mira's Hand. Thanks to the Ebonrock though, I knew what happened when one group held so much power over another. Dehumanizing one's victims became a simple task: to push the boundaries, convincing oneself that their victim's pain wasn't like the pain they could feel. Until the time came when if one looked at their victims, all they saw were animals.

Was that how I had corrupted Sorrelo?

"What's our next step, princepa?" Jafa Velmira asked.

Mateo had been right about me all along.

Chapter 22 – Jakar

Three years ago

QUIN, AKHILIAN, CAUBI, and I stood in a circle within our room. Each had our right arm on the left shoulder of the person next to us. "Slaves no more," I said. "All of you deserve the power to forge your own future. They are nothing without us. Now is the time to show them."

They listened to me with fire in their eyes—a fire that burned brightly within my own heart. I was their leader and I would rescue them from this place. The masters had promised great rewards when we left the city, and this promise had enamored the other students, but the prospect left a bad taste in my mouth, and I didn't want to stick around to see the truth of the matter. It seemed too good to be true, and my friends agreed.

I'd summoned the will to escape knowing those around me would step into the void as well. They feared that step, but I didn't. Not anymore. I would show them the way.

"Master Orino will be waiting for us at the gate soon," I said. "We need to act fast. We'll only have a five-minute window when the masters change shifts."

If we wanted any hope of escaping Bloodreach, we needed to sever the head of the snake. Master Orino had once confided in me that only Master Galleir, as head master of the compound, could communicate with the kadiphs deep inside the crust. We had to kill Master Galleir if we wanted any hope of getting far, far away before the masters' masters started on our trail. But as far as Master Orino knew, the plan only involved him guiding us a few miles out of Bloodreach, where he would leave us with a map. What would he think when he came home to the Ebonrock compound to find his colleague dead?

My friends followed me down the hallway. Akhilian and Caubi carried two packs each—they would hide outside the masters' quarters while Quin and I slipped inside to kill Master Galleir.

The ever-present ruby glow of the Burning Mountains waited for us outside, casting long shadows in front of the faces of the compound's buildings. We snuck through the patches of darkness, keeping an eye out for masters and students, but the place was calm. Our final Imbibing was scheduled three passings from now, and the masters had given us little work to allow us rest. It only increased my sense of purpose to get Akhilian and Caubi out of here.

The masters' quarters were as modest as the students'. A long time ago, I had resented their power over us, but learned to shift my hate to the kadiphs. The kadiphs controlled the masters like the masters controlled us. Master Galleir still had to die though. Any master who beat us and treated us like dirt deserved death.

Green flames lit by refined bluestone and boron flickered in torch placements along the wall, and a collection of brooms and mops were stuffed inside a closet to our right. "You two wait in here," I whispered to Akhilian and Caubi. They nodded and shuffled into the small space.

Quin started chewing on her bottom lip. I offered her a reassuring look and it seemed to help. Feeding off each other's confidence was a habit we'd formed over the years—whenever one of us expressed fear or doubt, we would meet each other's eyes, and suddenly those feelings would fade away. It had helped me countless times.

I'd familiarized myself with the layout of the masters' quarters whenever they'd forced us to clean their quarters, and I knew Galleir's room waited at the far end of the building, marginally larger than those belonging to his brethren. None of the rooms had doors, and beyond each entryway, lumps cast in a faint green glow hid beneath blankets on stone cots.

Quin's hand snaked into mine and I squeezed it. Her palms were sweating. Or were mine? I pulled out the length of rockwood I'd fashioned into a stake that hid under my shirt and snuck into the room. Master Galleir slept on his side, body shifting in cadence with his breathing. The masters were light sleepers—almost as light as the students—and I carefully padded across the floor on my bare feet. Quin still held onto my hand.

We reached the bed and stood side-by-side. Before I could second-guess myself, I plunged the makeshift weapon into where I figured the bottom of his armpit would be.

He grunted. Before he could turn, Quin stabbed him in the back with a muffled hiss as I withdrew my stake. All the anger she'd accumulated over the years glinted in her eyes, and she stabbed again before I could attack a second time.

Several strikes later, and Master Galleir was nothing more than a body beneath a gory blanket. I realized that Quin and I had held the other's hand through the whole ordeal, our palms slick with sweat. "Let's get out of here," Quin whispered. Her breathing was labored and she trembled.

"One second," I said. I released my hold on her and pulled at an unsoiled part of the blanket.

The bound and gagged body of Master Orino stared at the far wall, clothes drenched in blood.

"No," I said, stumbling back. A shadow passed over us, and I turned to find a figure in the doorway. The kadiph with the hands of rock. I hadn't seen her in years, but she was unmistakable. Someone struck flint to tinder and a bright red flame appeared at the head of a torch, held by a man standing at the kadiph's side.

The kadiph started laughing. "Well, this is a shame."

Clinking and shuffled footsteps echoed through the hallway, and Akhilian and Caubi appeared, held at knifepoint by two more masters I'd never seen before. The kadiph entered the room, and the others followed to stand along the edges of the wall. Quin and I moved closer together, and each of us pointed our wooden stakes toward her. If the four of us could fight our way out of the compound, we could make a run for it toward the Outside. The kadiph would never follow us, if Orino's stories were true.

"This failure doesn't just rest on your shoulders," she said. She gestured toward the bed. "I don't think I've ever met someone more pathetic. Betrays us, then turns around and betrays you right back."

Quin raised her weapon higher, its surface shiny with gore. "You're lying. He wanted to help us. He was the only master who cared."

The kadiph rubbed her knuckles, and the sound of rock grinding against rock sent a chill down my spine. "He told Master Galleir someone might try to hurt him. Wouldn't share why he felt that way though. It's a good thing Galleir questioned Orino's loyalty enough to call me in. It took some coercion, but the man spilled his guts out. Metaphorically. Thank you for taking care of the literal part." She waved a dismissive hand. "It doesn't matter. What matters now is figuring out what to do with the four of you."

She paced in front of Akhilian and Caubi, each of whom trickled blood down their necks from the blades held to their throats. "First I would like to know one thing. Why did you want to escape?"

"Why do you think?" Quin asked. "The last Imbibing is in three passings. We didn't feel like dying, obviously." She had included herself among Akhilian and Caubi, even though she knew she could have survived.

This was all my fault.

"Figures," the kadiph said. "There's always a few of you before each Imbibing. The funny thing about a life like yours is that after a while, you stop questioning why some of your fellow students have disappeared. All of you are so painfully predictable. It's a good trait to have in those meant to serve."

It slowly started to become clear. Of course other students would have attempted a secret escape. I thought back to those who had disappeared in the weeks leading up to each Imbibing, and remembered how I'd assumed they had died from one of the many jobs the fellowship forced onto us. Why wasn't I smart enough to have considered this?

"Do you know where we find *masters* for the Ebonrock?" she asked, mocking the title. "They bend the elements like you. It would make sense that they were once students, yes? But they aren't any type of student. They are of a particular sort, solely comprised of those who try to escape before an Imbibing."

"Is that what this is?" Caubi asked. She flinched when the blade dug deeper into her skin. "Are you offering us jobs?"

The kadiph laughed again. "You'll have to prove to us you have a different type of courage first. The courage to commit to absolute loyalty. Do that, and you'll have a chance to live without risking death to another Imbibing."

"How would we do that?" Akhilian asked.

"I'll give you a hint. If only one student attempts to escape before an Imbibing, we kill them. The four of you will need each other if one of you is to become a master."

The realization made me sick. "Whichever deserter kills their fellow students becomes the next master."

The kadiph looked at me up and down. "I know you. Jakar, isn't it? Master Galleir said you were always the first to wake after each Imbibing. Honestly, I'm surprised to see someone of your caliber here." Her attention switched to

Quin. "Same goes with you. If anyone were to survive the Imbibings, it would be you two. But the answer to your question is yes, Jakar. It's the only way to redeem oneself. The alternative is death."

I looked from Quin to Akhilian, to Caubi. The color had drained from their faces, and I imagined I looked the same. These three had been by my side for more than a decade, watching my back and making this life worth living. "No," I said. "I won't do it."

"Me neither," Quin said.

The kadiph set her hands on her hips. "You'd face certain death instead of a chance to become a master? This branch of the fellowship will be moving on soon and the masters will be headed to the next city in only months. One of you could be there to help the next batch."

"Fuck off," Quin said.

I couldn't help but look at Akhilian and Caubi. They had been conspicuously silent in their responses.

"Well, all right then," the kadiph said. She turned to Akhilian and Caubi. "The offer's off the table for Jakar and Quin, but that's only better for you two. Now each of you have a fifty-percent chance at succeeding."

Before they could respond, the kadiph nodded and those holding knives to my friends' throats shoved Akhilian and Caubi to their hands and knees. The kadiph unsheathed a blade from her waist and let it clatter to the ground. "Better do it quick. The first to have second thoughts is the dead one."

They eyed the knife stupidly. Akhilian scrambled for the blade. Caubi leaned back and put her hands up. "Akhilian, please."

Akhilian stabbed her in the soft notch between her collarbones.

"No!" I said, lunging forward, but the kadiph turned around and punched me in the chest. It was like being struck by a meteor, and I stumbled backward onto the bed. Master

Orino's warm blood soaked into my clothing, and I crumpled to the ground.

As I tried and failed to inhale, I stared at Caubi as she tried to stem the spurts of blood, gurgling, face contorted in agony. She collapsed onto the rock and stilled. Akhilian started sobbing, holding his knees to his chest. Quin looked ready to kill everyone in the room, but the two men who had been holding Akhilian and Caubi hostage now held weapons to her throat.

"We have ourselves our newest master," the kadiph said. She looked down at me and smiled. "But congratulations are in order for the two of you. You were willing to die instead of kill your friends, and that's proof enough that you have the fire necessary to survive any Imbibing we throw at you. You'll continue as planned."

Akhilian gasped, eyes glassy. "You mean… I didn't have to kill her?"

The kadiph looked at him with pity. "You always have a choice. We needed a new master to replace Master Orino though, so consider yourself graduated. I doubt you would have survived for long around the other students anyway, once they learned what you did."

"You better kill me now," I wheezed. The kadiph had cracked multiple ribs, but I didn't care. "I'll never obey you. I'll kill every master the first chance I get."

She tsked. "So much spirit, Jakar. And so much to learn. We do have ways to make you obey. You think we'd allow our students to leave the fellowship with so much power, but without our absolute control over that power?"

"What are you talking about?" Quin nearly screamed. She cried through her rage, and inched forward as though ready to skewer herself on the blades pointed at her.

The kadiph's amusement faded. "Don't worry about that now. Just focus on surviving the last Imbibing. Unfortunately, we'll need to restrain the two of you before we can perform the flesh binding, so each of you will be going into solitary confinement." She clapped. "Your lives within the Black Depths will come soon enough."

Two of her men pulled me to my feet, which felt like the kadiph punching me all over again. Agony coursed through my chest as they dragged me past Akhilian, who continued to weep in a puddle of Caubi's blood. I felt the pull of Quin's power, like the twang of an instrument's string, and she cried out when the kadiph slapped her with the bone-crunching force of her stone hand. Quin went limp as another man caught her.

What did the kadiph mean by our new lives in the Black Depths? Was that the life of comfort the masters had promised us? And what was a flesh binding?

Anguish overwhelmed my curiosity. I'd failed my friends. I'd tried to lead them to freedom, but I had only led them to death.

Chapter 23 – Efadora

THE DOOR TO my bedroom creaked open, and I nearly picked up the jewelry box on my nightstand to throw it, thinking the intruder was Meike. But I remembered in my sleep-addled state that she wasn't my guard anymore. I looked up to see Mateo, of all people, standing there.

No one was allowed in my room except for Dala, my serving girl, but Mateo's piety—and the fact he was Augustin's master smith—seemed to open more doors than the Sovereign himself. "Go away," I said. "I'm sleeping."

"You've been sleeping a lot these past several passings, princepa. Your kidnapping was hard on you, but life must go on. Come on. Your brother wants to speak with you."

"He can speak to my tomb when I'm dead. At least then I can't tell him to go away."

The light from my sitting room backlit Mateo's figure, making it difficult to see his expression. "You've slept this entire passing," he said. "If you don't start acting like your normal self, people will wonder if something's wrong."

"Manasus changed me. I live a life of extreme comfort now."

The master smith left without a word, and Dala replaced him, lighting the torches along the walls. I stared at the light's reflection dancing along the copper tub's side as she picked up my basket of dirty clothes for washing. "Sorry, Efadora," she said. "Would let you sleep in more, but they're making me do this."

"It's fine." Maybe it was for the best that I left my bed. My head pounded from all the sleeping.

A quick wash in the tub revitalized my senses. Goosebumps rose on my skin from the heat, reminding me of the scabs running from my left collarbone to the start of my right armpit where Carmen's father tried to cut me open. A scar I would soon be proud of. Scars provided better camouflage inside the Pit.

Not that I had a future in the Pit anymore.

Ten minutes later, I emerged from my quarters to find my personal guard standing at attention—a man who had trailed my shadow nonstop for a week, and whose name I still didn't know. The man seemed content with not speaking to me, which made him my favorite guard in the palace. Mateo waited in the hallway, hands clasped behind his back.

"What does Emil want?" I asked.

"It's not my place to divulge."

"Funny you say that after you broke that promise to my father."

Mateo's brow twitched. He had told Emil that Ig, our family's servant, somehow possessed elemental power and worked—in the master smith's words—as a hitman for Father. My father had sworn Mateo to secrecy, yet Mateo spilled the beans as soon as my father joined the dirt.

"It didn't make sense to maintain Ig's secret after your father passed," the master smith said as we walked. Busts of animals native to the crust, from wolfbats to razorback centipedes, lined the hallway, watching us. "I honored my word until I decided your brother needed to know. Ig's likely the most dangerous man in Mira. If you saw what I saw in Augustin, you'd agree."

The prospect of Ig —the quiet, stone-skinned servant

from Sulian Daw—wielding impossible powers fascinated me. The man could apparently hold magma without being harmed. Hopefully I'd be able to see for myself.

"Speaking of breaking promises, I'm surprised you haven't tried to sneak out," Mateo said.

Emil and Magnate Bardera had assumed my willingness to stay in the palace meant I was finally afraid of the dangers in the city. "No point."

"No? Being cooped up in here for so long seems to be driving you half-crazy."

"Yep."

"Why all the sleeping? I always remembered you as more of a caged fox whenever someone told you that you couldn't do something."

"I don't want to talk about it."

"Is it because of that friend of yours?"

"You heard what I said, master smith. Drop it."

I would've normally felt odd reprimanding an adult, but he was being an ass. Carmen was the last person I wanted to think about right now.

Inside the throne room, Emil and Magnate Bardera sat opposite each other at one of the long tables, the place cleared out of the nobility who often attended the magnate. Emil's forehead rested in his palm as he read a sheet of paper laying on top of a map of Mira. He was frowning deeply. "What's going on?" I asked.

He looked up. "Oh, hi, Efadora. Good to see you're up. I've been talking with the magnate about a message we received from Radavich this morning."

I slid onto the bench beside him and he offered the single sheet of paper.

Jancarlo and Lucas dead. Sara marching south with mercenary army. Plan to raid Granite Road.
Stop her.
-Ig

Magnate Bardera leaned forward, the skin around her eyes wrinkling as she brooded. "Do you think your sister had your uncle and Magnate Jancarlo killed for supporting Olevic Pike?"

"I wouldn't put it past her," Emil said. "Though I'm not sure how she would have managed it."

"Not sure?" Mateo asked. He paced in front of the dais leading to Magnate Bardera's throne. "You know what Ig is."

Emil rubbed at his whiskers. My brother once sported a thick, well-trimmed beard, until he had to shave it to sneak out of Augustin. Just another casualty of our family's betrayal. "If Jancarlo Haresh is dead, then Radavich's audencia—they call it the Assembly of Stars there, right?— they'll have to figure out who will succeed him. Jancarlo didn't have children."

"Apparently times are good to overthrow royal families."

I touched the end of Ig's message. "Ig wants us to stop Sara? He said she's planning to pillage the Granite Road."

Emil's forehead creased. "How would Sara be in charge of a mercenary army? If she is, I can't imagine her recklessly marching them onto the Granite Road."

"So either Ig's a liar or Sara is doing exactly what he's saying. This note's several passings old, too." I drummed my fingers. "What about the courier who delivered it? Maybe they know something."

"Left already to continue his deliveries," Magnate Bardera said. "He warned us there were rumors of Magnate Jancarlo's death when he left Radavich. He did say the city was on lockdown, that only approved government workers and courier services were allowed in and out of the capital. Crime was escalating on the outskirts of the city, but he saw no sign of a mercenary army."

"That doesn't mean Ig wasn't telling the truth," Emil added.

Mateo left the front of the dais and leaned down beside my brother, setting a hand where Emil's shoulder and neck met.

"We have to hope Sara doesn't use Ig to reach Augustin. It would spell disaster for your claim to the throne if she did."

"How do you figure?"

"The people of Augustin hate Ig for executing Bolivar. A couple months under Olevic Pike's rule won't make them forget that. Not to mention the entire Foundry will hate him as soon as they find out what he is."

Mateo gave Emil a reassuring squeeze, but Emil shrugged the hand off and left the bench. "People will be able to see that Ig is a good person," Emil said. "We can tell them about the flesh binding."

"That's wishful thinking and you know it. Ig can single-handedly destroy your chances of ever ruling Augustin. They'll only see him as evil, as an agent of the Great Ones, and that will poison the reputation of anyone associated with him."

Emil stalked to the rock garden pond built beside the throne, where fish, crustaceans, and bioluminescent flora collected in a miniature ecosystem. He studied it without a word, his back to us.

Mateo continued, "Hypothetically, let's say Sara did raise a mercenary army. Mercenaries have to be paid, correct? Where would she get the money?"

I knew Sara well—the answer was easy. "That's why they're raiding the Granite Road," I said. "Imagine all the stuff they could steal along the way."

My theory left them stewing. The idea of Sara robbing the Granite Road so she could bring an army to Augustin wasn't as horrifying as it sounded though. As long as Sara kept her army well managed, they would keep the damage to a minimum. And Sara could lead any group of people as well as Emil. *Not every solution to your problems will be a savory one*, as she liked to say more than anything else.

Magnate Bardera's pen broke the silence as it scratched against parchment. The plight of the Adrianns couldn't put a hold on her responsibilities as magnate. It made me think of a time before the coup, when life was calm. Boring. "If Ig's message speaks the truth, then this mercenary army is already well on its way to Augustin," she said without looking up.

Emil turned around and faced us. "Which is why we need to leave."

"Are you serious?" I asked.

"Getting word about Sara's army is what we've been waiting for." Emil returned to the table and bent over the map. "We'll ride west until we reach the border of the Radavich territory, then turn south onto Radavich's Granite Road. Sara's army should have already passed through by the time we reach it. We'll ride south on the army's heels until we catch up, and then we'll find out why Ig felt the need to tell us to stop Sara."

Conflict worked its way into the lines of my brother's face. Ig's note had disturbed him a lot more than it had me. "C'mon, Emil," I said. "It's our big sister. We needed an army and she found one. Like you said, this is exactly what we've been waiting for."

"You're right," he finally said. "We should trust Sara. If we go, are you sure you're all right to leave Manasus? If you stayed, you would have to stay in the palace a little longer, but I'm sure the magnate could let you to see more of your friends."

"No," I said with every ounce of conviction. "I don't have friends here. I'm going where you go." I tried to make the matter as clear as crystal on my face. My life here was done.

Emil eyed me, and for a moment the image of Carmen sobbing in her cell hit me like a cold shock to the system. I scowled to myself. "I was hoping you'd want to come," he said after half an eternity. "This is a family matter."

Magnate Bardera paused in her work. "Did you still want the cartographer you requested, Emil?"

"Yes, ma'am. My plan is to stay off the main roads when we leave Manasus, to avoid bounty hunters. Everyone knows

Efadora is staying with you. I wouldn't be surprised if word has gotten out that I'm here as well."

"Then you'll have your cartographer, as well as a contingent of riders to escort you."

"That's more than generous. Thank you."

The magnate offered a kind smile. "Manasus is a small territory, and I'm sorry I cannot help in a greater way. For now, at least. Consider this recompense for what happened to your sister." She waved at her guards. "You two. Go get Meike as well as Oversergeant Eslid."

The man who I assumed was Oversergeant Eslid arrived first. He wasn't a very large man, with silver rings in his brown braided hair and toned arms exposed by a sleeveless tunic. Tattoos of flowering vines wrapped their way around his biceps. Magnate Bardera left her seat and clapped him on the back. "Good to see you, Oversergeant."

"Pleasure, Magnate."

Bardera waved Emil over. "This is Prenz Emil Adriann. The girl at the table is the Prinzessa Efadora, as you've probably guessed."

Eslid cocked his head at my brother. "The Rock Snake? I imagined you as older. A little bigger, too."

My brother eyed the magnate, but Bardera only took a step back. "Sorry to disappoint," Emil said coolly.

The oversergeant gave my brother a long look, then his gaze went to Emil's waist. "Is that it? That a Meteor Blade?"

Emil had sanded down the paint and rare metals of the scabbard until it looked plain as a commoner's, but the hilt still gave it away to anyone who knew what to look for. It was made from bone and black leather, identical to Bardera's, although the two Blades differed at the pommel. My family's sword had a polished black jewel while Bardera's was made from jade. My brother eyed the small smile on Eslid's face, then returned it, grinning as he pulled the blade from its sheath. The Blade's edge gleamed faint blue, the glow barely visible, the flat of the sword polished to a shine.

"Forgive me," Eslid said, bowing. "Been months since the magnate last entertained me. My eyes have been sore to see such master craftsmanship." He nodded toward the wall mount over Bardera's throne where her Meteor Blade hung in its ornate scabbard.

"Craftsmanship we'll never see again, if Mateo's to be believed," Emil said. If I remembered correctly, the Meteor Blades had been crafted by smiths working the Star Mines and gifted to the six magnates over a hundred years ago. The Star Mines was a place of power where the Foundry mined its rhidium—how the Blades' rhidium edge was forged was a mystery, since rhidium oxidized as soon as it touched the air, but nobody could ask the smiths of the Star Mines how it was done. Only the master smith and his council of senior arc smiths knew where the Mines were located, as the smiths who made their pilgrimages there never returned, except to deliver rhidium shipments once per decade. It was the final resting place for members of the Foundry, and Mateo would die before he gave up its location.

"Have you used it in battle?" Eslid asked.

"A couple of times."

"What I would have done to see that. For a Meteor Blade to see battle is a rare thing. Of course the magnates do not fight on the front lines, and the territories have seen relative peace since the forging of the Blades. The edge bites especially hard, does it not?"

Emil offered the blade by its hilt. "Hold it. You can feel its power if you close your eyes."

Eslid stiffened. "A warrior does not loot the hand of another."

My brother paused, confused. "Sorry, Emil," Bardera said. "It's a soldier's custom here in Manasus. When you take another's blade, it is only after you've bested them in a sparring match or defeated them in battle. You'll come to understand Eslid and his riders over the coming weeks."

Emil nodded and sheathed his blade. A moment later, the

sound of chains dragging over rock came from the hallway outside, and my former guard entered the room between two escorts, shackles still on her wrists and ankles. She looked smaller without her plate. Bored too, but otherwise unperturbed by the last two weeks she'd spent in her prison cell.

"Ah, Meike," Magnate Bardera said, glaring at the woman. "And how are you feeling?"

"Fine." Meike took in the room's occupants through the dirty bangs of her shoulder-length hair, and her gaze lingered on me for a split second longer than usual. Having spent so much time with her, I knew what kind of dark thoughts bubbled inside that skull of hers.

"Free her," the magnate said.

Meike rubbed at her wrists after she was freed, then folded her hands in front of her and waited.

"Your imprisonment was time for you to reflect on past actions," Magnate Bardera said. "While I do hold you responsible for Effie's disappearance, I also recognize that her kidnapping was not a betrayal on your part, but simply from incompetence."

Meike's brow twitched at the words, but she offered no other reaction. Bardera continued, "I'm not oblivious to the specifics. Effie was rather clever in losing you, but that wasn't the first time, was it? She has a history of disappearing. Enough times to participate in gang activities, even."

Mateo and Emil turned on me, and Magnate Bardera offered me a disappointed look. Then the faintest hint of amusement glimmered in her eyes, but faded when her attention returned to Meike. "Would you like a second chance?"

Meike bowed. "Of course, Magnate."

"Good. You'll be escorting the Adrianns while they attempt to reconvene with their sibling."

Her mouth hovered open. "You want me to leave the city?"

"If that's where the Adrianns go, then yes. You go

where they go. Oversergeant Eslid and his riders will be accompanying the four of you as well."

The bench screeched as I wriggled out of it. "You don't have to do this. She can stay here if she wants. I'm sure Eslid can protect us just fine."

"Meike needs to prove herself capable of protecting a life if she's ever meant to return to my service again." She made a shooing motion toward the guards at the door. "Wait outside. You too, Oversergeant."

Eslid bowed and left, followed by the guards. When the doors echoed shut behind them, the magnate continued, "I'll need you to do something important for me as well, Meike. Something that cannot leave this room. You'll be my eyes and ears while the Adrianns retake their homeland, and you'll return to me once they deem your service satisfactory. I need you to find out from Prinzessa Sara Adriann what the political situation looks like in Radavich—how well supported the late Magnate Jancarlo was by his assembly when he declared support for Olevic Pike. Also, whether Sara Adriann's army weakened the city's defenses on their march out."

Meike nodded, but her expression was brittle. "Yes, Magnate."

"May I ask why you want to know these things?" Emil asked.

"Radavich has been placing heavy tariffs on our exports for a long time," the magnate said. "Something Magnate Jancarlo refused to budge on since Manasus was never in a position to negotiate. We've always relied so heavily on their exports of oil, rockwood, and ghost grains. But now I see an opportunity to change that dynamic. No doubt their economy has suffered from the deaths of their magnate and secretariat, and now I'm pondering whether further destabilization of Radavich could have dramatic benefits for the surrounding territories. Augustin included."

"And why do you want to know about the capital's defenses? Are you considering going to war with them?"

Bardera let out a sharp laugh. "That's a heavy question. Let's just say I know how to recognize when there's blood in the water. Tulchi will smell it too, and if there were ever two territories that didn't get along, it would be them. I'd rather seize this opportunity before they do while everyone's eyes are still on the chaos in Augustin. I've sent people to Radavich to investigate what is happening there, but your sister may have insight that could be valuable."

"All right," Emil said. He approached Meike and offered his hand. "You did what you could to protect my sister, and I know how much of a pain she can be. She's gotten the best of me on more than one occasion."

The guard studied the hand—it was clear I wasn't the only Adriann she disliked—but she finally reached out and accepted it. This trip would be a valuable service to Bardera, but the magnate could have sent a number of people. In truth, Bardera was exiling her.

"Magnate," Emil said to Bardera. "If it's all right with you, I'd like to leave as soon as possible."

Chapter 24 – Efadora

It only took minutes to remember why I hated traveling on foxback. I sat behind Emil, holding onto him while his mount loped in front of the dozen soldiers, and we headed out the gates of Manasus, passing between sheer granite walls dozens of feet tall where soldiers watched on from crannies carved into the rock. The lack of control shot my anxiety through the roof. I always relied on my hands and feet to move around the city, and now I bounced in my seat and clutched onto my brother, powerless. I hated feeling powerless. I'd asked for my own mount, but all the foxes were too big.

The cartographer Bardera had hired for us—Carina was her name—led the group, followed by Oversergeant Eslid, then Meike, then Emil and me, and then the master smith. Eleven of Eslid's riders tailed us. Every fourth man carried a torch that lit our way as we wound up and down tunnels and passed homes with oval-shaped doors. Everyone in the contingent wore plain gear, but the squads patrolling the capital's outskirts acknowledged us wordlessly when we passed. The tunnels started to rumble, and we came to a cavern dominated by the Elvas River—a thirty-foot-wide channel of rapids that cut from one end of the cavern to the other, so loud that I needed to press my mouth to Emil's ear for him to hear me. We crossed a rockwood bridge damp with mist that carried a steady stream of travelers, traders, and caravans to and from the capital. On the other side waited a wide tunnel leading to the Granite Road, and in the cavern's darker crevices, there were a handful of other more menacing tunnels that everyone avoided, separated by tangles of coral trees, matted with moss, and buzzing with insects. Carina picked the narrowest one of them all and led us down it.

For what seemed like hours, Carina took us along snarls of tunnels, ridges, caverns, and cliffs, all of them devoid of a single person. The last time I'd conversed with a cartographer as part of my tutoring, the man had told me that about one percent of the crust had been explored, and that if you traveled more than a mile off the Granite Road you might as well surrender to the fact that something big and crawly and poisonous was going to rip you to shreds. I caught flashes of movement in the undergrowth, but they didn't bother us, or we were moving too fast for them to attack. The group barely paid them any attention—if they weren't concerned, then neither was I.

"Not so hard," Emil said over his shoulder.

I relaxed my grip on his sides. "Sorry," I said through clenched teeth. Faults above, I wanted my own mount.

Finally, thankfully, the group slowed to a walk. "Gah," I said. My thighs were killing me. To think we had a handful of passings of *this* between us and Sara. We were currently in a cavern that caused my breath to fog in front of me, and a river flowed against a wall to our left, with glowing algae growing beneath its surface that caused reflections to ripple along the ceiling. A field of ghostly mushrooms twice my height grew to our right, and glowing spores floated above our heads.

"You're sure we're not lost?" I asked Carina.

The leather of her saddle creaked as she turned and leaned to the side so she could see me behind my brother. "We're alive, yeah? That means we're not lost."

Her throaty accent sounded strange, but it explained why her black hair had shocks of crimson running through it. "Where are you from?" I asked.

"From a country called Yarokly, east of Mira. Ever heard of it?"

I shook my head.

"I'd hardly call it a country by Miran's standards. It's smaller than Manasus. Your Sovereign's flirted with us in the past, but The Rift will always separate Mira from the rest of Ra'Thuzan. Makes negotiations difficult."

"Is Yarokly near Sulian Daw?"

She laughed. I had no idea what she found funny. "Not nearly so far east. It's between Karatoa and Xeriv. Near the Black Depths, east of the Dead Bogs."

This time I shrugged instead of shaking my head.

"What are they teaching you in school? I swear, Miran brains are mushier than most."

"It's hard to care about what happens in the rest of the world when we never interact with it," I said.

"Smart words from one so young. And an unfortunate truth. Those of Mira's territories think themselves superior to the rest of the world simply because they spend their lives isolated from it."

"I saw a bobbit worm antennae sticking out of the water farther upriver. You're sure this is the right way?"

"My job is to take you and your brother on the right path," she said as she pointed a rolled-up map at us. "Not the safe one. We shouldn't be putting so many warm bodies together in places like this, but I suppose that's what the soldiers are for."

"We'll be fine," Emil said to me. "Her elemental power has been guiding us since the capital. I can feel it. She uses her maps from the Archives to cross-reference the quartzite compositions in the walls around us."

"You can feel her power even though you're bound to different stuff?" I asked.

"Sure I can. All elementals use the same intermediary. The Foundry calls it the Influence. I think Ig once called it an eelektri-magnetic field." He struggled to pronounce the phrase.

I turned to Mateo, who rode alongside us. "Did Ig ever tell you how he got his powers?"

"From those cultists he was raised by," Mateo said.

I tried to picture what the manservant had been like as a child. He and I had never been close during the several months we lived together in Augustin, but one thing about him used to always stand out. Pain meant little to him, or at least pain that wasn't caused by his flesh binding.

"Apparently the place Sara and I rescued him from was a lot *more* than we realized," Emil said. "It explains why Father was in such a hurry to leave Sulian Daw when we found him."

"What do you mean you and Sara found him?"

"We found him in a cage in an abandoned compound on the edge of Som Abast, the city we were in. It was ugly. I couldn't believe he was still alive. We think his masters kept him in solitary confinement for months."

Could I have lasted months alone in a prison cell? Definitely. Learn to value yourself above everyone else, because you're the only one you're stuck with, Sara always said. I was faithful to that creed, and it had made me stronger and more independent than anyone else my age.

The members of Titanite looking at me, deadness in their eyes. The shriek of Carmen's voice telling me she never wanted to see me again. Why did these stupid memories keep plaguing me? The pit of my stomach twisted.

I was tired of this pain. Maybe I wasn't as strong as I thought.

Everyone dismounted at the other end of the cavern upon Emil's orders. We set up camp by the river's edge, away from the rampant flora, and I made my bedroll beside Emil while the riders started a fire. Mateo laid his bedroll at my and my brother's feet, putting himself between us and the rest of the cavern.

"Why is it such a terrible thing that Ig is so powerful?" I asked Mateo. Emil was setting up his sleeping arrangements, and he paused.

"I'll answer your question with a question," Mateo said. "Why do you think the smiths of the Foundry are pacifists?"

"Because you don't believe in violence?"

"But we sell the highest quality weapons and armor in Mira, perhaps even in all of Ra'Thuzan, that we forge with our own hands. We've facilitated more violence through the creation of these tools than anything we could have done ourselves."

"Then I don't know."

"You should be familiar with one of the Foundry's core tenets—that devoting oneself to a single craft is one of the highest callings in life. Mastering the forge takes years of work, and we do it to grow closer with Fheldspra. When you're hunched over that forge, with the heat blasting you while you strike the metal with everything you have, you feel Him." His mouth turned up as he lost himself in a memory. "Order always flows into chaos if one isn't vigilant, so the smiths put most of their energy into their craft. If we didn't, it would allow us time to... consider other applications for our abilities." He nodded toward Emil, who listened as well. "It's why your brother feels the darkness pull at him. Life in the forges was supposed to be his destiny after he became a metal worker, but your father took that away from him, and it came at a cost."

I thought back to when Emil had attacked Carmen's father. "You're sure that's a supernatural darkness?" I asked my brother. "You knew Father. Even if you weren't a metal worker, you still would've inherited all those ugly things from him."

Mateo answered instead. "The darkness pulls at those with power who are unable to focus that power, and people like Ig only make it worse. He intensifies the darkness."

Emil had been digging his fingers into the end of his unrolled bed as he listened, the muscles in his arms flexing, and he turned to glare at the master smith. "No, he doesn't. You think he's affected me? If anything, Ig's shown me better than anyone what controlling your emotions looks like. One's thoughts are irrelevant. People should hold you accountable by your actions, not what's going on in here." He jabbed a finger at his skull.

"I'm not here to argue, only to advise. He corrupted your father and he'll corrupt your sister."

I wanted to tell Mateo I agreed with Emil, that his words sounded like a load of crap, but adults never took my opinions on life seriously. Fifteen-year-olds were incapable of having wisdom, apparently. A memory came to me, of Söres on the ground at Titanite's hideout, blood leaking from his head, and my near-overwhelming urge to cut his head from his shoulders. I knew better than anyone how easy it was to think bad thoughts. Thank the depths I didn't act on *all* my impulses.

Emil rose, taking angry steps toward the soldiers to help stack tinder for the fire. "Have you heard of the Schism?" Mateo asked me.

"Hasn't everyone?" I asked.

"Fair point. How much do you know about it, beyond the fact it's responsible for the Foundry's loyalty to the territories' magnates?"

I shrugged.

"It happened about eight hundred years ago, long before the Sovereign conquered the territories and created Mira. It started with a man. A smith, in fact. No one knows his name because the Foundry wiped his identity from history. But the Schism, the event he started, stayed in the books so that the smiths would always remember what happens to those corrupted by their own power. As the story goes, this smith came to the realization that there were powers hidden deep inside every member of the Foundry, beyond the ability to master the forging of steel. This created a thirst for power, and the master smith of that time excommunicated him from the Foundry. This smith disappeared for more than a decade. When he returned, he and the group he belonged to were all elemental. This group could not only control steel with incredible power, but could control other things too. These men and women collapsed tunnels with the swish of a hand. They wielded the lavas themselves without being burned. This smith and his followers almost destroyed the territories because he hated the Foundry for keeping itself in the dark. What he didn't realize was why the smiths did this, and he exemplified that reason. He didn't see the pursuit of power as a bad thing at the start of his journey, but by its end, he killed hundreds without second thought."

"A group of all powerful elementals? Reminds me of the Sovereign and the primordia."

"It does, doesn't it? The Foundry's long wondered whether the Sovereign discovered his power in the same place as this ancient smith."

"So what happened to the smith?"

Mateo shook his head. "He leveled the capital city of Saracosta, for one. Killed all of his former brethren. If you ever travel to the country's capital, you'll see the scarring of what he did even now. After he brought Saracosta's magnate to his knees, the smith disappeared. No one knows where though. Some believe he fled to find more power since the desire to rule no longer attracted him. The smith wanted to understand the nature of the universe. He never came back, so it's suspected that his quest ultimately killed him and his elemental friends."

I let out a *hmph*. "Interesting story."

"An interesting lesson about power, too. After the Schism, the smiths in the remaining territories vowed to serve their magnates without question. We've been criticized for not participating in the wars over the years, but it's how we've survived. We're powerful enough that if we ever tried to move against the Sovereign or influence territory politics, we'd be destroyed."

"But you would fight the Sovereign and his primordia if you could."

He pursed his lips. "I'd be remiss about the truth if I didn't admit that even after two centuries, there still hasn't been a consensus on whether we should follow him… but no. Our current plan is to wait it out. The Sovereign will be dead soon. How he managed to extend his life to over two hundred years is one of the most sought-after secrets in Mira, but it's clear he won't last much longer. It's why he's so focused on preparing his son, Bilal, for the throne. Hopefully Bilal will be a kinder soul."

The soldiers finished setting up camp, and they sat on their packs around a newly-made fire, drinking from waterskins and chewing on dried meat. Carina studied her maps, oblivious to the small talk around her, and I watched her from across the fire, hoping she'd look at me. I wanted to talk to her—learn more about life outside the territories, but her focus was unbreakable. Meike sat on her bedroll almost twenty feet away at the edge of the fire's light, sipping from her waterskin.

"Meike," Emil called out.

"Yes?"

"Why don't you join us?"

"Emil…" I muttered, but Meike rose, dragging her pack over so she could sit with us as we sat around the fire. None of the soldiers offered her a spot in the circle—they kept their backs to her as she circled the group, pretending she didn't exist or laughing to themselves and smirking. It surprised me until I remembered that to these soldiers, Meike had been unofficially banished.

Mateo shifted his seat over. "Here," he said, deflating the soldiers' fun.

"Magnate Bardera told me you're her best swordswoman," Emil said when the woman joined us. "Is that true?"

Meike chewed on her jerky for several moments before answering. "Spent the past twenty years perfecting my form. It's been my life, aside from serving Magnate Bardera. My years of commitment should answer your question."

"Commitment can't compensate for being shit at your job," one of the soldiers said, and the others suppressed their laughs. Oversergeant Eslid's eyes crinkled as he drank from his waterskin.

Meike glowered like usual but didn't respond. "All that armor weighing you down," another soldier said. "Never understood that. Makes you look ridiculous."

Meike's armor was packed up at the moment, but looking at the rippling muscles outlined by her ratty white undershirt and brown pants, one reason for the armor was clear. She was in better shape than anyone else sitting at the fire, including Emil and Eslid. Their taunts were also strange to hear considering the nose ring she wore, its metal reflecting the light of the fire—jewelry that Manasan soldiers only wore when they bested three soldiers at once in a sparring match. The only other nose ring in the group belonged to the hulking figure on the far side of the fire, a man named Brux.

"Armor makes me a one-person barricade in the right tunnel," she said.

"Because we're at war, and that's clearly what's needed," the first soldier said. "Excellent decision-making as always."

While the others eyed their friend, doing a much worse job at suppressing their laughs this time around, I watched Meike. Her composure cracked, and just for a second her brow twitched upward in anguish. Her expression leveled out and she turned to Emil. "May I be excused?"

Emil nodded.

Meike returned to the bedroll. "I'm not going to intervene when it comes to some light ribbing," Emil said to me in a low voice, "but there's clearly some division in the ranks right now. Can Meike be trusted to do her job?"

I readied an answer but stopped myself. Did I really want

to say no? It made me bristle to think back to when she'd stopped me from robbing that pervert Niall, or when she'd scared Carmen away from the palace, but that didn't make her bad at her job. In fact, the only reason anyone thought so was because of what I'd done to her.

I watched her as she sat hunched over in the near darkness, her back to everyone, almost like she was hugging herself. "She's a pain," I said, "but she knows her way around a sword."

Soon everyone turned in for the night, and I seemed the only one in the whole camp who couldn't fall asleep within the first five minutes. An hour later, the rawness in my legs caused me to toss and turn, and the faint songs of snoring from a dozen men made me wish I had a pile of rocks to throw at them or to at least bury over my head. Eventually I rose when the urge to pee hit me.

Two black silhouettes sat at the edge of camp, a short distance from the giant mushrooms that glowed like ghosts, and a small flame flared in one of the silhouette's hands. I approached the sentries, one of them smoking a pipe. "How is it out here?" I asked.

"More'n dandy," the man with the pipe said, head wavering.

I caught the whiff of something strange. "Is getting high part of your job description?"

"Your brother wants to take us halfway toward the mantle where there's nothin' better to do," the other one said. It was hard to make out any details in their faces through the faint glow of the spores floating overhead. "You wouldn't take the last few joys in our lives away, would you?"

"Whatever," I said, and padded off.

Perhaps Mira's drug problem was worse than I realized if two soldiers thought it normal to smoke while on watch. Did the Regheta gang put their hooks into those men? Did my sister?

I circled the camp until I reached the river, then headed upstream for someplace private. The river was beautiful, with crystal clear water and glowing patches of bioluminescence growing on the bottom. While I squatted in a place more obscured from camp, I started thinking about how plant life out here seemed so odd at times. It reminded me of the Proliferation—a theory my tutor told me about that tried to explain why the remains of so many creatures in the crust weren't more than a couple thousand years old. A puzzle paleontologists still hadn't cracked. Strange to think of Ra'Thuzan as anything other than completely hostile.

A faint clicking emerged over the sound of rushing water.

I pulled up my trousers and peered upriver. The field of mushrooms dominated the cavern like a thousand ghostly lanterns, but the light only intensified the darkness of the path running along the river. The clicking sounded like a pickaxe striking rock. I moved backward, toward camp.

The frequency of the clicking increased until it transformed into one continuous sound, and I broke into a run. The clicking suddenly appeared in front of me and I skidded to a stop. It surrounded me. I put my back to the water, and the glow of algae glinted off the thirty-foot length of chitin that had cornered me.

It was a centipede. Body as thick as my torso and with a hundred legs, each as big as mine, it had curled itself into a crescent and cornered me against the river. To my left, the pincer-like forceps of its mouth clacked together and its antennae waved back and forth, trying to find me.

I turned to jump in the river, but before I leapt, a yell echoed in the cavern. Steel glinted in the darkness, held by a figure backlit by the mushrooms. The sword arced down and bit into chitin, and the centipede's head whipped toward the attacker.

Meike, fully donned in her plate, braced herself as the centipede struck. Its head bounced off her breastplate, and one of its forceps fell to the ground from Meike's riposte. Meike hacked again, but the centipede threw more of its weight against her, causing her to stumble. A dozen legs wrapped around her and she dropped her sword. The centipede moved in for another bite, and Meike grunted and yelled.

The centipede's thrashing body collided with me as I ran for the sword. I recovered, dodging its violent movements as it continued to strike at Meike over and over again. I grabbed the sword out of the dirt and swung for its head.

The blade severed both antennae. The centipede straightened, still holding onto Meike, but its head waved around in a craze. It smacked into me, knocking the breath from my body and sending me tumbling again.

"Not fucking happening," I muttered, grabbing the sword once more and charging. Meike's blade was heavy, and my swings were slow, but I managed to hit the thing in the head. Its thrashing intensified, but the legs holding onto Meike relaxed enough for her to untangle herself and crawl away.

"To me," Meike said, and I rushed to return her sword. She chopped at the monster—each strike stained the ground with dark fluid and severed more of the centipede's segmented body. Soon the thing flailed in two pieces, and the ten-foot-long section belonging to the head stilled.

Dirt and scrapes covered Meike's armor, and she rubbed at her lower back. "Did it bite you?" I asked.

She turned full circle, examining herself. "Don't think so."

Yells from the camp pierced the sound of rushing water. I took off and Meike followed.

Half a dozen centipedes, each at least twenty-five feet long, thrashed and struck at the attacking soldiers along the edges of the camp. The sentries I'd spoken with earlier lay in the dirt, face down, and a yelp came from a fox bound by a curled centipede. That's when I noticed only a few of our mounts remained tied to our makeshift hitching post, cowering or snapping at their attackers.

A bead of fluid struck me in the face as Emil nearly bisected a nearby centipede. The Meteor Blade blurred blue in the darkness, nearly impossible to track, and it left the monster in sizzling pieces. He moved on to another holding one of the foxes in its cage of legs. I grabbed my dagger from my pack and ran for the centipede's lower body while Emil left deep wounds near its head. My blade bit into the legs wrapped around one of the stone foxes until the animal flopped onto the ground. The fox didn't move, the fur on its shoulder bloody from where the centipede had injected its poison.

Meike freed another fox, and the animal limped off, whimpering. A dozen feet away, a centipede struck at Mateo, but the master smith deflected its attack with the flat of his sword and inhuman grace. An uppercut to the head left the centipede in spasms.

Severed limbs, headless segments, and purple centipede goop covered the edge of camp by the time the fighting subsided. Only three of the six centipedes had been killed—the rest fled into the forest of mushrooms with portions of their bodies. But the centipedes managed to take out seven of our stone foxes as well as the sentries. The foxes had been trapped by the hitching post, helpless. Only three of the eight that survived were uninjured.

Under the light of a restarted fire, Mateo and Emil examined three soldiers who moaned and writhed in the dirt. Angry, fist-sized lumps grew on the soldiers' arms or legs where they'd been bitten, and my brother helped the master smith apply a white powder to the wounds. The unharmed soldiers applied the same powder to the foxes.

"Is that enough to stop the poison?" I asked. From my understanding, they were using powdered papaya—a common treatment for centipede bites. But those centipedes had been far larger than anything found near the capital.

"No," Carina said without looking up from her maps. "They'll need antivenin if they want to avoid the risk of their hearts stopping or necrosis setting in." Emil opened his mouth, but she added, "I'll let you know when I find the nearest town where we can buy some."

I helped one of the soldiers drag the dead sentries to the river's edge. We lay them side-by-side and threw blankets over their bodies.

"How did this happen?" Mateo asked.

"I paid those two a visit right before we were attacked," I said. "Whatever they were smoking smelled awful. They were high as ice, I think."

The flames made my brother's glare look like it was carved from stone. "Who else brought drugs with them?"

No one moved.

Emil pulled his blade out and pointed at one soldier, then another. "If you did, throw them in the river now. We'll be traveling together for a long time, which means I'll find them eventually, and if you wait until then, I'll kill you where you're standing. That I promise. I won't let anyone else put our lives at risk like that again."

Still no one moved, their exhaustion etched with some of their earlier fear.

Emil paced back and forth, his rage deepening until I saw flickers of the man who killed Carmen's father. For a second I thought he might strike someone down to set an example. He stopped and took three even breaths. "Please." He sheathed the Meteor Blade. "Throw it in the river and I'll remember you as someone who put the safety of your comrades first. It'll be an admirable thing. You'll have my respect and the respect of those around you. I understand how difficult my request might be."

One man stood—he avoided our gazes as he dug a coin purse out from the bottom of his bag. He walked to the river, threw the purse in, and returned to his seat to stare at his feet.

"What's your name?" Emil asked.

The man struggled to meet my brother's eyes. "Petamare, het."

"Thank you, Petamare. I don't want to make any presumptions about how important what you just threw away was to you, but if you need help from me in the future, or anything at all, don't hesitate to let me know. I want to do whatever I can."

Petamare gave a meek nod.

Emil returned to treating the bitten soldiers, and I watched him as he examined one of the men's bites and applied more powdered papaya while frowning to himself. My first thought when it came to the dead sentries was how they'd earned their place in the depths for putting us at risk, but when Emil had confronted a third addict in the group, he didn't treat him like a criminal. He saw Petamare as someone who needed help.

I suddenly felt embarrassed for how much I wanted to rule the Manasus underworld. I'd never seen this much of the other side of the business before.

Meike took a seat beside me. Her white undershirt and brown pants were drenched in sweat, her hair damp. I would've expected her to smell bad, but all I caught was the faint aroma of jasmine. I supposed someone like her was too poised to let body odor fly. She took a swig from the waterskin in her hand, a silence settling between us. I almost let out a *thank you* for earlier, but the thought of thanking Meike left a bad taste in my mouth.

"You had your armor on fast," I finally said. "Were you sleeping in it?"

The guard watched my brother leave the soldiers to sit beside Carina. The cartographer angled the map toward him and ran her index finger across the leathery material. "Didn't like the way everyone was looking at me earlier," Meike answered.

"How'd you know where I was?"

"Was awake when you left camp. Made me uncomfortable how far you went. Decided to make sure you weren't disturbed while you took care of your business."

My cheeks grew hot. She really did take her vows to Magnate Bardera seriously. "I'm glad you didn't tail me like that in Manasus," I said. "I probably wouldn't have had many friends otherwise. You would've broken my gang up in a heartbeat."

"I... might've turned a blind eye a time or two. Didn't want to be too intrusive. That had to change though when Magnate Bardera ordered you confined to the palace."

Meike had tried to give me freedom? It was hard to believe, considering how smothering she was at times, yet I remembered how easy it was to lose her in the Pit before heading to Titanite's hideout.

Emil stood. "We need antivenin and more mounts to purchase. There's a town half a passing's walk from here, but there's one problem. It lies on Manasus's old thoroughfare, from before the Sovereign built the Granite Road, and it's built out of some old Sihraan ruins. That means the possibility of ruin folk and whoever else uses the old thoroughfares for trade and travel. That's a lot of people who might not take kindly to us. It's our best bet for getting back on schedule though."

Ruin folk, or fringe folk, lived in ruins and other fringe towns beneath the territories, and they were people who wanted no part in the Sovereign's rule. They still technically belonged to Mira, but they were notoriously difficult to find, as ruin folk hunted cartographers for sport. The Archives had a strange obsession with mapping out the Sihraan Empire, and ruin folk didn't much appreciate that. If Carina was made nervous by our change of plans though, she didn't show it.

Few words were spoken while everyone broke down camp. A few of the uninjured knelt among the bodies of the centipedes, sawing off pieces of red chitin and packing it up—something to do with their tradition of claiming the weapons and armor of the dead they defeated, probably.

We finished strapping the wounded soldiers to the backs of the foxes that could handle the weight, and I kicked dirt onto the fire, darkness swallowing the bodies of the slain foxes and sentries we left behind.

THE BITTEN SOLDIERS were vomiting over the sides of their mounts, their skin shiny with sweat by the time we reached Lo Toddul.

Geodes—some as long as my arm and others the size of small houses—grew at odd angles on the cavern ceiling, shining light on the town below. Ancient stone ruins littered the depression where the town sat, crusted by newer buildings of rockwood and black stone. Herds of mole-rats grazed on the cavern's hills around us as we followed a road leading down, a stream of rural folk passing us headed the other way. I felt sweat collecting on my lower back and pulled off my coat, the heat this far down in the crust sitting in the air like a blanket.

A man not much taller than me led a strange breed of donkey attached to a pull cart that was filled with blankets, utensils, and other household wares. He looked to be some sort of tinker, and he stopped as our group began to pass him. He spoke rapidly, nervously, in a language that sounded vaguely familiar to Augustin's old tongue but too far different for me to understand. The man's body language wasn't hostile. My brother looked to Carina and Mateo, but they shook their heads. "I'm sorry," Emil said to the tinker. "I don't understand."

Oversergeant Eslid nudged his way to the front of the group and asked a question in the ruin folks' language, the words coming to him easily. The local replied and touched Eslid on the shoulder before continuing onward.

"You can understand him?" I asked.

"Knowing the tongue of the ruin folk is part of the reason I'm employed by Magnate Bardera. The man said strange people are here. Dangerous."

"Strange to them could be normal to us," my brother said. "Let's go."

Lo Toddul's buildings were built from a strange, pockmarked brown stone with obsidian trim, sitting either against or on top of old ruins that had been worn down from the eons. Mannequins stuffed with moss were attached to posts throughout the town, and I noticed a person carrying a stone crown struck through with blood-red crystal, trying to fit the thing onto a mannequin's head. More crowns sat in a crate at the person's feet. "What are those?" I asked.

"It's for a holiday common with the ruin folk in western Manasus," Carina said. "They worship a pantheon called the Aspects. The stone god Brexa, Terias the Burrowing Sphinx, among others. Brexa was Fheldspra's lover and mortal enemy. She represents order while Fheldspra represents chaos. The Great Ones are their children."

I snorted. "They worship more than one god? And they think the Great Ones are Fheldspra's children, not us? That's the funniest thing I've ever heard."

"It's a big world out there. Worship of the Aspects is much more common than you think. Your territories aren't the center of the universe, even if your Sovereign insists otherwise. Lots of beliefs out there. Lots of strange happenings to justify those beliefs."

In Lo Toddul's center, a group of foxes drank from a trough at a hitching post in front of a building, saddlebags heavy on their haunches. The building looked like a general store. Lo Toddul's residents walked to and from the other structures, decorating their town in preparation for their holiday, but they gave the general store a wide berth.

"Maybe whoever's inside'll sell their mounts, if we was convincing," Petamare said.

Not likely, I thought. Only a breeder would part ways with a fox this far from a city. If Emil couldn't convince the owners to sell, would he be willing to steal the foxes if it meant reaching Sara?

"You three," Emil said, pointing at the soldiers. "Stay here and guard the wounded. The rest, come with me."

Seven of us entered the shop. The owner sat behind a counter near the front door with terror in his eyes. Beyond the shelves, the store transitioned into a cantina that was patio-style, with its back walls missing—floorboards gave way to dirt, and every table had been pushed together to accommodate a group a dozen strong. There was a bar by the rear entrance, and the barkeep sat low in his seat like he was trying to make himself as small as possible.

The group's black clothing absorbed the light from amber geodes growing along the walls. Scars riddled skin not covered in dark fighting leathers, and curved sabers were strapped to their backs, forcing them to lean forward onto the tables. A man and woman sat at the head—the only two without obvious weapons—and the man was the largest person I'd ever seen. He and the woman next to him sat on boulders instead of chairs, which seemed odd.

Mateo grabbed Emil's arm and squeezed. "I recognize that man. The big one. He was Bolivar's friend."

Emil squinted. "You're sure?"

"I only saw him with Bolivar once, but you don't forget a man that size."

Judging by how quickly Emil's face went from curiosity to worry, the same thought had crossed his mind too. Tuli Dempra, the man who sent the Fiador Fianza after him, Sara, and Father, was Bolivar's friend. I almost refused to believe it given the chances, but Mateo sounded pretty sure of himself. Wasn't Tuli supposed to be a smith?

I glanced at my brother. Back in Augustin the only thing he'd cared about more than swordplay was his beard, but now he only had about a week's worth of whiskers and his shaved scalp had half a finger's length of hair covering it. I, on the other hand, was distinctly Efadora, but Tuli Dempra hadn't put a bounty on my head. That was all Olevic.

"We could steal their mounts," I said.

"They'd hear us," Emil said in a low voice. We shared a look, and he said, "We'll find out what Tuli Dempra wanted with our family another time. Meike, go talk to them. See if they'll sell at least some of their stone foxes."

My former guard approached the group. The scars on the men and women's faces looked like someone had taken a knife to their bodies hundreds of times, while the skin of Tuli and the woman next to him was smooth as marble. Everyone turned to look at Meike. "Moment of your time?" she asked.

"And who are you?" the woman asked. Her hair was grey

and wiry from age, but her face didn't look much older than Sara's.

"Ex-military from Manasus. I'm under contract to protect a cartographer." She nodded toward our group.

The woman glanced our way, then nudged the mountain sitting beside her. "Do we believe her, Aronidus?"

Tuli Dempra rested his arm on the table, the wood groaning. So 'Tuli' was a false name after all. "Nektarios and Lilianthe wouldn't hire agents who would strut so obliviously through the front door." Tuli's—no, Aronidus's—voice was soft, like that of a young boy's, and his words had trouble carrying.

I recognized the name Nektarios. That was the primordia who met with Father on behalf of the Sovereign. He delivered messages and formal requests to the territory, and twice a year brought delegations from Saracosta to audit the tax logs of the capital and the towns along Augustin's Granite Road. He occasionally liked to leave a business or two destroyed as a parting gift. The man was unstable, but so were all primordia.

I took in the two again. Their flawless skin, the boulders that seemed to strain under their weight, their mention of Nektarios. "Fhelfire," I whispered. Aronidus and the woman were primordia.

"Very well," the woman said to Meike. "Carry on."

Meike didn't move. "We were riding toward Radavich, but centipedes killed some of our mounts. Would like to buy some of yours."

"No," she said, and took a drink from her mug.

"Please, hera. It's very important we make good time."

Those sitting with their backs to Meike looked over their shoulders. "Oh, is it?" the primordia asked. "We have business in the Manasus capital to attend to. Business that I promise is much more important than yours. You're free to go about it now."

Meike came back the same time Carina finished perusing the shelves. "I didn't see any antivenin in here," the cartographer whispered.

My brother waved for us to follow, and we headed for the store's entrance. He stopped in front of the owner who was still cowering. "Do you know where we can find antivenin?" he asked.

The man shook his head in confusion.

Emil waved Eslid over and the guard leaned over the counter, talking in a low voice. The owner responded, and Eslid grimaced as he turned around. "Says our friends in the cantina bought the last of what was left in Lo Toddul."

"Great," Emil said, pinching the bridge of his nose.

Outside, we passed the line of foxes at the trough and headed for the rest of the group. One of the bitten soldiers massaged at his chest as he sat on his mount—the bite on his forearm had changed from red to purple. The injured foxes lay together, licking at their wounds and whining.

Nobody noticed me leave the rear of the group and walk toward one of the primordia's foxes.

"Efadora, stop," my brother called out, but I had already unclasped a bag hanging off the fox's haunches. Inside were documents sealed in protective film, packaged food, and supplies wrapped in what looked like howler fur. When I didn't find any antivenin, I re-clasped the bag and moved to the next one.

Several vials of antivenin sat inside a leather case in the third bag, coupled with sharps of condor quills used to inject it. I stuffed the leather case into my waistband and covered it with my shirt, but paused when I saw a journal at the bottom of the bag. Tuli Dempra liked to write in a journal.

Opening the book brought me to the earmarked passage.

Plans awry. Instead of heading northwest to Tulchi, the eldest princepa moves south to her homeland, mercenary army in tow—

I re-clasped the bag and walked away with the journal. This was potential suicide, but we needed to know why Aronidus had placed a bounty on my family.

A door creaked behind me, and I turned to find the woman primordia eyeing the journal clutched to my chest.

I experienced a near-overwhelming urge to run as she strode toward me. Footsteps pounded on dirt, and Emil and Mateo appeared at my sides at the same time the primordia reached us.

The master smith yanked the journal out of my hand and offered it to the woman. At the same time he took a step forward, angling his body between me and her. "Please forgive my niece. She has problems with behavior. It's why I brought her on this trip, to keep an eye on her. She meant no harm by it."

The woman accepted the journal. "So you claim responsibility for her actions?"

"Yes, of course."

"Good."

She grasped Mateo by the throat and lifted him off the ground, and her foot struck Emil's chest, launching my brother a dozen feet backward. The master smith kicked at the air as his fingers worked to pry the woman's hand off.

I collided with the side of the woman's body, but it was like trying to move a wall of rock. It seemed impossible to have so much weight in a body so small. I grasped at her shirt and pulled backward in an attempt to throw her off balance, but she didn't budge.

Fabric ripped, and a tear ran a third of the way up her shirt. Pale scars mottled the skin beneath, similar to her friends inside, but these scars were different. They looked like branches of lightning trailing down the length of her back.

She tossed the journal behind her and used her freed hand to pick me up by the throat too. Her grip was a cold vise, and my vision blurred. As I started to black out, the pressure on my neck disappeared and my world turned upside down. I hit the ground, tumbling until I rolled to a stop.

Dizziness sent me stumbling as I scrambled to my feet.

My vision started to clear, and I saw Mateo's body still. "Consider this a lesson in life," the primordia said to me. "Learn to take responsibility for your own actions. Innocent people die, otherwise."

"I never said I didn't want to!" The retort came out a half-shriek, and the cavern swallowed the sound as my vision turned glassy. I wiped away the tears, but more appeared. Mateo's face was a hideous purple. "Fight me, ragworm. *Yadra*!" I started throwing out every curse word I knew.

The door to the store opened again, and Aronidus stepped out, ducking his head beneath the top of the frame. "Stop, Otalia," he said with his soft voice. "Killing a smith invites too much trouble from the Sovereign."

Otalia rolled her eyes and tossed the master smith. Mateo struck the ground face first, and I was rushing to him before his body came to a rest. His eyes remained closed, and fresh cuts covered his face and hair from where he'd struck the ground. Emil limped to our side a moment later, clutching his chest, face contorted in pain. We helped the master smith onto his back.

Aronidus joined Otalia. He picked up his journal and brushed it off. "The primordia have free rein to execute anyone they suspect of stealing," he said. "Given that this journal holds no monetary value, you'll be left with a warning. We won't be so kind next time."

Mateo awakened in a bout of coughing—one of his eyes was stained red from a broken vessel and blood leaked out of the lacerations covering his head. Emil struggled to pull the master smith to his feet, and Eslid replaced me to help. "C'mon," Emil said. The three of them slowly made their way to the rest of our group.

I reached the soldiers first. "Meike, Carina, and… whatever your name is," I said. "Round up the foxes and let's get out of here."

The injured foxes protested when the soldiers tried to move them, but they eventually struggled to their feet and limped alongside the bitten soldiers riding the unharmed mounts. Mateo massaged his throat as we headed out of town, his other arm hooked around Emil's neck. I looked round to see Aronidus tuck the journal into his back pocket, then Otalia follow him inside.

"The primordia won't... get away with this," Mateo struggled to say, and broke out in another string of coughs.

"I'm so sorry," I said, my voice quivering. "I shouldn't have done that. I don't know what I was thinking."

"It... was nothing. Someone needs to... stand up to those... abominations."

The primordia had been allowed to abuse Mira's citizens for centuries, but that didn't matter to me anymore. If Mateo wanted to do something about it, I would help.

"Did anyone else notice who that very large man was?" Emil asked.

"The man who put bounties on our family," I said. "What would primordia want with you guys? Didn't you tell me he was surveilling all of you before the coup started? He could have claimed you then, whenever he wanted. It's not like anyone could've stopped him."

He rubbed at his chest, watching one of the bitten soldiers on a fox sleeping against the beast's neck. "You're right, Efadora. He's one of the most powerful beings in the territories, but he's restraining himself for no reason. He's staying off the Granite Road too, for no apparent reason. It doesn't add up."

"Remember what that woman Otalia said to Meike?" I asked. "She and Aronidus made it sound like some of the primordia don't get along. Are they trying to kill each other?"

No one in the group answered the question. Stories and rumors circulated the primordia like a cloud of flies, but none of them mentioned that they fought with each other. What did the Sovereign think about this?

"I saw something in Aronidus's journal," I continued. "He knows Sara is marching on the Granite Road with a mercenary army. He wanted her to go to Tulchi for help instead."

Emil readjusted his hold on Mateo, but he managed to nod. "I have a bad feeling. Why would one of the primordia want us to get Tulchi's help?"

"They're using you," Mateo said. He used his free hand to touch a rag to the cuts on his temple. "People call territory politics a game of chatraga. The royal families think themselves the players, but the primordia have always relegated them to pawns. The magnates just don't want to admit it."

Our group reached the lip of the bowl the town sat in, and I finally felt safe enough to pull the leather case out of my back pocket. "If it means anything," I said to Mateo, "what happened back there wasn't for nothing." Despite my tumble, the glass vials inside the case were still intact.

The pain on the master smith's face disappeared. "Oh, Efadora." His smile faded when he looked at the town. "We should move quickly."

We stopped at a fungus farm a mile outside Lo Toddul.

Emil and Carina sat on the crystalline surface of a glowing geode, poking at and drawing lines on Carina's maps once again. Mateo spoke with a farmer in front of a home built out of what looked like an ancient utility building; behind it, a defunct, pillared aqueduct descended diagonally from ceiling to floor. The ingenuity amazed me—did the ruins of some ancient city await right under our feet? It was impossible to know where the aqueduct led without a few wagons' worth of pyroglycerin.

A field of light-pine mushrooms grew around the pillars supporting the aqueduct, covering half the cavern floor. Mateo was trying to buy any surpluses the farmer might've had since our supplies would evaporate long before we reached Sara, considering we had to walk.

I leaned against a fox while the animal chewed on cured mole-rat meat. Meike joined me, standing on the other side of the fox, and she started running a brush along the animal's flank. We didn't speak, and I passed the time by watching the master smith speak to the farmer. The skin on Mateo's neck had turned dark purple and the cuts on his face had stopped bleeding. He winced whenever he turned his head.

"You did the right thing earlier," she said. I realized she'd been watching me watch Mateo.

"You think so?" I asked. "If those soldiers didn't get that antivenin, it would've meant fewer people to wind you up."

Her brush paused. "They deserve death for their words?"

"I was joking."

She started up again, bristles rubbing against fur, the fox giving Meike a lick on the leg. "Words don't bother me."

I snorted. Faults above, but that was a load of crap. I waited for her to look up, to show her indignation so I could see the lie in her eyes, waiting until I realized she was avoiding my gaze.

I knew in that moment I would never give her a hard time again.

Emil gathered the group. Carina stood beside him, trying to catch almonds with her mouth that she threw in the air. "So the plan's changed once again," my brother said. "Those primordia are riding for Manasus, which means they'll find out Efadora and I left the capital. Aronidus probably hasn't lost interest in his bounty on my family, so he'll likely come for me. I'm assuming he's avoided chasing after the Princepa Sara because she's surrounded by her army, but he will probably realize I'm easy pickings if he connects us to the group he encountered in Lo Toddul. It wouldn't be a stretch for him to realize we're trying to catch up to Sara's army and will be traveling the Granite Road now that we're down foxes. He'll also know we won't make good time and we'll be vulnerable for several passings."

He glanced at Carina, who managed to catch an almond.

"This means that avoiding the Granite Road is more important than ever." He picked up the map and held it in front of his body. "Instead of trying to catch up to my sister on the Granite Road—" his finger moved due west along the Granite Road until it reached Radavich's territory, then moved south along the path Sara's army was taking, "—we'll take a series of tunnels that cut a more direct path toward Augustin." His finger moved southwest from the area we were presumably located in Manasus, in a straight line toward home. It moved parallel to Dagir's Pass, but without high elevation gear and enough mounts, we would all be ice-cubed.

My brother folded the map. "Expect regular run-ins with the wildlife."

The soldiers looked at each other, nonplussed.

"I know this is asking a lot after what happened," Emil said, "but we need to reach Sanskra as soon as possible. Last time I saw the Princepa Sara, we agreed to meet there once she mobilized her army. That's where she'll be waiting until we arrive. Every moment she delays there means Olevic Pike will be better prepared in his defense of the capital. Will you go with me? A soldier should follow their superior's orders, but I lost that privilege when I got two of you killed." He waved everyone off before protests were given. "If I want to become magnate, I need to learn to take responsibility. Consider this practice. So I'll ask once again—will you go with me?"

Nobody spoke. I almost said yes, but this moment wasn't meant for me.

Petamare stepped forward. "I go where you go, het."

One by one, the rest of the contingent voiced their agreement. Even the bitten soldiers looked confident—they now walked instead of rode, and the skin around their bites had lightened.

The thought of no longer catching up to Sara on the Granite Road made me uneasy, but I had Ig's note to thank for that. Why go through all the trouble of sending it? I tried my best to shrug off the feeling. This was Sara—she'd taught me most of what I knew, at least most of what was useful, including how to live life beyond the nobility. She was the wisest person I knew. The commoners loved her because she did them favors as Mira's Hand. I wouldn't stop trusting her because of the word of someone who, by all accounts, should've hated my family.

Emil's shoulders dropped a degree when everyone agreed to the plan. "Good," he said. "Let's move."

Chapter 25 – Jakar

As I STOOD in the town of Cragreach, skin prickling from the heat of the fire devouring the building in front of me, I could only think of the primordia and the Sovereign's military, and how none of them had come to stop Sara's army.

Mercenaries shouted commands to one another on the single road running through town, stacking furniture they'd pillaged onto a line of carts that accompanied the army. Next door to the burning building, the red-brown brick of Cragreach's *maedhall* darkened from the flames but remained otherwise unscathed. I left the throng of mercenaries and headed for the maedhall's front door. Inside, I paused on the entryway, my hand moving to the hilt of my knife, and listened for Fredrick—the commander of coin for Rodi's gang. I heard no voices, and stepped forward, ready to hunt.

The maedhall was built like those in the other two towns we'd raided on the Granite Road—paintings of honeycomb lined mud-brick hallways, illuminated by old-fashioned torchlight. A set of stairs descended into a cellar at the rear of the building, where voices floated up to meet me. I pulled my knife from its ratty sheath, relishing the moment.

Ghostly lightcaps crusted the floor of the cellar where mead barrels lay side-by-side. Fredrick was at the other end with his back to me, pawing at a young woman who had wedged herself between two barrels. With each swipe of Fredrick's hand, the woman lashed at him with a kick.

"The saving's in the cellar," Fredrick said in a low voice. "You lied three times now. Means three fingers. Keep it up."

The young woman noticed me and peered past his shoulder, prompting Fredrick to turn around. "Ig? What do you want?"

"Three of your gang mates are dead," I said, my voice hollow. "Faye, Aidio, and Orla."

For a moment, the distress on his narrow, scarred face mirrored the girl's behind him. "How? They were alive when we took Cragreach."

He stepped back as I crossed the floor, but not quickly enough to avoid my blade flashing into his stomach. He cried out as I pushed it deeper into his soft flesh, and I put my hand over his mouth. He tried to twist away, but I held him in place.

I let him drop to the floor, where he moaned and leaked blood onto the rock. Soon, acid from his ruptured stomach would start burning its way through his insides, making the last minutes of his life agonizing.

His face contorted, almost inhuman. "Why?"

I knelt, and his hand grabbed at me sluggishly. My knife came down and drove clean through his wrist to pin it to the ground. He gasped, but the sound was driven from his body when his struggling intensified the pain. "Sara's Words protect your boss," I said, "but they don't protect you. I'm going to kill every single one of your friends, and then I'm going to destroy this army."

A wet eye shined in the darkness between the barrels. Fredrick would have raped, tortured, and left the maedhall girl for dead, just as he'd done to the winery girl in Hamagard.

Fredrick's moans turned into wails. My blade moved, but he was too weak to push away my hands as the weapon separated the muscles in his throat. A pool of blood reached out from his body, and the girl wept.

Four of Rodi's crew down and four to go with precious little time to do it. Sara's army would make quick work of Cragreach upon the princepa's orders—this was the third town we'd hit on the Granite Road, and we were already behind schedule. She'd been furious when she learned her army had spent two whole passings in Hamagard, but it was her fault. She led the army yet disappeared for multiple passings to scout for ways around town defenses using her elemental power. She trusted too much in the jafas and jafos to stay faithful to her orders. Trusted me too much.

Following my confrontation with Rodi, I did everything I could to make Sara think I'd obey. Never arguing, never second guessing, always faithful, all so I'd have a chance to do the unthinkable. Was I bitter she found it so easy to believe I was still a coward? I tried not to think too much on the answer. Either way, everything was different.

Outside, mercenaries had already loaded up most of the furniture and coin onto the caravan. The flames next door had doubled in size, washing me in heat, and smoke collected along the cavern ceiling. Ash and embers fell around me as I crossed the city street, where more mercenaries stood guard around groups of bound locals.

Last I heard, Rodi's crewmember Calum had commandeered a noblewoman's vacation home at the edge of Cragreach. I passed the last building in town, and a plane of ancient, solidified magma sloped upward. A circular door waited at the top, built into the east cavern wall. I jiggled the handle. Unlocked.

Plush carpets ran down the hallway, with vaulted ceilings covered in crystals that shed emerald light throughout the home. Several people awaited me in the sitting room, strewn about like a collection of discarded marionettes, guts and blood leaking onto carpet and stone. One man's chest had been cracked like a wishbone from blunt force trauma, another woman's neck ripped open with a garrote. I stared at the scene for several moments, letting the rage build.

In Coracas—our first target just south of Radavich's capital—none of the residents had died. Then in Hamagard, Altabor's crew had killed a handful of farmers who refused to give up their food. The mercenary army was getting worse, would continue to get worse. Dozens of towns stood between us and the Augustin capital.

I would stop them though, starting with Rodi's crew.

Calum was in the bedroom, laying on a bed at the opposite wall, a bottle of Hamagard wine in hand. His head swiveled toward me, a lazy smile on his face.

The remaining three members of Rodi's crew lounged in the room with him.

"Look at who we got here," Ehliat said as she drank from a mead bottle while relaxing on a desk chair. Her hand axes rested on her lap. "Enjoy our handiwork?"

Everyone was drinking, but Calum seemed the only one drunk. Keeping my voice level was hard. "Did those bodies belong to the nobility who lived here?"

"Get a load of this flame-forsaken prick," Ristafo said. He sat nearest me, on top a dresser to my left with a sword leaning against his knee. "The indignation."

"Was a family from the capital," Ehliat said. "You wanna hear something rich? They fled the city after the martial horn sounded. Bribed a guard to sneak them out so they could stay here until the heat died down. How hilarious is that?"

"You deserve to die," I said.

The dresser rattled as Ristafo pushed off from it. "You gonna be the one to do it?" The uneasy edge in his question undermined the bravado.

"Four against one? I'm not crazy."

He tried to mask the way his body relaxed. "You got balls you do, considering Mira's Hand has them in a vice most the time."

"Didn't stop me from putting down that animal Cassandra."

Ristafo punched the mirror above the dresser and grabbed his sword. He lumbered toward me but stopped five feet away.

"Careful. Maybe we turn you to pieces either way, give Sara the old oh well. Not much for her to do after the fact."

I smiled. Hatred filled his eyes, and he took two more steps forward.

Bringing him within arm's reach.

My blade slid out of its sheath, and before Ristafo could bring his sword up, my weapon severed his jugular. As he fell, I threw my blade toward Alfo, nudging the steel with my senses as it flew. The knife buried itself in his chest.

A mead bottle shattered, and Ehliat charged me with a scream, an axe in each hand. She hacked over and over, but I deflected the steel with the flats of my hands. I moved backward, forcing her to step over Ristafo's body. One of her axes moved in a downward strike, and I deflected it to the side and rammed the heel of my palm into her nose.

She stumbled backward, but recovered and spat bloody phlegm on the floor. Blood dripped over a sneer that stretched her mouth. Calum scrambled off the bed, but only managed to hit the floor in a tangle of sheets.

"You're dead, toad," Ehliat said, and threw one of her axes.

Her technique was impeccable—a form that could only take dozens of hours to perfect. And the weapon would've killed me if I wasn't elemental.

I tilted my torso to the side and caught the axe's wooden haft. Before she could react, I twisted the weapon's head the other direction and threw it back. It split the woman's face in two.

Calum lurched to his feet, but crashed into the dresser, bouncing off and hitting the floor again. I picked up Ristafo's sword.

"You're gonna regret this, slave," Calum said. His eyes had difficulty focusing.

Lousy last words, those. Ristafo's blade sent his head rolling over rockwood and carpet, leaving a snail's trail of death.

My chest heaved as I stood over the bodies. I'd done the unforgivable, had betrayed Sara, but all I felt was excitement—

an exhilaration that built until I choked out a laugh. Was this what it really felt like to do what was right by my own free will?

I couldn't touch Rodi, and the bigger jafos and jafas like Jafa Velmira were too hard to reach, but I only needed to kill enough for the infighting to start and then everything would fall apart. The Granite Road would be safe. Rodi was still finishing a meeting between the crew and company leaders to prepare their mobilization, but if I acted quickly, I could grab one or two of them while they searched out their crews.

I clipped Ristafo's belt to my waist and sheathed the sword, then returned to the sitting room where the smell of shit and gore had worsened. I wrinkled my nose, but knelt over the closest nobleman and closed his eyes. "*Seri do-neuro, filepa mor fiera-di Fheldspra*," I said. The words sounded awkward—I'd never spoken the Augustin death chant before, and I struggled to dredge up the words from my memory.

I repeated it over each victim, thinking of Emil as I did so. Hoping he'd approve of this tiny act. How would he feel if he knew I planned to stop the army meant to return Augustin to his family?

He'd say I was doing the right thing. The Adriann family wasn't lost yet.

I stepped outside, but froze. Sara huffed her way up the ripples of solidified magma, Rodi walking beside her. "What are you doing, Jakar?" she asked, leaning on one knee.

The princepa frowned when I didn't answer, and moved up to meet me. "You know I asked you to not carry a sword," she said, breathing lightly. "It makes some of the jafas and jafos nervous."

Rodi clapped me on the shoulder and reached for my waist. "Stick with moving pebbles around," he said, pulling the blade out. The empty sheath slapped against the side of my leg. "And cheer up. Wouldn't want to see you get killed giving the wrong person the same look you're giving me now."

"May I go?" I asked Sara. "Jafo Altabor needs me to help his men finish loading the carts on the west side of town."

It took her a moment to respond. "Sure... just be careful. You'll hurt yourself if you go wandering around while the crews are pillaging. Most of them don't recognize you yet."

"Wait," the crew leader said. He rubbed at some blood smearing the blade's edge. "Why were you in that house?"

"Fredrick mentioned some of the locals were fighting back," I said. "He asked me to warn the rest of your crew."

"Some girl killed him in the maedhall, so he was right," Sara said. "You would figure he'd take his own advice."

The jafo's eyes zeroed in on me. "He's lying."

"Jakar?" she asked.

"No," I said quickly. "I'm not lying."

"Ig. Tell the truth."

A tremble rippled through my body, extinguished by a hot flake of ash that stuck to my cheek. "I paid Rodi's crew a visit," I said, and glanced at the blade in Rodi's hands.

The sword clattered to the ground and Rodi ran for the home. The sound of rockwood striking rock echoed down the hill as Rodi disappeared inside. "What did you do?" Sara asked.

"You found time to visit your army for once."

"Yes. For you. Your elemental power fades after three passings, remember? You told me that. Now answer the question."

My trepidation faded, and my feet suddenly felt more stable on the rock. There was something calming about getting caught. It meant I no longer had to pretend. "They killed the nobility in that house, Sara. They had to die."

"Do you have any idea what you've done?" she asked in a whispered hiss. She watched the entrance to the home, waited a moment, and continued. "Rodi has the power to make the jafas and jafos aware of the fact they don't need me to pillage the Granite Road anymore. It doesn't matter what he and his crew deserve."

"Then let me kill him."

She picked up the weapon, which had slid several feet down

the rock, and spent the ensuing silence looking over the town. A building collapsed, devoured by fire, and voices argued over a set of orders. My only regret was wasting time to savor the deaths of Rodi's crew. I'd been so close.

"You have to promise you won't do anything like this again," she said. "I'll deal with Rodi. All right?"

"No."

She turned. "No?"

"You promised you'd control your army, but people are already dying. You're losing them, and for some reason you won't acknowledge it. We need to stop this before it's too late. If you don't want to help, then I'll find a way to do it myself."

Something in her face changed. It was subtle yet profound. She no longer looked like the person I'd spent weeks traveling with, just the two of us. She moved close, and her hand pulled at the twine around my neck, revealing Emil's ring hiding under my collar. "You're not the person I thought I knew," she said. "I thought you wanted to give Augustin back to my family."

"Maybe your family isn't meant to rule Augustin."

The tip of the sword stabbed the ground and a *clang* rang out, punctuating the anger on her face. "I can't believe you just said that."

I met her eyes. I'd been afraid, once, but not anymore. "I thought you believed in me," she continued. Her warm breath hit my mouth, and it smelled like mint leaves. "You gave me a gift, you know. Without you I might not have had the courage to tell people who I really was. You said that people would follow me and that they'd love me for being both a princepa and Mira's Hand. But now mine and Emil's name would fade to dust if you had your way. Didn't you once say the only thing you cared about was returning my family to the throne?"

She was right. I'd once obsessed over helping sit Emil on his father's chair. I almost answered yes but caught the word before it left my mouth. I had no idea what I wanted anymore.

Destroying Sara's army was all that mattered, but after that? The idea of serving her purpose, no matter how small, made me sick to my stomach.

She took my hand into her scarred one, caressing my knuckles. For a moment, we were back in the cartographer's den. "You're cruel for making me choose," she said. When she exhaled, her breath came out shaky.

She let go.

"They're dead," Rodi said. He was walking down the hill. Anger didn't overwhelm him like I expected, and he stumbled over the uneven rock, some of the soul gone from his eyes. When he looked at Sara, he regained some of what he'd lost.

"The others in my crew?" he asked me. "Aidio, Faye, Orla?"

"Dead."

He started toward me, but Sara inserted herself between us. "Don't."

The crew leader obeyed. Was he afraid of upsetting her now that he didn't have a crew, or was there something more there?

"You need to stay," I said to Sara. "Keep an eye on me so I don't ruin your plan." If I couldn't dismantle her army, I could at least force her to watch the damage they inflicted. Maybe then she would change her mind.

"Follow," she said.

We walked down the hill to the edge of town, to a ridge overlooking the Granite Road as it snaked down a series of switchbacks into a canyon, thirty-foot-long stalactites hanging from the ceiling and dripping water into clear pools at the bottom. The Granite Road disappeared into one of the tunnels waiting below, leading to Beledor a few miles away— the army's next target. A group of scouts in light leathers were on the ridge restocking the packs on their mounts. Jafa Vichya broke away from her crew and nodded to Sara. "Hand."

"I saw the last of your scouts return. Did they find anything?"

"The people of Beledor are aware of what happened here and are barricading themselves, as you suspected. Gonna have a bitch of a time with this one. If we find any side tunnels around their defenses, even if it fits one at a time, it'll move things much more quickly."

"Thank you, saiora. Finish your resupply and be ready to leave as soon as I'm done with these two."

Jafa Vichya nodded and left, and Sara turned to us. "Stay with me," I said before she could speak.

"I can't. My elemental power is too important to the scouting party. But I need you with the army in case primordia show up." She deliberated for several moments. "Rodi, watch after Jakar while I'm gone."

I made a disgusted sound. "Kill me instead."

She bristled. "You betrayed my family by trying to stop my army. You tried to get in my way when I only wanted to save Augustin from a man who slaughtered dozens of people to seize the throne. I thought you cared about me."

I failed to come up with a response. Of course I cared. How could she accuse me otherwise?

Her argument made no sense either. Why would she go after a man for killing Augustin's commoners when she was willing to forget those who died in the pursuit?

"Ig, you'll obey any command from Rodi as if it was a Word from me."

The power of her command made its home within my bones, deepening my loss for words. My heart started to race as I considered the consequences of what she'd done.

"I have to go now," she said. "I'll be back in three passings." She sighed, misery flashing across her face, and she handed Ristafo's sword to Rodi before heading for one of the mounts. She placed a foot in one of the stirrups and pulled herself onto the fox. The scouts and Jafa Vichya formed up behind her, and she glanced back at them before her gaze settled on me.

"Hmm," Rodi said. "That was unexpected."

Dread loomed over me like a great hand, and I considered reaching for the sword as it hung from Rodi's grip and making a run for it. Before I could move, the jafo said, "You won't stop me or this army from pillaging the Granite Road." He thought for a second. "You're welcome to kill if it'll get Sara to the Augustin capital, though. Might need to have you hunt down any deserters."

The weight of the command pressed against the top of my spine, and I shuddered. A small whine left me, and I almost cried.

We watched the scouting party canter down the road, cross the canyon floor, and disappear into the passage dimly lit with red. As soon as they disappeared, Rodi said, "Jump on one foot."

The flesh binding squeezed the back of my head when I refused to move. Before it could punish me, I hopped once, trying to hide the glassiness in my eyes.

"Damn," he said. "Don't even have to use that command word. Lay on the ground."

I lay on my back. White-hot fury replaced my panic, and I looked up at him, all the hatred in my life concentrated in that one moment.

His boot collided with the side of my ribs, and I pulled myself into a ball. Another hit to the back made me grunt. The jafo struck me over and over, and I waited in silence, imagining what it would feel like to strap him to a chair with a dull knife in my hands.

He stepped back to catch a breath, chest heaving. "Stand."

I struggled to my feet, wiping blood from a split lip. My body felt tender and bruised, and my breathing hitched from a broken rib. It didn't matter what he did to me though. None of it mattered.

He made a tired wave with the sword. "C'mon."

We walked down the road running through the middle of town, the buildings lining it full of broken windows, splintered doors, and the beaten spirits of those gagged and bound in front of them. The occasional house popped and crackled with fire. Hundreds of mercenaries amassed on the road, their boots churning mossy landscapes and gardens to mud, preparing to depart. Jafa Velmira spoke with her second-in-command in the Radavich old tongue, next to a half-filled cart while inspecting a haul of pillaged swords and staves. My limping caught her eye.

Rodi turned up a footpath leading to a building with a sign hanging off a single rope, swinging above the doorway.

Gulrotavas
Fremde med kolg tomage velkemen!
The Carrot Tavern
Come with cold and empty bellies, or prepare to share!

A group of locals sat in mud against the front of the inn, their hair dusted with ash, and blood-smeared dirt staining their faces. It was a cluster of families, with sets of parents and a few dozen children ranging from babies bundled in blankets to young teenagers. Those carrying newborns were the only ones without their hands tied behind their backs, and couples leaned against each other as they eyed us.

Rodi ran a finger through the blood on Ristafo's sword and wiped it on my forehead. "You're gonna spend the rest of your life dreaming of the faces of my crew, wishing you coulda taken it all back." He offered the weapon and pointed at the man sitting closest to the door, a burly fellow who looked like a cook, possibly the owner. "Now take this sword and kill that man."

The families started—the cook scooted closer to his wife, their three children pressing in from the other side. The taste of acid crawled up the back of my throat. "Rodi, please," I said. "Don't do this."

"You got five minutes to complete this task."

"You said you'd spare us if we listened!" the cook's wife screamed as she clutched a child to her chest. Her words caught the attention of dozens of nearby mercenaries, who clustered around the line of carts to see what was going on.

I turned my back to the families and faced the crew leader. "Just take it back," I said. "I'll do anything. Just take it back."

He pushed the oiled leather of the sword's grip into my hands, squeezing my fingers over it. "This is the price they pay for those we lost taking Cragreach," he said loud enough for the families to hear. "Blood for blood."

I stepped away, sword in hand, and glanced at my wrist.

"Don't even try to harm yourself," he added. "And never play poker, friend."

I stuck my wrist out and brought the sword up, but lightning struck.

Overwhelming pain.

It faded, and I found myself on the ground, vomit in my mouth, my skull thrumming with a hangover of agony. The punishment had only lasted a second, disappearing as soon as the sword was out of my hands, but that moment had been worse than any conventional pain I'd experienced in my life. "Better hurry," Rodi said as he stood over me. "We got places to be."

I crawled on the ground, reaching out for the sword, taking as much time as possible, panicking as I tried to figure out what to do. More mercenaries had shown up to watch, the sounds of labor quieting as people whispered to each other. The owner lumbered to his feet, his arms still bound behind his back, and stepped forward. His wife grabbed for him. "No, Fahreti," he said. "I'm dead either way. Least my children can know I died standing." His back was to them. They couldn't see the way his mouth trembled, his eyes filling with tears.

I pulled myself up, using the sword for support. "Do it," the owner said. "Do it," he repeated, more quietly, his voice shaking, matching the fear that had to be in my eyes. "You can't save me. Better you than one of them."

I let myself move without thinking. The sword came up and around, sliding along the man's neck until the artery was severed, spilling blood down his body. He crumpled to his knees, and his wife and children screamed, rushing over to press their bodies to him during his last moments, their arms still bound behind them. The three children cried, the wife sobbing, and she looked up at me. "*Jeval.*"

The hollowness in my chest deepened. It was Sorrelo all over again. I couldn't be that man again.

"Good, good," Rodi said. "Kill the rest of the family now. You got five minutes."

The mother and children's cries intensified, and they pushed harder against the still form of the father, as if he could protect them. "I can't," I said, my voice cracking.

"Can so," the jafo said. "This is just the beginning. Cragreach will be a ghost town by the time you're done."

Some of the men and women in the other families tried to scramble to their feet while those around them broke down, begging, but Rodi kicked them down or punched them until they stumbled back. The mercenaries guarding the captives moved closer, setting their hands on the hilts of their weapons, but they looked at each other and at Rodi with wide, questioning eyes. The kids who were old enough to understand tucked themselves as tight as they could against their parents, pleading into their chests, and the littlest ones watched on, trying to figure out why everyone was so upset, some of them starting to cry anyway. Jafa Vilmera and Jafo Hedasian whispered to each other as they watched the spectacle, but they didn't intervene.

I didn't move, taking in deep breaths. I thought killing Emil was the only Word I couldn't obey, but I realized that wasn't true. I couldn't do *this*. It didn't matter how much the punishment terrified me, especially so soon after the previous one. All I had to do was let it take me one more time. Hopefully my death would rob Rodi of the need to murder these people for what I did to his crew.

Knowing the punishment would be coming, and knowing I could prevent it if I really wanted to, made me tremble violently. I tried looking at the terror in the children's eyes, at the way they tried to curl in and hide behind the backs of their parents, but it did nothing to give me courage. My knees went soft and I almost lost my footing. I focused on the staccato sounds of my erratic breathing, trying to force my diaphragm into even, forceful breaths as my teeth chattered uncontrollably, the thump of my blood pounding in my ears. *One last time*, I thought.

It struck.

The pain wrapped me in an eternity. It was all I knew. All I'd ever known.

Then I came to, opening my eyes and wondering where I was. Wondering if I was dead.

But death hadn't come for me—Rodi still loomed over me like a god.

His mouth was moving. "—five more minutes," he was saying.

Sobs wracked my body. "Please…" I croaked. The flesh binding squeezed the back of my head with its horrifying grip. Rodi knelt and lay Ristafo's sword next to me. I rolled to my side and stared at the weapon through the tears. Behind me, the families wept.

I gripped the sword's handle.

Part 3

Chapter 26 – Ig

THREE SMITHS IN soot-stained robes and bared feet stood before Sara and me, beneath an archway in the Foundry's private chapel. As the smiths listened to the princepa, a mosaic of stained glass backlit by magma that coursed through the walls struck their faces with light. I could see the fear, even as they attempted to mask it. Sara asked the unprecedented

"The city guard will defend Olevic Pike out of duty, even though they should follow me," Sara said. "We have the numbers outside the city. My strike force can attack the gates, and we'll only need your help fighting our way into the palace. If we do it quickly there won't be many casualties."

The council of senior arc smiths chewed on her words. They were a group of three that had formed following Mateo's disappearance, created whenever the master smith left Augustin. But I could tell they didn't want to make the decision without Mateo present.

Sara pressed on. "You fought for my family when Olevic betrayed Augustin to stage his coup. You defended us. What I'm asking for isn't that far-fetched. It's the right thing to do."

"Mateo asked us to suspend our vows during the coup," one of them said. "It was necessary then, but this is different. You aren't asking us to defend you. You want us to attack. To be the aggressor." He was the oldest of the group, a man in his mid-sixties but built like a riverboar.

Another smith—a tall, sturdy-looking woman ten years my senior—met my gaze. I told myself her suspicion was imagined. What would they do if they knew what we'd done to get here? If they knew about Cragreach? The memory almost overwhelmed me, and I wavered on my feet, trying my hardest to hold myself together. I looked away to stare at the assortment of colors in the mosaic. Then I retreated into that quiet place in my mind. A favorite place of mine lately. Picturing it when I closed my eyes was easy after so little sleep in so many passings. I could feel the rockwood beneath my hands and feet. Could experience the intense hunger from being starved by the kadiphs. It was a terrible place, but it distracted me from remembering.

"When the reformers attacked us in the Foundry several weeks ago, do you remember what Mateo said?" the princepa asked. "Protect the Adrianns at all costs. Help us and you'll be fulfilling your duty."

It didn't take long for the smiths to reach a decision. They would help.

"We'll spread the word to our brothers and sisters," the lead smith said. "Ten minutes is all we need." The imminent violence didn't rattle their nerves, but I could tell it disturbed them. They would know some of the men and women they'd be forced to kill.

Sara and I moved to the back of the chapel where the lava fall flowed. It spat globules of heat and fire into a narrow, glowing cavity below, now split in two like parted curtains to reveal a hidden passageway beyond. Our strike team waited in the tunnel's shadow. We'd spent an hour climbing through old mineshafts threatening to cave in at any time just to find the secret passage Mateo told us about several weeks earlier. We'd encountered two Augustin smiths on the Granite Road—one of whom didn't know about the secret passage, and the other providing detailed directions before Rodi killed him.

Sara gestured toward the darkness, and the strike team headed in single file, jumping over the cavity and avoiding the magma falling on either side. I watched the molten rock fall, its heat on my face, the strike team fading into my periphery. The longer I watched, the more the sound of boots on stone faded into the background until all I heard was gurgling magma. There was something different about the fire. Or did I imagine it?

Survive.

I blinked hard, but the dancing light didn't go away.

Persevere. For the sake of everyone.

There was a voice in the fire, a whisper in the flames, barely audible. But that didn't mean it was real. Most things didn't feel real lately.

A hand on my shoulder. "The hard part's over," Sara was saying to me. I blinked again and the dancing light was gone. Sara was watching her strike force crowd into the room. "Looks like that smith Tuli Dempra didn't work with Olevic, otherwise the Listener would've known about this passageway. Lucky us."

Emil and Sara had once arrested Mateo in this chapel, before all this began. It felt like so long ago. I closed my eyes once more to catch a glimpse of my quiet place, if only for a moment.

When I opened my eyes, Rodi loomed out of the tunnel, the last of our strike team of eighty, and he made a motion as if tipping a hat toward me. It angered me until memories made the back of my throat fill with stomach acid.

Sara looked from him to me, and something in my eyes softened her. "Rodi, we'll take it from here. Go let the others know the front gates will fall soon. Make sure they're ready to go."

Rodi frowned. "I haven't cracked any skulls in a while. Don't make me pick my ass with the rest of the army."

"The plan's changed."

"At least let me go with you and the smiths to the palace. I'm good with a club. Might need me next to you."

"You're going to help the other crew and company leaders secure the upper levels once Jakar gets the gates open. Kill whoever resists, but your main objective will be to let everyone know the Adrianns have returned. Ensure they peacefully wait out the fighting."

He let out a mock sigh. "Fine." His hand clapped my shoulder and I shivered. "Good luck, friend." The passage's darkness swallowed him.

"Take the gates as quickly as possible," Sara said to me. "Come to the palace afterward so I'm not sandwiched between any fighting on the first and third levels."

I nodded and turned to leave. She gripped my upper arm, stopping me. "You can't give me the cold shoulder forever. You have every right to be angry, but I don't want you getting us killed by not communicating."

My mouth opened, but I closed it again when I found I had nothing to say. She had no right to judge my coldness when she'd made no effort to speak to me alone since Cragreach.

"Ig, talk to me." The command was half-hearted but firm.

The pressure on the back of my head appeared. My most intimate adversary. But I had nothing to say. The damage had been done. Nothing could reverse Cragreach or the trail of fire the army had left in our wake.

"I just don't understand," I finally said. "You once said to me you wanted to overthrow Olevic Pike because of the commoners he killed during the coup, but you have to know what happened in Cragreach. People have died since then too."

She stepped in close so no one else could hear. "This army is made of mercenaries, not soldiers," she whispered. "They lost control of themselves, just like you said. You were right and I can admit that." Her breath smelled like the cinnamon bark she liked to chew, and its warmth touched my neck. "You don't know how lucky we are that they kept their sights on Augustin."

I snorted at the absurdity, nearly overcome. "You should've let me keep going after I killed Rodi's crew. I would've given my life to stop the jafas and jafos."

The look on her face tensed with that last sentence. "No. You would've gotten yourself killed for the effort. You're not that powerful." She squeezed my arm and left.

My strike team threw aside prayer blankets and leaned against placements of stone carvings as they filled the chamber, jittery with anticipation. This was a game to them. The council of smiths returned, and they looked ready to voice an argument. But they didn't. "We're ready," the senior arc smith said.

Sara led us through halls of dark stone and red light full of the smell of metal and fire. Her numbers swelled as smiths joined from branching hallways and rooms, and soon I could no longer see the swing of her dark hair through the bodies. Every smith brandished a weapon—most carried a one-handed hammer and shield, some with longer, two-handed hammers. There wasn't a blade in the bunch. They all wore the same expression of worry and resignation. Sara had asked a lot from these people, had forced them to choose sides after several weeks of tenuous peace between them and the Listener.

The blanket of warmth lifted when we reached the drafty front shop and its darkened forges. Augustin had blockaded the city entrance a few hours ago, sometime after our army passed through Sanskra, so most of the city's inhabitants would be hiding in their homes by now. Only a few patrons roamed the shelves, and they froze to watch smiths and mercenaries alike pour out of the back hallways. They cowered in the corners and stared at the ground, as though hoping we wouldn't see them. Several smiths approached them and offered quick, soft-spoken words.

If only Sara had led an army of smiths along the Granite Road instead of the killers at my back. Why had I spent these past two years judging the Foundry for their beliefs? It didn't matter whether or not I believed in their god. What mattered was the result. I hated the eighty sellswords I led toward the gates, all of whom moved restlessly, chomping at the bit, hoping to add more notches to their belts of anguish.

But I wasn't leading them for Sara anymore. I led them for Emil. When he came home, he would find a way to fix this. He would find a way to fix me.

We passed through the pillars of the Foundry's entrance and into the wide cavern beyond. Augustin's gates sat to our left at the bottom of a long, gradual descent, and to our right, the upward slope leading to the city's first level. Normally this road would have been clogged with heavy-laden caravans, fresh and weary travelers, and yelling purveyors of food stands trying to sell everything from kabobs to fried root. Now the wheel ruts worn into the rock looked naked. Everything was empty. I could almost taste the tension.

I nodded in signal to the men behind me and took off down the slope. They raised their swords and whooped, running after me.

None knew of my flesh binding—only the crew and company leaders were aware of it, and even then, it was an inkling. The fighters following me believed I'd slaughtered countless innocents willingly, and my reputation continued to feed their courage. Did goodness exist anywhere among the lot? Or had they been torn down to the foundations like me?

The entrance into the city resembled Radavich's. The tunnel zigzagged, and within each segment, artificial barriers fifteen-feet high had been constructed. But while the barrier's sheer wall stalled an invading force, the side pointing toward the city allowed soldiers access to the parapets. Those on the first barricade scrambled to create a defensive line when they saw us charging. While the strike force shouted, overcome by the thrill of the fight, I stayed silent. I carried no sword or shield.

Our line charged up the steps and crashed into them. I blocked the stabs of pikes, pushing the flats of the blades away with the palms of my hands. Wrists and ankles broke as I knocked soldiers to the floor. They'd had the advantage of the high ground, but only thirty men manned each barricade. Normally, that would have been plenty against a force ten times our number, if we'd been attacking from the other side.

It was over in minutes. Where the end of the parapet met the tunnel wall, two soldiers pressed their backs against the rock. One of my men surged past me, and his sword flashed as he cocked it back, but I grabbed his arm before it could lash downward. "No," I said.

The mercenary paused, but didn't argue. "Surrender," I said to the soldiers.

They nodded emphatically.

Another mercenary, still drunk on the fight, tried to squeeze past us to deliver a killing blow. I grabbed his wrist, twisted it back until I felt the snap of his bone under his flesh, and shoved him over the wall. He fell fifteen feet to the rock below. When he bounced off the ground and came to a rest, he started screaming. No pressure appeared on the back of my neck—Rodi had forbidden me from harming the army until we reached Augustin, and here we were.

The rest of the strike force faltered. Some of them stepped away, nervous, and for a moment I considered. I could hurt them. I could kill them.

"Let them surrender if they ask," I finally said. My tone made it clear what would happen if they disobeyed. "And move fast. The rest are going to hear him."

The strike force dismantled the drawbridge door built into the barricade, and I regarded the soldiers I'd saved. They were several years younger than me, each only seventeen or eighteen. A year or two younger than Emil. "No one else will hurt you," I said. The continued wailing of the man drove home my point.

At least I had saved two.

We continued to the next passageway, and it was the same story. Three defenders managed to surrender before anyone slaughtered them, and this time nobody attempted an execution. Five barriers stood between us and the start of the Granite Road, and when we reached the last one, forty-seven out of my eighty had fallen. We took eighteen prisoners in total.

The drawbridge door to the final barricade fell. Its echoes shot into the vast cavern, where the walls and the ceiling flared out, covered in moist rock, flowering roots, and glowing crystals, the start of the Granite Road shooting through the center of the cavern floor, crusted with coral and mycelium trees. Sara's army camped just beyond the range of bow fire, and they cheered when they saw us. Their advance lacked any semblance of rhythm or organization, and the mercenary leaders led the way—a group of twenty-three jafos and jafas who led their horde toward my home.

All I could think about in that moment was killing them all.

When the army reached the drawbridge, they shoved and fought to move inside first. The mercenary leaders led them back the way I'd come, working under orders from Sara to kill any who resisted but to keep collateral damage to a minimum. Retaking a city didn't mean anything if they destroyed it in the process. Much good a command like that did.

Twenty members of my strike force stayed behind to man the front gates, looting discarded pikes. The steps to the parapets creaked as someone climbed up the back side of the barricade. Rodi. He noticed the three bound soldiers sitting in the corner. "We taking prisoners now?" he asked.

If this had been weeks ago, the realization of what he wanted would have caused my composure to crack, but now my mind only retreated into my quiet place. I could feel the cold wood of the Ebonrock cage under me, the air wet in my nostrils and full of the sound of dripping water. A place I never should have left. "Kill them," he commanded.

My body was a machine as I unsheathed the knife and leaned over the three soldiers as they looked up at me, tears already in their eyes. I'd promised them safety as long as they obeyed. They shied from my blade, pushing themselves against the rock, kicking at me with their bound feet. Their eyes pled. Those eyes fluttered when I slit their throats.

Rodi nodded in satisfaction, and my strike force watched me, aware of the contradiction in my actions. They would have expected at least some protest from the man who had broken a comrade's wrist to ensure prisoners were taken and protected. Whatever they saw in my eyes made them keep quiet. They'd seen my work in Cragreach.

I followed Rodi as we headed back into the city. He paid no heed to the other prisoners held captive by the mercenaries now manning the other barricades, and I realized he had only wanted the others dead out of fleeting pettiness.

I tried not to think about that.

The path brought us up and into the city until it flattened out on a road of limestone bricks comprising the first level's walkways, the tunnel's sloped ceiling giving way to the sharp edges of cut stone where the first businesses of the trade district waited. All of them were closed. Blood smeared the corner of a shoemaker's shop, and several of the city guardsmen lay on the ground, armor dented and muscle and flesh gouged open. Mercenaries clashed with clusters of guards along the circumference of the first level, but the fighting was sparse on the upper levels. The wind carried a cacophony of screams and cries as citizens caught outside scurried to find shelter.

Mercenaries streamed up the ramp to the second level, uninhibited—Sara's army had struck before anyone could fortify the ramps to the palace level. I moved to the wrought-iron railing at the edge of the ridge and peered up. Almost thirty feet of space separated floor from ceiling, with gnarled bushes growing out of cracks in the rock between levels. I balanced on top of the railing, and grunted as I kicked off and sailed upward, bypassing the ramp entirely. It was my first time using elemental power in the open city, and I had always wondered if I'd be able to make it from one level to the next. My fingers grazed the lip, barely catching, and I heaved myself up.

Platoons from Augustin's military corps charged three dozen smiths—the brunt of the Foundry's order—and poured down the third level ramp where the barracks were. The smiths dodged their strikes with a metal worker's finesse, but since they were unpracticed, struggled to land blows of their own. They were losing.

The mercenary army near the ramps fought in a frenzy, but discord and melancholy threaded its way among the Augustin soldiers and the smiths. I could sense the stilted hesitation in the battle. A distaste that would evolve into horror in the hours after the fight.

But still, the soldiers attacked the smiths, following orders to defend the city. Doing as they were told. Before the smiths' line could buckle, I charged in.

Weapons were sometimes awkward things in a battle. My hands granted greater control to parry and deflect attacks, and offered more choice in whether to land a killing blow. While the swords of one side crashed against the shields and hammers of the other, I sailed into the thick of it, feet sliding over the limestone like oil on water. My body flew low to the ground, and I swung around legs and waists, punching hamstrings and breaking ankles. I was a leaf in the wind. Laughter burst from me at the exhilaration, then the sobbing came. For a moment, I really could forget.

If only I'd been asked to fight like this on the Granite Road.

More enemies focused on me when they realized the stone-skinned man with no weapon was causing their line to crumble. Several tried to impale me against the ground, but I jumped, body spinning over everyone until I landed safely behind the smiths. The armada's defense folded and the smiths managed to push them toward the third level ramp. A number of smiths discarded their hammers and began fighting with their fists, using shields for protection. They were following my example.

A small group of smiths clustered around the palace doors, and I caught a glimpse of Sara's hair. The city guard who had been posted in front of the doors were either dead or had fled. When I joined the princepa, a crate of pyroglycerin was stacked in front of the ornate, rockwood doors. Where she'd found such a supply, I had no idea. "Just in time," she said. "You look like you're in a better mood."

"For a second I felt like I was in control again."

She ignored the jab and looked to the door ruefully. She still acted guilty whenever she used a Word, which was odd, considering she never acknowledged how Rodi had controlled me in the same way. But I was past the point of trying to understand.

At least her guilt meant she cared.

Flourishes of masonry talent covered the palace front, with patterns of decorative cornices and recessed walls for us to hide inside. The group divided into several of the recesses and a smith started to count down. At zero he ignited the fuse leading to the pyroglycerin. Five heartbeats later, an explosion rocked us, blowing chunks of rock off the ridge that bounced across the chasm floor below.

A full garrison waited for us inside—a barrier of heavy armor and stern faces at the end of the marble hallway. To my left, torches reflected off the palace's famous stone mural detailing Augustin's history; opposing forces on opposing ends of its story. The garrison was an impenetrable wall with no way to flank them. Sara waved a command and we stopped.

"I'll deal with this," Sara said. She stepped forward.

"You recognize me, don't you?" she asked in a raised voice. "I'm Sara Adriann, the princepa of Augustin. Why are you fighting? You should be defending my family."

The soldiers' demeanors changed subtly. Sara's words worked at the sharp lines in their bodies, but did little else.

"You see the smiths behind me, right?" she continued. "They're loyal to the magnate above everyone else, except Fheldspra. And they're fighting for me. Stand down and fight for the right side."

"We've heard about the rumors on the Granite Road," a sergeant called out. "We won't let you or that evil behind you infect this place."

She looked in my direction. Was he talking about me?

Flying steel rippled on the waves of my elemental senses. I shoved Sara out of the way as a six-foot length of spear flew over the line of soldiers, aimed for the princepa.

Time seemed to slow as my mind processed a dozen thoughts in an instant. My life flashing before my eyes, I realized. But instead of a string of memories, I only experienced self-reflection.

All I had to do was let the spear fly true.

My hands clamped down where the haft met the spearhead, the blade's cruel point an inch from my chest.

The sound of wood clattering against stone echoed through the chamber as I dropped the weapon. Sara recovered, and I expected a command for us to charge the line. "Did they just try to kill me?" she asked no one in particular. Anger swelled among the smiths. Even I was surprised. But these were Olevic Pike's most loyal soldiers—those who had lifted the man up during his coup.

"Jakar," she said. "Can you break through that line?"

I shook my head. With concentration and slow work, pushing through them was possible, but I would've had to be within arm's reach.

"And if you had a source of heat?"

"Wait here," I said, and pushed my way through the smiths.

Outside, the fighting had intensified while Sara's army struggled to prevent the corps from spilling onto the second level. Each level possessed three ramps and a half dozen set of stairs along its circumference, and the mercenary army protected the crescent piece of this level where the palace resided. I jumped from the ridge's railing.

Falling was easier than jumping with my elemental power. When my feet met the black rock, a push from my power cushioned my fall. I rolled forward and recovered, running for the river.

Heat bathed my body as I stood at the lava's edge. The magma bubbled and spat—horrible pain and death for anyone who touched it. Anyone except for me. Me, of all people.

Those meant to serve didn't deserve this power. If Fheldspra existed, why didn't He make the Adrianns go through the Imbibings if they wanted to control the elements? If they were strong enough to lead, why couldn't they carry this burden?

I plunged both arms into the fires. When I pulled back, molten rock covered me from my fingers to halfway up my biceps. My elemental senses flared outward and pain nipped at different parts of my arms.

When I came to within fifty feet of the sinkhole's wall, I jumped. Soldiers and mercenaries paused in their fighting to watch as I arced toward the second level and skipped over the railing to land on the ridge.

Inside, the smiths stepped out of my way, whispering to one another when they noticed my glowing, magma-coated arms. I broke through the line and stepped beside the princepa. Fear pulsed through the faces of the soldiers.

Pikes poked through the shield wall as I charged. Ten feet before I reached their points, I skidded to a stop and thrust my hands in front of me.

Men screamed as those directly in front of me flew backward. I continued forward, and when someone tried to stab me with their pike, I swatted the steel edge away, the repulsion spinning the weapon out of the man's hands. The haft of another pike burst into flame when I parried a blow.

Sara and the others joined the fight. The hole I'd created widened, and the princepa leaped with her elemental power, vaulting over an unbroken section of the line. The soldiers turned to defend themselves; several against one. Another pushing motion sent them skidding across the floor.

The smiths finished dispatching the defenders, and the magma sloughed off me into two piles. I continued onward with Sara, rubbing at my hot forearms. The skin started to sweat profusely but felt mostly undamaged. More guards waited farther inside the palace, but none were as organized as that first line.

Those outside the atrium doors stepped aside to let us by. We found Olevic Pike inside, watching us pour in as he stood in front of his granite chair. He had done some redecorating—portraits of his daughter hung on two of the square pillars holding up the room, over the carvings of Fheldspra battling the Great Ones. Toys and puppets lay scattered next to the dais, and protective railings had been placed around the magma pool against the wall so a child wouldn't accidentally touch it. The place had been made child-friendly, to the point where the atrium looked almost alien. A place where a father loved his daughter.

"If it isn't the magnate himself," Sara said. "Where are your guards?"

The man looked down his nose through a pair of spectacles. "They left when they learned the smiths had joined the fighting. The rumors are true, I see. You're Mira's Hand."

"I guess the secret's out. Please don't judge me too harshly for breaking the law, Listener."

"You know, I'm not impressed often," he said, his tone and demeanor morphing. "You turned the Granite Road into quite the interesting place." It seemed he no longer cared to put on a show for the smiths. Maybe he knew what was coming. "I had the pleasure of hearing all sorts of stories from those who stayed in front of your wave." His gaze fell on me. "I could have learned so much from you, *Dor di Fero*."

"What did you call me?" I asked.

"Refugees talk of an elemental accompanying Mira's Hand. It means 'The Iron Sorrow' in the old tongue. I would've loved to see how you worked for a nickname like that." He eyed Sara. "I never knew you were capable of mass murder."

The council of smiths pushed through their brothers and sisters to stand at the front. "Liar," one said. It was the tall, sturdy-looking woman. "You're trying to erode our faith in the princepa. We've helped many refugees who fled from Sanskra. None mentioned mass murder."

"Plenty knew of the incoming army. Few actually saw that army's destruction for themselves." He shook his head at Sara. "The Iron Sorrow and Mira's Hand are two people, but they're not really, are they? I saw the control your father had over Ig, and it made me realize something. The Adrianns are just a bunch of puppeteers, aren't they?"

My breath caught. Did he know about the flesh binding?

Sara nudged me forward. "Please go retrieve our dear friend from that pedestal he's put himself on."

As I grabbed Olevic from the top of the steps and dragged him down, he studied me. The refugees had a name for me. The Iron Sorrow.

I shoved Olevic to his knees in front of Sara. "I looked into your past when I saw what you did during the coup," he said to me. "Sent friends through The Rift to Sulian Daw. You can break the chains holding you down."

I stilled. "What?"

"Keep my daughter safe when you do. I can die happily knowing she's safe. Gut the princepa while you're at it, as a favor to us both." Before I could answer, his attention shifted to the smiths behind Sara. "My body count doesn't hold a candle to the Adrianns. Stand for evil like her and an eternity of ice and darkness awaits you. Isn't that what your Sky Scrolls say?"

"Oh, shut up already," Sara said, and spat on the man. Saliva dripped down Olevic's face, and Sara pulled out her blade, yanked the Listener's head back by his hair, and stabbed him in the right eye, shattering his spectacles. The man's body smacked against the marble.

The princepa took a deep breath and her shoulders slumped. "It's over." She smiled at me. "It's finally over. We got our home back."

The smiths looked at the puddle of blood growing under Olevic's head, and at Sara. Then at me. A chorus of emotions simmered under the surface.

"Go put down any remaining resistance in the city," Sara ordered. "Spare anyone if you can."

The smiths hesitated for one second, then two. They turned and left.

Chapter 27 – Efadora

OUR LITTLE GROUP ducked behind an outcropping of rocks near the shore of Sanskra Lake. The Granite Road wrapped around the cavern's edge, but we only had eyes for the firelight glimmering in the middle of the lake, the minerals in the cavern's ceiling twinkling above, and the town of Sanskra, calmer than it had any right to be. A distant scream shattered the illusion.

I pulled myself onto the largest rock where darkness still offered a bit of cover, and Emil followed suit. "Did you hear that?" I asked in a low voice.

"Yes."

"Does that mean we caught up to the army?"

"Sanskra can't fit an army. Looks like they already marched on, left behind a garrison in town." He pointed to the far end of the path that shot across the lake like a black arrow, where the plateau began. "I see barricades, but nobody's manning them."

We joined the others as they watered their mounts behind a grove of coral trees, illuminated by a cluster of white quartz. Mateo sat on his knees at the darkness's edge where the grove met the Granite Road, forehead pressed to the ground. He'd prayed every passing since Lo Toddul.

"They've garrisoned the town, but it's hard to say with how many," Emil said.

"Why leave men behind?" Mateo asked as he joined us. He rubbed at the gravel stuck to his forehead.

"Maybe to prevent Olevic from flanking the army." He eyed Carina, Petamare, Brux, and the rest of the soldiers. "Eyes and ears open. We don't know what to expect, so keep your guard up. Follow my and Mateo's lead. Understand?"

"Yes, Het Adriann," the soldiers said in unison. We attached our foxes to rockwood spikes nailed into the ground, and Emil took the lead as we followed the series of interconnected bridges on the north side of the lake. Torches lined the rutted pathway, but someone had doused the flames. We found the local guards on the town's edge in a tangle of limbs in the rocky soil, pincushions to a volley of arrows.

"We knew this would happen," I said to my brother. All of us had hoped Sara would keep as much blood as she could off the Granite Road, but guards took the defense of their towns seriously. Casualties were inevitable.

"I know," he said, voice flat. He gave the hand signal and we kept moving.

Sanskra's buildings looked mostly intact. We hid behind a general store with broken-in windows, and Petamare pointed through the shop. "See the carts in the middle'a town?" he whispered. "Twenty-five'r so. Maybe more."

The windows on the front and back of the store lined up to provide a peephole to the town's center. Sanskra's Fheldspra statue, glowing from rock infused with fire opal, shed light on a collection of carts brimming with carpets, chests, dinnerware, and rare metals. The carts were surrounded by half as many men and women in worn fighting leathers, scuffed with the dirt of their travels.

"Looks like you were right," Carina whispered to Mateo. "That caravan must be how the mercenary army is paying for itself."

"Where're all the people who live here?" Brux asked.

Emil fiddled with the hilt of his Meteor Blade. "They must've taken refuge in Augustin before the attack. C'mon. No point in delaying this."

My brother left his cover, tailed by the rest of us, and he walked toward the town center, hands raised. The mercenaries turned at the sound of our boots crunching in the gravel, and scrambled from where they lounged around the carts, grabbing for their weapons. One let out a sharp whistle.

"I'm looking for Sara Adriann. Princepa of Augustin," my brother announced. "I'm her brother, Emil."

The nearest sellsword jogged to Emil, and his sword rang from its sheath in an upward cut. My brother jumped back, inhaling sharply, then lunged forward into the pocket of the man's backswing and wrested the sword from the sellsword's grip. He struck the man in the nose with the weapon's guard and kicked him to the ground.

I pulled out my dagger in one hand and my brass knuckles in the other. The mercenaries advanced on us, weapons ready.

"Listen to me," Emil said. "I'm the princep of Augustin. I'm Sara Adriann's brother. Isn't she in charge of your army?"

A pair of sellswords approached him. "You're a dead brother," one of them said.

They swung at Emil simultaneously. My brother deflected one blade with his left palm and parried and riposted the other with the sword he'd taken, plunging his weapon through the right man's leather chest guard. The man fell, and Emil cut the other one down, then discarded the sword and pulled out the Meteor Blade.

"Take prisoners if you can," he said over his shoulder as he settled into a fighting stance.

A dozen more sellswords grouped together, then let out a battle cry and charged. Our group rushed forward to meet them.

Emil and Mateo's swords blurred as they fought, striking with such force that one mercenary dropped his weapon, grunting from the vibrations. My brother once told me his elemental ability let him add power to the swing through the weapon's fulcrum. Soldiers like Meike, on the other hand, fought with muscle and staccato movements—she caught an enemy's sword with her cross guard and shouldered the mercenary to the ground, skewering her foe in the stomach.

An advantage to being so young, and short to boot, was how often people saw me as an afterthought. I arced around the fighting, pretending to be a frightened little girl caught in the chaos, and moved behind three mercenaries advancing on Meike. The mercenaries stabbed at the same time, and Meike knocked their weapons aside.

The nearby fighting pulled our friends away, leaving Meike's flanks unprotected, and the three sellswords moved in. The guard backed off, sensing the danger, but the mercenaries didn't let up. I almost shouted in a desperate attempt to distract them from hurting Meike, but reined myself in and sprang into action. None of the sellswords noticed as I snuck in behind them.

My dagger slid along the hamstrings of the closest two, and they banged their knees on the ground as they collapsed, shouting in pain. Meike decapitated one, then blocked a strike from the unhurt mercenary. She continued the one-on-one as I stabbed the other mercenary I'd debilitated, and she managed to cut the man down in four moves. Meike nodded to me, breathing hard, and wiped at the sweat on her forehead, pushing her hair out of her eyes. "Thanks. Was close."

I nodded back, smiling.

Doors slammed in frames as more enemies trickled out of the buildings, but their counter-attack lacked coordination. They staggered outside, confused and angry and some half-dressed, almost unable to comprehend their fallen friends around the carts, many of them drunk or high. They desperately formed up and charged. My brother attracted most of them, flanked by Brux and Petamare and others who protected him doggedly the way he had looked out for them on the trip here—a spear tip snuck its way into the line and drew a line of red along Emil's arm, eliciting yells from Eslid and Toria, and the two Manasan soldiers collapsed on the spearman and plunged their steel into his soft flesh.

Emil broke ahead of his men. He fought with the same rage I saw in Manasus, and I wondered what had set him off this time. I sometimes worried over why I enjoyed hurting people and whether that made me a bad person, but my concern faded as I watched Emil. If he could revel in the darkness and stay a good person when it counted, I could too.

The blood of almost thirty mercenaries seeped into the dirt by the time the fighting subsided. Meike and Mateo bandaged up the soldiers with supplies from a local store, and my brother stood over the nine wounded mercenaries we had restrained. The sellswords sat in a ring at the base of Fheldspra's statue, staring at the bodies of their friends. Emil leaned on his sword, and the tip sizzled as it dug into the blood-smeared rock. "When did the main army march for Augustin?"

Nobody answered. I kicked the nearest one in the back of the ribs.

"Several hours ago," the man said as he cringed, revealing two crowns in his mouth.

"I can't imagine them breaking through Augustin's main gates if the city's had proper warning," Mateo said to my brother. "They might still be there."

An older mercenary from Augustin with a salt and pepper beard looked up from his lap. "There was talk that Mira's Hand knew a secret way into the city, just outside the main gates. Haven't heard from anyone since they left though."

"Shut up, Gabriel," Crowns said.

Mateo's face paled. "The twists. Sara must've led them through the mine shafts to the Foundry's back entrance."

"Any idea when reinforcements might arrive here?" Emil asked Gabriel, but the mercenary shook his head.

"Emil. Efadora," Carina said as she hurried toward us from the edge of town. The alarm in her voice caught everyone's attention. "Both of you need to see this."

My brother and I followed the cartographer along the side of one of the buildings until we reached the edge of the plateau. The black surface of Sanskra lake rippled with movement.

Dozens of bodies floated in the water. Fish, eels, and all manner of creatures from the deep ripped at the flesh of the dead.

Emil turned and stormed to the center of town. The group of sellswords watched my brother round to the front of Crowns and kick the man on his back. Crowns cursed, and my brother set a boot on the man's chest and touched the mercenary's shoulder with the edge of his blade. The mercenary cried out as skin sizzled and burned.

"Who's in the water?" my brother asked.

"Ones who wouldn't listen," the man said through clenched teeth.

"What does that mean? The people who lived here?"

"Yes!"

"Who authorized that?"

The man squeezed his eyes shut as tears came out. "Please, make it stop!"

The tip of Emil's blade parted from the man's shoulder, and my brother stepped away. "What's your chain of command look like? Who gives you your orders?"

The sellsword sat up and his face contorted. "Our... crew leader does. Jafa Balchi. She gets her orders from Mira's Hand."

Emil knew of Sara's alter-ego by now. I'd told him on the trip here. "And did Mira's Hand order you to kill the locals in Sanskra?" he asked.

The man shook his head.

"But you did kill some? How many?"

"I..." The man looked to his friends, but they avoided his gaze.

I wanted to kill him. For a moment, I thought my brother would do the deed—he squeezed his sword handle and his stance tightened like he was ready to swing. But he held back.

"Was this normal for you?" Emil asked. "Killing those in the town you raided?"

The older mercenary named Gabriel stirred. "Yes." His compatriots shot him looks of death.

"Why?"

"You shut your mouth," Crowns said to Gabriel.

Emil swung his fist, connecting with the side of Crowns's mouth. The mercenary's head snapped to the side and he rolled on the ground. When he sat upright again, he spat out blood. Both his crowns rolled into the dirt in front of him.

Gabriel continued, "We were real careful with the first couple towns. Or our crew was at least. But things changed in Cragreach when the Stalker executed the people there. After that, the jafos and jafas relaxed their rules."

"The Stalker? Who is that?"

"Right hand to Jafo Rodi. Real name's Jakar, I think."

Emil shared a look with Mateo, and I knew what they were thinking. Why would Sara let one of her subordinates get away with mass slaughter? "This Jakar," my brother said. "You say he killed everyone in Cragreach?"

Gabriel nodded. "Cut them down, every single one. Men, women, children. Little babes too. He's cold as they come."

"And what did Mira's Hand say when this happened?"

"Dunno. Mira's Hand didn't spend much time with the army, far as I know."

A stab of pain touched my thumb, and I realized that in my restlessness, I'd poked myself with my dagger. How many people had died on the Granite Road?

Stop her, Ig's note had said.

"Keep an eye on them," Emil said to the soldiers, and he gestured for Mateo and me to follow him until we walked out of earshot.

"I'm a flame-forsaken fool," my brother said. His Adam's

apple bobbed up and down, and he let out a shaky breath. "Sara was supposed to keep her army under control."

"We weren't in a position to stop them even if we wanted to," the master smith said. "And we don't know the whole story."

I remained quiet, struggling to rein in my nerves. I was the one who'd reassured Emil back in Manasus that Sara wouldn't let anything bad happen on the Granite Road. I squeezed my hand into a fist and pushed the thoughts away. "Where were Ig and Sara when that Jakar fellow killed those people?" I asked.

"I don't know, but we need to find Sara," Emil said.

The master smith turned toward the circle of captives. "And what about them?"

"We don't know if they had a hand in killing the people of Sanskra, but the evidence isn't in their favor."

My hand moved to the brass knuckles in my pocket. "Do we kill them?" I asked. Sara hadn't ordered the deaths of any Sanskrans, according to Crowns, which meant she had a cancer in her army. I'd have no problem with cutting it out.

"Depends," Emil said.

We returned to the captives, and they eyed us nervously. "Who's responsible for those floating in the lake?" my brother asked.

Nobody answered.

"Gabriel?" Mateo asked. "You've been helpful so far."

A small sound escaped the older mercenary's throat, but he didn't speak.

"Emil," I said, kneeling in front of Crowns. I picked up one of the teeth Emil had knocked out. "Look at this tooth."

My brother squinted until the look on his face deepened into something more disturbed. Gold crowns were the norm among commoners, but platinum was a status symbol among the upper echelons of the nobility. Emil had one himself. A mercenary couldn't dream of affording platinum crowns.

Emil unsheathed his sword and pointed it at Crowns. "Open your mouth."

Crowns hesitated, but obeyed. Blood painted his gums, but not from any wounds caused by his knocked-out teeth. It was as if he'd set the platinum-plated teeth into the empty spaces to humor himself.

They were his trophies.

"Animal," my brother said. Crowns's mouth was still open when Emil struck. The swing was violent, uncoordinated, and sent two-thirds of the man's head rolling awkwardly across the ground, the rest of Crowns's neck a gory ruin. Some of the sellswords struggled and cringed, cursing in their old tongues, but our group held them fast.

I took in the scene with new eyes. Every captive wore rings on their fingers, noses, and ears—gleaming metals contrasted by dirty faces. The look on my brother's face betrayed similar thoughts.

"Execute them," Emil said. "Everyone except Gabriel."

The sellswords scuffled in the dirt in an attempt to flee, but our group was already in position. A dozen weapons struck within the span of a heartbeat.

Emil stood over Gabriel. "Was I wrong for killing your companions?" His question sounded tired. Empty.

Despite the fear in the mercenary's eyes, he shook his head. "All have sins to atone for."

"Even you?"

Tears appeared in Gabriel's eyes, and they ran through his beard. "I'm sorry," he said to Mateo. "Forgive me."

Mateo's expression hardened, but he didn't answer.

"Can I borrow your knife?" Emil asked the master smith as he sheathed his sword. Mateo handed it over, and my brother knelt before Gabriel with the borrowed knife, running the tip of the blade along the mercenary's dirty pant leg. "Tell me more about this Jakar."

Gabriel stared at the metal. "He itches for any chance to kill, they say. Thirsts for it like water. Jafos and jafas told us if anyone deserted, they'd have the Stalker track them down and flay 'em."

"Did you ever meet someone working directly for Mira's Hand? His name is Ig."

"No, saior. Your friend mighta been with Mira's Hand while she was scouting ahead of the army."

Emil's arm rested against his knee as he knelt, but his forearm flexed repeatedly as he gripped the knife and deliberated. Finally, he grabbed Gabriel's hands and sliced the twine with one stroke. "You're free to go."

"Saior?"

"Take the road east and you'll find a town called Thornhang. Let the people there know what happened in case they don't already. Ensure they ready their defenses. That is how you'll repay me for sparing your life."

Gabriel picked himself up and offered a small bow. "Thank you kindly."

Emil watched the sellsword head for the path leading out of town. I shook my head. "You should've killed him."

"We need someone to warn Thornhang. If he does then he'll earn his freedom. He gave us good information too."

"Spilling his guts doesn't clean the blood off his hands."

My brother turned away. "I'm tired of killing. Let's just find our sister."

Sanskra had worn Emil down, but I was just getting started. I wanted to hurt something. The feeling intensified as I thought of the mercenaries dumping body after body into Sanskra's black waters.

Carina leaned against one of the carts. "I'd like to make a suggestion," she said. "I think the dead of Sanskra deserve recompense for what happened to them."

Emil crossed his arms and waited expectantly.

The cartographer nudged her head toward the cart. "So let us offer them payment."

Emil rubbed at the beard he had cultivated over the last month. "Throw it in the lake?"

"Absolutely."

"That could take a while."

"Time well-fucking-spent."

Brux, Petamare, and the others smiled at Emil's order, and they started the first two carts toward the northern entrance, where the guard railing surrounding the town ended. Emil's spirits lifted too. It felt like a travesty for all this wealth to go to waste, but that faded when I pictured how furious it would make the mercenaries.

But this act would also undermine Sara's authority when those she commanded realized everything they'd worked for this past month had disappeared. And I didn't admit to the others that as I watched the first cart roll over the edge and splash into the black abyss, I felt like I was betraying my sister.

WE STOOD OUTSIDE the entrance to the twists, off the side of the Granite Road where the embankment led to a series of tunnels that had once been a hub for mining tin and other metals. One such tunnel was the start to a maze that apparently led to the Foundry. Emil would've killed me if he knew I'd explored these tunnels years ago, back when I discovered my love for exploring. But I knew then how exploring such an unstable cave network could be suicide. Still, I felt a sense of ownership over the twists, and so felt strangely outraged as I studied the wall of rubble before us.

"They caved it in," Mateo said.

Emil climbed the embankment onto the road. Distant veins of exposed magma and pyremoss illuminated Augustin's gates at the end of the cavern. "I knew Sara wanted to attack the capital, but part of me never believed she'd actually pull it off. Augustin's built like a fortress."

"This is Sara we're talking about," I said.

I'd expected him to begrudgingly agree, but my words only quieted him. Neither of us had spoken about Sara on the ride from Sanskra—both of us had too many questions about her inability to stop the massacres both there and in Cragreach.

"What about the passage we took out of Augustin?" Emil asked.

Mateo climbed down the embankment. "I don't think it opens from the outside. We could try blasting it open with Carina's pyroglycerin, but we'd be doing that under a magma chamber. It could kill us and whoever's in the throne room."

The plan sounded risky, but was there another option? I'd spent most of my twelfth year searching for other ways into the city, but had found nothing. Augustin was iron-clad. The only person who traveled in and out of the capital without accountability was Nektarios, the Sovereign's primordia.

"Carina," I said quickly, "do you know about any tunnels close to the surface, northwest of Augustin?"

"I'd have to look at my maps to say for sure."

I knew the tunnels existed, but it had been a couple years since I'd explored them. "The primordia travel near the surface, but nobody's bothered looking for them because everyone's terrified of Nektarios. But I can say for sure that there is an entrance the primordia use that's hidden in the northwestern section of Augustin, in the Lid. I've seen him going in and out of it, through one of the alcoves they made prison cells out of. I've been inside the tunnel too. It runs straight. I'm betting that if we find a passage as close to the surface as the Lid is, that's also directly northwest of Augustin, then we'll be close to the primordia's tunnel. Close enough for Carina to find it, and then we can use her pyroglycerin to break inside."

"Wait," Emil said. "You went inside the primordia's tunnel system?"

"I made sure Nektarios was gone first."

My brother messed up my hair. "It's not fair how Mother and Father saved up all the brains and courage in the family and gave it to their youngest. You know that?"

I tried to ignore my blazing cheeks. "Uh, thanks."

Chapter 28 – Efadora

THE SMELLS IN the tunnels Carina led us through brought me back to my explorer's phase. The cartographer touched her torch to the sconces lining the walls, and soon fire danced on pillars guarding collapsed, long-abandoned antechambers. We were in a series of old tunnels beyond the northwest edge of the city, according to Carina. Mateo said this place was once part of Augustin until the Schism collapsed most of it, but Carina insisted some of these ruins were a lot older, given the pictographs carved into some of the architecture.

Insects hiding in crevices stirred when the flame's light exposed their homes, moving in tangled masses of appendages and bodies of chitin. My skin normally would've been crawling by now, but a few weeks off the Granite Road had done well to desensitize me. "X marks the spot," Carina said, her ear and hands pressed against the wall as she stood on top of Brux. She smacked at a millipede as long as her forearm, which fell off the wall and scurried away. "There's a large cavity on the other side of this wall. Upward angle, with about a meter of rock between us and it. Definitely not natural."

She pulled out a few vials of pyroglycerin—almost the last

of her supply—and snuck them into a cubbyhole near the ceiling. A wave of bugs fled out of the hole, but Carina barely noticed. She unraveled a spool of fusing and dropped it to the ground before jumping off Brux. "If you'll do the honors, Meike."

Meike touched her torch to the fuse's end. Carina scurried away and hid in one of the antechambers, which seemed like a good sign to follow.

I flinched when an explosion blasted us with a pressure wave that nearly ruptured my eardrums. We made our way back to find rubble strewn throughout the tunnel, the air thick with dust. "How aren't all cartographers deaf by now?" I asked Carina.

"What?"

"And if someone in Augustin heard that explosion?" Mateo asked.

"Doubt it," my brother said. "If anyone noticed, it'd be wandering primordia."

His words sobered the group. One by one, we climbed through a hole barely wide enough to fit our largest group member, Brux, and once recovered, we stood together and studied our surroundings. I remembered being equally perplexed by the primordia tunnel when I'd first discovered it.

The tunnel extended into what looked like eternity in both directions, perfectly straight and rounded. At no point did it narrow or widen, with only subtle lumps and depressions along the walls. It was made of granite. Emil crouched and rubbed his hands along the surface. "How?" he asked.

"The Sovereign and his primordia built the Granite Road," I said. "Wasn't Saracosta a little backwater town before he turned it into a massive capital for his country too? This tunnel sits on the low end of the spectrum of impressive stuff they've done."

"How far have you explored?"

"Not far." The tunnel squeezed at the echoes, squashing them into nonexistence. "This is farther than I've gone."

He peered down the tunnel leading away from the city. "And that's supposed to lead all the way to Saracosta's capital? That's hundreds of miles away."

"Helps make sense as to how the primordia can travel from capital to capital inna couple passings," Petamare said.

Our group walked two abreast as we trekked toward the city. It was oppressively quiet, and everyone kept looking over their shoulder into the void.

Did Aronidus and Otalia know by now that they'd scuffled with Augustin's princepa and princep in Lo Toddul? The idea of them travelling toward us, moving at incredible speeds, awakened a primal fear in me that was hard to ignore. What were they doing traveling off the Granite Road to the Manasus capital, and why not use this tunnel system to get there? It probably had to do with the non-elementals accompanying them.

Mateo and Emil walked at the front, and everyone filled their time with nervous conversation. I tailed the group but didn't mind. Meike slowed to walk beside me—either she, Mateo, or my brother had kept me within arm's reach since Lo Toddul.

"Did well back in Sanskra," she said

"Yeah, we did."

"Sorry. Pardon the accent. I meant to say you did well back in Sanskra."

"Oh. Thanks."

An awkward silence followed. We'd traveled on good terms the past few weeks, but talking to her was hard. I still wasn't sure if she forgave me for how I'd treated her in Manasus, or for causing her quasi-exile. "I'm happy my brother let me fight," I finally said. "He gives me more freedom than anyone else. Probably because he's the Rock Snake. I'm sure he thinks he can protect me no matter what."

Meike frowned. "Right."

Her reaction was odd, but it tickled a suspicion of mine. "You don't like him very much, do you?"

"No, no, princepa. It's not like that at all." Her cheeks colored from embarrassment. It was a funny look on her.

"You can be honest," I said. "I won't tell."

"It's difficult to explain to those who don't believe in Fheldspra."

"I probably know enough to understand."

She checked on anyone listening. The soldiers weren't frosty toward her anymore, but they never made much effort to include her in the group the way they had Carina. I used to think people didn't listen to what Meike had to say because she didn't like to talk, but now I wondered if it was the other way around. "Tell me," I said. "I want to hear it."

"The Foundry holds the pursuit of mastery over one's craft highly. I heard your brother became an apprentice then left after his Trial."

"And?"

She chewed on her lip for a few moments. "About fifteen years ago, my parents were killed by a bobbit worm while three of us were travelin' through the crust. I didn't sleep for weeks after that. Couldn't stop despairing, wondering if I could've been faster." A small sound left her throat. "I almost did the same as the princep. Became a smith so I could better myself as a fighter. Would've been a terrible transgression to take advantage of the Foundry in such a way." She looked down. "Sorry, princepa. I shouldn't be saying these things about your brother."

"It's all right," I said. "But you have it wrong. Emil didn't try to join the Foundry just so he could become an iron worker. Smithhood was the most important thing to him growing up, but my father pulled him out. He was really miserable about it for the longest time after that."

She craned her neck to search my brother out. "Didn't know that."

"You should give him more credit. That's an order."

She cracked a smile. "Yes, princepa."

No light signaled the end of the tunnel, but gusts of wind

started to cut through us, as cold as my memories of past excursions in the Lid. The uniformity of the tunnel fell apart, and we stepped onto a flat plain of black ice. Icicles drooped from a ceiling fifteen feet above our heads. Ice covered all sides of the cave, afire with the reflections of our torches. The wind still came in spurts, but bit harder with each step. At the end, we turned a corner and stepped onto a small ridge overlooking Augustin.

"It's cold as shit up here," Carina said, jaw trembling.

Ignoring the hypothermia-inducing temperature, the view from this ridge always enchanted me. Billions of stars twinkled in the sky, interspersed with clouds of red and green that the Guild of the Glass studied and called nebulous stars. Ceti shimmered with waves of light overhead, the largest star in the sky, while Saffar—a burnt, red juggernaut of a moon—was hiding like it always did between passings. Augustin's ice sheaths spilled over the sinkhole's edge, growing hundreds of feet down the sides of the chasm, leaking water and mist far below. Somewhere around here was a path leading out of the sinkhole, reserved specifically for prisoners who chose ice as their preferred method of execution—they would walk out to join the small graveyard at the start of the icy wasteland, freezing in under a minute, adding to a timeline of statues extending centuries into the past. Or so I was told.

I picked my way down a narrow set of stairs. There were no protective rails this high up, and one slip would've sent anyone falling to their deaths, but everyone in our group kept their nerves hard enough to stay focused.

Augustin's top layer, the fourteenth level, was nothing more than an alcove wrapping a quarter of the way around the sinkhole. Stone masons had flattened the ground out, but the place was empty. The same story waited on the next three levels. On the tenth, packaged meats and anything needing refrigeration filled the shallow corridors to the brim. Several lifts hung from pulley systems that businesses rented from the city, but all were still, the ropes frosty with disuse. All looked quiet from this height, but it was hard to tell how much of the fighting had calmed since Sara's army broke into the city.

The eighth and seventh levels contained the Barrows, where the poorest of Augustin lived. When we reached the eighth level, a low din appeared over the whistling of the wind, and I paused. "Do you hear that?"

Eslid pointed toward a nearby alley. "There."

Emil started for the opening where teal flames danced on the walls. "Come on. Those torches aren't usually lit."

The alley twisted to the left and right, where it led to a tangle of corridors lined with homes that had previously been boarded up. Someone had removed the planks from the entryways, and the grimy windows glowed with light. Emil set a hand on the nearest door. "Do it," I said.

Dozens of Augustins waited in the room, crammed together and chained to the walls, stripped down to their undergarments. They quieted when the door opened. "What's going on in here?" my brother asked.

"Nothing at all," one of the residents said. "Nothing to worry 'bout here."

Dried blood and bruises covered most of them, and some shivered violently. Emil was letting the cold air in. He shut the door and turned to us. "Looks like we found the Augustin corps. They're in bad shape."

"We should leave," Carina said. "What usually accompanies captives?"

The answer rounded the corner leading back to the ridge, the group of ten moving with purpose. "Ho!" the lead man called out. They didn't wear secular steel, but high-quality weapons and armor from the Foundry, as well as furs for the cold. Half of them sported bloody bandages from the recent fighting. This level probably crawled with patrols tasked with keeping an eye on the cluster of makeshift jails.

The patrol leader's eyes found me. "You all with us?" he asked.

"Obviously," Emil said. "What kind of question is that?"

"Who's she then?"

"Doesn't matter. That a problem?"

Apparently fifteen-year-old mercenaries had a way of standing out. Carina, Brux, and the others leaned forward as they waited, ready to pounce on command—these people might as well have been the same mercenaries we'd encountered in Sanskra.

"Just curious, is all," the man said. He had long brown hair and a bandage over one eye. "I did want to know what you were doing. Spotted you from the ridge, heading down from the twelfth level. Curious."

My brother shrugged, backing off from his initial hostility. "We were exploring. Seeing if there was anything worth grabbing."

"Mira's Hand ain't allowing anyone to loot the city." He nodded toward the nearest door. "That why you been poking around here? Looking to skim a bit off the top?"

My brother's falter was subtle, but he recovered quickly. "I didn't see anything worth taking, so we haven't technically broken any rules."

The man's head tilted up and he studied us even more closely. "Ah. What's your name? What route you working?"

Meike's fingers twitched toward her weapon, but none of the mercenaries noticed. The patrol leader's attention remained on my brother, and Emil matched it with equal intensity. "We don't answer to you, so it's none of your concern. That an issue, or should we work it out?" He set a hand on his sword.

The leader shook his head. "Not necessary. Just play nice and don't steal anything, or Mira's Hand'll have Jakar pull you apart." He signaled to his patrol, and they continued down the corridor until they disappeared.

"Close one," Brux said in his gravelly voice as we headed back to the ridge.

"Might've been worth it to ruin our cover," I said. "Those people don't belong here."

We reached a set of stairs leading to the seventh level. The others had shrugged off the confrontation, but not Emil. "Those patrols own the city," he said.

Mateo surveyed the lower levels as we descended the steps. "It looks like everything's on lockdown right now. I wonder if this is how Radavich looked before Sara mobilized her army."

Another patrol circled the chasm farther down. "I don't like this," my brother said. "Augustin shouldn't be this quiet."

"It's only temporary," I said. He nodded, only looking half-assured. In truth, I felt the same way. I'd pictured thousands of people celebrating their liberation and the return of my brother and sister, but all I felt was a tension in the air. Hopefully Sara would kick her army to the curb as soon as everything returned to normal.

How important was her army to her?

"So, we're in Augustin now," I said. "Do we just walk through the front door of the palace?"

"Not after the way that garrison received us in Sanskra. Let's gather intel first. Learn more about Jakar and find out what happened to Sara and Ig."

We passed more patrols on our way down, but they gave us no more than a second glance. We moved like mercenaries, so people assumed we were. Emil led us to the third level down Plate's Folly Row, a popular alleyway where commoners usually came to celebrate holidays like Mira's Founding. We were currently the only souls walking down the wide alley. He stopped at the end in front of Drinker's Hole, a bar with torches hanging on either side of the door, ablaze with the white sparks of thermite normally used for shellfish diving.

The only person inside the bar was the barkeep, who tensed as soon as he saw us. The place was taken care of, with a bar made from a red-brown rhizome wood, meticulously polished, as well as high-quality tables and chairs. It was strange seeing the place so deserted. We weaved through the pillars and took our places at a table in the far corner.

"What'll you have?" the barkeep asked when he approached our table. He was a wiry, older man. Scared shitless too.

Emil looked him up and down. "Some information. Has martial law been declared since the invasion?"

The man nodded meekly.

"I'm guessing that's why business is so slow."

"Yes, saior."

"Do you know of any Augustins who've been treated poorly since the occupation started?"

The barkeep ran a hand through his thinning hair. He seemed to relax a tad, perhaps due to our demeanors. "After the fighting? I mean, it's been difficult to talk to friends and family since the lockdown." He looked away, embarrassed. The lie was easy to see.

Emil stood and took one of the man's hands in both of his own. "You can trust us. We're not who you think we are."

The barkeep frowned. "You look familiar."

"I'm from Augustin, like you. My friends and I snuck into the city and we're checking on residents to make sure they're all right."

The man looked back and forth between us all. "You're not kidding, are you?"

Emil shook his head.

The barkeep exhaled sharply. "Thank goodness. I was worried these invaders had killed anyone who could hold a sword."

"Is that what's been happening? We found prisoners in the Barrows, but they looked well enough off."

"The survivors are, sure. When the smiths joined the fight against them, it cowed everyone quickly. Nobody wants to raise their sword against the Foundry. But it's the destruction of the Fiador Fianza that has so many people worried about what this invading army might do."

Emil let go of the man's hand and sat back down. "The Fiador Fianza was destroyed?"

The barkeep nodded. "Sara Adriann overran them shortly

after she took over. Had most of the bounty hunters killed, far as I know. Don't know much beyond that. Who are all these outsiders and why are they fighting for the princepa?"

My brother and I shared a look. Of course Sara would have taken revenge on the Fiador Fianza. She didn't forget grudges. Just like Father. "What have you heard about the princepa?" Emil asked.

The man's eyes glimmered. "Word spread several hours before the battle that Mira's Hand led the incoming army. You know, the Augustin smuggler. Everyone thought Mira's Hand wanted to avenge the Adrianns, but then when they took the city, none other than Sara Adriann herself was the smuggler." The enthusiasm faded. "I understand the need for men from the crust, but her soldiers worry me. There are rumors of some dark happenings on the Granite Road, but I don't know what to make of it. I'm willing to give our new magnate the benefit of the doubt, though. Mira's Hand has done much good for the city over the years, even if the nobility denounced her."

"New magnate?"

The barkeep eyed us, confused. "Sara Adriann, obviously. Who else would succeed Olevic Pike? Emil Adriann is missing, and people say Efadora Adriann is in Manasus. The audencia just has to vote and the princepa will be the new magnate."

"That's enough," Emil said. He pulled some money out of his pocket and set it in the barkeep's palm. "Payment for the information, and for the business you've lost from this invasion."

The barkeep's mouth hovered open, staring at the pile of standards and bits. He bowed his head. "Thank you. Thank you so much." He shuffled into his back room.

"Magnate Sara, eh," Carina said as she planted a boot on the edge of the table and balanced on the back legs of her chair.

"It won't happen, Emil," Mateo said. "One word to the Foundry and they'll make sure the audencia never votes your sister in. Her association to Ig will undo everything once they learn what he really is. Ig's been a poison to your family for too long, but at least for now we can use it to our advantage."

"What's so wrong with the idea of Sara running the territory?" I asked.

The words sounded wrong as soon as I said them, but the prospect of Sara succeeding Father touched on old resentments. Nobody seemed to consider Sara a worthy ruler, as if they all knew Emil was Father's favorite and accepted without question he would be the next in command. It wasn't fair. Sara had the skillset, had connections with every rung on the social ladder. She wasn't afraid to get her hands dirty. She was Father without the paranoia.

But she hadn't stopped those deaths on the Granite Road either.

"Nothing," Emil said, trailing off, staring at his hands in his lap.

Mateo looked down his nose at me. "I don't think I need to convince you of your brother's qualities, but what's most important is that Emil is a godly man. Sara isn't. The Foundry is the single most important institution in Augustin, and to support it is required of anyone who wants a long, healthy rule."

"Ig is Emil's friend," I said, "so much good that logic does. The smiths will just need to learn to accept Ig."

"They won't. I promise you that. It's why your brother already agreed to denounce Ig."

I waited for Emil to meet my gaze, but he didn't look up. "When was that decided?" I asked.

"We had many good talks on the way here," Mateo said. "It'll be a kindness to Ig, really. Ig won't be punished for what he is—he'll be sent back to Sulian Daw where he can be free. It's a scenario that will make everyone the happiest."

"I bet. Sounded like Ig was super happy last time he was there."

Emil finally met my eyes. His cheeks were red with embarrassment, and he scrunched his face up, annoyed. "He doesn't have to go back to Sulian Daw. He can go anywhere. Be anyone he wants. I can't change the fact that the commoners hate him for killing Bolivar, and that the smiths will despise him for his power. There's no future for him here."

The group shifted uncomfortably while Emil and I stared at each other for several seconds, the muscles in my brother's jaw working, the set of his brows deepening. For the first time in my life I was disappointed in him. Ig was his friend and now Emil was abandoning him. For some reason that struck a nerve.

Emil looked up to Mateo, had looked up to Father, but at least he could recognize the crap coming out of Father's mouth.

Meike broke the silence. "We should find out when the audencia plans to vote Sara in."

"Good idea," Emil said without breaking eye contact. It was clear he had no interest in budging, but it wasn't a hill I was willing to die on either. Ig was little more than a stranger to me.

"I'll help," I said to Meike, bowing out of the staring contest. "I know most of the hidden passageways around here. I can draw them up if you let me borrow one of your maps, Carina."

Carina rummaged through her pack and laid out a map on the table. Mateo stood. "I need to go to the Foundry," he said. "If Sara had to go through my smiths to invade the city, and if the smiths know what her army did on the Granite Road, then blood was spilled. My brothers and sisters need me."

"Can you make it down there all right?" Emil asked.

"I know how to hide when I need to."

"Be safe then."

A cold breeze moved through the bar when Mateo left, disturbing the map as I bent over it. As I sketched lines and scrawled Xs on the parchment with a charcoal pencil, I thought of Sara and how much I wanted her to be magnate after all.

Chapter 29 – Ig

"THE AUDENCIA WILL not vote you in. Not if we have anything to say about it," Senior Arc Smith Panqao, lead smith of the council, said. The man folded his scarred, soot-stricken arms in front of him. "We know about the Granite Road."

Sara sat on the same chair her father had posed on a thousand times in the past, elbow propped on the white-and-brown wool blanket covering the chair's arm, chin resting against her palm. She looked stoic, like Sorrelo, but without her father's tautness. Senior Arc Smiths Panqao, Porcia, and Celestana stood on the dais, heads tilted up at Sara while I hid in the shadow of the nearby pillar—my usual place under Sorrelo's service. A puddle of Olevic's congealed blood stained the marble by the smiths' feet—a stain Sara refused to clean up—and the smiths pretended not to notice it.

"I thought the smiths avoided politics like brimstone," Sara asked.

The smiths' postures tightened. "Interesting you say this after taking advantage of our help," Senior Arc Smith Porcia, the tall woman, said. "But yes, you're right. We generally don't offer our opinions to the audencia. Perhaps this gives you an idea of how extraordinary the circumstances are."

"We've all been through a lot recently, so I understand the importance of placation. What if I ended the lockdown? I was considering a transition to a simple curfew while I finish negotiations with the audencia anyway. Would that make you happy?"

"No," Panqao said. "Nothing will make us happy. Not after the Granite Road. It was a curiosity when the Sovereign and his primordia didn't intervene when Olevic Pike seized the throne, but they *will* come now, once they hear of the sins your army and the Iron Sorrow committed. That I can guarantee. If their armies don't destroy this city while purging you, your sellswords soon will. They grow more vulgar, intrusive, and violent with each passing. It won't be long until they start doing what they do best. Remove them from the city immediately."

"My family worked hand-in-hand with the Foundry for decades," Sara said. "Whatever happened to taking your vows seriously?"

Senior Arc Smith Celestana snorted. "Our vows were never to you. Our loyalty was always to the throne, and you do not deserve to sit on it."

"This matter won't go away. That I can promise," Panqao said. He turned his back on the princepa, and the others followed suit.

As they headed for the door, I reopened the book I'd had nestled under my arm, a weighty tome called *Timelines of the Territories, 5334-5533,* its pages covered in water stains and grime. I'd found it in a bookshop on the fifth level ridge, the shop's door left open during the siege, the shelves frosty and ruined from the wind. The owner never returned, likely killed during the battle, which was a shame because I wanted to ask about what I'd read. The timeline in the book started twenty years after the start of the Sovereign's reign and detailed key events in Mira.

There were hints and rumors in the pages, of conflicts between the territories fought by thousands, all stopped in their tracks by one person, the Sovereign, the answer of how never stated. Maybe the author didn't know. The page I had earmarked was on the Conflict of the Ivy Passage, fought between Radavich and Tulchi seventy-four years ago—the one Rodi mentioned the first passing we met. It didn't say much about the conflict itself or how it ended, only detailed the successions of the magnates for both territories—Magnate Chantel Seregal of Radavich and Magnate Khalid Shaw of Tulchi. Both started their rule within a week of each other, both complete strangers to the territories their respective Chambers had elected them to lead. I couldn't find any record of their noble families prior to their elections, which was odd considering nobility loved to write themselves into history books. There was no record of either magnate's family in Saracosta either, supposedly where the Sovereign brought them from.

I closed the book, thinking of Panqao and how convinced he was the Sovereign would come for Sara.

The doors to the atrium creaked open. Rodi appeared, passing the smiths as they left the throne room, and he was frowning. The jafo took the smiths' place on the dais. I doubted he even registered the pool of dried blood under his feet. "Got a problem. Big one."

"My life's one big problem at the moment. Might as well pile more on."

He watched the door as it shut behind the smiths, waiting for the echo of rockwood to ring through the chamber. "Everything we took from the Granite Road is gone."

She straightened in her chair. "What?"

"Balchi's crew is dead. All twenty-nine carts gone. Only Allo's crew knows right now, and they've already started a search. I told them not to tell the others, but it's only a matter of time."

She slumped. "Fantastic."

A warmth appeared in my belly. My cheeks stretched. Happiness. That was what I felt. Exhilaration to the point of giddiness. A contentedness filled the hole in my stomach, and even though I knew it'd be brief, I reveled in it.

Rodi should've been enraged, but no. The news barely perturbed him. "You can count on me, whatever happens. I'm with you 'til the end, Magnate."

"You don't sound like much of a crew leader anymore, you know that?"

"People change, Hand. Contract work's unsatisfying when faced with the prospect of helping a magnate who can make a real difference in the world. Someone who can make the territories great again. You're a legend in the making, Hand."

So Sara had been right about Rodi. The man was just looking for a leg up in the world, to join the ranks of the nobility he loved to hate. I expected her to call out to me that she'd been right all along—*Look, Jakar. Proof of the commoners' envy*—but she didn't rebuff him. She smiled, the corners of her eyes crinkling, and it made me realize that Rodi would be the one with the last laugh. All he had to do was stroke Sara's ego enough times and he would get whatever he wanted.

"Nothing we've done will matter if the audencia won't legitimize me," she said.

"You're on the throne already. Not like they can kick you off."

"Politics don't work like that. I can't maintain long-term power if I don't have the support of Augustin's judiciaries, and by extension the people. Government rule is about more than force."

Rodi took two steps up the stairs. "You deserve this position. More than anyone who has ever sat where you are now. We need to find a way to solidify your place here."

The hand not holding the book had been pressed against the dark-grey limestone pillar as I leaned against it, and my fingers pressed into the rock without me thinking, leaving deep gouges. Sara draped her legs over one of the chair's arms. "What are you suggesting?" she asked sarcastically.

"The Listener betrayed your family and the city when he staged his coup, but we know he couldn't have done it without help from the audencia. The audencia deserves Olevic Pike's fate."

"Only part of the audencia would've supported him."

"I know, I know. But how're you gonna remove the fat from the protein? Traitors among the audencia will never show themselves. If the smiths are pulling back their support, you'll have to do whatever it takes if you want your family ruling Augustin again."

His last sentence struck a chord—she straightened in her seat and leaned on her knees, her expression settling into one of contemplation. I left the shadows. "No," I said.

Rodi turned, startled. "Not a word belonging in your vocabulary, friend."

Sara said nothing as I approached the dais. "Don't listen to him," I said. "This isn't you, Sara. It's too late to change what happened on the Granite Road, but it isn't too late to change the future."

Rodi cut in. "This is your city, Sara. Take his advice and your family loses it. Something has to be done about the audencia."

"There has to be another way," I said.

Sara drummed her fingers against her leg. *Why was this even up for debate? She was better than this.* "Rodi's right about the complicity of the audencia," she finally said. "Only some of them were responsible for Olevic's coup, but all of them had a hand in allowing him to rule while we were out in the crust almost getting ourselves killed."

"There are dozens of judges in Augustin's Chamber," I said. "They all have personal guards too. That could mean hundreds dying."

"Sounds dangerous," Rodi said. "Especially if they hole themselves up somewhere. Need an elemental if we want to punish them for what they did."

I imagined what it would be like to take a serrated edge to

Rodi's neck, to saw into it until I broke through his spine, and my body trembled, the rage building. "Say it," I said to Sara. "Give me the Word. Order me to murder everyone standing in your way."

She cocked her head, expression controlled. Difficult to read as usual. My feet brought me onto the first step. "Do it."

I wasn't sure what I was doing, but I liked it, whatever it was. The impulse to stand up to Sara had disappeared weeks ago, despair ruling every waking minute of my life since Cragreach, but this time was different. This was my purpose—a purpose I'd created for myself.

The princepa only stared, flickers of pain cracking her mask. She glanced at Rodi.

"I'll be a nice guy this time around," Rodi said. "You don't have to kill them *all* right now. Just the ones in the audencia who outright oppose Sara and her goal to become magnate. We'll reassess the situation after. You have three passings to complete this task, so best be quick about it."

The faintest pressure appeared on the back of my neck, one that would only intensify as time ticked down.

"I don't understand," I said to Sara, my voice shaking. "Don't you feel guilty? You're Mira's Hand. You protected the kids of Augustin from using the drugs you smuggled. You used to leave gifts for the people of the Barrows."

She didn't answer. Only watched me with hard eyes.

"You care about the people," I said, "but for some reason you let hundreds of them die and many more get wounded or their lives destroyed on the Granite Road. Doesn't that mean anything to you? Can't you *feel*?"

"I tried to tell you from the beginning," she said. "I never hid who I really was."

I blinked. I thought of those conversations on our trip to Radavich, of why she was Mira's Hand. It was because she wanted to do good in the world outside the rings of the nobility through a profession her father hated... but she never said that. She said it was because commoners don't remember magnates, they remembered those who made a name for themselves in the upper levels, who affected their lives on a personal level. A reputation as someone who was a champion for the little people would immortalize her among the masses. Heat crept into my neck and face. No, that couldn't be why she did it. There was more to her than selfishness.

"Sorrelo was on the verge of something important right before he died," I said. I wiped my nose with the back of my hand, tears drawing lines of heat down my face. "I think he started to realize what you and Emil and Efadora meant to him. That his family was more important than ruling complete strangers. I think if he was still here, he wouldn't be impressed with what you're doing. He'd tell you that making greatness for yourself could be about the quality of the people in your life, not the quantity."

Sara stood. She descended a few steps until she was next to Rodi, and she set her hands on her hips, her brow set in anger. "You served my father for two years. I've known him my entire life, so don't pretend to know him better than I did. *I* know what he would've wanted, and *I* know he would've said our family was meant to rule Augustin, whether it was Emil or me or Efadora. The Granite Road was necessary to make that happen. Leaders have to make hard choices sometimes, and sometimes the people will hate them for it. It comes with the territory."

If it was a simple matter of doing what was necessary, she wouldn't have spent all that time avoiding me on the Granite Road, only sticking around long enough to ensure I didn't lose my power. She didn't want to see what her army was doing because she knew it was wrong. A silence followed. One I couldn't break. My mind had numbed.

She continued, "I'll do what my father couldn't. I'll do right by both the nobiletza and the commoners. The territories will know me as both their ruler and as Mira's Hand."

What could I say in response? I couldn't breathe. Her eyes softened the longer she looked at me, and her forehead wrinkled, her brows lifting up. The stony expression had been a façade after all. She did care. Rodi shifted uncomfortably— he was witnessing something he had no right to see. I wanted him to leave. He wasn't allowed to see the side of Sara I knew was coming.

"We should've had this talk sooner," Sara said. "I'm sorry for avoiding you."

"Why avoid me if you didn't care what happened on the Granite Road?" I asked.

She only looked at me.

"Why do you care about how I feel above anyone else?" I asked. I choked out the question, the words almost nonsensical. The atrium blurred, and I wiped my face. "What about all those people I killed? They felt too. It played out in their eyes, over and over while Rodi made me execute them." My voice was louder now, yelling, the noise coming out hoarse, my throat tender and in pain. "It was the same feeling on a hundred different faces."

More silence. The princepa wrapped her arms around her torso, hugging herself, and after several seconds, said, "Ig, you won't be bound to any future commands Rodi gives you."

Rodi swelled at the order, but he didn't argue. The pressure on the back of my neck didn't disappear though. I was still bound to his previous command.

"You can leave the city after three passings," she continued. "You can live a happy life and you'll never have to see me again. I won't stop you." Her voice grew quieter as she finished. She returned to the top of the stairs like she was ready to sit back down, but she only waited there, her back turned, arms wrapped around herself.

Sara wanted to give me freedom, to let me make my own purpose, whatever that may be, so long as it didn't interfere with her plans. But if I couldn't interfere with her plans, then it wasn't a life worth living. I'd found a purpose in doing what I thought was right, but it was too late to matter. It had been too late for two years.

The door waited for me. Neither of them asked me where I was headed.

The choice was obvious. I should have ended it when Sorrelo forced me to throw an innocent man in the river. My fate belonged with Bolivar Adriann's.

Chapter 30 – Ig

MY PATH BROUGHT me between the two broken onyx pillars outside the palace entrance. The home of the monarchy and its mouth of broken teeth, spitting me out for the last time.

Rodi's commands had done their work to prevent me from killing myself on the Granite Road, but Words faded with time, and Rodi never thought to renew that particular Word since Cragreach. I was willing to bet part of him hoped I would do it. He had gotten his revenge.

Sara never knew I'd tried to take my own life right before killing all those people. I wondered if I should've told her, if it would have changed anything.

Mercenary patrols roamed the second level like militarized gangs. They continued to maintain order, but there was no money in guard work. They pushed the envelope with each passing hour, knocking on doors for security checks and harassing the residents. The perpetual tease of the window shopper. What would happen when they learned of their missing spoils? The army was a ticking time bomb.

Smiths walked around the middle and upper levels, pulling squeaky carts laden with food and care packages, catering to the needs of the city. Some of the ones on the second and first levels paused, dropping the cart handles on the cobblestones to watch me pass. What did they think of me? Of the Iron Sorrow? The question only made me surer of what I had to do.

What did they think of Sara Adriann?

I was pathetic for letting myself fall in love with the person I served. It had blinded me, making me think Sara was someone she wasn't. I was just like those slaves in Sulian Daw who fell in love with their masters as a way to protect themselves. The angry part of me desperately hoped my death would hurt Sara the way she had hurt me, but that was impossible.

Farther down the chasm, smoke billowed from the Fiador Fianza's entrance. Whatever happened to Tuli Dempra? Did his bounty have anything to do with Olevic Pike's coup? Would he stop hunting Sara and Emil now that Augustin was theirs? Questions for someone else to answer.

I thought of Emil's bright smiles, of his warm hand clasped on my shoulder as we shared jokes or when he pulled me into conversations with noblemen who tried their best to ignore the manservant to Sorrelo Adriann. I was past wishing he'd showed up to stop Sara, but shelfire, what I would have done to see him one last time, even if it didn't change anything. I was sick with the need to see his face. To be with my only friend.

My feet met the obsidian platform at the river's edge, a wall of heat hitting my body. A blue-white piece of ice the size of a house from the nearby ice sheath lay nearby, melting in a black pool, the lava next to it bubbling and exploding from escaping gas. How long could I protect myself after jumping in the river before it ate through my body? My power was almost unparalleled, only rivaled by the Sovereign and his primordia. A power that had convinced Sorrelo to kill those whose only crime was to speak against him. It had caused Lucas Adriann to betray his family. It allowed Sara to think marching on the Granite Road was the easiest answer. My power had twisted their minds, just as fear of my flesh binding had twisted mine.

But was it my fault?

No. No, it wasn't.

I choked back a sob. My knees touched the ground, and I felt at the grains of dirt covering the obsidian's glassy surface. It wasn't my fault. To be human was to struggle with self-control, and the outcome of that struggle was what defined you. To be a good leader was to at least try to understand the consequences of your actions, to get a grip on the true power you held, and to use it responsibly.

Still, I had to do this. Ascribing fault didn't matter anymore. The outcome was still the same.

Two groups of smiths watched me from the ridge. The mercenary patrols expressed less interest, but of course they didn't care—they didn't know the significance of the platform I stood on.

Death by ash, or by ice? Sorrelo whispered.

The longer I imagined what hearing that question would be like, to receive a death sentence from Sorrelo Adriann, the more absurd the idea became. Every master in my life had abused and manipulated me, but they all shared one thing in common: an intense fear of losing me. It didn't matter how much they played with my mind or pretended I was nothing. No person in their right mind would kill a flesh bound elemental as powerful as me. If I wanted to die, it had to be by my own hand.

Sara's power over the mercenary army would crumble. I smiled, and old words from my oldest friend came to me. *You always have a choice,* Quin once said. She was right. I'd had the freedom to choose since the first passing of my flesh binding, I'd just been unwilling to take the hard path—the one that waited at the bottom of the river.

I could finally do some real good for this city. For the first time in two years, I felt truly free.

"Ig?" a voice asked.

The Word nearly sent me leaping off the platform, but the voice was too high. Too innocent. Not Sara. I rose to find two smiths, both out of breath and clutching at their robes. A man and woman, both young. The man looked vaguely familiar.

"Yes?" I asked.

"Don't do this," the man said.

I almost laughed at the absurdity. A smith, of all people, trying to convince me not to kill myself. "No offense, but you have no idea what you're talking about, or of what I've done."

He took a step forward, but paused, almost like I was a rock snake ready to strike. "That might be true, but I know what you didn't do. All those mercenaries wanted to kill me and you didn't let them. You broke bones before you let them lay a hand on me."

The smith was from the invasion, when my strike team overran the first barricade. He was one of the guards who surrendered to me. He continued, "My sister gave me these robes as a disguise. She and I can look out for each other now."

Now that I examined them, the two did look related. Both with sharp noses, narrow cheeks, and the distinct auburn hair of a Tulchi. The girl moved closer to stand next to her brother. "I was one of the smiths who fought with you on the second level, and I saw you break the line that almost overwhelmed us. You did it alone without killing a single person." She let out a pained laugh. "You followed the smiths' vows on that passing more closely than anyone else in the Foundry." Another step brought her onto the glossy obsidian. A clever plan. Human contact often folded one's confidence in these situations. A trick I'd seen time and again among the Ebonrock.

"None of that matters," I said. "For every one person I saved in Augustin, ten more died on the Granite Road."

"Are you really responsible though?" she asked. There was a knowing look in her eyes. I stilled.

"You aren't defined by your flesh binding," she said. "You saved my brother's life. You're not beyond saving."

"You... you know?"

She took another step. By now she only stood ten feet away.

"The master smith told us. He says you're an agent of the Great Ones, but we know that's not true. The Adrianns are the cancer. A lot of the older smiths sided with the master smith, but many of us who saw you fight think otherwise. You have friends, Ig."

A knot appeared in my throat. "Mateo's in Augustin?"

She nodded.

If Mateo was in Augustin, that meant Emil was too.

The young woman hurried forward to grab onto my elbow and wrist, her grip gentle. She didn't try to pull me away from the river's edge—only stood there, hoping her touch would be enough. I watched the runoff from the nearest ice sheath cast mist on the chasm floor.

Emil was the one person who could fix this mess. He could also stop Sara's Words once he learned the secret to issuing a command. A sacrifice of flesh would be required—he would need to carve into his body the name of the creature responsible for my flesh binding. The creature called Ig that lived at the bottom of Som Abast's Lake.

If Emil could issue a Word that conflicted with Sara's, the ensuing punishment from the flesh binding would show Sara that her brother would always be there to stop her. To stop me. Brother and sister would work something out.

Thought of the flesh binding's pain made me tremble.

The wind whistled, billowing my robe, bits of snow sticking to my robe, turning it into a portrait of the sky, and brother and sister seemed content with the silence. My trembling finally stilled. If Mateo was in the Foundry, he could tell me where the princep was. I would convince the master smith at best and force him at worst. He wouldn't give up Emil if his conviction in my corruption was strong enough, but there was still hope.

I would be with Emil again, one way or another.

"I'm going to the Foundry," I said.

They nodded, looking relieved when I stepped off the dais. I weaved through puddles of ice melt and across the basalt, flurries of snow from the ice sheaths whipping at our clothes and hair. The ramp waited ahead, but when I saw who rushed down the palace level ramp to the trade district, I skidded to a stop. Rodi and Sara. The princepa locked eyes with me.

"Jakar, what are you doing?" Sara asked as they came to meet us. "Someone said you were standing on the execution platform. Why?"

This was bad. Very bad. What would Rodi do if he knew Emil Adriann was around to challenge Sara's claim? If the answer was violence, could Sara stop him? "I—I was going to end my life. Make sure no one else had to die."

"Ig, you are not allowed to hurt yourself intentionally," she ordered. Anger filled her expression, but I could see alarm there as well. The underlying terror.

"So why didn't you do it?" Rodi asked. "What changed?"

"Because your command prevented me."

Sara narrowed her eyes at me, then at the smiths. "What are you talking about? What did those smiths say to you?"

"They told me that what happened on the Granite Road wasn't my fault. That the smiths think it was yours."

"Ig, tell me what they told you."

I desperately willed the pressure on the back of my neck to let up. "They told me what I just said... and that Mateo is back in Augustin."

"*Dora-sa*," she whispered. "Jakar, follow. And don't make me use another Word."

SEVERAL DOZEN OF Sara's best men waited in a line behind us, spilling through the columns of the Foundry's entrance and forming an impenetrable barrier on the flagstone steps. Several smiths watched us warily from behind the countertops, their forges abandoned.

"Come on out, Mateo," Sara shouted. There was no hurry in her voice—she knew Mateo couldn't escape. The twists had been caved in, and Olevic Pike had collapsed the back tunnels leading from the palace to other parts of Augustin. Mateo could only exit through the main entrance, unless the smiths somehow had another secret passage.

A retinue of smiths filed out of the hallways, and they parted to reveal the master smith. The past few months had roughened the edges of his face—scruff covered his jaw, and scabbed cuts and scrapes covered the side of his head and knuckles. He eyed the princepa worriedly, but when his gaze found mine, all emotion died.

Part of me wanted to struggle. To run. Hopefully Mateo understood I didn't want to be here, would've done anything to stop the inevitable.

The smiths didn't stand with the same uniformity as before, with pockets betraying the tension through subtle body language. They didn't reek of the 'us versus them' attitude they'd exuded when confronted with a common enemy. Rodi had imprisoned the siblings I'd met at the river, and while Sara was out of earshot, he let me know they'd die as soon as we took care of matters here.

"Hello, Sara," Mateo said. "Ig."

"You didn't tell me you were back in town," Sara said.

"Augustin's changed since we parted ways. Revealing myself didn't seem the safest choice, considering what I've been hearing about the Granite Road." He crossed his arms. "Your army is telling stories of a man named Jakar who's responsible for a slaughter in one of the towns. They call him the Stalker of Cragreach. I've heard other names too. But I'm willing to bet Ig, Jakar, the Stalker, and *Dor di Fero* are all one in the same. Does that sound accurate?"

I answered for Sara. "You're right."

He shook his head. "That means you could've stopped all of this. To think of all the faith Emil put in you."

I did my best to quash a familiar guilt. I was not evil.

"Speaking of which," Sara said. "Where is my brother? I'd like to talk to him."

"I don't know." He wore the lie as a badge of pride.

"Please tell me. You're a family friend. You know I wouldn't let anything bad happen to him, or to you."

"It's not you I'm worried about," he said, then pointed at me. "It's him and everyone else standing behind you. I can't give up Emil's location until your army leaves Augustin and Ig has been executed."

"Not possible. The audencia will arrest me. My mercenaries obey orders, anyway. They aren't a danger."

"From what I hear, some of your army's already left Augustin after they found out what went missing. It's only a matter of time until the rest leave."

Sara went still as a scorpionfish. "And what would you know about that?"

"I know they'll have a hard time recovering their wagons from the bottom of Sanskra Lake."

Leather creaked as the mercenaries murmured questions and obscenities to one another. "Someone just signed their death warrant," Rodi said.

Sara raised her hands toward the men. "We'll get to the bottom of this," she promised. She turned to the master smith. "Do you have any idea what you just did? They won't let you survive the next passing."

"I had no reservations about your men's intentions. It was going to come to this eventually. I'm willing to die standing between them and the city."

"Give the man what he wants," a mercenary called out. Others growled in agreement.

Sara's force outnumbered the smiths, but if the smiths retreated into their hallways, the odds would even out. It would be a long and bloody battle.

I knew Sara's choice before she said my name. "Jakar. You need to kill Mateo. It's the only way."

The master smith's mouth parted in disbelief at the proclamation, but I'd suspected this moment would come as soon as I told Sara his location. It terrified me nonetheless. I didn't move.

"*Jakar*," she warned.

Still, I didn't move.

"Don't be a coward," Rodi said. It took me a moment to realize he spoke to Sara.

"Ig, kill Mateo," she said.

My knife left its sheath and I parted from Sara's side. With my simple robes and little blade, I looked like a child compared to the others, but the smiths watched me warily, tensing with each step I took. Some looked concerned, afraid of what the Stalker of Cragreach might do.

Mateo didn't move. A small part of him probably wanted me to kill him, if only to validate everything he believed in.

I was supposed to tell Emil the truth behind the flesh binding so he could stop Sara, but he wasn't here. Would Sara let me die if I disobeyed? The answer had once been no, but there was nothing about Sara I was sure about anymore. Would she be as sadistic as Rodi and try to feed me the Word over and over until I obeyed?

My heavy footsteps brought me to the halfway point between the two groups, and I stopped. "Is Emil safe?" I asked the master smith.

"As safe as he can be while you're alive."

"What about Efadora?"

He hesitated. "Yes, she's safe."

I nodded to myself. Knowing Emil was well would have to be enough. Wondering how Sara would react no longer mattered. All I knew was that I couldn't kill Mateo, couldn't kill for Sara, couldn't kill for anyone. No amount of pain would change that.

The prospect of punishment loomed over me like a cloud, but the message I needed to send was too important. "Tell Emil I love him," I said.

I turned away. Sara set her hands on her hips, but the defiant stance didn't translate to her face. She was worried. My free hand moved to my neck, and I grabbed the twine, pulling out Emil's ring. My fingers had trouble closing over it, my hand shook so badly.

"I won't do it," I said. "I'd rather die than kill one more person for you." I almost snarled the words. The rage I'd felt toward Rodi returned in full force, but it wasn't just that. It came from an anger and hurt I'd harbored since my time with the Ebonrock. From the injustice of having countless others control who I'd become. "You have no right."

Something in my voice disturbed Sara. But there wasn't time to see her reaction.

Pain slammed into me like a battering ram.

Chapter 31 – Efadora

THE BACK OF the mercenary line waited for us at the top of the Foundry's flagstone steps. Whatever they watched had their attention good. Emil and I stopped beside a stone column behind those to the far right, and a few looked at us curiously, but said nothing.

Emil peered through the line of men and women, almost frantic. Earlier, when I was sneaking through the commandeered military barracks on the third level, playing the confidence game so none of the sellswords would question why a teenager roamed their hallways, I'd overheard a mercenary named Rodi calling for dozens of fighters to follow him to the Foundry, prompting me to book it to Drinker's Hole as fast as possible. Emil was the only one there, the rest of our group out on a 'patrol' gathering intel, but he came with me to the Foundry anyway, terror for Mateo in his eyes.

As short as I was, I could only see the smiths clustered around their counters of weapons, the tunnels behind them glowing red with pyremoss. Farther along the line of sellswords, somewhere in the middle beyond my line of sight, Sara spoke. "And what would you know about that?"

Mateo stood at the head of the smiths, unafraid. "I know that they're going to have a hard time recovering what they stole from the bottom of Sanskra Lake."

"That shitter," someone nearby murmured. Someone else called out more loudly, "Someone just signed their death warrant."

My sister sighed, and something about hearing it caused my heart to leap. I could easily picture the expression on her face—the pursed lips, the raise of her brows, the slight shake of her head. It was Sara. The same old Sara. At that moment I realized how badly I'd missed her. "We'll get to the bottom of this," she said, though I couldn't tell where the words were directed. "Do you have any idea what you just did? They won't let you survive the next passing." Her question sounded like it was aimed at Mateo.

Why would the master smith admit what we did? It didn't take long to figure out. As soon as the mercenary army found out what happened, and they would find out eventually, they would go searching for their spoils. Searching meant visiting other towns that, in their minds, harbored thieves. The end result was obvious. More death and destruction. Mateo wanted to draw everyone to him.

"I had no reservations about your men's intentions," the master smith said. "It was going to come to this eventually. I'm willing to die standing between them and the city."

"Give the man what he wants," the man in front of Emil called out. Everyone around us erupted in cheers.

A tense silence followed. The smiths waited for the verdict that would eventually come. No one could stop the violence to follow—every moment of inaction injected more restless energy into the men around me.

"Jakar. You need to kill Mateo. It's the only way," Sara said.

My brother gripped the pommel of his Meteor Blade, but he didn't unsheathe it. Only rested his hand there and watched. I wasn't surprised by Sara's words—executing Mateo before a fight broke out could be enough to save the smiths around him. But I realized we could stop the man named Jakar. I itched at the chance to kill the Stalker of Cragreach.

"*Jakar*," Sara warned.

"Don't be a coward," someone said. It was the mercenary named Rodi, Sara's right hand man.

"Ig, kill Mateo."

Emil let out a small whine, and the gears started turning. Ig was Jakar? If that was true, it meant he was the one who killed all those people. Dozens, maybe even hundreds of people.

He was bound to our family.

That meant Sara had killed all those people.

Our family's manservant came into view, taking slow steps over red runes and black rock. Almost a hundred feet of space separated the groups, but Ig took his time. Forges lined the side walls of the room, their cavities red hot, and rumor had it he could draw power from the fires themselves. He looked so small compared to everyone else, but all of us knew he was the most powerful. And in the ways that mattered, the weakest.

He looked both different and the same since the last time I saw him. His long hair was pulled back in a ponytail—the style he'd always worn—but it was unkempt, dirty, and matted. The man was covered in grime, his clothes unwashed, looking like some of the Ash addicts on the eighth level. He had more scars on his arms. His body language most closely resembled his old self, as he had always walked with a slight hunch, hands positioned as if ready to protect his torso. A trick, maybe? He wanted his enemies to underestimate him, and when they least expected it, he'd destroy them.

Emil's knuckles whitened on his sword. "He can't do this," he whispered. But Ig certainly could, according to those stupid Sky Scrolls that said he existed to spread evil among the faithful of Fheldspra and to corrupt those around him. I could see the conviction settling in Emil's bones, Mateo's words turning to stone in his mind.

A twisting sensation appeared in my gut. The more I thought of Sara doing nothing to stop Ig from killing those people—of giving Ig those orders—the worse the feeling became. I felt sick. Sara wasn't the kind of person to do that. Right?

Ig stopped halfway between the smiths and the sellswords. He studied Mateo, but the master smith didn't look afraid. "Is Emil safe?" he asked, his words small.

Emil's breathing stilled.

"As safe as he can be while you're still alive," the master smith said with the judgment of the world in his voice.

"What about Efadora?"

The question caught me off guard. Why would he care about me? My brother took a step forward.

"Yes, she's safe," Mateo said.

"Tell Emil I love him."

Ig turned around—to face Sara, I suspected. A trembling hand moved to his neck, and he pulled at a necklace hanging there. No, not a necklace—my brother's charm I'd assumed he'd lost.

"I won't do it," Ig said. "I'd rather die than kill one more person for you."

His face filled with emotion, just like Emil when he was in the thick of battle. But where my brother succumbed to a wild wave, Ig looked in total control. It was the fire in his eyes. A glimpse of the man I'd built up in my mind when hearing stories of the Iron Sorrow. "You have no right," he said. His voice came out as a rumble. Unstoppable, like a volcano ready to erupt. He spoke in a way that left no question.

Panic filled his eyes and he collapsed.

The small scream that left his throat was not a sound any person should've been able to make. It was a small, constant, shuddering shriek that sent chills down my spine. His body convulsed in ways that made him look inhuman, and I wondered what was going on inside his head at that moment. People I'd seen Olevic Pike torture hadn't made sounds like that before they died, and Ig had subjected himself to it willingly.

"For crying out loud, Sara," the man named Rodi said. "Put him out of his misery already. You heard him. He ain't interested in helping you anymore. He's useless."

Metal sang against metal, and Rodi appeared, marching toward Ig. "Rodi, stop—" Sara yelled, but Emil blocked my view. My brother forced his way through the line and ran toward the other man. The mercenary reached the manservant, but before he could swing, Emil collided with him. Hard. They were close in size, but the blow knocked the man named Rodi off his feet and sent him rolling.

My brother's sword was out now, the edge of the Meteor Blade gleaming. "All of you stay away from him," he hissed. He circled Ig as the man continued to writhe until my brother was facing Mateo and the smiths. My breath caught. "Don't even think about touching him," he said. Desperation threaded his voice, making it tight.

I'd never seen Mateo more shocked, his mouth parting until it hung slightly open. "What are you doing?" he stuttered.

Emil looked ready to take on everyone at once, including the smiths. He also needed help. I almost forced my way through, but a hand settled on my shoulder. Meike appeared behind me, along with Carina. Sweat slid down the woman's face as though she'd been running. "No," she whispered. "Deadlier here, behind them."

Meike was right, but part of me didn't care. I wanted to stand next to Emil, to show myself to Sara. Maybe if I could talk some sense into her, our family wouldn't be standing on opposite sides of this fight. I could bridge the gap between my brother and sister. But nothing could be done about the blood that was about to spill, and I could kill more from here. It was the best spot to help Emil.

"Emil?" I heard Sara ask. I still couldn't see her.

"How could you?" Emil asked, enraged. "You made Ig kill all those people on the Granite Road. And you wanted Mateo dead? Remove your Word, now. Save him."

Those in front of me stepped forward. Emil positioned

himself between them and Ig, and he caught a glimpse of me, Meike, and Carina. It strengthened his conviction. My dagger was already out, and I planned to stab it into the nearest back as soon as the fighting started. "Stay away," he said to the advancing mercenaries. They didn't stop, moving slowly.

A projectile blurred across the floor at the same time Emil twisted, and he sent an arrow tumbling upward with the flat of his blade. Everyone froze, and in the silence I heard the creak of a string as a mercenary somewhere further down the line nocked his bow again. Another sellsword yelled, his voice loud and ugly, and the rest charged. Mateo grabbed a fistful of one of his brother's sleeves and pulled him as he ran forward, then the rest of the smiths were following.

My blade snuck past the edges of the secular steel worn by the man in front of me and sunk into the soft flesh above his hip. He spun as he cried out, his arm almost smashing into my face, but I ducked and shouldered him, knocking him over. The two nearest him turned at the commotion. Meike stepped past me and brought her blade down on the skull of another, sending blood spraying across the back line, but only a few of them noticed. The rest were already driven into a frenzy, itching to get at the smiths, consumed in a roar of noise that filled the chamber.

I scrambled forward while Meike and Carina took care of those who'd lingered. Meike shouted something at me but I ignored her. The only thing that mattered was Emil, who was standing between two rows of teeth as they snapped shut. The first sellsword reached him—it was a big man trying to barrel Emil over, but my brother braced himself and somehow, miraculously, impaled the man through the stomach while squatting and lifting up, sending the body catapulting over him. He straightened at the same time the dying mercenary crashed and slid across the tiled floor, his Meteor Blade arcing and cutting through the haft of a halberd as it stabbed at his face. The head of the weapon went spinning. Emil twisted his shoulder away just as an arrow flew past him, and a smith at the head of the advancing line tried to dodge too but took it in his arm, making him stumble.

The line of mercenaries and smiths crashed into each other, but the sellswords closest to my brother stayed just out of reach as Emil swung at them with both hands, warding them off. Emil stepped backward, moving past Ig until he was standing over the man, and kept swinging at the mercenaries as they shouted curses at him. Ig was still seizing. Emil checked the line of smiths, but they had been a heartbeat slower to the fight, and the mercenaries threatened to completely surround him at any moment. I shoved my way between two mercenaries, no longer trying to kill them, scrambling desperately, breathless from my heart in my throat. Fhelfire, I wasn't going to get to him in time.

Sara's voice was distinct enough to pick out through the noise. "Rodi, *no!*"

I caught sight of the man through the bodies. He held a red-hot blade from the nearest forge, the metal deformed from having sat in the fires too long. My sister's command didn't stop him. He pushed the blade through Emil, its glowing end sprouting out of my brother's chest.

Sara shouted. So did Mateo. The fighting shuddered with new intensity. My blade buried itself to the hilt into the man closest to me, then it was killing the one beside him. The other mercenaries moved too fast to notice the death behind them. My heart raged in my ears. Chaos encircled me, but I could only see Rodi. He was all I cared about. I would make his death so painful they would make songs about it. His death would be as famous as the Sovereign. My peripherals registered Emil, who was draped over Ig as our manservant continued to writhe, Ig oblivious to the events around him. My brother wasn't dead. I caught a glimpse of the blood pooling under him and Ig, and I looked away, my mind going blank. White-hot.

Sara shouted a command and Ig's body stopped convulsing. He didn't wake though. He'd been under the spell of his flesh binding for a full minute at least. I looked at my brother again. He'd been knocked onto his back in the chaos, his head turned to the side, and he now watched Ig, expression fixed in relaxed surprise. The look didn't change.

Rodi had disappeared in the press of the fighting. I screamed in frustration. I would find the man or die trying. A hand grazed me, and it had the desperation of someone familiar—Meike, maybe—but I kept moving forward. Not even Meike could stop me.

Someone's elbow drew back to stab an enemy, and it struck me in the side of my head, sending me sprawling. I crawled forward and recovered, continuing onward. People were dying everywhere. It was impossible to tell who was winning.

"Efadora?" Sara yelled. She was to my right, blade in hand, blood dripping down the side of her face.

When she tried to grab me, I pushed her away. "Stay away from me!" I screamed. My face was wet and hot. Someone else had killed our brother, but it felt like Sara had struck the blow. Why hadn't she stopped her friend? Why was she even on his side to begin with?

Sara was on the verge of tears, but my words didn't stop her. She grabbed at me again and managed to wrap her arms around my torso. For a moment, I considered burying my blade in her gut.

My vision turned glassy as I looked again at Emil's ruined chest, the dark blood pooling under him, and his endless stare.

"Someone grab her," Sara ordered, her voice full of frustration and desperation. Why was she still ordering them around? Why wasn't she killing them?

Two pairs of rough hands grabbed onto me, and Sara let go. I struggled, kicked, and yelled, but they were bigger and stronger than me. Someone threw a bag over my head and carried me away.

Chapter 32 – Jakar

Two years ago

I PASSED THE time by counting drips of water.

The darkness gave no indication of where the kadiph's men had imprisoned me, but I suspected my wooden cage sat in the middle of a small cave. I hated how excited I felt when my wardens visited to offer food and water. Anything to break up this impenetrable dream of darkness.

Then there was the dripping. Sometimes those drips felt like my last tie to reality—the one thing standing between me and insanity. Other times it felt like insanity's cause.

Caubi was dead. Akhilian had betrayed us. Quin... I had no idea what happened to Quin. If we were going through the same thing, then she had gone through our last Imbibing a few passings ago. Or had it been longer? Time was impossible to track in here. Had she survived? The last element had been potassium. That combined with the other five elements had made the final Imbibing the most excruciating experience of my life. But I survived. Somehow, even though there wasn't much to live for anymore.

The words sounded ridiculous as soon as I thought them,

as usual. No matter how bleak life became, I would persevere. I lived because of Quin. Akhilian and Caubi were lost, but not her. Strangely enough, escape still felt possible. They had imprisoned me, but they hadn't stolen my wits. I could still save Quin and escape, and this time there'd be no mistakes. As long as I was capable, I'd resist them. The kadiph had ensured I would never lose that fire.

The door ground against the stone floor as it opened. I squinted at the figures lit by the torches in their hands, but the light was too painful to make them out.

"How is my favorite student doing?" a voice asked.

It was the kadiph. So she hadn't disappeared inside whatever hole she'd crawled out of.

Echoing footsteps approached my cage. Then a sound I never expected to hear—the sound of keys scraping in search of the lock. I tried to rise to my feet, but my joints and muscles screamed. I'd been lying prone for who knew how long. Standing was nearly impossible.

Searching hands found my arms and pulled me up. It wasn't the stony grip of the kadiph but of the two accompanying her. They dragged me out of the cage and toward the exit. I tried to resist, but exhaustion had worked its way into every crevice of my body. "Where are we going?" I asked, my voice raspy.

"It's your big day," the kadiph said. "It's time for your flesh binding."

They brought me through a long sequence of hallways I didn't recognize while the torches lining them stabbed at my eyes, and we approached something I never expected. Stairs leading downward. There were no underground chambers in the Ebonrock compound, far as I knew, and I was pretty sure we were still within the grounds. We descended, and the men carrying me by the shoulders kept my weight off my feet. They had no trouble, for I'd lost a fair amount of fat and muscle during my imprisonment.

A room waited at the bottom, hallways on all four sides.

Every hallway ran out of sight. The kadiph headed for the left one and I was forced to follow. As we moved, I noticed the woman's hands had changed. She had smooth porcelain skin instead of semi-cooled, vitrified rock.

Impossible. As often as I'd seen the woman in her molten armor, the heat should have eaten through her skin and bone long ago. I tried to think quickly. They were afraid of Sulian Daw's lightning storms, but I couldn't begin to guess how I would take advantage of that.

"Is Quin alive?" I asked.

"Yes. It really is tragic the two of you felt the need to escape."

Was it really that hard for her to understand why we tried? Maybe it was. She didn't seem the type to know what a friend was. "How long has it been since the last Imbibing?"

"About a week. Hopefully your imprisonment allowed you time to think about your choices."

We passed through hallways and continued our descent. How deep beneath Bloodreach were we going? My sense of direction was almost turned upside down. The kadiph stopped in front of a door, its grey wood almost blending in with the featureless rock, and turned to me. "Try not to panic when we enter this room. You'll only end up hurting yourself."

She opened the door, and what waited on the other side made me long for my cell.

The room was uncut by stonemasons, with a ceiling like an inverted bowl and covered in tiny stalactites. A dozen people worked along tables at the room's sides, studying metal instruments that were connected to wires that snaked across the ground. These countless wires dipped into a pool of black water running along the far wall, and in that pool was a bulb of ghostly white flesh. The bulb floated in the water, ten feet tall and nearly touching the ceiling as it splashed water onto the rocky floor. It moved lazily. No limbs protruded from its body.

I tore my gaze away. The people in the room wore thin, tattered shirts, and on the backs of their necks I could see scars. The scars' roots grew out of their hair with branches that disappeared under the cover of their clothing. The metallic boxes they watched were covered in dials and buttons, meters and gauges. A strange technology I'd never seen before.

My attention couldn't help but return to the fleshy mass rising out of the water. "What is that?"

"Obsidian Lake's most esteemed resident," she said. "We call it Ig. You'll soon understand why. Ig comes to us when it's called for."

It was impossible to tell how big the creature was. "I don't understand," I said.

"Of course you don't. And if you or the masters did, that would cause problems. Hope is a nuanced art we have to teach you students. Too much of it and you spawn ideas of escape. Too little and you end up offing yourselves. Dishonesty necessitates progress."

"We were never meant to leave Sulian Daw, were we? There was no reward for surviving the Imbibings. It was a lie."

She stood in front of me. The monster continued to sway in the water behind her. "Wrong on both counts, Jakar. The students were always meant to leave, just not to a place you would like."

"Where?"

She smiled. "To the Black Depths. Or to its edges at least. Deep near the mantel where, as you might've heard, the Great Ones reside."

The Great Ones. Behemoths in the pitch black of the subterranean ocean. I'd heard stories before my kidnap, but they were all myths. The only legends the masters pushed were of Fedsprig—the elemental of light known as the Great Ones' enemy—and His domain, where we could live with Him and the other gods that were His children, so long as we remained obedient.

Pores covered the mass behind the kadiph, almost breathing in rhythm with the lapping of the water. The wires in the water shuddered with its movements. "Is that a Great One?"

She let out a hearty laugh. "Oh, no. Not even close. Ig is merely a stain of the Great Ones. The most distant of descendants. The barest hint to a greater power."

"Why is it here?"

"To provide your graduation present."

A chair covered in straps waited to the left of the pool. I started to thrash, but the two holding me didn't loosen their grips. "What are you going to make it do to me?"

"We'll be leashing you. Honestly, what did you expect? Binding to those six elements made you quite powerful, even if you don't realize it yet. Trying to control you would be like trying to control fire. We need some way of stopping the burn. So, mental castration it is."

Old blood stained the wood of the chair. "You're going to steal my mind?"

"To steal something implies you owned it in the first place. But to answer your question, your mind will still be there so long as you can hold onto your sanity. Losing it is a common side effect. Some recover, others not so much. But if you can listen and labor, that's all that matters."

"The flesh binding… is it like binding to the elements?"

The kadiph strode over to the chair and pulled at the straps, checking them. Standing so close to the monster didn't bother her. "Yes, actually. Human flesh is made up of elements, as is everything else."

"I thought those bound to the elements can't affect organic matter."

She grunted as she yanked at the leg straps, but they didn't give way. "Another lie. The only reason elementals can't affect organic matter is because organic matter is composed primarily of elements that are impossible to bind with: oxygen, carbon and what have you. Those elements would kill anyone who tried to bind with them. It's why rhidium is so deadly when consumed by itself, as the rhidium attempts to bind with the most abundant element in your body: oxygen. But if something *were* to be bound to every element in human flesh, including oxygen, then the impossible becomes possible. The whole is greater than the sum of its parts." She gestured toward the monstrosity. "Exhibit A."

"That thing is an elemental?"

"The Child doesn't look it, right? Ig holds godlike power, in a sense, not unlike its ancestors. And the Child listens to us when we seek favors, for instance when we request for it to leash the minds of those who would help us locate its ancestors deep within the crust."

When she finished inspecting the chair, my captors brought me to it. I started thrashing again, shying away from the tower of white flesh beside me. They strapped me in, but I was too weak to fight back.

The kadiph knelt before me. "The Child is going to connect with your mind. It's important you remain calm so it can build a bridge between you and it. The more you resist, the more painful it becomes."

The restraints cut into my wrists as I pulled at them, and the wood bruised my flailing legs, but it was useless. "Please, I don't want this. I'll be a good student."

She looked at me like I was an idiot. "Nobody cares you tried to escape. It changed nothing. This was your fate all along."

The water rippled, and the tip of a tentacle rose out of the water. It had the same pale color as the rest of its body, and strips of wet, glossy flesh hung from the bottom of the tentacle. It slithered through the air, grazing my shoulder, and I held back the urge to vomit. The kadiph held me by my temples. "Hold still."

Jolting violently, I shook off the woman's grasp and bit into the meat of her thumb, but it was like biting into rock. I clenched down with all my strength until my gums hurt and my teeth felt tender, but I couldn't even break skin.

She laughed and gently pulled her hand away. "You get one

last struggle in. Seems like a fair trade for your sanity." She grabbed me by the temple again, and this time I couldn't shake her. Black winds, she was strong.

My body trembled as the tip of the Child's appendage slid along the back of my head. It felt weighty and warm. What looked like black hairs were plastered to strips of meat hanging from the appendage, and several of them rose until they stood on end, and I felt them prod me when the appendage continued to brush against the back of my head. I jerked and jolted, but the monstrosity waited patiently. I wasn't going anywhere.

Half a hundred black hairs stabbed into the back of my neck.

I screamed.

The scream echoed into eternity. I was floating. Floating in a vast emptiness, robbed of sight, smell, taste, hearing, and touch.

But I felt its presence.

The presence of something enormous. Something incomprehensible.

Ena-ujiwelub-sihev-hes-por-duroc-sayo-gir? *Onaw-ladiro-pe-fa-ret-lapabat-ivon.* *Tasera-eyoye-ga-uzone-ranapay-nepelec-yudafat-rin-egeyi-acare.* *Leteso-ginu-ieba, revie-osufope-bar-tanace-ere-rogela-nidet-citeha-oteme-nu. Tirohan-sitimu-de-erinoler-ocetari-be-ruhe-porer?* *Ciereri-rituwed-tocufif*

I couldn't hear its voice. It had no voice. But the words resonated through my mind, attempting to overwhelm me.

Cay-riri-aniget-tezetud-awel-edamef, arereta-eta-icotelim-cedero-esidav-rem-hac-adag, idunanie-enete-ico-bosac-noh-atis-po-petade

ig ig ig ig ig ig ig ig ig ig ig ig

Ig

My soul screamed.

* * *

SOMEONE OPENS THE door.

Kadiph?

No. Two visitors. Male, female.

"What do we have here?" woman asks. Heavy accent. Doesn't sound like kadiph.

Footsteps. There is torchlight moving outside cage. Shadowy figures.

"There's a prisoner in here," a man says with harder accent. Almost too hard to understand.

"Maybe he'll tell us where his friends are if we break him out."

"No, Sara. He might be dangerous. Someone's going to find us snooping around here."

Laughter. "Are you that worried?"

Metal scrapes against metal. Woman grunts.

"Here, try this," man says.

Painful spikes of sound echo in my ears. Man is striking lock. Door to cage squeaks.

Door is open.

Warm hands pick me up. I can't resist. Has the time come? Am I going to Black Depths?

The two carry me into hallway outside. Set me down. No one else is around. Remembering kadiph is as painful as torchlight. Threw me into solitary confinement after flesh binding, decided I needed to be broken further before my trip. Said I'd only be in cage for six months.

How long has it been?

The man and woman kneel over me. "He's more dead than alive," woman says.

"What should we do with him?" man asks. No, not man. Boy. Shy of manhood by a year. Both dark hair and strange skin. Related?

"Well, he might tell his captors we were here. That wouldn't bode well for Father. Might make his negotiations a tad more difficult."

Boy nods. "You're right. I guess we'll have to get him out

of here."

Where are the guards? Somewhere in compound. They will be furious when they learn what happened. Kadiphs will come.

Boy and young woman carry me through hallways. Up a set of stairs. Outside.

Outside.

Light from Burning Mountains turn the field between us and Obsidian Lake red. A familiar sight that makes me want to cry. The winds from Outside stir up black waters of Obsidian Lake. What lives down there…

They drop me when I start screaming. Boy straddles me and presses hand to my mouth. "You're going to get us killed if you keep doing that." His eyes are kind. He doesn't want to hurt me. Struggles with Sulian language. Foreigners. Masters, maybe?

"Who are you?" I ask when boy takes hand away.

Boy glances at older girl. Sister? "Just a couple troublemakers looking where we're not supposed to," he says slowly, awkwardly, in Sulian. "You can thank Sara for that."

"Where are you from?"

"Oh, sorry. We're not from around here. Father wants us practicing your language. Is it passable?"

I nod.

They sneak me out of compound, half carrying me. Move between shadows. Have months made my guards sloppy? Months… I was inside cage for months.

I feel frantic. These two are giving freedom from compound. Escape. The impossible. "Easy there," girl says. Sara.

Boy says something in strange language. Sara laughs. Responds. Boy notices me studying them. "I'm Emil, by the way. Don't be afraid." His nose wrinkles. "You've been sleeping in your own shit, haven't you? Those fucking savages."

They increase their pace. Too exhausting. So much

movement. My legs look narrow. Covered in sores. Standing hurts too much. Last time I saw someone... when a guard fed me. Stomach hurts with hunger. Guard will return soon with meal. They'll find me gone.

So much movement. Head dizzy. Everything black.

I WAKE. I am in bedroom. On the ground. Others are in room.

They are speaking in strange languages. More angry voices are on other side of closed door, but people in room with me ignore it. It's the brother and sister, Emil and Sara, arguing with third occupant in room. Sara lets out annoyed gasp. She leaves with Emil.

"You're awake," voice says. Third occupant kneels down to inspect me. Older man. "Sara and Emil were fools for stealing you. Of course, the Sulians were fools for forbidding them from entering that compound." Has accent, but speaks Sulian easily. "That guaranteed their interest. Now they have to go out and convince our hosts that the rumors of a missing slave have nothing to do with us."

I roll onto back. Spasm with coughs. Man stands and waits. "My name is Sorrelo," he says. "I'm a guest of your city. My children have put me in quite a predicament. If I let you go, you'll no doubt tell your masters what happened."

Sorrelo's children. Children.

Tosiset-ga-leyiro-etinur-adocir-sieceli-onurori-rec-tanet; lahirix-repu-rahalem-ori-gerabe-neh-gedemus ig ig ig ig ig ig ig ig ig ig ig ig ig ig ig ig

Child.

I let out shudder that turns into scream. Sorrelo sets foot on my chest. Squeezes the air out. Doesn't take much. "Do not. Do that," he growls.

The Child. It told me. More children like it, all over world. Those they flesh bind are sent to shores of the Black Depths. Kadiphs would command us to dig dig dig dig in search of ancestors. The Great Ones. Kadiphs worship them. They find slaves for them. Slaves totally bound to the kadiphs.

But I'm not bound yet. Child has planted the seed. Now a kadiph will reap its bounty when I arrive at the Black Depths.

No. I would do anything to avoid that. Child showed me what waited for me. I know.

I move into sitting position as Sorrelo kneels beside me. "Put your hand... on my neck," I say.

He looks ready to ask why, but does as I say. His hand cradles back of my neck. Can feel rough fingers feeling at branches of scars on my skin.

"Repeat after me," I say. "*Cocilas hepug lese bayarog noqo celat.*"

His brows furrow. Is he wondering if trick? "Cocilas... hepug lese... bayarog... noqo celat," he struggles to say.

"*Rohar ho le rata.*"

"Rohar... ho le rata."

Flickers of lightning travel up my spine. I do not care. Giving power to this man means keeping it out of kadiph's hands. "If you request my services, I will be bound to you," I say to him. "When you ask, it will be done."

His eyes calculate. He is confused; never encountered anything like this. He is a foreigner though. It means if I serve him, he will take me away. Far away from here.

"You're saying you will serve me?"

I nod weakly. So tired.

"That... sounds great, I suppose, but you seem to have one foot in the river already." He props me against bed and rises to stand over me. "I have no use for you."

He doesn't understand. Doesn't know the power the Ebonrock gave me.

My hands press against the floor. A floor of stone. My elemental power can feel its constituent parts. Pieces of a puzzle I can control. After last Imbibing, I feel stronger, though body much weaker.

My fingers push into stone. Sink in. So difficult. Sparks

ride up hands and onto floor. Sorrelo watches, eyes wide.

I scoop two handfuls of stone out of floor like mud. Present them as gifts.

"Ah," he whispers. "That changes things."

Now for hardest part. The sacrifice. I hope he will forgive me.

I shove Sorrelo onto ground. Pull knife from sheath on his belt. Use last of strength to hold him down. I am weak, but he is old and I am desperate. Can't fight me off. I grab his arm and carve.

He is terrified. Shudders through clenched teeth but doesn't cry out. He is too afraid of knife in my hand. Too afraid of what I can do.

When Child's name, Ig, is shiny on his arm, surrounded by bloody runes, I collapse onto ground. Sorrelo wrenches knife from my hand and puts blade to my throat.

"What was that?" he asks. So angry. So very angry.

My eyes flutter from exhaustion. Binding is settling into my bones. Skin on back of neck prickles. Traces of lightning. It is forming.

"An offering to the Great Ones required," I mutter "You spoke the Words of their language, and now you've sacrificed your flesh. I will soon be bound to you. Your first request to the Child will finalize the bond."

Bright blood drips from his cuts, but he ignores his pain. He is strong after all. "I should kill you."

"Just let me serve you. Make a request to the Child and the magic will be complete. Then take me away from here."

He studies me for several moments. Still angry. "How do I make a request to the Child?"

"Say its name. I carved it into your body. Then give your command."

"Ig..." he says, reading arm. Looks up to sky, as though speaking to invisible god. "I would have this man serve me until the day I die. And when I die, I would have him serve my children."

Sighing, I collapse to floor. Vibrating energy in the back of my head snaps into place. The binding is complete. I will serve this man's family. I am at peace with this. The kadiph of the Ebonrock never die. This is better.

Emil and Sara return hour later. Sorrelo is helping me drink water. I still sit against bed, but now I'm on rug. Sorrelo moved it to cover marks I made in floor. He tied ripped cloth over his sacrifice and hid it with sleeve. Told me to hide power from Emil and Sara.

"I think they believed us, but they're acting a lot frostier now," Emil says. Looks at his father. "They're going to ask you some hard questions during your next meeting with the Sulian ambassador."

"There isn't going to be another meeting," Sorrelo says.

"There isn't?"

"We're leaving. We've been here two weeks and made little progress. I'll be cancelling all further meetings too. Find the rest of our procession and spread the word. We'll be leaving as soon as everyone is ready."

Sorrelo already helped me change into unsoiled clothes. Was gentle with me. I made a good choice binding myself to him. He and his family will be good to me. They don't speak in native tongue, speak Sulian around me instead. They want to include me.

Emil collects belongings from around room. "I'm glad you convinced me to tag along earlier," he says to his sister. Glances at me. "We saved a life."

"No, you saved a life," Sara says. "I probably would have left him there."

"But you didn't even argue when I suggested we take him."

She shrugs. "I'll probably regret admitting this, but let's just say that maybe, just maybe, I want to be a better person when I'm around you." She smiles. Her eyes twinkle.

Emil smiles back.

Chapter 33 – Jakar

WHEN I CAME to, part of me already knew Emil was dead.

I'd dreamed it. Not of his death, but of him. Of his kind eyes when he discovered me in Som Abast. I never dreamed. Not since my flesh binding. So when he appeared in my unconscious, I knew something had gone horribly wrong.

Rockwood bars surrounded me. I almost panicked at the thought of being back in the Ebonrock compound—that everything in the last two years had been a product of my mind breaking further than I ever thought possible—but my arms and legs weren't atrophied, and light filled a room bustling with people. I pushed myself to my hands and knees.

I was in a cage in the middle of the audencia chambers.

Built into Augustin's second level, directly opposite the palace was the freghesa—one of Augustin's oldest districts, where the capital's judiciaries handled the constant flow of civil disputes, created and changed city bylaws, listened to pleas from the mayordomos of the towns throughout the territory, and where they held criminal trials.

The entire audencia was in attendance.

Three rows of desks sat before me, each row slightly lower than the one behind it. All thirty-six audencia members didn't pay my cage much attention, milling between chairs or speaking in whispered conversation along the wall behind the desks. A tapping foot here, a twitch of an arm there. The audencia was nervous. Someone had rolled my cage to where the accused of Augustin sat during their trial, but where someone normally sat chained to a chair, I'd been thrown into a cage. Behind me were several rows of pews occupied by members of the nobility, where citizens of Augustin could watch the public judgments of the audencia. I counted over a hundred in attendance. Guards lined the room, watching over the crowd with spears in hand.

Was the lockdown over? Some of the city guard had been released, no doubt to provide protection to the audencia chambers. The nobiletza looked harried too. Disheveled. Not the usual aura of those used to comfort in a secure city.

Beside me, in a cage of metal instead of wood, sat Rodi.

"Finally awake?" he asked. Even imprisoned, the mercenary still spoke with an air of ridicule. He'd been offered the comforts of a cushioned chair bolted to the cage floor, his ankles shackled to its legs.

What had happened to Emil? My heart hurt. Pain stabbed at my chest. My mind tried to retreat into its quiet place, but every time I thought of Emil's kind eyes, it pulled me back to reality. There was no escaping this. The pain in my chest continued to thrum.

Sara stood among three of the audencia's judges to the right of the room. Her body was worn, her damaged hand hanging at her side. She looked stressed. Upset. Her conversation with the judges only seemed to aggravate her.

"Sara," I said, my voice raised, a surprising amount of strength in it. It cut through the din. "What's going on?"

I sounded like the old Jakar. The thought should've reassured that part of me who had mourned his death for two years, until I realized that who I was then, who I was now, no longer mattered. Nothing mattered anymore. I was nothing. Strangely, that was the thought to reassure me. I struggled to my feet and rested my face against the bars, the chatter in the room quieting. "What happened?"

Sara crossed the floor to stand beside my cage, avoiding eye contact with me and watching the audencia take their seats, her good and bad hand clasped behind her back.

The last of the judges settled into their chairs. It was like sitting in a shallow bowl, looking up at the audencia sitting at their ebony desks, and the spectators eyeing me from their raised pews of stone. "Let's begin," the transcriber sitting to the far left said as he scribbled at a stack of parchment.

"Where's Mateo?" I asked Sara. "Where are the smiths?"

She kept looking forward, ignoring me.

A man sitting front-and-center among the audencia leaned on his desk. "To start, we would like to extend our thanks to Sara Adriann for bringing this matter to us. Proper formalities have more or less fallen apart this past week, and we are taking Sara's gesture in good faith that she intends to return full judicial control to those elected to carry out such rulings."

Sara bowed. "Absolutely, Judge Abeso."

While Judge Abeso's mildness toward Sara was alarming, the man's peers looked far less pleased with the princepa. Bags hung under their eyes, and they refused to relax the tightness in their postures. The guards ringing the room looked even more haggard than the judges.

Despite the disconcerted looks so many judges aimed toward the princepa, none of them called for Sara to be arrested. She must have struck a deal with the audencia.

"Where to start," Judge Abeso continued. "We have much to decide on."

"Let's start with the death of my brother," Sara said.

The pain in my chest spiked and I sagged against the bars. Emil was the reason I'd held hope throughout Sorrelo's abuse. Why I'd turned my back on freedom at Dagir's Pass. Why I'd stepped away from the river. What was the point of living if I had no one worth sharing my life with? I didn't despair at the question, though. There was nothing left inside me capable of despairing. There was nothing left inside of me capable of anything at all.

"Very well," Judge Abeso said. "Princep Emil Adriann, contender for the Augustin throne, was killed two passings ago during a confrontation between the smiths of the Foundry and the princepa, who was backed by her mercenary army. An army she recently used to depose and execute Olevic Pike. A matter we'll address later. We have eyewitnesses claiming the Radavich mercenary, Rodi Kanna, killed Emil Adriann. We also have accounts claiming Ig, manservant to the Adrianns and nicknamed the Stalker of Cragreach" —he sneered the nickname— "was the one who killed our princep. Two very conflicting reports."

My fists tightened. No words could express my outrage. Someone had accused me of killing Emil?

"So, let's hear it, you two. We'll start with the mercenary," Judge Abeso said.

Rodi shrugged. "What's there to say? Ig killed the princep. Every one of Sara's men can attest to that. Could've asked any smith too, but they're not here. Not even sure why it's a matter needing discussing."

Rodi's tone reeked of smugness, and he glanced in my direction as he finished, the corner of his mouth turning up.

He killed Emil.

Sara thundered with controlled fury. It was a partial relief seeing her anger toward Rodi, and I realized now why she was trying to work with the audencia. They were the only ones capable of punishing him.

"What of you, *Dor di Fero*?" Judge Abeso asked.

A small sound escaped my throat, and I blanked on how to explain something so obvious. "I… I didn't do it," I said. "I was unconscious. Ask the smiths."

"They have chosen not to attend the trial."

I waited for him to ask for elaboration—to express curiosity over why I'd been unconscious—but he only glared. It didn't matter to him, I realized. I was the Iron Sorrow, which meant I had to be Emil's murderer. Several of the judges glanced at the back of Abeso's head, their lips pressed together, but none of them interjected.

At least I had Sara's testimony, judging by her anger.

"Would like to speak to the princepa for one moment, Judge," Rodi said. He had to have known what Sara would say.

"Make it quick." Judge Abeso turned his attention to those sitting around him and they spoke in low voices. Some of them clearly wanted me dead, but the way the others looked at me made me wonder if the cause wasn't lost.

A faint pressure caressed the back of my neck as I watched them; Rodi's order to kill those who didn't support Sara still stood. Rodi had included a three-passing time limit with the Word too. If Emil had died two passings ago, it meant I only had hours left to fulfill the command, assuming I left this chamber alive.

Sara crossed the front of my cage to stand in front of Rodi's. "What?" she asked in a furious whisper.

"Don't do this."

The din from those around us obscured Rodi and Sara's voices, but I could still hear the conversation. "And why's that?" Sara asked. "You killed him, Rodi. I don't care how loyal you were or how beneficial you were to my cause. I would take one of him over a million of you and your sellswords."

He leaned in closer. "I'm not asking you to help me for my sake. Asking you to help for the sake of everyone around us. See anyone familiar in the audience?"

The attendees among the pews gossiped with each another, many of them avoiding my gaze, but some had familiar faces under their costumes: Jafos and jafas of the mercenary army. I saw Velmira, Bacarest, Anila, and a dozen of the others who operated the arms and legs of Sara's horde. Members of their crew accompanied them too. It was hard to tell how many in the crowd were true nobility or death in disguise.

"You were done soon as we lost what we pillaged from the Granite Road," Rodi whispered. "Our boys and girls know what happened now, and they're angry. The smiths were smart to hole up in their little church, otherwise they'd be dead by now. They wanted the master smith's head and you couldn't give it to them. They're gonna rip this city apart if anything happens to me."

"*Batra*," Sara spat in the old tongue at the same time I muttered, "Bullshit."

"Why do you think my friends are here? While you were ending the lockdown and putting the city back in motion, I was talking with them. Waiting so long to have me arrested was a mistake, and now you've lost the loyalty of your army. Left 'em out to dry before they could receive what was promised."

"It's not too late to pay them," Sara said.

"Wrong. Nothing will compare to what we took on the Granite Road. Now they have no choice but to find a way to pay themselves. Let me live and I'll convince them to head back into the crust, and we'll find a town or five for recompense. Or kill me and watch them destroy your city from the inside out. Either way, they get what they want."

Sara tried to summon up a counterargument. She had none. Finally, she looked at me. I could see the choice in her eyes.

Her nostrils flared at the mercenary. "I hate you."

"Can live with your hate just fine."

She returned to her spot beside my cage. "Are you finished?" Judge Abeso asked.

"Yes, Judge."

"And?"

She took a deep breath. And another. She froze.

It didn't last long. "Rodi did not kill the princep."

"No!" someone screamed. The younger princepa sat in the corner of the room at the end of the front row. Efadora. Two guards surrounded her, and they looked ready to restrain her as she stood in front of her chair, staring at her sister like she was ready to kill her.

Knowledge of my imminent demise didn't scare me, especially knowing Rodi's command would kill me anyway. My execution would mean an escape from everyone in the world. It would mean rest. When you were nothing, rest was the only path left to take.

"How could you do this?" Efadora asked her sister.

Judge Abeso steepled his fingers. "Are you claiming support for your family's servant, princepa?"

"No shit, Abeso," Efadora said. "That crooked fucker sitting next to Ig deserves his intestines wrapped around his neck."

"You would do well to address me by my title, Princepa. Frankly, I'm disturbed you would defend *Dor di Fero*, of all people." He massaged his brow. "Well, this is not good. Not good at all." He craned his neck toward the rest of the audencia. "How shall we go about in judgment of Princepa Sara Adriann?"

"We'll need to discuss further behind closed doors," one said.

Sara stepped forward. "What are you talking about?"

"I'm referring to the next part of our judgment," Judge Abeso said. "Rumors from the Granite Road cannot be ignored, and some members of the audencia find you responsible for what may or may not have transpired. This coupled with the master smith's insistence on Ig's innocence has led us to decide that we will be electing Efadora Adriann as the new magnate."

A small laugh erupted through the room. "Take your election and sit on it, Abeso," Efadora said. Whispers of outrage threaded through the nobility.

The master smith said I was innocent? It was a gift I didn't know I needed. Despite everything, a warmth appeared in the back of my chest, dulling the pain there. Thank Fheldspra he hadn't attended the trial. Despite everything, all I wanted right now was for the smiths to stay safe.

Judge Abeso glowered at the younger princepa. "I suppose that makes the decision easier." He brought his attention to Sara. "You are the last Adriann for the throne. There is another option, of course, and that would be to rid ourselves of your family once and for all. However, Olevic Pike's rule was a miserable affair, the way he spent far too much time trying to strip us of our power so he could hoard it for himself. The audencia's place will always be here in the chambers. As such, we are open to officiating your rule as Augustin's new magnate."

Several voices from the judges spoke up at once. "Are we?" one of them asked. "This seems like a discussion we should continue in private."

"We are," Judge Abeso said. "Sara is willing to work with us, so learn to accept a gift when it is given."

Sara as magnate was their last resort, but this didn't seem to bother the princepa. She bowed low. "You'd forgive me for so much? I'm honored. Anything to put all this behind us and bring Augustin back to its former glory."

"Good. Then prove your pledge to the wellbeing of this city." He gestured toward me. "There is Emil Adriann's killer right there. He must be executed for his crimes."

"This is only a hearing," one of the judges said. "We haven't even deliberated on sentencing yet. You cannot decide Ig's punishment."

"I believe I can, actually," Abeso snapped. "I'm in charge of this meeting, am I not? *Dor di Fero* thought it okay to execute Bolivar Adriann without a trial, so consider this poetic justice."

Those outraged by Abeso's sentence quieted. They were afraid of him, I realized.

"You'll be the one to execute him," Judge Abeso said to Sara.

Sara hadn't moved for several seconds, frozen like a critter trying to stay unseen. "... I will?"

"That's what I said."

"He should be thrown in the Lid while the audencia meets for sentencing so they can decide a date and time for his execution, if they even think that's what he deserves."

"So he has plenty opportunity to escape? No. You're the one who let him into our city, and your path to redemption can start now by executing him. Prove to us you don't condone his behavior. His right to death by ash or ice is forfeited. Put him down right now and we can leave this blight in our memories."

Sara turned full circle, then set her feet like she was ready to run. We shared a look, and the life drained from her face, her lips parted in disbelief. She slowly unsheathed her sword and held it like the hilt was covered in thorns.

It was her family's blade. A handle of bone wrapped in black leather with an even blacker gem for its pommel, the edge of the blade glowing a faint blue. Parts of the edge looked chipped and the flat of the blade was scratched and stained. She positioned herself at the front of my cage.

"I can't do this," she said in a low voice. She breathed fast, shallow breaths.

"I'm already dead," I said. "Just promise me you'll kill Rodi next."

She shook her head. "The army would never leave peacefully if I did that," she whispered.

"Right. Protecting the people is why you're doing this. Can't miss out on all the love and adoration of those strangers."

She swallowed. As she stood there with wooden legs, eyeing the Meteor Blade, delaying, anger started to work its way into me. She acted like she cared, like she was doing the hard thing, but for every good deed she committed, that was one more deed she benefited from.

She brought the blade up, holding it with her burned hand, the sword trembling, and I stepped away as its edge moved between the bars and grazed the rockwood with a hiss. I didn't move beyond her reach, though, my hands still gripping the bars.

"Are you ready?" she asked. She blinked, the corners of her eyes wet.

I nodded. She was giving me a gift at this point. Anything to get away from her.

Her tears welled up until they slid down her face, the Meteor Blade wavering in her hand. Then she stabbed as hard she could.

My hands snapped out, my palms catching the flat of the blade, and I gasped as the tip stabbed into my flesh at the base of my ribcage, the caustic burning making me shudder. Fhelfire, it hurt! I stepped back, but I didn't release my grip. Warm blood leaked from the wound, and I could feel it pooling along the contours of my abdomen beneath my clothing.

"Ig, let go of the blade," she commanded.

I didn't let go.

No pressure appeared on the back of my neck.

No pressure.

"Jakar?" she asked. She paused, waiting for the inevitability of my flesh binding's punishment.

Nothing happened.

"You... you tried to kill me," I said dumbly. The pain in my solar plexus hummed, but I could only think about the lack of pressure from disobeying a command. The audencia watched in silent confusion, and Sara froze as she held her breath. She tugged on the sword but I continued to hold it between my palms.

The simple fact that she wanted the sword and I didn't want to give it back nearly overwhelmed me. It was all I could do to stay calm, and I almost ended up letting go. "Ig, give it to me," she said in a shaky voice.

My arms and legs worked with a mind of their own. I pulled away, yanking hard, and she must not have realized I was capable of disobeying, as she didn't hold on tight enough to keep the blade in her hands. I trembled with ecstasy, my body buzzing with disobedience through the pain. How was this possible? I turned the Meteor Blade around and grasped it by its hilt, the bone and leather worn and its pommel gleaming flawlessly. Emil had held this sword for months, and I could almost feel the warmth of his grip radiating into my palm.

"Sara," Rodi muttered in a warning tone.

Judge Abeso spoke over the rising chatter, and I realized he was trying to quell the tide of restlessness rippling through the chamber. My ears didn't register his words though. My sight and hearing keyed in on the man in the cage beside me—the flexing of Rodi's forearms as he watched me, his gaze full of spite. The creak of his chair as he leaned forward, wondering what I would do next.

The sword rose to hover horizontally by my ear until I held it like a spear. Rodi jumped to his feet, unleashing an incoherent yell.

The blade traveled between the two sets of bars and impaled him in the throat.

His clogged screams echoed through the audencia chambers as chaos broke out, and the mercenaries jumped to their feet, pulling out concealed weapons. The guards charged at the sudden threat in the pews, pushing past the innocent, or ran to protect the judges, but a mercenary in costume brandishing their blade looked no different from a noble drawing out a knife to defend themselves.

"Defend the audencia!" Sara shouted. She glanced at me, but a trio of mercenaries jumped the wooden barrier in front of the pews and shoved their arms into my cage, trying to skewer me with their weapons. I snapped someone's wrist, disarmed him, and plunged the blade into his forearm. The man collapsed with a scream as he clutched his wrist, his artery severed. The rest backed off when they saw me with a weapon in my hand. More sellswords reached Rodi, but the man was leaking blood off the sides of his cage, the Meteor Blade still protruding from the base of his neck as his skin sizzled like meat on a skillet.

Why did the flesh binding fade when Sara stabbed me? The Adrianns had had countless opportunities to kill me in the past two years... the only difference now being that Sara had tried to execute me instead of letting the flesh binding's punishment take me. Did the willing execution of a faithful servant break the hold of the flesh binding?

A triumphant yell escaped my lips, and my arms trembled from the adrenaline, but the yell faded as the fire in my chest intensified. Pressing a palm to the wound hurt like the core, but I needed to apply pressure if I wanted to live long enough to escape. The smell of burnt flesh penetrated the muskiness of blood.

My flesh binding prickled on the back of my neck, and I realized Rodi's command still lingered.

The audencia clustered at the back corner of the room where most of the guard formed a protective line around their desks, and a string of orders left the shouting mouths of several judges, impossible to hear over the fighting. I removed my blood-slicked hand from my chest and grasped my rockwood bars, shaking them, and the flexing of my muscles sent another stab of agony through my wound. "Help, someone," I grunted. My voice was too weak to pierce the chaos.

Efadora was still separated from the audencia and their line of protection, the two guards surrounding her fighting off a coordinated attack from a wave of mercenaries. Efadora tried to help, but one of the guards shoved her behind him, and a sellsword snuck in, sticking his blade into the man's gut. Efadora shouted as her guard fell, backpedaling when her other one took an axe to the head. Two sellswords grabbed the princepa and dragged her thrashing body over the railing, toward the building's exit.

What few guards were lingering near mine and Rodi's cages fell to the swelling number of mercenaries. The chamber doors burst open and more mercenaries flooded in. A woman leaning against a nearby pew struggled to cock her crossbow with clenched teeth—who managed to smuggle one of those in? She watched me, her eyes full of hate as she locked the crossbow's string into place.

A young man in a bulky robe snuck up behind her and turned her neck into a bloody ruin with the garrote in his hands. The woman dropped to the floor. Her killer brandished the crossbow and aimed it at the opposite side of Rodi's cage, where I noticed a young woman fighting off two mercenaries with a short sword. The man with the crossbow was the soldier I'd saved during the siege of the capital; the woman with the short sword his sister. He sunk a bolt into the spine of one of the mercenaries attacking his sister, then the sister cut down the other one a heartbeat later. The brother picked up a discarded two-hander and slid over the railing, and I realized he was wearing steel under his robe. The siblings faced three mercenaries preparing to assault my cage and rushed forward.

The woman moved with the grace of a Foundry metal worker. A mercenary swung at her in a downward slice, but she palmed the weapon to the side and opened his guard up enough for her to plunge her sword into his stomach. Her brother swung his two-hander hard enough to send another mercenary off balance, and his sister came in to slash the man across the face. The last one caught an arrow from behind, from one of the guards rallying the judges.

The smith rattled the lock to my cage. "My power won't open it."

"They made it with an alloy we're not bound to," I said. "It's tungsten carbide, I think. Hit it with a hammer."

The girl found a hammer covered in dark, arterial blood nesting in the grip of a slain mercenary, and brought it back to the cage. The first strike sent a sharp ring through the chambers and blood flicking across the floor of my cage. The second strike shattered the lock.

The brother caught me as I stumbled out on weak legs. "We should leave," I said.

Death filled the chamber. Bodies leaked puddles of blood in the spaces between pews or lay draped over benches. Many wore the expensive fabrics of the nobility, but I couldn't tell how many of them were mercenaries or collateral. The audencia looked smaller than before, and I caught a glimpse of an opened door in the back where judges filed through one by one. Sara was already gone. Mercenaries vaulted over pews and railings in a frenzy, trying to break the line of guards protecting the retreating audencia, and only a handful noticed us near the exit. The Tulchi smith was a whirlwind of death as she guided us forward, her short sword in one hand and her hammer in the other.

Outside, gangs of mercenaries fought along the ridge like packs of wild dogs. A hundred corridors were built into the second level, some as wide as the Granite Road and others as narrow as a side alley, and many of them had people running in and out of view with torch and steel in hand, the frenzied sellswords breaking in windows and setting fire to homes. Smoke crawled along vines covering the ceiling until it escaped into the open air of the chasm. I squinted, sweeping the level, but there was no sign of Emil's younger sister. "Did either of you see where they took Efadora Adriann?"

Both companions shook their head.

The smoke was thickest at the palace waiting several hundred feet down the ridge. It billowed as black as the palace's broken obsidian pillars, occasionally spitting out spluttering nobility rushing out of the haze. Four mercenaries prowled the entrance, cutting down each batch of nobles as they emerged.

I took off. Each step sent a horrible stabbing sensation into my chest, but the euphoria of running of my own volition overcame it. The sellswords didn't notice me approach, and I elbowed the first one in the mouth as she turned. I gripped her wrist, breaking it while she stumbled backward, and she let go of her sword, stumbling. The sword fell into my hand and was stabbing into her jugular before she hit the ground. The Tulchi brother crashed into another one, impaling him, and his momentum sent the man stumbling into the mercenary next to them. The sister pounced on the fourth—she swung the hammer at the same time the sellsword swung at her, and the hammer hit the sword hard enough to send it flying out of the man's grip and sliding across the mosaicked rock. He yelped in pain, the sound intensifying as he took the smith's other weapon in the armpit. He slumped, and the mercenary who had been knocked to the ground tried to scramble to his feet, but the Tulchi smith was already there, bringing her hammer down on his skull. The hammer made a sound like cracking lobster tail.

More nobility materialized from the smoke, and they collapsed onto the stone in fits of coughing, shying away from the bodies of their friends and the sellswords.

"What are your names?" I asked the two as they knelt over the gasping nobles.

"Ester," the smith said. "My brother is Damek."

"Thank you. I need to find a way to stop this army, and it has to be soon." Phantom fingers tapped against the back of my skull, reminding me of my unfinished work. Release from the flesh binding had saved my life, but it had also sealed my fate—Sara had lost her power to give a Word, which I suspected meant she couldn't take it away either.

I'd find a way to stop the army before Rodi's command killed me.

"Mateo's working on it," Ester said. "The smiths were using your trial as a distraction so they could rescue the corps held captive in the Barrows. They're escorting a caravan of weapons and armor up the levels right now."

"Why were you at the trial then?"

She rubbed the back of a man who couldn't stop coughing, staring at the body of another several feet away, the dead noble's clothes twisted around his limbs, dirty and bloody. "The master smith believed rescuing you would only get the smiths killed, but Damek and I needed to see the trial for ourselves. We had to see if the rumors of the princepa's corruption were true." Her gaze sharpened like broken glass. "The Foundry won't sit by anymore. That I promise."

Hope dulled the despair. Maybe I could die happy knowing smiths like Ester would be around to stop Sara from becoming magnate.

Damek tore a strip of cloth from the robe he wore over his breastplate and greaves of secular steel, using it to fashion a tourniquet for a woman's leg. "We're with you to the end, Jakar. We can head—"

An object struck the second level ridge like a meteor, sending vibrations through the ground and chipped rock into the air.

Not a meteor. A person. Shorn hair colored an ancient grey, with the features of a man in his prime and a face chiseled from stone. He stood on concentric rings where the ground had bowed under his landing, and he waved at the cloud of dust that rose around him.

It was the primordia, Nektarios.

Chapter 34 – Efadora

TWO MERCENARIES DRAGGED me by my wrists through a wide corridor on the fourth level. I thrashed, kicking and screaming, and managed to bring my heel down on the foot of the woman to my left, right on the joints of her toes. "Above and below," the woman hissed, and hit me in the face with her gauntleted fist.

Stars exploded in my vision, and I tried to scream, but the sound came out more like a gurgle at the end of a tunnel. Dizziness overwhelmed me. My vision slowly cleared, and I found myself looking up at the ceiling, my butt and legs sliding over the tiled road as they continued to drag me by my arms. "Best coin's always with the dead. Where is it, princess?" the woman asked.

My left cheekbone buzzed with pain and the side of my mouth felt wet. There was a hard piece of food in my mouth and I spat it up. A tooth. It rolled down the front of my tunic and bounced on the ground. The corridor opened into a plaza, the ceiling vaulting up until it was dozens of feet above our heads. We were in the Catacombs of Fire, where rows of catwalks lined the walls leading into burial chambers for the lower nobility and wealthy commoners. "Rich get buried with some of their jewelry, right?" the woman asked. She and the man dragged me to the fountain in the center of the plaza. "Show us which."

There was the sound of boots slapping on stone, then the woman was tumbling, still holding onto me, yanking me hard to the right until she let go and I rolled across the ground. Cold, dusty stone met the tender side of my face, and I pushed myself up.

Meike kicked the man in the chest and off his feet, then brought her sword to bear in time to parry the woman stabbing at her torso. She attacked the woman in return, sparks flying as her blade scraped over the sellsword's steel chest guard and vambrace. Meike only wore fighting leathers—her exposed arms gleamed with sweat and grime and she had nothing but cloth and leather to protect her from the fully armored sellsword, yet she was the one advancing hard, savagely, her opponent stumbling backward, teeth gritted in rage. The edge of Meike's blade found the soft meat in the woman's thigh, and the woman crumpled, gasping. Meike spun, and the sellsword's head hit the ground.

She faced the man, but he was already running for the entrance into the largest tomb, where torchlight danced inside the dark cavity. Her eyes found mine and she raced to me. "You all right?" she asked, kneeling.

"More, coming," I struggled to say.

My words were interrupted by a gang of mercenaries that rushed out of the tomb the man had disappeared inside. There were six of them, and they were protected by secular steel, long blades in hand. Meike helped me to my feet while they cornered us in a semi-circle with our backs to the trickling fountain.

"Caught ourselves a coupla live ones," one of the mercenaries said, and laughed. The others grinned, and I offered my own bloody smile, though all I felt on the inside was fear.

Meike pulled me behind her and widened her feet into a battle stance, the muscles of her sword arm flexing. She gave the blade a twirl and let out a battle cry. It was gruff, filled with the promise of violence and a hint of desperation. The sellswords moved in, jeering at us like we were caged animals.

A group of shield-bearing mercenaries wearing pauldrons and tassets of red chitin appeared at the end of the corridor, rushing to join the first. They reached the plaza, but then steel glinted from behind the rockwood shield of the lead man, who plunged his sword into the neck of one of the armored sellswords. The newcomers crashed into the others and Meike bolted forward to join the battle.

"You scare me sometimes," Undersergeant Eslid said to Meike when the last sellsword lay cut open at his feet. Petamare, Brux, and the rest of the riders surrounded us. "In a good way, I think." He clapped her on the back.

Meike nodded in acknowledgement, still trying to catch her breath, but when Eslid looked away a smile flashed across her face. "We all stay together now," the undersergeant continued. "Best way to navigate any jungle is to move as one."

"Might I suggest helping Mateo and his smiths?" Carina said as she cleaned the flat of her blade using the calf of a dead man.

I cupped some water to swish it around in my mouth and returned it to the fountain much redder than before, then stole a mercenary's dagger from their belt and surveyed the dead at our feet. Now Sara's men had gone from killing Emil to almost killing me. Just thinking of my sister made me clench my jaw until the socket with the missing tooth made my gums ache. She'd pay for what she did to Emil, to the people on the Granite Road, to Ig. She wasn't my sister anymore.

We ran to the ridge where smoke from the levels below created a hazy curtain rising to the sky, and screams from the nobility and commoners echoed into the chasm. "There," Brux said, pointing. Through the haze two levels up, a caravan of carts and the unmistakable red-brown robes of Mateo's smiths marched along the sixth level. "Might be able to fight our way up," the big man said. "Don't look promising though."

Countless packs of sellswords, some several to dozens strong, waited between us and the smiths, ravaging the city. They were most concentrated on this level and the one above and below us, where there were still valuables worth stealing and the city guard had almost no presence. "The pulleys," I said. The ropes dangled a hundred feet to our right, swaying with the wind. "We'll ride them up."

Halfway to the pulleys we came upon a group of mercenaries struggling to ignite the curtains to a stage built against the ridge. We came up behind them—Eslid's riders still looked like every other gang running around—and the riders cut them down, smiling and laughing as they did so. Now *this* was justice. The kids of Titanite could never stomach blood and death the way Eslid's riders could, the way I could. These were my people.

A series of ramps jutted from the ridge where a dozen ropes snaked up and down the level. One of the ramps had its pulley and counterweight attached to this level with a pile of stacked blocks waiting next to the empty counterweight. Perfect. Letting the counterweight sink to the floor would bring us to the Barrows on the eighth level, then we could circle back to the smiths.

"Each stone's a hundred pounds," I said. "There're eleven of us, so throw on about twenty-five. That should do the trick."

The riders set their shields down and started stacking blocks on the counterweight. Fifteen blocks in, when they were breathing hard and their faces and necks were covered in sweat, another gang of mercenaries, this one fifty strong, flooded out of one of the alleys. The sellswords stopped in front of the stage where their slain friends lay on the ground with dying torches still in hand, saw us, then pointed and broke into a run.

"Fhelfire," Darien said, scrambling for his shield. The others followed suit.

"Form up," Eslid barked. "Shield wall."

Eslid's riders stood shoulder to shoulder, bringing up their shields and bracing themselves. The front of the mercenary group collided with the riders, whooping and hollering, the sounds quickly turning into ones of surprise and pain when the riders answered by separating flesh with their swords. Men and women fell back, uncoordinated, smearing the ground with blood, being pulled back by their friends who yelled obscenities at the riders. The next wave moved more carefully, trying to poke at the shield wall for any sign of weakness, their glee gone. One sellsword sent a wad of spit flying at Brux's shield—the big man stepped forward, shouting, and the sellsword slipped in blood trying to back away. He hit the ground, cracking his head against the rock, and Brux took one giant step forward to skewer him before rejoining the wall.

A volley of arrows struck the line, but rockwood was too dense for them to stick, and the shafts ricocheted across the rock. "Right side," Eslid shouted, and that's when I noticed some of the sellswords moving along the arc of the ridge to reposition themselves. Meike grabbed me, pulling me close behind Eslid and Brux and the others just before another volley hit us from the side. Haflid cried out, a shaft sticking out her side, and she collapsed.

We were trapped like rabbits. We still needed to add more stones to the counterweight, but even if we miraculously got the platform moving under the threat of bow and steel, the mercenaries would cut the rope as soon as we were away.

"Grab her shield," Eslid said at Meike. Meike picked up Haflid's shield, its owner lying face down on the rock, and tried to join the line, but Eslid shouted, "No. Onto the platform with Efadora."

Meike grimaced, but nodded. She tried to pull me away from the stinking heat and labored breathing of the oversergeant and Brux, but I almost refused. I couldn't do this again. I couldn't lose more people who cared. But I let her pull me onto the platform under the protection of her shield. "You too," Eslid said to Carina. Darien let out a wet gurgle, an arrow impaling his neck to the other side, and he collapsed. The shield wall stumbled trying to close his gap.

"Take it," Meike said to Carina, handing her the shield. The cartographer took it without complaint. "Keep her safe."

"Meike," I shouted, but Meike was already stepping off the platform.

Eslid smashed a man in the face with the lip of his shield and used the lull to turn around to shove Meike with all his might. She was bigger than him, but he had enough desperate strength to make her trip and land on her butt on the platform once more.

"Brux," Eslid screamed, half-crazed. The big man dropped away and Eslid and Petamare filled the gap in one fluid motion. Brux threw his shield to the ground and shouldered the counterweight with a roar.

Eslid took a foot's worth of spear in the stomach, curling him over the shaft. "No!" Meike and I said at the same time Brux sent the counterweight off the side of the ridge and us toward the sky.

Chapter 35 – Jakar

THE PRIMORDIA STOPPED in front of us, surveying the recovering nobility and the scattered bodies. He turned full circle as though noticing the chaos for the first time. "Why is it a man can't leave the territories for a few weeks without it all falling apart?" He walked past us and through the broken onyx pillars, the smoke swirling as it swallowed him.

"What are you doing?" Ester asked when I turned to follow.

"I need his help finding Efadora."

I entered the acrid smoke before the smith could protest. The air singed my nostrils and burned my eyes, each step ripping at the wound in my chest. Heat washed over me and shadows danced in the haze. I squinted as I held my breath, but I could barely see more than a few feet in front of me.

Past the first corridor's carved murals was the main hallway where tapestries, carpets, and furniture burned. The vaulted ceilings collected most of the smoke, allowing me to see Nektarios moving toward the other end of the hall. Three mercenaries struggled out of an antechamber a short distance in front of him, struggling with a metal sculpture. The prize was a five-foot tall model of a Great One—a writhing mass of tentacles and flesh—and looked to be made of copper with

435

a layer of quartz crystal under its base. They dropped the sculpture to draw their swords, and their aggression triggered the primordia.

Nektarios moved faster than the mercenaries' hands twitching toward their blades. He gripped one of them by the back of the neck, and I could hear bone break all the way from here. His victim fell as the primordia's fist struck a woman's skull, hard enough to spray blood and brain onto the last man, who let out a horrified yell. The survivor fled through the smoke into an adjacent hallway.

Such incredible strength. Nektarios stalked after the mercenary, and I hesitated before following again, my heart thumping. Here I was about to throw my life away. Again.

I found Nektarios in a chamber unscathed from the flames. Pyremoss grew behind stained glass windows that depicted Ra'Thuzan from its core to the volcanic surface, casting a warm hue on the man as he stood on a bloodied carpet over the mercenary, who was now very much dead. He cocked his head at me. "I recognize you. Sorrelo Adriann's personal attendant."

I tried not to dwell on the mass of odd angles and broken bones at his feet. "There's an army outside that's about to kill a lot of people," I said.

"They will be dead very soon."

I relaxed. When all hope was lost, the primordia, of all people, had come to save the city.

"The tip of the pyramid must crumble first," he continued. "I shall work my way down afterward. Though it seems one Adriann has already met their fate." He gestured behind him. "Would you happen to know where the rest are?"

A sarcophagus sat on a raised platform at the end of the room, made from clouded Guild glass and igneous rock. On the shelves behind it sat tools of the dead's chosen craft and symbols to represent their life—in this case a polished sword of Foundry steel, a bust of white agate made in the likeness of a burrowing hawk, and a bar of platinum surrounded by piles of freshly minted standards. The hawk was a symbol of courage, the platinum a symbol of wealth. Emil.

"Sara Adriann," I started, my voice wavering, my insides numb, "was in the freghesa. I don't know where she is now. The same goes for Efadora Adriann."

Nektarios shook his foot, flicking away the blood that had stained his boot, and took a step away from the body. "So is it Sorrelo or Emil Adriann who lies in the tomb?"

"Emil. Sorrelo passed several weeks ago."

"Ah. Then only half the challenge. Unfortunate."

"What do you mean?"

He strode toward me. "You will fill me in on what has happened while we walk to the freghesa."

"Are you going to kill the Adrianns?"

He stopped in front of me, a head taller but seeming twice the size. "I suppose a trade in information is a fair deal. The Adrianns will die, yes, but you may rejoice in their good fortune. Death is preferable to what the Sovereign will have in store for Augustin. Now, tell me about this mercenary army and their deeds."

"What is the Sovereign going to do?"

He frowned. "Your position as servant is the only reason you are alive right now. My temperament is rarely so agreeable. You would do best to listen."

I didn't move. "Will the Sovereign do another purge?"

Nektarios let out a *hmph*. "Surprising. I did not know such stories still existed."

He grabbed me by the neck and threw me across the room. My vision spun, but I instinctively opened my Eye, sensing the elements around me—the calcium in the stone, the iron in the torch holders, the silicon in the glass I flew toward. I smashed into the sarcophagus but cushioned myself with my power. I bounced off and collapsed on the stone.

It felt like someone had stabbed a pike through my abdomen. I gasped, a new spurt of blood pouring out of my wound. Panic forced me up and I braced myself for an attack—the primordia no doubt perplexed by how I'd survived—but the man was already gone.

The glass had a shallow Jakar-shaped imprint, but the depression had spider webbed, dropping tiny shards onto the floor. Dark fabric poked through the openings. I left a bloody handprint on the sarcophagus as I pulled myself up and grasped at the ring twisted up in twine around my neck.

"I'm sorry, Emil," I said. The clouded glass hid his face, but I knelt over the head of the sarcophagus and pressed my forehead to the cold surface. "Rodi for you, the primordia for Efadora."

I brought my elbow down on the bottom corner of the coffin's lid and a sliver of glass as long as my forearm broke off. I picked it up and limped for the exit, toward fire and death.

The flames continued to rage throughout the palace, at their most intense in the main hall. Nektarios had stopped near the front, his back to me, while Ester and Damek faced him— Ester brandished her short sword in one hand and her bloody hammer in the other, Damek with his two-hander, their weapons of steel and Damek's armor dancing with the colors of the inferno. None of them saw me. I crouched behind a bust, pressing my hand hard against my wound, and stifled a gasp.

"So much defiance in this city," Nektarios said. I could barely hear him over the roar of the fire. "I am under orders to avoid your kind, but I will break both of you if you are still in my way after ten seconds."

"Where's Ig?" Damek asked.

"The servant? He is dead. He thought it smart to do exactly as you two are doing right now." Nektarios's body wound tight as a spring, but he didn't pounce.

I moved into the open and caught Ester's eye, but her gaze didn't linger. "You'll die for your evil," she said. "For two hundred years you've terrorized the territories. No more."

The primordia's shoulders shuddered with laughter. "Oh, child. I'll enjoy pulling you apart."

As the man's laughter faded into the din, I snuck up behind him and stabbed the glass into his back, driving it in with the force of my elemental power. He didn't stumble like I'd expected. Despite being razor sharp, the glass only sunk a few inches into his flesh.

The back of his hand struck me in the shoulder like a hammer. I flew until I rolled across the smoldering carpet and bumped into the statue of the Great One, the pain in my shoulder stealing my breath away. I tried to stand, but a pair of hands grabbed me by my robe's collar and lifted me until I was half a foot off the ground. I was held at eye level, and Nektarios stared at me with his lupine eyes. Ester and Damek charged. Without looking, the primordia sent out a powerful pulse of elemental power, far more powerful than anything I could have done.

Damek was flung back by the armor he wore, crashing into the wall beside the entryway. A flaming tapestry dropped down and engulfed him. Ester's sword struck a different wall, burying a foot into the rock, and her hammer turned a piece of pottery on a pedestal into dust. She cringed in pain, but when she saw her brother beneath the tapestry's flames, she rushed to him.

"Coming to Augustin has been a treat," Nektarios said to me with smiling eyes. "Years and years of shepherding the cowed masses, decades of monotony, an eternity without meaning. I hope that army fights with the same fervor as you three. This I pray to the Mazesh, to those who made themselves God."

"You won't have a chance to find out," I said, grabbing onto the primordia's wrists, phantom daggers cutting into my shoulder.

I drew in Nektarios's heat, drinking in his energy the same way I took Rodi's in Radavich. The ground trembled as I siphoned it away, sending pedestals to the floor and more tapestries fluttering to the marble in my attempt to make Nektarios catatonic.

I balked. So much heat was trapped in his body, enough to rival the fires in the palace—a vast well of energy needed for him to live, required to power muscle denser than steel. It filled me up until it threatened to rip me apart from the inside, and I struggled to siphon it into our surroundings as the hallway continued to quake. It was too much to draw out in a single moment.

Nektarios looked down at my hands. "You are an elemental? And not one from the trade schools or the Foundry. They cannot siphon energy at your rate. Nowhere close." He pulled his right arm away, continuing to hold me with his left, then grabbed the wrist of the hand I still had clutched onto him and squeezed.

I gasped as bone broke. I lashed out with my unhurt hand, but striking him in the jaw was like hitting rock. He laughed. "A prize for my brothers and sisters, found in the most unexpected of places. You will be our shepherd from the abyss. You know of the Rha'Ghalor?"

"Who?" I cried out.

He pursed his lips. "Too good to be true, perhaps. We will discuss at length the origin of your power once Augustin is docile."

He dropped me and I awkwardly hit the ground. My hand and my shoulder throbbed as I tried to lean against the statue, the pain temporarily overshadowing the burning in my chest. Fhelfire, I was close to done. Nektarios turned to face Damek and Ester, the shard of glass still protruding from his back.

Ester held her hammer and Damek his sword. Ash coated Damek's hair and face, but he looked otherwise unharmed. Ester simmered with fury. Nektarios took a step forward, then Ester let out a yell and charged.

Her brother followed, but not with the same fearlessness. Ester reached Nektarios first—the primordia sidestepped her swing, ducked beneath the next, then caught the head of her hammer with the palm of his hand. He ripped the weapon free and used the hammer's handle to bat away Damek's swing as he followed up. He seemed to relish fighting the smith as he played with the two almost lazily, smiling at Ester's frustrated grunts.

There was no stopping the primordia. Weapons did nothing to his body—a hammer could do as much damage to him as it could to an anvil, and even if Damek landed a hit, his blade couldn't penetrate the man's flesh. Nektarios's body was as dense as a mountain, more solid rock than human.

Like the kadiphs.

The primordia kicked Ester in the chest, sending her flying into a pedestal. Her head bounced off the stone and she crumpled to the ground.

The kadiph who ruined my plans to escape the Ebonrock had possessed hands of partially vitrified rock that had transformed into flesh as hard as steel, and I'd nearly broken my teeth biting her on the passing when I received my flesh binding. Those hands weren't hers—they'd been created for her, somehow.

I pulled at the ring hanging from my neck until the twine broke, then pressed my fingers into it with my good hand while it rested on my other palm, working carefully so my broken wrist wouldn't overwhelm me. My bruised knuckles ached as I plied the metal, but the energy I'd leeched from Nektarios gave me strength. The ring warped slowly, becoming bigger, two prongs growing out opposite ends. Once the shape was right, I set the charm on the statue, the prongs resting between two tentacles of the Great One, and I closed my eyes.

After leaving Sulian Daw and recovering enough of my mind to think on my past mistakes, I'd despaired for weeks wondering what I could've done to stop the kadiph. I eventually found the answer hiding in Master Orino's advice about the storms, within the name of the intermediary all elementals used to affect the elements they were bound to— the electromagnetic field.

The charm started to spin.

My body still hummed with the energy I'd drawn from Nektarios's body, and I fed it into the iron as it spun faster and faster. The hairs on my arms stood up. I stood on the base of the statue, feeling the energy feeding into the magnetized, spinning iron and silver convert to electricity, building a charge throughout the copper and my body.

Damek swung at the primordia in desperation. He wasn't a metal worker though, and if Ester looked like a child fighting the primordia, he looked like an infant. Nektarios caught the blade easily with the crook of the hammer. He slapped Damek in the face and disarmed the young man, then brought his newly acquired sword down just below Damek's shoulder, cutting the man's arm off.

"Nektarios," I called out. "You've tried to kill me twice and I'm still here. You're pathetic."

The primordia stood over Damek, who lay on his back with his mouth moving and his eyes glazed over in shock, and looked back at me. "A distraction to delay the inevitable only causes more suffering."

"Your master will kill you for your failures."

The primordia bristled. He stepped away from his prey and marched toward me. "What would you know of my—"

I slapped him in the face the same way he had Damek. The air snapped. There was a sound like marble scraping against marble as Nektarios's body clenched, and his eyes rolled around in their sockets, arms and hands curling inward. He tipped backward. He hit the floor like a statue, hard enough to make it vibrate, and his leather armor ripped open from the shard of glass that pushed through his back and sprouted out of his chest.

Cords of muscles bunched up in his neck, arms, and legs. He still clung to Damek's sword, but the hilt grew out of the bottom of his hand like putty. His eyelids twitched—he was still alive, even with a foot-long shard of glass piercing his chest. I ran for Ester's fallen hammer before the man could recover.

I brought the weapon down on Nektarios's head with a grunt. A small indent appeared on the primordia's forehead and his eyes rolled more violently behind partially opened lids. Another swing, and this time bone broke.

The crackling flames ate up the calm. I stared at the primordia's ruined face, too stunned to move, until Damek's moans snapped me out of it. The man was delirious from blood loss. "Come on," I said, and wrapped his intact arm around my neck, pulling him to his feet. His sister lay in a crumpled heap as we passed, her robes smoldering.

I set him down beyond the broken onyx pillars and returned for Ester. With a groan, I slung her over my unhurt shoulder. Tears formed in the corners of my eyes from the pain in my arms and chest, but I soldiered on. Outside, two nobles had appeared, standing over Damek and tending to him. They were the same ones we'd saved not ten minutes earlier.

"Make him a tourniquet," I said to one. "Tie it tight or he'll die."

They struggled to rip strips of cloth from the robes of a nearby body, and I surveyed the area around us. The chaos had intensified, but the mercenaries had avoided the smoke pumping out of the palace entrance, off to pillage and burn the untouched parts of Augustin.

My stomach sank at the realization I'd killed the only person capable of stopping them.

"Take them somewhere safe," I said to the nobles.

I limped for the nearest stairway, hoping to find Mateo and his smiths somewhere in the upper levels. They and the corps were Augustin's last hope.

Chapter 36 – Efadora

THE LEVELS TURNED into a blur of alternating stripes as we rose toward the stars. The platform stopped suddenly, sending the three of us into the air and making me damn near skewer myself on my dagger when we landed. We fell in a heap, almost rolling off the platform as it swung back and forth. A four-foot space separated us from the railing. Meike grabbed onto me, then tossed me at the same time I jumped, and I sailed over the gap for one heart-stopping moment before landing on the ridge.

"They're dead," Carina said once she and Meike made it over. Her eyes usually had a detached look to them, her mind somewhere in the crust most of the time, but not now. The ink bottle tattoo on her forearm rippled with anger. "I'm going to unscrew their heads from their bodies."

The platform dropped out of view, followed by the sound of whistling rope, and moments later the end of the cut rope whipped around the top wheel of the pulley system before dropping away. So Eslid and his riders really were dead. Rage nauseated me until a deep, sucking emptiness replaced it, getting worse and worse until I felt a sob coming. I couldn't bite it back. Meike kneeled at the ridge's edge, whispering into Haflid's shield which she now wore, then returned to us, her expression full of grim determination. Seeing that helped. As hard as it was, I pushed back the anguish. Now wasn't the time to let grief take over.

The Barrows were quiet. The commoners up here were hiding in their homes, pretending the fighting below didn't exist or barricading their doors. The alleyways leading into the makeshift prisons for the corps waited on the opposite ridge, and I caught a glimpse of several mercenaries heading into the twisting halls, their swords drawn.

Wind whipped at us, the ice on the backside of the sheaths that grew past the ridge glistening blue and white as we ran behind them, our breath fogging as we reached the other side of the Barrows. Shouts of terror reached us from the maze of alleyways. I led Meike and Carina down the nearest one, where frost coated the stone where salt hadn't been thrown down, torchlight fluttering. The first jail wasn't far—several doors along the corridor had been thrown open and blared with the sounds of fighting.

Several bodies lay slumped in the first room of the house I entered, all of them put to the sword. I entered a dark hallway, feeling Meike's presence behind me, and found a barrier of bodies as two mercenaries hacked their way through the POWs toward the room at the far end, their backs turned to us.

"Surprise, fuckers," I said as I sheathed my dagger between the ribs of the sellsword to the left. My blade slid out and plunged into the side of the right man as he turned his body. The first one swung wildly as he fell, and I narrowly avoided a sword to the head. The second man made a much quicker business of dying.

I came to a room in the back where the last of the house's POWs had fled. They had managed to dislodge the rockwood boards from the wall that linked their manacles, but the board kept them together like caught fish on a line. The door had been ripped out of its frame.

"Stop!" I yelled as one group started to rush me. They paused. The sight of a teenage girl turning the corner instead of two blood-crazed mercenaries stole their momentum. "I'm not here to hurt you. I'm here to save you."

"You lying?" a particularly pathetic-looking prisoner asked.

"Of course not," I said.

"Prove it," another said.

I turned to Meike and Carina. "Go help the others." They nodded and disappeared down the hall. I went back to glaring at the POWs, swallowing my annoyance. *We don't have time for this*. Sara always said that as soon as someone pitied you, you lost their respect forever, and suddenly my irritation at their weakness made sense.

How much of me had been formed by my sister?

"The invading army isn't policing the city anymore," I said, trying to sound like Father, summoning some of that absoluteness he'd been so good at. "They're turning on Augustin and killing anyone they want. That means all of you. Fight now while you have the chance." I finished with a kind look. Something Emil would have done.

No one responded. They were too wary to move, too wary to trust.

What could I say to spur them into action? What would Emil have said?

"I get how hard the invasion was on you," I continued. "They made you fight Augustin's princepa. She was the rightful contender to the throne and she had the smiths on her side. But everything's different now. This army is going to burn the city and destroy our home. Help the smiths and help the Adrianns. Save Augustin."

Telling them to help my sister ignited a spark I almost lost control of, but I reminded myself this wasn't for her.

Their expressions evolved from those of beaten mole-rats to those of people who suddenly remembered they were trained soldiers. Their postures straightened, and their last reserves of strength buoyed to the surface.

"Take what you can from the dead in the hallway," I said. "Use it to save the others."

"Who're you?" one asked. "You look familiar."

I left the room to find the key to their locks on one of the sellswords' bodies. It had been a year and a half since I'd roamed these streets or walked at my father's side, so of course they didn't recognize me. It would stay that way, too. I was no longer princepa.

After I freed them, several POWs scavenged weapons and shared pieces of armor from the dead men. Outside, Meike and Carina were nowhere to be seen, but clashing steel echoed from the other homes. The freed soldiers slipped past me, moving with restless energy, itching to save their friends. Their eagerness spurred me into action. I eased inside the next house in the alleyway, searching for blood.

We killed the sellswords swiftly and without remorse. They had entered the jails is pairs—masters of death at close quarters, but easily overwhelmed when they found themselves flanked. Prisoners who had managed to dislodge the hardwood boards rushed the mercenaries while we attacked from behind.

Soldiers flooded into the corridor outside, some equipped with gear from those slain. Of the approximately seven hundred men and women imprisoned in this back alley, a third had been slain at the hands of twenty-six mercenaries. A massacre.

I found Meike and Carina among the stream of prisoners headed to the ridge. Blood sheeted the side of Meike's neck from a cut in her hair, but she barely seemed to notice and it looked like the bleeding had stopped. "You're all right?" she asked. "Lost you for a bit there."

"Physically? I'm just great," I said. "Has anyone seen the smiths yet?"

"No," Carina answered, her voice nasally from a broken nose. "They should've been here by now."

The POWs gathered at the ridge. The pillaging continued below, but the air up here was still relatively quiet. Meike moved to the railing and surveyed the POWs, exhaustion heavy in her eyes. Mist from the nearest ice sheath beaded her hair, quickly turning it white, and her eyes raked the soldiers. "Where're your sergeants and company commanders?" she asked.

The question moved through the crowd, and several men and women were singled out. One broke apart from the crowd. She was small for an adult, only half a head taller than me. "We're still here," she said.

"Good. The smiths are headed up right now with supplies. We need to meet them as soon as possible."

Many of the soldiers looked at one another. "You sure about that?" one of them asked.

I could see the fear, misery, and shame on everyone's face. The battle with the smiths had taken a lot from them.

Carina leaned over the railing and pointed. "They're in trouble."

The smiths were still on the sixth level, stalled. Two groups of mercenaries had surrounded them in a pincer movement, pressing in on the tiny group who struggled to hold them off with hammers and shields.

"Major Cata, pleased to meet you," the small woman said as she reached Meike, Carina, and me. She climbed on the railing, unconcerned with the drop behind her. "Tavich, Riobat, Balruma!" she shouted. "Front and center!"

Two men and a woman pushed their way to the front to stand before Major Cata. "Reform your companies and locate your former platoon leaders," the major ordered. "If they're dead, promote new ones from the squads. Have your platoon leaders locate their squad leaders and repeat the process for any who were killed."

"Yes, Major," all three said simultaneously. They faced the crowd and started shouting orders, motioning for the platoons to separate and form up.

As the battalion finished organizing, another group of mercenaries appeared at the top of the ramp from the seventh level, a hundred feet along the ridge. They paused at the sight of the POWs. There were a hundred of them, and they gaped at the battalion's newly formed lines.

A sellsword blew a horn. Its low, haunting sound bounced off the face of the sinkhole. If any mercenary wondered whether danger lurked in the Barrows, the horn answered that question. The sellswords charged.

The company commanders shouted without hesitation. A smattering of soldiers who had armed themselves from the fallen death squads positioned themselves at the front. Everyone else was unarmed. All three companies—almost five hundred in total—let out a bone-chilling roar and charged.

Meike, Carina, and I followed Major Cata as we ran on the army's edge. Dozens of sparsely-equipped soldiers and hundreds of their unarmed compatriots crashed into the scores of mercenaries.

In minutes, three-quarters of the sellswords lay dead at the battalion's feet, the rest of the attacking force fleeing down to the seventh level. More soldiers donned gear from the dead. "I don't think it's a secret anymore that the prisoners escaped," I said.

"Aye," Major Cata said. "This will get much harder. We need to maintain our momentum."

Those most heavily armed took the lead, but each ramp only supported nine soldiers walking abreast. "Move, move!" Major Cata chided. Her voice lit a fire beneath the army, and their pace quickened. Some slipped on ice or collapsed from the trauma of so much movement, but others helped them to their feet.

The battalion reached the sixth level, panting hard and drained of energy, and the company commanders halted them to regroup in formation. No one had a chance to rest. One order from Major Cata and the battalion advanced on the western portion of mercenaries pressing in on the smiths. The west side of the mercenary pincer movement found themselves surrounded now, and some turned to face us while others focused on breaking the smiths' line.

The battalion smashed into them, working to tear the line apart. Only a fraction of them were armed though, which made fighters like me invaluable. I jumped into the fight, Major Cata barking an order at me to stop, but I ignored her. A mercenary bellowed as he hacked downward, attempting to cleave me in two, but I sidestepped it and stabbed him in the thigh. He fell to one knee and my dagger found a place in his jugular.

The sound of ringing metal exploded in one of my ears. Carina's sword hovered over my head, having blocked a killing blow from a man I hadn't noticed. Swords shrieked as the sellsword pulled his weapon back, but a throwing knife dug into his cheek.

"It's best to have someone watching your back when you jump in like that," Carina said. Her eyes sparkled with insanity, intoxicated. She nudged me forward.

Soldiers picked up weapons from slain enemies as we worked our way inward, and our push strengthened with each passing minute. Soon our swords and my dagger devoured the western company of sellswords. By the time we made it halfway to the smiths, who only numbered a dozen now, I'd bloodied my weapon on four mercenaries. Carina fought to my left, Meike to my right, and soon I lost count of how many sellswords we cut down. Over the roar of the battle I could hear Carina weeping.

Two mercenaries launched themselves at me, but then Meike was there throwing the weight of her body into them, causing both to stumble into the blades of the soldiers. Blood covered the right side of her head and neck, her eye swollen shut, but still she fought. The smiths moved with elemental grace, but Meike was all technique and brutality, and a new frenzy overtook her as she carved her way through the mercenaries. I almost couldn't believe there was ever a time when Magnate Bardera doubted her. I thought of Emil, of how perfect he and Meike could've been as sparring partners, as friends, and then I was the one throwing myself at the sellswords, a snarl leaving my throat.

Mateo and his smiths fought against several pull carts piled to the brim with weapons and armor. Half the smiths lay dead among the wheels, and Mateo fought over them, planting his one-handed hammer into the skull of the closest mercenary. When he saw us crushing the last of the western pincer, he let out a hoarse yell, injecting new energy into the others.

The line of mercenaries on the other side retreated, full of confusion and fear. The fresher, unarmed soldiers grabbed weapons off the pull carts and rushed after them. Meike watched them go until her sword clattered to the stone and she collapsed.

"I'm fine," she said when I helped her sit up. She looked at me, her good eye full of glee even though the skin around her other one had ballooned, half her face was covered in blood, and she couldn't even stand on her own. "Just tired, is all."

I hugged her as hard as I could.

I pulled away, and Meike looked down, hiding her face. A few moments later she looked back up. "You should get yourself bandaged up," she said, wiping at her good eye.

I keyed in on the line of fire trailing up my left arm. Someone had left a gash along my bicep, and it leaked blood on my forearm and hand. "Are you going to be all right?" I asked.

She nodded. "Just need to catch my breath."

Mateo was standing near the carts. He shifted his weight on his back foot to allow two soldiers who'd grabbed weapons to surge past him, then he stumbled back, colliding with the side panel of a cart. He slid to the ground.

"Everyone's trying to take a nap on me," I said as I stood over him.

He looked up with blood-rimmed eyes. "It's good to see you're safe." The bottom of his red-brown robes had been ripped and sliced to tatters, and blood stained the edges of the tears. He watched more of the corps trade in the secular blades they'd pillaged for Foundry steel and don more pieces of armor. "You saved them," he said to me.

"I didn't want you hogging all the glory. That's selfish."

The fighting moved to the ramp leading to the fifth level, where Major Cata's battalion pushed against the line of crumbling mercenaries. Carina fished a roll of bandages out of one of the carts and started wrapping my arm. Mateo sat low to the ground, unable to avoid staring at the bodies of his brothers and sisters, and the city's lights reflected the sheen of tears in his eyes. "Some runners told us the mercenaries captured your sister and the audencia," he said.

I took several long, even breaths, considering. I should've been happy she was finally getting what she deserved, but all I felt was fear.

As much as I hated Sara, I didn't want her to die.

The last of the mercenaries retreated down the fifth level stairs. Carina tied off my bandage, and I ran for the ridge railing. Carina followed, and Meike pulled herself to her feet to join us.

"Faults above," I whispered. Thousands of mercenaries were amassing on the chasm floor, waving their weapons in the air, chanting, smoke from hundreds of buildings licking up the sides of the sinkhole. The city had done far too good a job at hiding their true numbers. Major Cata's battalion had taken control of the upper wings, but chaos ruled everything below the sixth level.

Seeing the army made me realize just how diminished Augustin's military corps had become. Between the sellswords' assault on Augustin and the slaughtered POWs, most of the city's military was dead. An uneasiness stirred in my gut at the thought of Augustin falling.

A roar of voices echoed up the sinkhole as the mercenaries prodded the audencia along at sword-point. Toward the river.

Chapter 37 – Jakar

FOR THE THIRD time I knocked on a door, and for the third time no one answered. I tried to shoulder it with my good side out of frustration, but gasped at the ripping pain in my chest. The caustic burning had worsened. It felt like acid eating me alive.

On the level above at the opposite side of the chasm, the freed POWs charged a group of mercenaries standing toe-to-toe with the smiths. I didn't have the strength to help though. If I didn't dress my wound soon, the blood loss would kill me.

My fist pounded the door, smearing it with blood, and I slumped onto the steps. Where else could I go with what little strength I had left? I needed a house in the eastern section of the upper levels, where a magma vein running toward the surface fed into the homes of those able to afford the prime real estate.

Several seconds later, the door opened.

A noblewoman peeked through the doorway as I dripped blood on her front steps. "Yes?" she asked timidly. She probably knew of the fighting, but I wasn't a mercenary carrying a sword and a thirst for death. Just a lone, bleeding man.

I pressed my palm against my wound again, my skin slick, then pulled myself up and stumbled into her house. "I need help."

"How would I help?" she asked. My boots left red prints on her bat silk rug as I moved through her living room, where flickering candles lit my path. The woman had piled furniture near the front door for a barricade. It looked like she lived alone.

The knife I'd stolen from a dead mercenary came out of the sheath under my robe, eliciting a gasp from the woman, but I continued onward. A pleasant warmth filled her home, and the temperature increased as I made my way to the back room. There, a thread of lava circulated through aqueducts surrounding a pool of bubbling water. Debris and solidified rock crusted the aqueducts—city scrapers hadn't come by recently to clean them. I knelt before the basin that fed lava into the first aqueduct and pushed the blade into the viscous surface, leaning the handle against the basin's edge. My knuckles made it difficult to hold the weapon, but the pain in my arms and shoulder was dwarfed by the agony in my sternum.

Pulling my robe off filled me with misery, but by the time I finished, the weapon was red-hot, its tip glowing white. "What are you doing?" the noblewoman asked. She had finally summoned the courage to join me in the back room.

I answered by touching the blade against the wound on my chest. A satisfying pain burned away the torture of the rhidium and left behind rippling red and white skin. After a few more finishing touches, the wound was fully cauterized, and I turned my torso from left to right, the pain still impossible to ignore but it was no longer acidic. I was lightheaded, my throat chalky and my stomach gnawing away at my insides, but at least I wouldn't die. Not yet.

"You're the Adriann servant, aren't you?" she asked. "I recognize you from Bolivar Adriann's execution."

"Not anymore."

My heart quickened as old habits braced my body against

this defiance, but no punishment came. I was finally a free man. It would be short-lived, but at least I could die knowing I was beyond Sara's reach.

"Do you have any men's clothing I can borrow?" I asked. She hesitated, but nodded.

Several minutes later, I stepped outside sporting a mole-rat coat with notched lapels, as well as trousers custom fit for a nobleman with narrower legs. The outfit looked ridiculous, but it'd have to do.

A crowd grew on the chasm floor like a fungus. The mercenary army was gathering—shouting, chanting, and drunk on a frenzy I'd witnessed time and time again on the Granite Road. The frenzy of invincibility. A huddle of people broke apart from the throng, and their frail figures and distinctive slate-gray robes identified them as the audencia. The mercenaries forced them toward the obsidian platform at the river's edge.

If the entire audencia was executed, including those like Judge Abeso, Sara would no longer have the support to rule Augustin and she would be deposed. The smiths would ensure that. And with my last Word being fulfilled with their deaths, I would live to see another passing.

All I had to do was watch. If they died, it wouldn't be my fault.

All I had to do was let more people die.

Letting the audencia die could be so easy—I hated most of them, I knew, and how some of them helped a man like Olevic Pike launch a coup while others refused to listen to my testimony during my trial. But to let the judges who were innocent die for their sins? Old words of Emil's came to me, from when I'd asked him what he would do about the reformers if he became magnate. "I'd work with them as best as I could," he said. "Helping those you like is easy, but to help those you dislike is a truer definition of character."

He was right, but still I didn't move. I was finally free from Sara, and I didn't want to give that up. I shivered.

This was about more than helping a few innocent people.

I thought back to the way I'd turned away from freedom on Dagir's Pass, and how I'd done so because I wanted a purpose worth fighting for: to return the Adrianns to the throne. But that wasn't the real reason I did it—I did it because the idea of living my own life had terrified me. Of living for a purpose that was my own.

If I let the audencia die, it wouldn't just be my purpose I would be serving. It would be the mercenary army's. It would be Rodi's. If I let them live, it would be serving Sara's.

Neither option would feel good, but so it went sometimes. I would just have to do what felt most right.

The door to the noblewoman's home protested as I pushed it inward. The furniture she'd started stacking again tipped over, and she reached for her sword leaning against the wall. I rushed inside before she could grab it and ran for the back room.

When I dipped my arm into the basin, the lava flowed over my flesh, coating it. Sparks of pain shot into me like sharp pinches, but the heat soothed the pain in my broken wrist. When enough molten rock covered my right arm, I repeated the process with my left.

I entered the noblewoman's front room and she screamed. "Please open your door," I said.

She rushed to the door. "Just leave me alone," she sobbed.

The lava on my arms flared when I reentered the gusty winds outside. The door lock clicked this time, followed by sounds of the noblewoman rushing to reassemble the barricade. I took a deep breath and started sprinting toward the edge of the walkway. When I reached the ridge, I skipped onto the railing and leapt.

The chasm's maw waited below, the sight taking my breath away. I sailed hundreds of feet through the open, frigid air, my overcoat flapping in the wind as I arced over the city, and I sailed toward the ninth level until I skidded over ice and stone. Then I turned around and took off again.

I landed in the space between two ice sheaths on the

thirteenth level, crashing into the uncut stone of the far wall. I recovered and ran along the ridge where the sheath created a makeshift tunnel—a wall of rock to my right and a wall of frost and ice to my left reflecting the colors of my lava-coated arms. The ground was fractured and stressed from the weight of the ice, from eons of its slow descent, and I drank in the heat of the molten rock until I brimmed, dancing on the edge between maximum potential and self-destruction. I stomped on the limestone connected to the sheath. Elemental force rode through the soles of my foot and the ground let out a deep crack, the fractures widening. I struck again.

My leg vibrated with each blow as I worked my way along the sheath, the ice protesting adamantly by the time I reached the other end, the sheath groaning like a wakening giant. The magma dimmed with each break I made in the rock, and it started to harden around my arms. Halfway along the sheath, another crack echoed through the tunnel, this one several octaves lower, and it was loud enough to rattle my teeth. I stepped back as the ice rumbled, coming alive.

The sheath started its slow, inexorable fall, and my world shook like an earthquake, shards from the ceiling bouncing off my shoulders as an entire section of the thirteenth level started to destabilize.

As the sheath tilted toward the open air, I jumped and catapulted off the limestone over a chunk of ice as large as a building. The ice sheath hadn't cleaved into one section, but had shattered into hundreds of blue meteors, and my momentum carried me through the rain of death. Ice pummeled my body, but there was nothing I could do. My trajectory took me out of the zone of danger until I sailed in free fall beside the crumbling mass.

The bodies far below moved in slow motion, attempting to scatter. The ice moved too fast. Through the debris, I caught a glimpse of the audencia near the river. The first of the broken ice sheath crashed into the bottom of the chasm, rocking the capital.

Blue boulders ricocheted off each other, tumbling across the floor and through the lines of mercenaries. My power flared outward as I neared the ground, and my body hit at a tumble amidst the large-scale panic.

I ran. The rain seemed never-ending, and ice bounced dozens of feet over my head or rolled past at crushing speeds. The air was rife with pain and death. Men and women shouted, screamed, fled, but so many of them fell.

The farthest flying pieces came to rest a short distance from the first level ridge. The avalanche still rumbled, but not as fervently as before, and I managed to reach a safe enough distance to stop.

The dead were everywhere—bodies crushed or struck by the debris. A hill of blue ice and stone covered almost half the chasm floor, favoring the north side where the sellswords had mostly concentrated. Hundreds of voices searched for their friends or for answers, and the leaders of the mercenary army stared at the scene from near the river. The audencia, in the same state of shock, stood beside them.

Sara was with them. She took advantage of the confusion and bulled her way into one of the jafos, her hands still tied behind her back. The man she collided with stumbled backward and tripped into the lava with a scream. I took off toward them.

The other jafos' and jafas' swords were already out, and they turned their attention onto Sara, who had now cornered herself against the lava. They eyed her hungrily. "No!" I yelled.

They faced me, and the closest jafo entered a defensive stance. His blade sunk into my fist of rock, but not far enough to penetrate, and my other fist struck him center mass. He tumbled into the river. My arms erupted in agony, both from the heat and my broken bones, but I was a master of pain. I'd been shutting it out all my life. Three more of the mercenary leaders swung at my neck and legs, and I hopped to dodge the low swings, deflecting the third with a forearm.

When I landed, I shattered one woman's arm and caved in the skulls of the other two.

Sara dodged Jafa Velmira's blade as it made a silvery arc. The tip of the weapon grazed her as the jafa followed with an upswing, and a cut blossomed on her face, running from cheekbone to the center of her forehead. "Jakar!" she shouted.

The innermost layer of magma wrapped my forearms in its terrible embrace. I struggled to scrape off my gauntlets of rock, and they pulled at my skin as I freed my arms. What waited beneath was flesh burned far worse than anything I'd experienced before.

Another blow caught Sara in the thigh. The cut separated a fold of her skin from its muscle, and she let out a muted scream. Before Velmira could ready her blade to strike the killing blow, I picked up a discarded dagger Jafa Tamera clutched in her dead fingers and threw it. The blade buried itself to the hilt into Velmira's side and she staggered. I reached her, pulling the dagger out and plunged it back into her abdomen. I stabbed her again. And again. And again. She fell.

The rest of the mercenary leaders took off into the field, dodging hills and boulders of ice, and left us with the audencia. Sara looked at the burns on my arms and the ice-melt soaking my clothes as she wiped away the blood dripping over her brow and down her cheek from the wound on her face. She reached for Jafa Velmira's sword to prop herself up and pressed her other hand against her thigh, grimacing. "Is your flesh binding... gone?"

Rodi's command was still so crisp in my mind, I could almost hear it. *Kill anyone in the audencia standing between Sara and her goal to become magnate.* "No. Not until the audencia is dead."

Before Sara could respond, I faced the twelve men and women on the obsidian platform, who had heard everything. They tensed. "Go where you want," I said. "I won't stop you."

A mixture of confusion and relief spread across their faces, and they scurried from the river's edge without a word. Their path arced away from the broken army on the chasm floor, toward the nearest ramp.

Gears turned in the princepa's head. Maybe she wondered how much time I had before the flesh binding killed me. "Ig, I no longer want you to harm the audencia," she said.

I answered with a flat stare.

"Did it help?" she asked, her voice lowering.

"No." The grip of the command continued to build in the back of my skull. "Enjoy being remembered."

She wiped at the cut along her temple and forehead again, the heel of her good foot tapping as she leaned against the sword. She clenched and unclenched her jaw.

"Wait!" she called out to the audencia. The judges had only made it a few dozen feet, and they paused as the princepa limped past me to reach them.

"I don't want this anymore," she said.

The group parted, and Judge Abeso appeared, moving his way to the front of his peers. "You don't want what?" he asked.

"I'm withdrawing my bid for magnate."

"You would change your mind after everything you've done to secure your seat?"

"That's what I said."

His eyes narrowed. He didn't seem to believe her.

A small section of an ice sheath that was slow to break struck the ground fifty feet away, shaking the ground. Everyone tensed. "After what you unleashed on this city," Abeso said hurriedly, eyeing the nearest ramp, "I'm inclined to believe that you're no longer fit to be magnate. But we will discuss this at length later. We'll be holding your word to it though."

"I swear on my life that my word won't change."

The audencia parted and Sara returned to the river's edge. "My goals no longer involve ruling as magnate, so the Word's moot," she said. "Did it make a difference?"

I could already feel the hand on my neck loosening its grip. "Yes."

I could tell she wanted to continue the conversation, but something in my eyes stopped her. There was nothing for her to say, or at least nothing I wanted to hear. Her gesture should have meant the world to me, but for some reason, I felt nothing.

But Sara was always stubborn. "I'm sorry. So much has happen—"

"Don't."

My voice sounded wrong as I said the word. No, not wrong. Different. It had come out hard, allowing no room for argument. The tone of Sorrelo Adriann.

She didn't press. I'd commanded her to stop and she had listened.

I once thought the Adrianns were destined to rule Augustin, but in reality they would have failed without me. Sorrelo would have been overthrown months ago if I wasn't there to make the reformers fear him. He nor Sara could have survived what they put me through, could have dealt with the torture and trauma I'd undergone while living with the Ebonrock.

They were weaker than me.

The gory blade fell from my fingers, clattering to the rock. I turned and walked away.

Chapter 38 – Efadora

SARA ALWAYS SAID that as someone so small, I needed to strike like a bobbit worm whenever it came to a scrap—that ruthlessness worked best for someone like me, synergizing perfectly with the Adriann disposition, and hesitating only meant the difference between life and death.

Ruthlessness had led my sister to make plenty of stupid decisions in the past, to the point where I suspected she was full of shit, just like with so many things. Advice that was perfect for one person could be totally wrong for somebody else. In this instance, though, I took my ruthlessness to heart.

We charged the field while the mercenary army struggled to regroup after the fall of the ice sheath. We fought between frozen boulders, striking down stragglers and putting the injured out of their misery. We hunted them down like animals. The morale of the sellswords among the lower levels crumbled, and they managed to escape through the main entrance—scooping up their friends garrisoning the gates and disappearing onto the Granite Road. Nobody followed them.

Those formerly imprisoned in the Barrows showed no mercy. The mercenary army had been given a chance to peacefully occupy the capital and they had pillaged it instead. Or at least tried to. Even the smiths seemed to relish excising those assholes from Augustin. I could see the fire in their eyes while they fought. Mateo especially.

Meike, Carina, and I sat outside a smoldering clothing shop in the trade district, passing around a waterskin. "Ow," Meike muttered as Carina sat against her back, moving a needle and thread through her scalp.

"You've been getting banged up to shit for weeks now and *this* is what gets to you?" Carina asked.

Meike looked back, and Carina answered with a provocative smile. My old guard narrowed her good eye, the other one still swollen, then turned around and offered herself to the cartographer. Carina brought her mouth to Meike's hair, and for a second I thought she was going to kiss the woman's cut, but she bit at the thread while pressing a hand to the side of Meike's face to hold her still. Meike pushed her face into Carina's hand, so subtly I almost missed it, and her mouth turned up ever so slightly.

Faults above, I needed to start minding my own business.

Weary smiths handed out cured meat and water to even wearier soldiers, and both commoners and shop owners busied themselves cleaning up shards of broken windows or clearing out debris littering the streets. Charcoal markings covered the foreheads of every Augustin passing by. Mateo stood near the staircase leading to the chasm floor, surveying the field of ice and snow while talking to one of his senior arc smiths and Major Cata. They parted, and the master smith pushed through the flurry of activity to join us.

"It's going to be a lot of work cleaning all that up," he said. "I'm not looking forward to digging up what's underneath it."

"It was worth what it gave us though," I said.

He grimaced, but nodded.

No one questioned why the avalanche fell, and I could feel the question hovering between us. *Where's Ig?* Ig had saved the audencia and crushed most of the mercenary army by himself, but there was still no sign of him. Did he get himself killed?

I had so many questions, and some of them involved Sara. However, if I found myself wondering about my sister too much, my body had a nasty habit of clenching until my teeth started to hurt and my heart pounded in my chest. She didn't deserve my concern.

But she survived, I was sure—even benefited from the tragedy somehow. She was good at that.

Many of the nobiletza emerged onto the streets, and once they realized the sellswords were gone, started helping the commoners, smiths, and the last of Major Cata's battalion. I expected Mateo to join in, but he seemed content staying with us. "Look," he said.

Ig limped down the second level ramp between squads of soldiers headed for the upper levels. He wore a clean tunic and pants, but his arms were mummified in bandages. The pain didn't show on his face. He wore a pack over his shoulder, and he noticed us resting against the front of the clothing shop. A young smith was with him too, wearing a bandage around her head.

"You survived," Mateo said to Ig.

Ig nodded.

When the silence grew uncomfortable, the master smith looked to the young woman. "Where is your brother, Ester?"

"Being tended to in the physician's halls," the woman said. "He'll be unconscious for a while. We need to talk in the meantime, Master Smith."

"About?"

Instead of answering, the woman looked to Ig. Ig peered up at the second level, toward the corner of the palace we could see from this angle. Fingers of smoke trailed out of the entrance. "There's a body in there that needs to be removed as soon as possible," he said. "If word gets out about who it is, the city might panic. It belongs to the primordia, Nektarios."

"You're kidding," I said.

"One of the primordia… is dead?" the master smith asked.

Ester nodded, scratching under her bandage. "Damek and I fought him alongside Ig. Ig was the one who killed him."

"How?" I asked. It was hard to believe those like Otalia or Aronidus—people who had ruled as the Sovereign's iron fist for two centuries—could be anything other than invincible. Then I thought of the mountain of ice and the person who created it.

"They have a weakness," Ig said. "Their bodies are vulnerable to electricity. I think it has to do with the number of electrical impulses required to move muscle as dense as theirs."

"Electricity?"

"Like lightning." He grabbed for an invisible something at his neck, but paused as if realizing something. "You can create it with magnetic metals like iron," he said to Mateo. "I can show you how."

"That would mean a great deal," the master smith said. "If one of the primordia is dead, then others will come. Maybe even the Sovereign's armies."

Ig frowned. "Nektarios told me the Sovereign himself would come. The only reason he hasn't already is because the primordia weren't around to report to him when the Granite Road was being pillaged."

I'd met the Sovereign twice in my life. The man was a walking sack of sagging flesh, but I imagined he looked pretty good for someone two hundred years old. Strange indentations and folds covered his head and body, almost like his skin was putty that had been pushed around a few too hundred times. The only time Father ever hit me was during the first time I met the country's ruler, when I asked the man why everyone was so scared of him when he looked so weird. I was seven. Father backhanded me in the side of my head, then proceeded to apologize to the man profusely, squeezing my arm so hard I had bruises on my arm for weeks. It wasn't until the meeting was over, after I stopped crying, when I remembered how badly Father's hand was shaking as he held onto me.

"Any news of Sara?" Mateo asked.

"She's alive," Ig said. He stared at the ground as he answered. "She doesn't have plans to rule Augustin anymore. That's all I know."

"After everything she did?" I asked. Carina jumped, eliciting a small sound of pain from Meike, and I realized I'd asked the question a lot louder than I was planning.

The question stole some of Ig's energy. "Honestly, I didn't care to ask."

"It doesn't change anything. I won't forgive her."

His uneasiness softened. "I agree."

"So…" I began. "Do you want me to call you Ig or Jakar?"

He studied me for a long moment. Sara's army knew him as one name while Father and Emil had called him the other. I'd heard Sara call him both. It had taken time to figure out, but I'd solved the puzzle while studying the mountain of ice in the middle of the chasm. The word "Ig" had something to do with his flesh binding.

"Jakar," he said.

Whether I was right didn't matter. Early on our trip from Manasus to Augustin, I asked Emil if he would ever give Ig a Word if he knew how the flesh binding worked, and he had been horrified by the question. "Friends don't force friends into anything," he said. "And there's nobody in the world who deserves a friend more than Ig." The idea of controlling Ig—no, Jakar—had disgusted him.

It disgusted me too.

"I pride myself as a master smith in my ability to listen to my brothers and sisters," Mateo said, looking at Jakar. "I shouldn't have ignored Emil."

"I'm sorry?" Jakar said.

"I'm saying I never really understood your flesh binding until our confrontation in the Foundry. I could have though, if I wasn't so willfully ignorant. I want to do better."

Some of the tension Jakar was carrying unraveled. "Thank you for saying that."

They regarded each other awkwardly, and in the ensuing silence my throat started to knot up as reality hit me with another wave. Emil was dead. Gone forever. Why was it in some moments I didn't give a shit about who lived or died, but in others the despair would wash over me until it threatened to double me over?

I looked at the pack slung over Jakar's shoulder and cleared my throat. "Going somewhere?"

"I'm leaving Augustin once I'm done helping the smiths."

I turned to Meike and Carina. Carina was whispering something in Meike's ear, and my old guard answered with a smirk, her good eye glimmering. "Oy," I said. "Magnate Bardera needs to know what happened here, right? That means you two have to head back to Manasus soon. I'm coming with you. Jakar should too."

"This is your home, Efadora," Mateo said.

"No, it isn't."

He took a breath, ready to argue, but stayed quiet.

"You're always welcome," Meike said to me. "I could use some protection."

I snorted. "I think between me and Jakar, we could manage it." I checked Jakar's reaction, and the man was nodding, smiling faintly.

"Traveling with friends would do me some good, I think," he said.

Chapter 39 – Jakar

IT TOOK TWO weeks for the nightmares to slow.

Dreaming about Emil had unhinged something in me. The people I killed in Cragreach plagued every dream of mine—they sat on their knees grabbing for my hands as I walked through the town's burning streets, begging for me to take back the pain. Rodi and Nektarios watched from dark ridges and dark places. I dreamed of Sara standing in front of her granite throne, back turned to me.

Our group camped beside a hot spring somewhere in southeast Manasus, still a week's trek from the city. I slipped into the water, my feet feeling for purchase on the scraggly rock, then I splashed water into my hair and on my body, scrubbing at myself awkwardly with my good hand. Carina belted a laugh from the other side of the cavern. She'd just finished telling the group some history behind the Archives—about how it was originally created to find the ruins of the Sihraan Empire so humanity could repopulate them—and now she was showing Efadora how she located quartz within the walls, holding a map taken from the pile of parchments stacked on her pack. Quartz compositions changed depending on location, and her maps contained endless lists of compositional values. Efadora tried to dig at the quartz with her dagger.

"She's tough," Meike said as she helped me change out of my wet bandages, chewing on a piece of sweetroot.

"Efadora?"

She nodded.

"I never really knew her," I said. "She shipped off to Manasus not long after I came into her family's service."

The woman let out a *hmph*, enlightened somehow. I didn't know much about her, other than the fact she worked as Efadora's personal guard in Manasus. It made sense why Efadora cared so deeply for the woman.

Meike gently peeled off the bandage on my arm, and I grimaced. "Her brother would be proud of her, I think," she said.

My heart and lungs sank, the pain in my arm suddenly not so bad. I tried to distract myself by watching Efadora stick her hand into a crack in the wall and, with a grunt, pull out a glittering crystal. "She reminds me of him," I eventually said.

She considered the statement. "She reminds me of her sister, too. They're all different sides of the same die."

I thought of my own parents, wondering if I shared similarities with them as well, knowing I could see them again if I wanted to.

I didn't. When they sold me, they sold my love along with it. If it wasn't for the friends I made among the Ebonrock, I would have given up years ago. To find love among those around you was the only way to survive such an unforgiving place. Such an unforgiving world.

"I'm leaving next passing," I said.

It was the first time mentioning it after two weeks of travel. Meike didn't act surprised. She watched the steam curling along the surface of the hot spring, the sweetroot staining her lips a darker and darker orange. "Where to?"

"I'm going to kill the people who created my flesh binding

and find the other slaves I grew up with." It was impossible to know how long the kids of the Ebonrock survived working the Black Depths, but I had to hold out hope that Quin and the rest were alive. Saving them and killing the kadiph responsible for my flesh binding was my new purpose. It was a good purpose, one that filled me with fire. I'd almost forgotten what that was like.

Meike rubbed pyremoss gel over my skin with the tips of her fingers, then rewrapped my arm with a fresh bandage. "Gonna be lonely on such a long journey."

I realized how little I was looking forward to it. These past few months had been nothing but movement, and while my body had grown strong as a result, the exhaustion went far deeper than physical. "I'm used to it."

ICE GREW AMONG white-glowing lightcaps where the tunnels ahead widened and split apart like branches. Meike stopped and the rest of us followed suit. The left tunnel led due north to Manasus while the right led east, crossing through Byssa until it reached the end of Mira, passed through The Rift, and wound its way through countries like Xeriv and Callo until ending at Sulian Daw.

Hundreds, maybe even thousands of miles, a portion of which passed through The Rift, the most dangerous stretch of land in Ra'Thuzan. I only had enough supplies to get me part of the way, too. I could hunt for food along the way, find some work to finance myself through the journey.

I faced my companions, adjusting the pack slung over my shoulder, and opened my mouth to say my goodbyes, but Efadora stepped forward. For a second I thought she was going to hug me, but she moved to my side instead. "I'm going with Jakar," she said to Meike and Carina.

"You are?" I asked.

"If you want me," she said, her confidence faltering.

Even though we had traveled together for the last two

weeks, getting a read on her had been hard. I didn't blame her—she was still grieving and coping, so it made sense for her to withdraw. But she was an Adriann. Sara had destroyed my binding to her, but Efadora could still take advantage if she knew how to make the flesh sacrifice.

If I brought an Adriann along, I could hold onto my elemental power though. I'd accepted the fact I would have to somehow stop the Ebonrock without it, but maybe that didn't have to be the case.

"Efadora, please," Meike said, her composure cracking.

"Manasus can't give me what I want," Efadora said softly.

"What do you want then?"

"I want to see the world. To learn. To become strong." She looked at me as she said that last sentence. "I don't want to learn more about flesh bindings," she added. "It's not about that. You're free as far as I'm concerned."

Did I want to travel with someone like her? Efadora was known to be temperamental. I saw parts of Sara in her, but what mattered was that I saw parts of Emil too. "All right," I said.

Meike let out a fog of shaky breath, and Efadora rushed forward and wrapped her arms around the woman's torso. Meike's brows rose and she blinked hard, but Efadora was too busy clinging onto her to notice. Meike rested her cheek on top of Efadora's head.

Carina offered a hand to me, and when I grabbed it, her grip was strong enough to make a normal man squirm. "Get her killed and I'll kill you," she said, smiling.

Meike parted from the princepa, and she knelt to her level. "I know this is a lot to ask, but if you can send a message to Manasus about your wellbeing, Magnate Bardera would greatly appreciate it."

"Just the magnate?"

She cupped one of Efadora's hands in both of hers. "I know you can take care of yourself. Still, would make me feel better to hear from you."

"Sounds like a promise worth keeping then."

The four of us walked side-by-side, and as we approached the fork in the tunnel, our paths diverged. Meike and Carina cast one last look at us, and we did the same. Then they disappeared.

Off we went, toward Sulian Daw. Toward a place parts of me were terrified to return to. But I was at peace with my fears, for I had a new purpose. One of revenge. And part of me knew that Efadora could help me in doing whatever I could to make the Ebonrock hurt.

And while I wasn't truly free yet, I still had meaning I had chosen for myself. A purpose I controlled. And without such purpose in life, living never really mattered.

Epilogue

THE TAVERN DOOR swung open, and the largest man Sara ever laid eyes on ducked into the low light of the alehouse.

He looked well-traveled, sporting a black, flat-brimmed bolero hat and a thick jacket to protect against drifting spores. His gaze lingered on Sara's table, which sat beside the bar against the far wall, and he offered a nod in acknowledgement before moving to a table across the room.

Sara had chosen this seat to keep an eye out for men like him—he clearly recognized her, though he didn't carry himself like a threat, despite his size. He could've been one of the countless curious who wanted to ask about her retraction from the throne, but she wasn't worried about those types. There were plenty others with a bone to pick for a thousand different reasons. She glanced at her two escorts, assigned to her by the audencia, as they sat at the bar a dozen feet away and pretended they didn't watch her every move.

She sipped at her whiskey, hoping the alcohol would work her guard down and put her at ease—a state of mind that was impossible to come by lately until she was staring at the bottom of a few whiskey glasses. In reality, she'd have the Lid to protect her in a few passings' time, then she'd be safe from everyone. She was in a strange purgatory right now, where the audencia clearly wanted to hold her accountable for the burning of Augustin, but her privilege as an Adriann kept her out of a prison cell. Best to stock her belly up with whiskey now to keep the fire going once they sent her to the stars.

She downed the rest of the South Bys Rye and held her glass up to the barkeep, who nodded and grabbed for the bottle on the back shelf. "A triple this time," she said when the barkeep stopped at the table and poured more of the amber liquid.

"I cut most people off right about now," the man said.

"It isn't as though I have responsibilities to address on the morrow. I'm a sail without wind."

He added two more shots to the glass, offering a look of distaste before returning to the bar. Maybe she could fully commit to the South Bys Rye and other bottles like it and blast her brain into oblivion for the next few passings. The people of the lower levels judged dawdlers and the indolent, courtesy of the Foundry and their teachings, but she was already the most hated person in Augustin. The only direction for her to go now was up, in more ways than one.

More whiskey slid over her tongue, and she savored the taste, trying to make the intensity of the sensation help her forget. A life of infamy was never something she'd wanted. When had her life gone so horribly wrong? When Olevic threw his coup? Before then?

"To you, Emil," she said in a low voice, grasping the cup. "And to you, Efadora." Her head drooped and she caught a glimpse of her only souvenir from the conflict—the beat-up dagger in her belt that she'd picked up from the river's edge. She whispered, "And to you. I could never say this to your face, but… I'm a coward. What you gave me was unconditional… until it wasn't anymore. I've never had someone give that to me before. I…" She stopped, letting more whiskey burn its way down.

A figure loomed over her. "A barkeeper who reads minds," she started. "A friend—"

It was the half giant who'd entered earlier. He set aside the chair opposite Sara and knelt on the floorboards, bringing his face level with her. "Would you care if I joined you?"

He spoke softly for a man his size. He also spoke without an accent, but she didn't recognize him, which made him out-of-territory nobility. "As long as you have something interesting to say, and as long as it isn't about why the Adrianns no longer sit the throne. I'm about ready to run myself into the ground if I hear that question one more time." She blinked, trying to clear her vision.

"I believe you'll find what I say interesting. It's a pleasure to meet you. My name is Aronidus. You probably know me as Tuli Dempra."

Sara grasped her cup, her hand a little wobbly. The glass was thick, but she was confident in her ability to break it over the man's head. It would just take some extra concentration so she didn't miss.

"I'm looking for someone," he said.

"You're pretty good at that, aren't you? The looking part, I mean. The finding, not so much. Though you did manage to track me down while I was very publicly throwing myself into the bottle. Bravo."

She looked around to see most of the alehouse patrons watching them. Sara already drew attention like ass on sulfur, but now this half giant was kneeling across from her, pulling the eye by his own right. "It's not you or your family I'm interested in anymore," he said.

"Call me relieved. Why *were* you interested in my family, anyway? Tell me and maybe I'll help."

He shifted his weight back, and the floorboards groaned in protest. The alehouse's low light and his bolero hat made it difficult to see the details in his face, but he looked to be in his early thirties. "Months ago," he said, "I heard murmurings of an elemental among the Augustin nobiletza who could control materials beyond the scope of any of Mira's trade schools. I improperly assumed it was a member of your family."

"Ah." Of course. She'd grown accustomed to his type by now—people wanting to know more about Jakar, confounded that the Iron Sorrow could do what only the primordia were capable of. Boy did they have a hard time reconciling *Dor di Fero* with the Jakar who saved the capital.

"So the entire time you were hunting my family down like animals, you were looking for Jakar," Sara said.

He nodded.

She couldn't help but snort in laughter, then hiccupped. "Interesting that you heard rumors of Jakar's power before the coup. I didn't hear so much as a whisper, and trust me when I say my ears were open. Why are you so interested in finding him?"

"Because I believe his powers came from a cult I'm very interested in locating."

He set his hands on the table as he leaned forward, and Sara's hand returned to the glass, grasping the bottom. He eyed her intently, and she could see a hunger in his gaze.

The more he leaned over the table, the better look she got of him. His eyes looked lupine—yellow like the eyes of a stone fox, unclouded by blindness. The eyes of a primordia.

"Well, that's not normal," she said.

He gripped the table, and the wood creaked, ready to snap. "You'll tell me where Jakar is, or you'll find me someone who knows." The air of command around him deteriorated to something primal, his eyes changing to that of a predator's.

Acknowledgments

WHEN I WAS an aspiring writer obsessing about what it would feel like to get published, the first thing I would do when picking up a new book was read the Acknowledgments section. It was so vicarious seeing everyone who helped an author's dream become reality, and it helped me imagine what it would be like to thank my own support network someday. It was a bittersweet thing. All that visualizing was exciting but also made me restless, given how *hard* it is to get traditionally published. Sometimes the pursuit made me float and other times it crushed me. So the first person I want to thank is you, if what I described sounds familiar. I'm sure your dream feels as real as mine, and I hope you get to someday write out your own Acknowledgments section. Keep hanging in there and keep writing. I'm rooting for you.

To my first professional champion, Joshua Bilmes. Several long and miserable years in the query trenches had me hanging by a thread by the time I met you at WorldCon in San Jose, where you were so gracious with your time and allowed me a chance to dip my toe in what would become a very illuminating partnership. I don't know where I'd be with my writing if I never met you. Thank you for your editorial notes, your advice, your wisdom, and so much of it before you even signed me. The amount of time an agent is willing to put into no sure thing is amazing. Thank you for everything you've given me since and for always being the specter willing to haunt people on my behalf. It's a wonder seeing the titles you've helped bring into bookstores. I wish the general public praised literary agents the way writers do.

To my editor, Michael Rowley, for loving my story, for your guidance in your notes, and for answering my incessant questions. Tag-teaming all the obstacles that come with publishing can actually be fun when you're working with someone who is as in-tune with how I want my stories told as you are. To Rosie Peat, Hanna Waigh, and Jess Gofton for all your marketing input (far fewer people would know about this book without your help), to Paul for the copy editing, and to the rest of the Rebellion team. And to Gemma Sheldrake for the AMAZING map and Larry Rostant for the phenomenal cover art. Both of you ran with my suggestions and came up with something far and above what I'd hoped for. Seriously, this shit is awesome.

To Mom. I'm sorry I had to lose you when I was so close to the finish line. Your children meant the world to you, and I know that chasing the things that made me happy, made you happy too... would've continued to make you happy. To Dad, for raising me to be as contemplative as you are. It's served my writing well. Also, for the stress I caused you while you watched me try to do something as impossible as get a book published. I bet at the start you were scared to death I might someday say screw it to a real job and become a starving artist. But I kept my day job the whole time, so ha. Ha ha ha. And to my grandma Carol. You are a truly wonderful human being. I have all sorts of people to thank in the acknowledgments section of my book, but if this was an acknowledgments section of my life, you and Dad take the spotlight.

To Melissa Susanne Wiggins and Amphora Graye for being early beta readers and getting my book in the shape it needed to be in when it landed in the inbox of the agent I would eventually sign with. To the Fake G discord, and especially Ben/Talhe, for being such a solid support group and sounding board. To Jeremy TeGrotenhuis and Scott Smith for being author friends whom I vibe the hardest with. To Eric Togami for being so supportive as well as a true and best friend. To Tony, above all other beta readers—your friendship and attitude toward my writing has been loud and relentless, and sometimes that relentlessness is exactly what a writer needs even when they don't show it. Whenever exciting news abounds, I'm glad I have your face to shout it at.

To the Pitch Wars community—to Judi Lauren, especially, for choosing me as a mentee in 2016 and granting me access to many long and fruitful friendships. Thanks to Michael Mammay for the invaluable advice over the years. Shout out to Jen DeLuca for giving my first 50 pages the green light to send to Joshua before I signed with him. To Amelia Coombs—we write very different genres, but you exemplify the beauty of Pitch Wars friendships perfectly. To Ian Barnes and Keena Roberts, my Pitch Wars mentor adversaries with whom I share joint custody of our black Jumper-cat.

Thanks to all the Starbucks locations I wrote in over the years. I made many, many friends there both as a coworker and as the resident writer-dude. Thanks to all the future coffee shops I'll be writing my next books in.

Finally to my wife, Meghan. Trying to get published is frankly pretty awful at times, but you were always there to throw me a life preserver. Thanks for supporting me as best you could during my darker moments—I'm sure you felt out of your depth sometimes, but you tried, and trying did more than you realize. You've done such a great job giving me the time and space to write, for creating such a loving environment that was always waiting for me when I wasn't typing away. Stephen King said that writing should be a support system for life, but he didn't specify what life is. In my case, it's you.

FIND US ONLINE!

www.rebellionpublishing.com

/solarisbooks /solarisbks /solarisbooks

SIGN UP TO OUR NEWSLETTER!

rebellionpublishing.com/newsletter

YOUR REVIEWS MATTER!

Enjoy this book? Got something to say?

Leave a review on Amazon, GoodReads or with your
favourite bookseller and let the world know!